west

Book 4 of the Morningstar series

LJ FARROW

For Nicolette Joy, the star of my best childhood memories

For Stacy Xavier, for inspiration to write my fiction and serenades on the train

For Becky, my 'Alan Rickman,' who remembers Amaoke's birthday every year

For Caren Jill, who never fails to bring an awesome moon to my attention

For Wasif, who gets it

Finally, for Elizabeth, editor-extraordinaire, for coaxing the best from me when I need it most and want it least

Contents

Weston kept the Charger on cruise control, and when they topped the rise, they could see across the expanse of golden plains. Kansas was about to become Colorado, with the spectre of the Rocky Mountains in the distance.

"*Kansarado*," his companion declared suddenly with confidence, breaking the companionable silence of the past hour. When Weston remained silent, she added, "It has to be better than *Coloransas*, right?"

Carter was so earnest that he spared a small smile; fond as he was of her, he could ill afford any deeper feelings for her, now or ever. It was a lie he told himself daily, a sin he confessed repeatedly.

"It seems I am late to this game anyway," she sighed. "You seem to know when regions have names already."

"Some do. For example, one feels sorry for Indiana – that state comes last in every amalgam. *Illiana, Michiana, Kentuckiana…*" He gripped the steering wheel more tightly than he needed to on this die-straight stretch of plains highway, inadvertently reacting to her defeated tone, wanting to distract her from any despair she felt.

"And then there's the obvious. You wouldn't want to visit *Wy-da-ho*, right? That one must be wrong. We must conclude it's *Idoming*. I think it is important that we do not give up on the responsibility to categorize these regions properly."

"Ok, then," she said, her tone suggesting she was getting back into the playful spirit of the game. "Surely *Wyorado* must be right, rather than *Coloring*."

"Keep it up, kid," he teased. "I have a feeling the student may overtake the master."

"Hmmm. Can you really call me 'kid?'"

He glanced over at her, and her eyes were dancing with mischief. He tilted his head questioningly and returned his gaze to the road.

"I'm only suggesting, Father, that you cannot possibly be that much older than I am. I don't think you have the age-authority to get away with it." She was teasing now.

"Age-authority? I think you just made that up," he retorted, challenging her, knowing he was wrong to take such an informal tone, allowing the pretense of an intimacy they were not to have, one that he should not encourage.

"No, really, listen," she said, sounding every bit like the teenager that she technically remained. "It's like being a cougar."

"What does a mountain lion have to do with age-authority?" Weston was unable to stifle a laugh.

"You are truly impossible," Carter lamented, this time rolling her eyes. "Perhaps you *are* an old man hiding in that disguise. I mean a *cougar*, an older woman who dates a younger man."

"Like in *The Graduate*?" he asked.

"What's that?" she asked, completely confused, and he laughed again.

"An old movie," he told her. "But I thought it was enough of a pop-culture reference that you might know of it. The fact that you don't probably supports my right to call you a 'kid.'"

"Anyway, supposedly you have to be, like, ten years older to be called a *cougar*," she said, waving him away, refusing to take the bait.

"And what happens if you are only six years older? What do they call you then? A *lynx*?" he asked, smiling to show her he was not ridiculing her, rather the idea. "Less than five years, a *bobcat*?"

"Speaking of making things up," she said, trying to keep a stern look on her face and failing miserably. "My point, which you have been avoiding, is that *you* are not ten years older than I am. Therefore, you cannot call me a 'kid.' *Quod erat demonstrandum.*"

"Wow. Latin. You've been practicing," Weston didn't try to hide the pride in his voice. Carter was many things, not the least of which was intelligent, but she had been broken down in the worst of ways. He tried to give back as many pieces as he could to build her up again.

"The Mother Superior quizzes me unmercifully," she admitted, her voice betraying her feelings about that relationship. "So I make it a point to learn mathematical and legal terms to spite her." She immediately crossed herself, and promised, "I will confess my spite, and may God bless her soul."

They drove again in silence for a time, and not wanting to lose the closeness of their conversation, he asked, "Remind me, how old are you now?"

She sighed in exasperation, as if trapped by the reality of it. "I will be twenty in forty-three days."

"So…help me with the math here," he said, as if he were struggling with it. "That makes you…nineteen?"

She merely shook her head, but was again unable to compose her face. *Not going to beat anyone at poker*, he thought, and said, "So a typical *kid* your age is doing what? Getting tattoos and drinking beer?"

"And kissing cute boys," she replied without hesitation, making him blush. It was excruciating. She gave as good as she got. Her response had obliterated his argument. But she wasn't done with him.

"What about you, Father? How old are *you?*"

He smiled, signaling his own defeat. "I will be twenty-eight in…" he paused to do the mental calculation. "About two hundred days."

She gave him a look that might have had some pity in it.

"Ok, alright, I'm twenty-seven!" Weston capitulated, laughing. "You don't have to tell me – the math makes the difference well under ten years."

"Q.E.D., Father, Q.E.D.," she said, mischievously. "It's okay. What happens in *Kansarado* stays in *Kansarado*."

And because there was nothing left to say, they drove on through that made-up region without further wise observation on their relative states of being, a priest and a nun on their way to face down a demon.

weston

In the beginning, before the Beginning, the Creator conceived of an intelligent species, creatures of pure reason, without free will and incapable of corruption, incapable of sin.

Among these, the angels, was one favored of God, Beloved, most beautiful, Lucifer, *the Lightbearer, also known as the* Morningstar, *or* Azazel, *God's dear one. It was renowned among the angels for its wisdom and loveliness. Its songs and deeds exalted the Creator's works.*

And when the Creator made humans, with their frailty and their free will, he asked his angels to serve them, and there was a division among their number. Those who watched in the Garden, who were close to humans and understood their true nature, came from many orders of Heaven. They could see that the

human was beloved of God in a new way, for their free will which was meant to reflect the image of the Creator.

The Morningstar was asked to prostrate itself to humankind, and serve them as it served God. But it was unwilling, denying its directive thus: Pureflesh are of clay, and we are of fire. And so it was cast out of Heaven, the doors of the Divine closed to it, and its names were stripped away.

It was ever after known as many, to confuse its human adversary: ha Satan, *the Opposer, or* the Devil, *False One, or* Iblis, *One Who Remains in Grief, or* Abu Murrah, *Father of Bitterness, or* Aduwallah, *The Enemy of Allah, and many more.*

Its division of angels were known as the Fallen, and these creatures, as they fell to earth, were transformed, and became the third beings, demons, invested as their human counterparts with the free will they had lacked in the ranks of the angelic order. Free will with which to choose between good or evil. Two reigned over the others, serving their master in obedience only to chaos. The first of these was Asmodeus, *the Death-Bringer, or* Forcas, *The General. Next its Lieutenant,*

Beelzebul, *the Tempter, the Obfuscator, sometimes confused with Lilith, because such misdirection suited their purposes.*

But the Morningstar fell farthest and fastest, lighting the dawn in its descent. So bright and terrible was its fall that the site where it touched down was forever known as the Place of the Fallen. Shrouded in mystery and lost to time, the humans searched often for it, in the deserts East of Eden. Many failed to find it, others went mad wandering in the wastelands on a fruitless quest, and those unfortunates who stumbled across it, accidentally or otherwise, met a terrible fate. The sands of time buried it, and over the millennia, it was felt to be only a mythical place with no physical location at all. And the Morningstar used this forgetfulness to further its own diabolical aims.

Cast out, it would rule the earth until the end of humankind, its punishment delayed until the final judgement of the Almighty, marked as damned for eternity. But the Morningstar tired of this prison and conceived of a great mischief to hasten the demise of the pureflesh. Its scores of demons took up its cause to prove the inferiority and weakness of humans. To reflect the fatal flaw within, the mistake they believed the Creator had made in endowing pureflesh with free will.

The Morningstar gazed upon their naked ambition, desire, fear, and ate of these, preying upon such weaknesses to induce all manner of atrocity. Rarely did its minions act directly, instead corrupting the pureflesh to hunt and kill their own. But they had a taste for the suffering of these mortals that was irresistible to the weakest of their number. Its demon familiars fed on the baser things that emerged from sin, and were given power by those who turned to them for earthly prestige, those who readily exchanged salvation for gratification.

And because the pureflesh had a heady sense of curiosity, a thirst for forbidden knowledge, and a lust for power over one another, many of these forswore their chance at redemption, taking an irrevocable step toward the Darkness.

It was the Morningstar's favorite game to prove to its Maker these fatal flaws in Its creation. No relationship was sacred. The Morningstar provided the spark of anger to the tinder of Cain's resentment, and brother would even kill brother. Thus, it divided the tribes of humans. No crime was ever committed for which the Morningstar was not the architect.

Successfully contaminating pureflesh with its own, it engineered a descendant of the Fallen, a hybrid of demonic origin, a Prince to ascend a throne of evil ahead of the Opposer's campaign against humanity, leading to the close of civilization...

1

ALISTAIR SERAPH WIPED SWEAT FROM his brow with an already damp handkerchief, and fixed his audience with what he hoped was a stern expression. After all, a rebuke was what was needed in these times, what was always most effective with these, the faithful, indeed, it was what they had come to expect.

He looked out upon the dozens that had gathered, these backwater zealots so hungry for his words, and he, while versed in the Scriptures, wavered in his own faith, but never his desires. Most of those gathered on this stifling, humid evening had made their way to the revival tent for solace, for vindication of their judgements upon others, for a healing promise, for justification of their prejudices. He willingly provided fodder for all of them, knowing that he had the gift of persuasion, knowing that they would give their last dollars to him in hopes that it would save them.

As usual, in his opinion they were a sorry bunch, poorly educated, inbred, overweight country folk who had spent their whole lives within a five-mile radius of this very spot, never attempting or desiring to leave the bayou, much less Louisiana. He used this to manipulate them, their fear of outsiders, and the proximity of that harlot's jewel, New Orleans, less than a hundred miles away, to remind them that tangible sin and excess were close enough to reach out and ensnare them. They wore cheap cotton clothing, grimed from sweat and repeated washings in hard water, their hair limp in the humidity, their complexions gray from the efforts of poverty, their teeth rotting away in their heads from poor nutrition, or methamphetamines, or worse.

On this night, however, there were two notable exceptions. The first was the presence of a luminous youngster who sat alone near the front of the revival crowd, surely too young to attend alone, but apparently enraptured by his every word. Alistair would not have been shocked to learn that she was no more than fourteen, and this observation did not discourage the lustful imaginings he allowed himself to have about her.

She was clearly the bloom of the county, transitioning from child to woman, on the verge of becoming something extraordinary to behold, but she was still young enough to lack the self-awareness of a girl only a year or two older, and had not bothered herself overmuch with hairstyle and exaggerated dress like the older girls did. Her simple calico shift and careless braid appealed to him; he was intimidated by females that were self-aware enough to tart themselves up, although he could not admit such a thing even to himself. He found himself fascinated by the small streak of dirt where her thin neck met her shoulder just above the hem of her collar; it was obvious that she had been working on this hot summer day, and had hurriedly washed up to come to this revival service. His feverish brain was already wondering if he could get her alone afterward, and whether she could be manipulated. He shuddered, knowing he should be repentant of such urges, knowing what a hypocrite he was, but easy prey was the only kind from which he could obtain gratification. He even liked it better if they cried.

The second surprise of the night came near the end of his sermon, when he was in the middle of a thundering exhortation of their collective sins. The women were fanning themselves madly, and he thought he heard one of them moan out her distress that he was finding the sin in the room, locating it in them, and clarifying the need for their continued mortification that salvation may forever be out of reach, unless...

And just when he was about to make clear the need for them to contribute fiscally to this ministry, and remind them of God's desire that they make tithes to cement their intention to see Heaven, he noticed a latecomer slip into the tent near the back. The man took a seat, quite alone, in one of the mismatched folding chairs, crossed his legs, and folded his hands over his knee, directing a concentrated gaze at Alistair, who was so surprised that he lost his train of thought and fell silent in the middle of his climaxing rant. But the stranger seemed to nod, encouraging Alistair to continue, so he shakily picked up where he had left off, soon regaining his momentum, such that the others in the tent scarce noticed the intrusion.

The man cut such a striking figure that Alistair was unable to turn his eyes from him. Despite the heat, he wore a bespoke three-piece suit, with a watchpocket, foulard tie, and matching pocket square. His hair was dark and wavy, slightly longer than the current fashion, but certainly not like those longhairs in the city. The hair alone was riveting, it seemed to move of its own accord, although there was no breeze to relieve the oppressing heat. Alistair decided that it was a trick of the weak electric lights on the man's hair, because when he concentrated slightly he could almost convince himself it was an illusion. The man did not seem to be affected by the heat; there was no evidence of perspiration or discomfort despite the formality of his dress. He was handsome, but there was something disturbing about his level gaze, as if he could see into Alistair's very heart. He did not appear to blink or look away from Alistair for a moment, apparently hanging on every word, with an expression of wry amusement on his face. The man's shoes were the shiniest items Alistair had ever seen, unmarred by dust or scuffs, and he had the strangest feeling that if he were to look, the soles would also be pristine, as if untouched by any earthly substance.

Alistair even forgot about his primary quarry down front for a moment, but soon his darker appetites allowed him to abandon the distraction of the extraordinary visitor and sneak a look at the girl. He felt almost immediately compelled to look back at the gentleman in the back, and when he did so, the man was openly smiling, a disturbingly knowing smile of satisfaction and understanding. Even from his vantage point at the makeshift pulpit, Alistair thought the man's teeth looked unnaturally sharp, a detail that he was sure he must be mistaken about, given the distance. Alistair was both drawn to and repelled by him, but he managed to finish his message with enough force to get a reasonable return when the collection plate was finally passed.

2

FOLLOWING THE SERVICE, AS VOLUNTEERS collected
flyers to be reused the next night, Alistair pressed the flesh, feigning
his delight over any number of inanities, family stories, invitations to
dinner, useless gossip with local ladies. He shook hands with as
many people as he could, it gave him an excuse to get close to any
potential victims and ensure that word was passed along about future
sermons.

He looked around for the young girl from down front and was
relieved to see she was engaged with some of the older women from
town. He started to make his way over to her when he noticed that
the stranger in the back hadn't left his seat. Alistair found he could
not resist his curiosity about the man, and swept down the center
aisle with his hand extended, and a plastic smile on his face.

"Hello, sir! Thank you for joining us," he said, a standard
greeting for one he suspected was some local VIP or bigwig.

"Alistair Seraph," the man said his name silkily, almost
seductively, and his voice was chilling somehow. "You seem to be
making a bit of a name for yourself in these parts." His eyes flashed
with amusement, and something else, too. Knowledge. Alistair felt
known, as though this man saw through him, to the parts he wanted
desperately to keep hidden, keep others from seeing.

"I thank you. That's most kind," he responded automatically.
"But I'm afraid you have me at a disadvantage. I thought I had met

most of the town elders at the council meeting when I applied for my permit to hold the revival here."

"Oh, I'm afraid I am privately affiliated," came the smooth reply, and then the man stood up in one fluid movement, reaching into a vest pocket to produce a small business card that he offered to Alistair with another of those knowing looks. He held it out oddly, between the third and fourth fingers of his left hand.

Alistair reached for it, thinking that he noticed something unpleasant about the man's fingernails, but when he looked more closely, he saw that they were merely longer than fashionable, but manicured and buffed to a shine. He wondered if the heat were starting to affect him. These scorching summers in the South were grueling for a traveling revivalist.

As he took the card, he could not help but glance over his shoulder to try once more to locate his intriguing young woman, and when he looked back, the man was staring after her as well, smiling an extremely unpleasant smile. "You've discovered Lilith, I see."

"Do you know her?" Alistair asked hesitantly, surprised when he heard the name.

"Her name suits her," the man observed, watching the girl with obvious pleasure. "First woman and all that. Lots of firsts to come for her, I imagine, if you get *your* way."

"I'm-I'm sorry?"

"No, you're not. And that's what I like about you, Alistair. You have potential. I think you could be truly extraordinary, given the right investment," the man said. "For the right sacrifice, I think anything you want would be within reach."

"Money certainly helps the ministry," Alistair said, reaching for the way to put this conversation back on track, grasping at what he thought was being offered.

"You're setting the bar too low," the man shook his head as though he were disappointed that Alistair had jumped to that conclusion. "You should ask for what you really want. Power. So much power that you can do what you want with impunity. The power to make others look away from misdeeds. The power to utterly destroy something for your own pleasure."

The stranger stopped, and Alistair realized with dawning horror that he had been found out.

"Are you some kind of cop?" he asked, wondering if there had been a complaint about him. Trying to mentally calculate where he might have overlooked something, not properly covered his tracks.

"On the contrary, I'm the one who wants to help you show the world how wrong they have all been about you. Your message should be heard, your following should be cultivated and grown. Most importantly, your passions should be sated. I think someone is patiently waiting for you," the man told him suddenly, and Alistair turned to follow the man's level, knowing gaze.

Lilith, if that was indeed her name, was waiting for him expectantly down by the pulpit. She looked at him directly, her expression almost forward given her youth and apparent innocence. She clutched a prayer book in her hands. Much of the tent had emptied out.

Alistair turned back to excuse himself, but the stranger was gone. Utterly gone.

So he forgot for a time about the strangeness of the encounter, and although he kept Lilith there talking for some time, it was not nearly long enough for the tent to empty completely. And when she finally said she had to go, the last volunteer was still packing bibles into an empty milk crate, which left him no opportunity to get her alone.

He was buoyed up by her promise to return before the ministry left town.

When he finally got back to his trailer for the night, and looked at the stranger's card, he almost laughed. It must have all been a practical joke. But he couldn't shake the part of what he remembered that scared him. And the card itself was not funny at all. In slightly antiquated typeface, centered on the front, it said:

Senester Morningstar
Malefactor

3

THE DREAMS BEGAN THAT NIGHT, and continued on subsequent nights, gradually devolving into nightmares. Alistair could little recall any of them, but they interrupted his sleep well enough to rob him of much-needed rest, and he awoke each time in heart-pounding terror, unable to put his finger on what the dreams had been about.

The hot days flowed together, and he continued his ministry, and halfway through the week following his encounter with Senester Morningstar he was approached by a young woman of indeterminate intellect, who seemed enamored of him, asking him what it was like to be famous. Someone had dyed her hair an attractive plum color, and she wore a ratty shrug of the same hue. Her asymmetric gaze was slightly repellent to him, but there was nothing too bright in her eyes to concern him. She was prey for the taking, and he wondered again, as he so often did, that it could be so easy. This was an opportunity for gratification.

He protested that he was given no fame, and lied about wanting such a thing, telling her that his work was to humbly bring the wayward to the Lord.

"That must be lonely," she observed coyly, and Alistair felt as though her voice was echoing in his head. His sleep deprivation was starting to affect him, but he noticed that they were in fact alone, and that she seemed to have attended the services unsupervised.

He took her hand and led her out behind the tent, ready to begin his speech about the many ways in which she could get closer to God. But as he began, she told him, "You can't save me. My daddy told me I am already ruined, that God don't take no retards no how. So you can do what you want to with me."

Alistair looked around. No people for miles, all the cars had gone. Just the sun on the grassy field and the drone of the cicadas. Yet he felt watched, and he saw something flash in the depths of her eyes that looked like cunning, something predatory.

But his corruptions drove him on, and she was strangely compliant, welcoming even. But then she transformed into what she really was, and it was beautiful, and frightening, and he couldn't stop, and she was laughing.

And all at once the voice of Senester Morningstar was at his ear, saying, "You should hurt her more, make her cry." Alistair stood up, guiltily, and turned a full circle, but there was no one there.

And the girl on the ground, when he turned back to see her, was bloodied and broken, a corpse, dead for some time, that distracted gaze flat and accusatory, her hair limp and dull, her clothes in disarray.

He screamed and screamed but failed to wake up, for he was not dreaming.

4

ALISTAIR CAME TO IN HIS TRAILER, disoriented in the late afternoon heat. He moaned, wondering how he had gotten back inside with recalling how it happened. His watch told him it was four o'clock, the early service had ended at two. He had another service starting in an hour.

He peered out the window of the trailer toward the back of the tent but saw nothing. He hastily fixed his clothing and flung open the door, hopping briskly down the steps to investigate his fears. He was apprehensive, sweating and shaking, unsure of what he might find.

But there was nothing to find. Nothing at all. No marks, no stains, no disturbances in the grass.

"But, it can't be, it can't, it can't, *it can't*," he muttered to himself as he headed back to the trailer and stopped short. Senester Morningstar, resplendent in a velvet leisure suit, perched casually on the fold-down steps to the trailer, cleaning those long fingernails with a shiny metal pick. It looked unperturbed by the heat, impeccable, not a drop of sweat on its brow even though the suit it wore had to be the equivalent of wearing a fur coat in the high summer of Louisiana.

And the illusion that Alistair had discarded as a trick of the light was no such thing. Its thick dark hair floated about its face independent of all logical knowledge about the forces that should govern it, weightless and free. The creature would not have looked out of place backstage in Vegas getting ready to perform in some fancy lounge act.

Alistair knew fear, and this terrified him. Morningstar, he knew, was a disambiguation sometimes used to refer to the Devil himself. And if Alistair's faith had failed him in finding God, he understood immediately what had found him. But his greed, his ambition, and his sense of entitlement were of such impossibly great dimension that at that moment he began to wonder how he could benefit from the situation.

"Have a pleasant afternoon?" the Morningstar inquired. "My associate delivered our gift. You'll excuse her, she has a flair for the dramatic, and your tastes run to the unfortunate. She inhabits them for sport, but unfortunately she plays too rough and these possessions kill them."

"I don't know what-" Alistair began, but the Morningstar stayed him by holding up a hand and making a dismissive gesture with a small wave.

"Oh, don't be boring," it said with a grimace, revealing very sharp teeth stained with some foul substance. Alistair smelled death and heard the screams of the girl once more. "If you insist on this course of denial, I will be forced to discard you, as well. That poor girl's body could yet be found. With traces of your lusts all over her."

"What do you want?" Alistair asked, wondering how he should behave to avoid being boring to this creature, thinking he seized upon the answer.

"What you want," the Morningstar responded readily. "Sweet Lilith is coming tonight. I don't know if she is looking for a paramour, but that never stopped *you*, did it? But I need you to open yourself up to something...even more unpleasant than you!" It laughed gleefully, and Alistair struggled to remain continent, so horrifying was its expression.

"Like what?" he asked, hoping he sounded more resolute than he felt.

"Like *me*," came the answer from beside him, and a strong hand clapped down on his shoulder. Alistair nearly jumped out of his skin, which made this new arrival chuckle darkly.

Alistair turned to look at the newcomer, wishing he could be somewhere else, anywhere else. This man (and Alistair was certain he was not such, was not a man) was as handsome as the Morningstar, with a mop of shining brown hair cut fashionably and somewhat androgynously. Its eyes were obscured behind smoky sunglasses, but its mouth twisted cruelly in what approximated a self-satisfied smirk. It, too, wore clothing out of step with the circumstances, although its suit was a summer-weight tweed, and it had disdained the jacket, wearing only the vest over a shirt with no tie. Its sleeves were rolled up, exposing very capable forearms, and large hands that were scarred and brutal in appearance.

"This is my closest associate, Forcas," the Morningstar said by way of explanation.

While Alistair was lax in his morals, he had been diligent in his religious scholarship, and he recognized the name immediately. It was used to refer to Satan's greatest general, and the cruelest. The being had another name, Asmodeus, the Death-Bringer, punisher of the pure of flesh. Which meant that the woman had to be Beelzebul. The Unholy Trinity.

"Thank God. You understand. I don't have to explain it all," the Morningstar sighed in mock relief. "Forcas, we are in the presence of a true scholar of divinity. But thinking of us as women and men is a waste of time. Those are rudimentary classifications that don't really apply to us, as we are both more and less than these."

"And really, that's where you come in," the Devil told him, lighting a cigarette. It smelled of cloves and other herbs. "Lilith must bear a child, an extraordinary being. A superhero, if you like."

"But I-"

"Don't want children?" the Morningstar inquired. "By that, I'm to take your meaning as those you will have to be responsible for? Or those that you know of?"

This was said so coldly that Alistair grew concerned that there may have been a child of his issue already in the world. But he had no time to dwell on this, because the two visitors were studying him expectantly.

"I still don't understand," Alistair protested, thinking that he did understand quite clearly, and suspecting that he was past any point of return. He had garnered the attention of this monster, *the* Monster, and was being offered an impossible choice.

"Now, Alistair, you're getting dangerously close to boring again," the Morningstar warned, and Forcas' hand on his shoulder was painfully heavy. "I offer you the lovely Lilith, in your bed, at your service…"

"Imagine how she must feel," whispered Forcas at his ear, and Alistair involuntarily recoiled. His instinct should have been to be repulsed by this, but he was aroused. They knew him too well.

"Are you suggesting a bargain, like – like Faust?" Alistair asked weakly.

"Goethe had no imagination," the Morningstar replied. "Faust didn't ever ask for anything interesting. But I guess when you are bargaining from a point of weakness…and you have nothing that we want…"

"And what do I get in return?" Alistair asked, finally allowing his lust for power to make him bold enough to inquire.

"All the power and fame that befits a man of your talent," the Morningstar replied.

"And I just have to procreate?"

"Such a fussy little word for one so familiar with the pejorative," the Monster laughed a bit. "It's slightly more complicated than that. You need to allow us to assist you in these endeavors. More specifically, allow Forcas to join you."

"You want me to let Forcas watch?" Alistair looked blankly from one to the other, not liking the taste of a demon's name in his mouth, not wanting the familiarity that it implied.

"Nothing so vulgar," the Morningstar reassured him. "I want you to let him participate. I want you to let Forcas *in*."

Alistair understood with awful, alarming clarity what was being asked. And he knew with dawning certainty how he wanted to turn it to his advantage.

"No. I want you, not him," Alistair nodded to the Morningstar, twisting out of Forcas' grasp. He approached the trailer. "I'll let *you* in. But I want more for that. I want to be remembered."

"Me?" The Morningstar smiled, and Alistair suddenly knew that this bargain was tilting dangerously away from him. He suspected that this was what the Monster had wanted all along. "Always aim for the head, I say. Forcas, you won't feel slighted, will you?"

"If no one minds an ugly baby, I don't," Forcas chuckled, and when Alistair glanced at him he was licking his lips with a tongue that was mobile and notched at the end, snakelike.

5

ALISTAIR ASSUMED THAT HE WAS leaving Lilith behind as he left behind her tiny backwater Louisiana town. His ministry rolled on to the next county, and the very first night there, he was surprised to see the tent flooding with people. The first group arrived nearly an hour before he was scheduled to begin speaking, and the local Baptist minister had loaned his church choir for the festivities.

They were already set up, and to his surprise, began to sing several upbeat hymns, dancing and swaying like the place was a juke joint on a Saturday night. Thus the faithful were accompanied by this celebration as they filed in, jostling for seats, until it was standing room only. He saw several gentlemen giving up their seats for the ladies.

And to his great misgiving, just as he arrived at the podium to address them, he saw her. Looking even smaller and paler, in a brown calico dress that was too big for her, she entered through the flap at the back of the tent. She walked confidently down the center aisle, right down to the front, where those who had set up front and center parted for her, just as Moses had parted the Red Sea, neat as you please, so that she could sit directly facing him.

She sat straight and expectant, looking up at him, her eyes unblinking. He wanted to feel that she was judging him, but her expression was serene, almost content. She held her prayer book in her lap, and placed her hands over it gently, waiting for him to begin.

He could see the dark bruises that still marked her collarbones, and one smaller one at the angle of her jaw. She seemed even more childlike to him now that he had a carnal knowledge of her, and he felt a new emotion burning at the edge of his thoughts. Shame.

Alistair couldn't know that Lilith had her own dreams, and had known he was coming into her life. She had been told. She could have a child. She would. She already knew it was certain, though she couldn't have articulated what made her so sure.

Daddy had taken some convincing, but he had come around. She had found herself trying to persuade him of something for the first time in her life, and she wasn't sure who was more surprised by this, she or him. But they two were all that they had, for as long as she could remember, and she knew he would support her plea. She also knew that he would reach his own understanding of the situation.

At a time when Alistair should have been proud and excited that his ministry appeared to be growing, his bargain bearing fruit, he was feeling anything but pride. Indeed, it seemed that all the positive developments were tainted. He shrugged these feelings off, and tried to live in the moment, enjoying sermonizing to the biggest crowd he'd yet faced.

And they loved him, calling out *Amen* and *Testify* at every opportunity. He thundered through his message, getting into it, strutting the stage, aware of how he must look with the choir in their silky robes behind him. It was scorching, but during the most somber parts of his delivery, his audience was absorbed, the women fanning themselves madly, some of them making eyes at him.

But no matter how high he felt, his eye returned again and again to that focal point down front. Lilith. Her expression never changed, nor did her eyes ever leave him.

The collection plate was passed, and people seemed to be feeling generous, and it was all in keeping with the Morningstar's agreement. The choir sang, the lights were bright, and when it was over, he had more invitations to tea and Sunday dinner than he could possibly accept. More subtle were the other invitations to call privately upon a single lady for 'prayer and fellowship.' Hadn't this been what he wanted all along?

When he looked for Lilith in the general melee after the closing hymn, she was nowhere to be found. He felt relieved, and guilt at his relief. He knew she did not drive, and wondered briefly how she had gotten to the service, but these thoughts were soon carried away as he received the accolades of the makeshift congregation. He probably should have dwelt upon that detail further.

It was over an hour later that he turned off the strings of lights, leaving the tent in darkness. He ducked out through a slit in the canvas into weak moonlight, focused on the short walk to his trailer. He came up short when he felt cold metal against the skin of his neck. He could smell gun oil and heard one of the most terrifying sounds a human being could hear, the pump action of a shotgun that is aimed at them.

"Reverend Seraph? If that is your name," a gravelly voice with a profound bayou drawl addressed him. "Convenient for a minister to have an angel's name. I'm going to ask you one question. Answer it right, and there might be a chance to answer another. Answer it wrong, and the bear shot in this gun will probably take your head clean off."

Alistair paused, and took a slow breath, afraid to turn his head. He was tempted to ask a question of his own, but a quick calculation told him that it was probably not the wisest.

"Smart. Don't think your fast-talk will work with me," the man said, and the barrel of the gun moved incrementally as he nodded. "Do you know who I am?"

Alistair found he had very little voice, but he managed to croak out her name. "Lilith, Lilith's ..." He gestured at the man, trying to show he was making the connection.

"You got it in one," the man sounded amused. "She's my baby girl. All I got since we lost her Momma in childbed. The pertinent facts here are that she is all of fourteen. Even in this fine state of

Louisiana they don't consider that the age of consent, and that means that what you done to her could send you straight up to Angola. I hear that the men there don't take kindly to insults to children."

"But she tells me that you indicated she might be your chosen bride, she seems to understand it like that. I think it's a terrible idea, but I'm a sentimental man, and I want to see her happy. What say you, Reverend?"

"I-I-I-" All Alistair's smooth talk had left him, and he could only stammer inanely.

"Now, that's sweet. You're overcome. I'll take that as a 'yessir,'" Lilith's father got quiet, and he pointed the barrel of the gun at a less lethal but certainly more personal spot. "But I never saw the kind of loving that makes a girl all covered up with bruises. But see, she tells me that she fell down several times on the way home."

"I'm gonna put this gun aside. And *you're* gonna fall down several times on the way to your trailer back yonder. Then you and me are gonna be finished conversing, with me especially hoping that I don't have to have any more talks with you. I tend to be a man of very few words. A man of action, you might say."

6

"YOU DIDN'T TELL ME I'D have to marry her!" Alistair's petulant tone elicited a ragged chuckle from the Morningstar. He was still nursing the considerable hurts he had suffered at the hands of the girl's father.

"No one said you *had to* marry her," the Monster crooned, favoring Alistair with a crooked smile. It's teeth were stained with something unpleasant, and the corrupt minister didn't want to spend any time speculating about what it could be. "I would imagine the conjugal rights alone would provide an attractive enticement. Don't tell me that shotgun made you impotent? Although I suppose if you had refused…"

Alistair started in with another angry reply, but his voice died in his throat when the passenger door of the Jaguar swung open and Forcas stepped out, smartly turning to the backseat and opening the door for *her*, the one who had ensnared him in the first place. All three of them. Even he knew enough to keep his mouth shut for his own good.

"I like you, Alistair," the Morningstar said, holding up a restraining hand to his companions. "You have the balls to be ungrateful to us? We, who delivered her to you, ready to submit. Through you we have engineered the birth of the next Coming, and you lack the understanding of its importance. You asked to be remembered, and you shall be. Your influence is growing as we speak." Its shiny eyes flashed, and Alistair was assaulted by the voices of a legion of souls screaming for release. He turned away from what he saw in the depths of those dead orbs, far too certain that he was witnessing his own fate, knowing it was too late to take any of it back.

But the Devil made good on its bargains, and soon Alistair's ministry was elevated in the consciousness of the people of the South, and he was filling revival tents and collection plates to overflowing. But the bad dreams were the unasked-for price he paid for this success. He had to relive his assaults over and over, seeing faces he had long forgotten. He dreamt of being buried alive, fighting the soil as it closed over his head, as it slid bitter and loamy down his throat, knowing he would suffocate long before he could scratch his way back to the surface. Worst of all were the visions of the serpent, Forcas with his forked tongue, twisted around him in his bed, and the sting of the fangs that woke him in a cold sweat, his own screams still ringing in his ears.

In the end, this success was what calmed his concerns about having a young wife and a child on the way. He was called away almost constantly, which spared him the fetters of domesticity under the watchful eye of his homicidal father-in-law. But Lilith seemed content. She had a husband and father to legitimize the child.

And there were seemingly no obstacles to his continuing extracurricular encounters with other women. The difference was that now he seemed to be seen himself as an object of desire, if not affection, and he had less need to prey on the weak. He returned to the tiny trailer night after night in a new parish, and all too often he was invited elsewhere to share the bed of one of his many admirers. He returned to visit his wife at intervals that he felt met the minimum of a duty that he did not really feel.

He understood his initial attraction to Lilith as predator and prey. Legal entanglements discouraged that perspective, and accordingly, her attractiveness to him diminished. That and his distaste for their impending offspring, which he felt was not really his own. He felt keeping his distance was justified. The child would come, and surely a child of such provenance would be protected by its own Dark Father; Alistair had no qualms about deferring whatever role was expected of him to its nefarious plans and he disclaimed the child to its fate.

W

It is dark. But it is warm, and never quiet. The distant hollow sounding of a drum, soothing, a background symphony more complex than just her heartbeat; I know the rushing of her blood, like the tides, hear the gurgling bubbles beside me, feel deep vibrations as she walks, the fluid around me rocking me gently as I sleep.

I hear voices, many are far away, but one or two are familiar, none more known than hers. She speaks to me when I forget, when I stretch, or have to kick, and sometimes, rocking back and forth, she sings to me.

The other voices are in my dreams, and I both understand them and do not heed them, the chaos and cacophony of a storm at sea, one that I weather and endure, a chorus of sorts, a choir, because I am not alone. I am many.

She is mostly sad, but joyful on occasion, and sometimes, when I feel her joy, I give a little push, and more and more, as if she understands the only language I have, she pushes back, rocking my little boat, here on the waves, sailing toward a new place.

Just as I become snug, curled around myself, content, the waves rush away, and I am stranded, the beating of her heart rushing along, occasionally in sync with another, faster staccato song, which is the song of my own heart, the sound of my own being, echoed back to me from the outside. When it is time to go, I feel another hand holding my own, its hand, the Other, the briefest squeeze, for luck, and to remember.

She is scared. I feel her fear growing, and I try to remain calm.

When it is time, I push off the deep end and surface in a new place.

7

THE BABY WAS CERTAINLY A happy one. He came easily enough, surprising the doctor up at the hospital. For such a petite young mother she'd expected trouble. But the doctor's biggest challenge had been convincing Lilith to eat, that she needed to gain some weight so that the baby's growth would be healthy. She seemed such a sickly thing. The baby's father was twice her age or likely a bit more, and he was an infrequent attendant at Lilith's visits, which was no loss as far as the doctor was concerned, the man gave her the creeps. The girl's own father seemed to be her main source of support, and what he lacked in education he more than made up for in devotion.

When all the measurements were taken, the doctor realized why it had been such an easy delivery; the child weighed just under three kilograms, but was a full 60 cm in length, the longest she'd ever seen. He was well beyond the hundredth percentile, long and thin, stretched out like county fair taffy.

And although he'd been relatively quiet, his vital signs were normal, and he pinked up as he should. There were no visual stigmata of birth defects or hallmarks of delay. APGARs were excellent, and he was physically beautiful, with a full head of dark wavy hair that was surprisingly long for a newborn, and large dark eyes. If the doctor noticed that he favored neither parent, as she had many times before, she kept this observation to herself. Reported statistics suggested that one of every five children born is not the child of the father who claims it; privately, perhaps cynically, the doctor suspected it was closer to one in four.

Lilith was delighted with her baby, and his birth heralded the end of the strange dreams she'd suffered when carrying him. But she soon realized, as all mothers do, that it was a bigger challenge to keep him safe outside her body than in. She chose the name Weston, having heard it somewhere and liking it. She had neither the patience nor the imagination to give him a middle name, so she didn't, not realizing that the oversight was going to cause more hassles than if she'd capitulated and made something up to fill the gap between first and last name.

He was all smiles as he grew, but she noticed he was flatter in his interactions with Alistair. Weston seemed to tolerate his father, and was patient when held or spoken to, but lacked the animation he displayed very early on with his grandfather, and with her. But much as she adored him, Lilith realized early on that he was, frankly, strange.

He slept through the night after only a few weeks, but disdained his bassinette, only able to rest when alone in his crib. She would creep up to it in the morning, in case he still slept, but he was always awake, sometimes training those dark eyes upon her as if he had been waiting for her for hours, more often ignoring her as he seemed to watch, mesmerized by something unseen above the crib, whether the pattern the sunlight made through the curtains as it touched the ceiling, or the motes of dust within it, she could not say.

More disturbing still was some uncanny ability to get out of the crib when still impossibly young, apparently too young to do so on his own. Yet many a morning she found him, out of the crib, underneath it, or over by the wall under the window, and once, after a panicked sweep through their mobile home, sobbing and breathless, she discovered him under her own bed. He was lying on his back, and when she pulled him out, dust bunnies swirling in his hair and clinging to his onesie, he looked at her with those disquieting eyes, reaching out a small hand to touch her cheek, as if to stay her tears and calm her.

He always had a smile for her, and would not infrequently gurgle and try to laugh. But he didn't speak, not a word. He started to eat, crawl, take steps, make puzzles, look at books. He was engaged with the world around him. He seemed always to know when she was sad, or worried, or angry.

There was no vocalization that approximated speech. No *da-da*, no *ma-ma*. Lilith would awaken in the depths of many nights and hear sounds coming from his room, which was adjacent to hers, voices, she thought. More than one, a confused babble that she could not pin down as words, but it approximated the rhythm of a conversation. Perhaps her own irrational fancy, the remnants of a recurring dream.

She would get up to investigate, and find Weston standing in the center of his crib, staring at the moon, quiet. Or beneath it again, his eyes open but not vacant, moving as though he were listening to something that only he could hear.

Lilith perhaps lacked the imagination or the energy to be afraid, so preoccupied was she with the long absences of his father, the lack of financial or other support, and her own exhaustion. The situations seemed strange, but the child himself was less and less so.

As he got older, these idiosyncrasies became a part of their daily rhythm, and perhaps became her reality with him. Because she loved him, she overlooked what made him different, as only a mother can, and was strong enough in her love and convictions that she never listened to the prejudicial proclamations of the doctors who checked him over. She ignored their concern with his lack of speech, simply knowing that he was neither deaf nor dumb, and would communicate as and when he was able.

W

In the crib, when she has gone, they sing to me. Teach me. A song.

First the beast the beast the beast
Next but never least least least
Dragon from the east the east the east
Demons all we feast we feast we feast

First the beast the beast the beast
Nor will the power cease cease cease
Dragon in the east the east the east
Demons all we feast we feast we feast

A hundred times. A thousand. Ten thousand. Their voices like fire, climbing over and around me, they bear me up and over the side, where I stick, sliding down, around, under.

Drag me to the window to see the moon. Leave me with the serpent beneath the crib. The talking serpent. How I know these things and can understand its words I cannot say. The language odd, old as time, but part of me, inside and out.

I lie on the floor, not crying, not sleeping, as they swarm me, moving on my skin, ruffling my hair, tossing my body back and forth in the dust.

8

WESTON WOKE ABRUPTLY, HIS TODDLER'S brain alert to the night light to his left, its weak glow cutting into the darkness, helping him to remember that he was home, in his room, safe. Or, at least, as safe as he ever was.

Something was wiggling his big toe, the same something that had reached into his crib to do it. But as soon as it sensed he was awake, it began to pull him, and he slithered off the mattress, clinging to it as he was drawn down, around, and underneath. He put his hands down onto the dusty floor, letting his body gently separate from the underside of the thin mattress, feeling the weight of them all around him as he settled to the linoleum.

The other was there, too, its eyes golden and glittering, snakelike slits that studied his face carefully, perhaps disappointed that Weston's eyes had no fear.

The demons were gentle this night, buoying him tenderly with their attentions, ruffling his hair. It was their way; if he struggled or showed any fear, they were rough, buffeting him with screams and other torments that made him beat the floor with hands and feet, and sometimes his own head.

At his last doctor's visit, the kind lady who took him aside while Momma spoke with the doctor had asked him all kinds of questions about how he got his bruises. He had laughed when she asked if his Momma ever hurt him, but shook his head to show that she wasn't doing it. He pointed to himself, and the air, but she didn't understand about the demons. No, he shook his head, not Grandpa either. Nobody else, then? He tried to show her no, but he wasn't sure she could understand. He didn't talk to her at all, as always afraid of what might come out of his mouth if he tried. Unsure what *they* might say to her. They did not think very nice things.

Weston knew they thought he was dumb. But Momma always smiled and told him how smart he was. The lady asked him to draw a picture for her, and so he did. She didn't like it. He pointed to his room, and his bed, and his window, and all the monsters that visited, how they wrapped themselves around him.

"*Finalborn, demonspawn, child of Adam,*" the serpent-man hissed. "You must embrace them, these fine friends of yours and mine. I picked them for you. They love you, and they are the most important part of you. You are a prince, and you will rule the whole world someday.

It whispered to him on and on, which was preferable to the incessant screaming that he often had to endure, keeping him from regularly sleeping. He was lulled enough to return to his slumber, and that's where Lilith discovered him the next morning, curled up on his side on the floor beneath his bed.

W

Entirely by accident, I discovered their weakness.

When they sang incessantly, and were ignored, as I got older, they would punish me. If I fought back they hurt me, so I stopped fighting. There were still many things they could make me do. I woke one night with a screwdriver in my hand, standing next to Momma's bed, watching the big vein in her neck. Momma was asleep. She was so tired. She worked so hard. They whispered awful ideas to me about what the screwdriver would do, how soft her neck was, how the blood would look, how it would feel on my skin, how it would taste. My hand started to move, the tip of the tool in my hand pointed at Momma, so I fought but it was like fighting ten of me. I jerked my hand away, spying the little faces in the wall, and slipped the tip of the tool inside the slot. The vibration in my arm burned and jumped, throwing me down on the floor, but I felt it, they hated it so much that they were thrown, outside of me, rather than in, even for but a moment.

I don't think I made a sound, but the horde gave a horrid wail, and Momma woke up. I kicked the screwdriver under the bed before she could see it. She thought I had a bad dream.

The next morning she had to call Grandpa; she couldn't figure out why the trailer had no power. The breaker was thrown, he told her. He looked for a reason, but by then I had put the screwdriver away.

It was the first moment that I had any control. Electricity could push them out, but I could never keep them there, and they were right back, singing and babbling away, screaming sometimes for days after I did that.

And the snake-man, when it came to wiggle my toes and wheedle and talk, of things I would do, learned that I had unlocked a way to send it back. Once it stole my blue rosary that Mommy had given me, from her Momma, and I found it looking over her one night in her bed. I only had to take the lampshade down. I had practiced cracking the bulb just so, so I could open the chamber with the glowing filament intact, the electricity live, a tiny infantry of electrons that its flesh could not resist. More than once I sent it screaming, and it presented itself less and less.

The demons were another story, to remove them I had to injure myself. After the screwdriver incident, my arm was tingly for days. It was just as painful as fighting them off, but I had control now. Like everything, it came at a steep price.

9

AS ALISTAIR GREW IN INFLUENCE, he distanced himself from his family, never spoke of them, and they were lost in the obfuscation of his lies.

His ministry grew, and he found a woman nearly as ruthless and ambitious as he was, fair enough of face to elevate him even further in the ranks of the evangelists, from a rich Shreveport family that had television contacts, and Alistair's fame was assured.

He now had the money to disentangle himself quietly from Lilith and the boy, and he assumed it would be the work of a moment to obtain a quick divorce and avoid any negative publicity or further embarrassments.

But Lilith held firm, insisting he take out a life insurance policy that named his son the beneficiary, and her lawyers were surprisingly tenacious. They too wanted a speedy resolution, knowing their own client could not afford many billable hours, so they threatened him with exposure. He didn't like having any paper to connect him to the child, but decided that paying for the policy would be painless using his new wife's money, and he remembered his father-in-law's shotgun full of bear shot, so he finally agreed to insure himself for a goodly sum, a Cadillac policy that would pay double for accidental death, and guaranteed payment even in the event of his own negligence. It would not pay off in the event of suicide, but all parties on the plaintiff's side were satisfied that the defendant's love for himself and his general cowardice were ample safeguards against such an outcome.

Indeed, now that Alistair was a man of means and the had the medium with which to spread his message, he naturally wanted to distinguish himself from all the other charlatans. He did so by claiming to be protected by God, by the armor of his faith.

As proof of this claim, he proposed that he had no reason to fear the serpent, because God was his protector and his savior. At the biggest revival event of the summer he planned to handle a venomous snake to demonstrate this faith to his congregants.

"You're going to protect me," Alistair inquired of the Morningstar before the event, making it less a request than an expectation.

"We are certain the outcome will be even better than you could imagine. People will be talking about this for a very long time," the Monster promised him, and Alistair was unfortunately unable to decipher the lie cloaked in that truth.

The Death-Bringer himself inhabited the serpent, which administered a fatal bite, ensuring the Morningstar's prediction was correct. Alistair received a great deal more notoriety in death than he ever would have in life, which, after all, was what he had asked for.

10

LILITH KNEW HER SON WAS smart. She despaired of him getting an education in the public schools, at least enough of one that would allow him to escape this place, escape the blue-collar, drug-addicted poverty that wasn't even its worst affliction.

So she took him up to Terrebonne to the Catholics when he was old enough to enter the fourth grade, believing that he would benefit there from a better education than she'd had, or her daddy before her.

The nun behind the monstrous gray desk in the reception area eyed the young woman and boy with a mixture of distaste and pity, but invited them into the office behind her to meet Father O'Halloran, the headmaster, without a contrary word.

Lilith and Weston sat in fraying chairs facing the priest, and Lilith was so nervous about being there that she jumped a little when the nun softly closed the door behind them. She had fleeting second thoughts, and for a moment wanted to leave, the unbearableness of her poverty and her own perceived unworthiness laid bare.

Weston's little hand crept out blindly and found hers in her lap, disentangling her fingers, comforting her, as he often did. She could swear the child *knew* when she was upset, felt her distress. Perhaps children could do that with their mothers; she had no frame of reference, as she had not known her own. Her daddy had been an enigma, she knew he was always there for her, but she'd never had any keen understanding of any of his inner workings.

Weston, for his part, drew comfort from the loud ticking of the clock on the wall, and the electric buzz it made, which changed slightly from moment to moment as the second hand jumped and jittered, as if shaking out the time in this jerking dance. He made note of all the wall outlets he could see, and those he could not he was able to guess their location based on the regular placement of the others. Father O'Halloran's lamp had a sturdy cord and the bulb was large and smooth.

"Mrs. Seraph?" The priest consulted the note that the nun had passed to him and then smiled at Lilith, seeing her nervousness. His eyes were kind, so she was encouraged to speak.

"I brought my boy to get him into school here," she told him.

"Are you Catholic?" he asked, not to be exclusionary, but rather because she had come a long way.

"Not really, sir. My Momma was, but I never knew her," Lilith shook her head resolutely. "But his daddy was a preacher." This last spoken as if the information would confer understanding. But she wanted it known because she hoped it meant they would let him come to school here, and perhaps it might make them treat him better.

"I apologize," Father O'Halloran said. "It's not a requirement for admission. It seems that you drove quite a while to get here. I wondered if it was because you wanted a Catholic education."

"I just want him to have a good education," she replied. "Better than mine, you understand. And I have money. He has his daddy's life insurance money to pay for it. It's in a trust, but we can borrow against that for schooling."

The old priest sighed, and looked at Weston. He could not remember a more beautiful child. Darkly cherubic. Although he thought the word was overused, it was appropriate in this case. He was also quite tall for his age. The child resolutely avoided eye contact, his gaze darting from the clock, to the window, to the plants, seemingly assessing and reassessing moment by moment.

"The tuition here is based on financial need, Mrs. Seraph. The church takes your information and determines your fees. In many cases, students with the greatest need can attend for free," he reassured her, and was gratified by the relief in her expression. She was poorer than most, but he could see she was proud, and she nodded. It seemed that what he'd told her sounded fair. He wondered at her age. She looked to be little more than twenty herself.

"He'll have to board here since we come up from Vermilion Parish," she said sadly, and now there was something in her eyes that was sizing him up. "But I don't want none of those priests to touch my boy in a bad way, understand? I'm aware of some of what has been going on with that. He'll come home with me of a weekend."

Father O'Halloran nodded. "We are most vigilant on that point, ma'am."

"I'll know if anything happens," Lilith said with conviction she did not necessarily have.

Rather than revisit that concern, the old priest turned to Weston. "Do you like school?" he asked, hoping to take the child's measure.

"Oh, he won't speak to you," Lilith interjected. "He don't talk but real rarely."

"Oh?" Father O'Halloran looked perplexed. "But his records-"

"They're real good, I know," she said proudly. "He reads books I can't near to understand. His writin' got him a prize up at Baton Rouge two years ago. He works real hard. He just don't talk 'nless it's important to him, I don't know what all."

"Well, that's just fine," the priest replied, and Weston saw that he really didn't mind, although it was a mystery to him. Weston liked the way the priest's eyes crinkled at the sides when he smiled. Weston looked at his Momma and nodded to her.

Weston could leave her to stay in this place, but he would worry about her. There was plenty of electricity around for when he needed it, and the energy was good. He knew *that* would change when he came to stay.

He shook Father O'Halloran's hand when they stood at the door to leave, and the priest told him he looked forward to seeing him in a few weeks.

On the ride back he knew Momma was relieved. She was also still worried. He watched her bunched up shoulders from the backseat as she drove them homeward. But she was happier than he knew, and he smiled when she pulled in at the day-old bread shop on the way into town.

"How about a little treat to celebrate your new school?" Momma turned to look at him over her shoulder with a sunny smile. "Help me pick out some Wonder bread?"

He nodded and clambered out of the car. He walked beside Momma and she was happily surprised when he took her hand. He was only nine but already slightly taller than she was. He knew that people thought he was older, and some of them frowned when he held her hand. But it made her happy, and the prospect of soft white bread made him excited enough that he swung her arm back and forth.

She had enough extra change for him to get a small package of chocolate cupcakes, and the clerk smiled at him as she handed them over.

But Momma stowed the bread on the shelf behind the backseat, and when they went into the bank to cash her paycheck, someone tore the plastic covering that she had used to repair the back window and took it. She didn't say anything, but Weston could tell she was crying as she drove them home.

They hadn't found the cupcakes he had placed below the passenger seat in front of him, so he shared them with her while she was on the phone to his Grandpa.

"…well, Daddy, if you have to tear through a plastic-wrapped window for some bread, seeing's how bad off we are, then I suppose whoever got it must need it even more," she said, laughing a little at something Grandpa said in reply.

Weston loved this about her, that she was truly good, always aware of the possibility that things could be even worse. He stole away while she was still on the phone, gathering up the duct tape and a new piece of plastic to repair the covering over the missing window for her.

W

As a baby, Momma would hold me and look in the mirror, show me to myself, and for the first time, I saw it. The Other. Its eyes were different, though. Like marbles, the blight of a cataract, flashing like the lens in the eye of a raven or a kite, moving, not focusing, not allowing true eye contact. It wants me to see it there, whenever I look in a mirror.

As an older child, I began to avoid reflective surfaces. I realized that I could slightly blur my focus to avoid visiting with it at least twice a day, while it waited there for me to finish brushing my teeth.

It wants to talk, and inside I am many. I am we. It talks of we, and I am frightened. It looks just like me, am I a part of the we?

After years of consciously adjusting my focal point, I have done something irreparable to my eyesight. But being half-blind is better than seeing the demons — not just my own cohort of them, but the Monster in the Mirror. The eye doctor tells Momma I will need glasses, probably for the rest of my life. Good.

Finally, when I brush my teeth, I cannot focus on it, there in my eyes, because I go to bed blind, leaving my spectacles on my nightstand. It is angry, and I can still hear it, but it wanted to be recognized. I hoped it would not be the last satisfaction I would rob from it.

11

LOUISIANA HIGHWAY 14 CARRIED THEM from Vermilion Parish toward New Iberia on the way to pick up Weston in Terrebonne. Lilith's father had driven up from Pecan Island to fetch her. They planned to surprise the boy since he saw his grandfather very little now that he attended the parish school.

It was a hot and humid Friday afternoon, too early for anyone to be trying to get anywhere and start a weekend. Thunderclouds were building to the southwest, out over the Gulf; they'd be coming home in the rain. That stretch of road was usually deserted anyway and they only passed the rare car now and then that was headed toward the water. It seemed her daddy's old pickup was the only vehicle traveling inland. They didn't expect much traffic until they got to the junction at US-90 anyway.

They took the right turn out of Abbeville and were passing north of Avery Island, and Daddy was telling her about some funny story he'd heard out on the boat when something in the road caught Lilith's attention. There was a bird or something out there.

But when she looked up, she saw she'd been terribly wrong. It was a *man* in the road, standing directly in the lane ahead of them, about twenty feet away, facing the truck that was bearing down on him.

Lilith shrieked aloud, and it seemed that time slowed down. Her father planted himself on the brake so forcefully that he was standing on it, but they were too close. The bed of the truck slid to the right, skewing them slightly, but at collision they were still traveling close to fifty miles per hour.

The impact was terrible, the sounds of tearing metal and the awful *whump* of the body striking the front grille, which crumpled inward and surprisingly gave way, splitting the cab apart and sending two big pieces of what was left of the truck spinning away from each other.

Lilith could still hear screams when she came to rest several hundred feet beyond the point of impact. In her confusion she did not realize they were her own. Without thinking, she struggled with the catch on her seatbelt and climbed out of the wreckage, glancing up and down the highway to see if there was any other traffic, but there was not a car in sight.

She felt uninjured, but scared and strangely jumpy, so she ran back the way they had come, looking for the rest of the truck, calling out as she jogged up the center line, "Daddy! Daddy?"

On the opposite side of the road, nearly perpendicular to the crash, she discovered the other half of the vehicle. The bed of the truck had swung away, pulling the remains into the ditch. The open cab revealed her father, slumped over, half-impaled on the steering wheel. He hadn't been wearing his seatbelt.

She stopped abruptly when she reached the edge of the blacktop, where the breakdown lane met the gravel, and sobbed despairingly. She picked her way down to him, seeing that he was dead, reaching out to touch the sleeve of his flannel shirt. "Oh, Daddy."

Too late she wondered about the man they had hit, and as she decided to check the road, a shadow fell over her shoulder and she turned, expecting it was another motorist who had stopped to help them, even though she had heard no engine noise.

Instead it was the man from the road, the one they had struck. Impossibly unharmed, he still wore the dark glasses that obscured his eyes and an expression of pure malice. Not a hair was out of place, his clothing was pristine, and he strode down the embankment toward her with murderous purpose.

Lilith was so shocked at this that she had no thoughts of self-preservation until it was too late, and vicious hands grabbed her by the throat and threw her violently to the ground.

She gasped for air as her attacker clenched his teeth in a feral grimace, and she slapped at him uselessly, overwhelmed by his sheer undeterrable strength. Her flailing managed to dislodge the sunglasses, but she wished she hadn't, because his eyes were the eyes of a serpent, the pupils dark slits at the center of yellowish orbs.

"Why?" she finally croaked out, not understanding.

"Because I am the Death-Bringer," it hissed at her, showing its forked tongue, it's voice a rough lisping sound. "You should have died in the truck, damnable woman, but I don't mind. I will help you along. I need you out of the way. Your son cannot ascend his throne if he has to worry about his sweet Momma."

W

I knew when I saw Father O'Halloran crossing the quad. I knew that he was coming for me. I watched his progress through the dormitory windows, knowing that he would only return to campus and walk through the downpour for bad news.

I had been waiting for Momma and Grandpa to arrive to take me home. The weather had been contemptibly hot, the Southern sun a furnace, miserable all day. The clouds piling up on the horizon outside during Trigonometry did not herald relief, but I hadn't cared. The misery of the day was a foreshadowing of my own yet to come.

Most of the others had already gone; I hadn't bothered to walk over to the cafeteria for supper. I hadn't wanted to get caught in the rain, hadn't wanted to endure another second of their contempt.

It was what I had been waiting for as long as I could remember, knowing that I would not be allowed to keep those I loved, knowing that to own me they had to remove anyone that interfered with their plans, excise them, along with the parts of me that cared for them. Crush me utterly, abandon me to my despair, from which would come my salvation in the arms of the Monster.

But Momma had taught me to love, and I held onto that love, hiding it inside of me, understanding that the world was deserving of it, even as I was not. I would give what I had to. I would sacrifice everything, including my life, but never love. By keeping it, I was caring for the one gift she had given me in truth, a legacy, the only thing she had to give, and in doing so, she had left in me the best part of who she was.

They would take everything else, but I knew they couldn't get that. They couldn't find it, recognize it, see it in me, because they had no understanding of it.

12

ERASMO JIMENEZ WAS THE LOCAL automotive mechanic in Terrebonne Parish, and the repair shop he ran kept everyone, rich or poor, on the road. He'd inherited the business from his father, who had died young of a heart condition. So by the age of thirty, Erasmo and his younger brother, Eusebio, had developed a reputation for hard work and fairness.

Erasmo was a character, small, dark, and funny. He had seven children, and drove an ancient green Mercury Grand Marquis with a portrait of Benjamin Franklin painted on the trunk lid in a cameo circle that mimicked a hundred-dollar bill. The art was completed by two stylized *100s* drawn at the corners. There was a Santa hat on the back deck inside the rear window year-round; no one really knew why he kept it there.

His clients included the parish diocese, and Father O'Halloran took Erasmo aside one afternoon while the staff resuscitated the priest's old Buick once again.

"How you doing, Father?" Erasmo asked, grasping the priest's hand warmly, his eyes genuinely searching for the answer in O'Halloran's weary face.

"I am tired of this heat," O'Halloran replied. "Or perhaps I am just old."

"Not a chance," Erasmo observed kindly. "You just need a vacation."

"Speaking of which," the priest said softly, "I will be taking a sabbatical over the next several months."

"Somewhere nice?" Erasmo was sincere in his interest.

"Boston," O'Halloran said gently, and they both laughed together.

"That's no vacation," Erasmo shook his head. "At least you'll escape the heat."

"Home-cooking, though," O'Halloran told him. "My maternal aunt is still alive, and she likes to feed me."

"So a blessing somewhere in there, Father," Erasmo nodded.

"Always. We simply must look for it. I have a favor to ask you," O'Halloran got serious. "I have a young man from the school that is special. He's very mechanical, very smart, and needs an outlet. He's a bit of an outcast, and he lost his mother recently. Maggie and I took him in because I didn't want to leave him in the dormitory with all that was going on. He's only fifteen, but he will graduate next year. I was thinking of leaving the car for him, and wondering if you could use an extra set of hands around here after school and on weekends."

"I don't know, Father," Erasmo glanced over his shoulder at the characters that he employed in the shop. "This isn't exactly the place for an altar boy."

O'Halloran looked at Erasmo over his spectacles. "I know a few have come through here over the years." Erasmo and Eusebio had both served as altar boys in their youth.

Erasmo laughed. "You remember everything, Father. I don't know how you do it." He scratched his head and said, "*Mamá* would put me in my own grave if she found out I denied you anything. Sure. Bring him over and I'll find something for him to do."

"Very good, my son. I will be calling on your mother later today, so I am pleased I can tell her how you will be helping me out," O'Halloran said with a wink.

13

"WESTON, THIS SUMMER I AM going to Boston," Father O'Halloran said suddenly one evening at dinner.

Weston nodded, feeling anxious about what the statement might mean for him. He had another year of school; at fifteen he was already well over six feet in height and had leapfrogged two grade levels in the five years he had been at St. Ignacio School. He had already declared his intent to go directly into the seminary at age sixteen, provided the Church would grant permission. It would make him the youngest person ever to be admitted to the path to orders in North America.

"You'll stay here with me? Is that alright?" Margaret O'Halloran was Father's sister, and she acted as his housekeeper and caretaker. Her hair was red, typically Irish and kissed by fire, she had told him. Such was the belief of those in the old country. She smiled with her entire face and reached out to touch his cheek, wanting to reassure him.

Weston could only nod again, he did not trust his words, afraid they would betray his anxious feelings, his fears. He comforted himself by counting the outlets in the dining room, those polygonal faces that were set at consistent intervals just below the chair rail. He grimaced without realizing he was doing so, it had been quite a while since this obsessive behavior had manifested, but his compulsions returned when he was nervous. With the priest out of the house, he hoped he could control his own demons. He felt responsible for Ms. Margaret, who'd been nothing but kind to him.

"I have arranged a summer job for you," Father O'Halloran told him. "You seem to do so well with machines, I thought you might like to learn more about them. Erasmo Jimenez is one of my old altar boys, and he runs the auto shop in town. He says he could use a hand down there. You can do Saturdays until school gets out, and then help out part-time whenever he needs you."

"Yes, sir," Weston allowed those two words, because courtesy demanded them.

Father could see that Weston was uncomfortable about something, so he said, "It's only a suggestion, my son. You can decide for yourself. I thought I would leave you the car."

At this, Weston's head came up out of his lap and he pushed his spectacles up onto his nose, betraying his renewed interest in the subject. "But I don't have a license," he protested, and the old priest could hear his disappointment.

"Ah, that. Well, Louisiana will allow limited driving on a work license for anyone more than fourteen. Erasmo is your employer and he has agreed to sponsor you, so I can take you for your examination sometime before I leave," Father O'Halloran said. "You won't be able to drive after dark, or go anywhere but your place of employment without an adult, but that shouldn't be an issue, should it?"

"Oh good, he can drive me to the market," Ms. Margaret said with genuine delight, getting behind the idea and Weston smiled. He knew she was trying to bolster his confidence.

"Yes, sir," Weston said, more animatedly. "I mean – no, sir."

"That's more like it," Father O'Halloran laughed. He handed Weston a small booklet. "I took the liberty of picking this up. These are the rules of the road that Louisiana will expect you to know for your written test. Piece of cake."

Weston accepted it, but his excitement was tempered by uncertainty. What if, behind the wheel, he couldn't control *them*? But this concern was pushed aside by his genuine delight at the prospect of taking another step toward independence and self-reliance, toward a time when he wouldn't need the charities of others anymore. It was not that he didn't appreciate such things; it was that he felt that his life had thus far been a burden for others to carry.

"Now, let's help Maggie clear the table," Father smiled at his younger sister. "Then, if you have another kindness for this old man, I'd love it if you'd join me for a walk."

Weston got willingly to his feet, ready as he always was to help, ignoring the voices that tried to worsen his doubt, interfere with his resolve.

W

I never say the first thing that comes to my mind, as that is what is served up by the demons. Instead, I wait a few moments until I know what I want to say before I speak. But I fear that this precaution may fail me, so at times I am rendered mute by my inability to master my dread.

I volunteered to be confirmed in the Church, and Momma didn't mind. I don't think she understood it, but she encouraged me, as she always had. I like the ritual of mass, the repetition, the rehearsed response. I always know what I am to say. I had no fear at my confirmation; my lines were written for me, a script to follow, a path blazing and bright, and I had no worry about what would come out of my mouth.

My familiars are subdued here. For the first time since my discovery of the deterrence of electricity I have found another noxious stimulus, sanctity. I am unsure whether these objects are driven by the blessings they have received or my own belief in them. It is likely a bit of both, but I suspect my faith is the stronger of the determinants.

And that first communion, when I was so proud to affirm my love for the sacrifice made by Christ, I welcomed the searing Host onto my tongue, accepting my suffering and all the suffering that was to come. I knew I would serve with my whole heart, if only to imprison those baser parts of myself in order to contribute to the greater good. I swallowed His body with my own blood.

Momma's expression at the time told me everything. She was proud of me. Now I am grateful that she was still with me then to see it.

I was unable to eat for three days, so painful was the blistering that first time.

I chose the plainest rosary of all, one of wood, not beads or stones as the other boys had, as it was the simplest and most beautiful. Pragmatically, it is also the poorest conductor of electricity.

14

"YOU'RE QUIET TONIGHT," FATHER O'HALLORAN observed, as they made their way along the shaded lane in the last minutes of daylight. Twilight hovered above the trees, with their flowered crowns that heralded the coming summer.

"I'm sorry, Father," Weston said absently.

"Where are you?" Father O'Halloran asked him, wanting something from him. "Not here, not present to witness the end of another glorious day. Not to mention that sunset."

"I-" Weston began, and then stopped. He was still too afraid to say what he wanted to, what he'd wanted to tell his friend for a very long time. The burden was becoming too heavy to carry. "I will miss you, Father."

"And I you," Father O'Halloran paused and looked at him carefully. "But you need to find your voice, my son. If your call to orders leads to your advancement to ordination, you will have to demonstrate that you can call others to the faith. You speak well. What are you afraid of?"

"So many things," Weston whispered, and Father O'Halloran strained to hear him. "I must tell you, Father, that I worry I will be unfit for the collar. I pray, I study the holy writings, I evaluate them in the ancient languages, but these are mere scholarships. What if I am unacceptable to God fundamentally?"

It was more words than the boy had spoken in a very long time, other than when reading aloud to his mentor late at night in the priest's library, perhaps more of a speech than O'Halloran had ever heard him make.

"Demons," the boy said, turning to make eye contact with Father O'Halloran. "They are always with me."

O'Halloran felt a chill, but dismissed it as the coming on of night, that first drop in temperature that raises the goosebumps on one's arms. He was concerned with the boy's earnest tone. But he suspected that these were the worries of a devout young man with the usual attendant adolescent guilt and dreams.

"Weston, a priest must first understand and embrace the one reality that he cannot escape. A fundamental truth that he is not meant to escape. A priest is a mortal man, with all the attendant challenges and weaknesses."

"Can you tell me about it, how you deal with sin, Father?" Weston's question was such a plea that the old priest's heart was touched by its urgency.

"A good priest embraces humanity, both generally, accepting all of its ugliness, and within himself," O'Halloran replied, pausing before he continued. "He avoids the sin of pride that can creep in and make him believe he has been elevated above others. You will find this is very difficult, because the culture of the priesthood has in many ways invested itself with this insidious belief, may God forgive me such an accusation. In this way, he can understand his own failings, of which pride and vanity are the most dangerous, I will argue."

"But my dreams of late, they are becoming worse, becoming…more…" Weston found that his own mortification about the things he dreamt of lately could not be so easily articulated. But Father had once been a teenage boy, so he understood what was not being said.

"Lust is certainly a common temptation, but perhaps also the most natural of the sins, and it should also be combatted with this understanding of one's humanity. There is an evolutionary imperative to procreate, and this imperative comes from the Creator, so it is not a bad thing, but it must be overcome." Here, Father O'Halloran paused, to allow Weston to comment, but he was unsurprised when the boy remained silent, so he continued.

"Even for the layperson, to ignore that he has human control can make a man a rapist. It is a simple thing, that no one should be asked or forced to give up autonomy over their own body, their own sexuality. Even in the sacrament of marriage, a wife should not be forced against her wishes, nor should such a thing be sanctioned by holy men or justified by the demands of procreation. To do so requires a turning away from humanity, a diminishing of the respect due another," he remarked. "But the priest denies himself as a sacrifice, as a vow of purity, to turn away from worldly things and take up the example of Christ. It is no small thing that the Church asks of us, which is why you will be questioned about your calling again and again."

"You make it sound easy, Father," Weston lamented.

"Do I?" Father O'Halloran began walking again, slowly, to allow Weston to fall into step beside him. "It is a daily struggle, even now, to forgive myself my human weaknesses. But the work is eased because I remember that I am just a man. If I understand the man, and do not deny his susceptibilities, I can be a better priest. It is my job, really, to understand the human condition, and make myself open to all its possibilities. It is the way that the soul finds God, in my opinion."

"Is that what you mean about my finding my voice?" Weston asked.

"In part. Being unafraid to say the wrong thing in order to find the right thing is an expression of self-love. Forgiveness for oneself must come first. You cannot love others, cannot really love God without first loving yourself with all of your shortcomings," O'Halloran told him.

"But what if something disastrous comes out?" Weston asked.

"Oh, my son," O'Halloran laughed. "That is a certainty. But you remember that you are not ultimately in control. Let God guide you. It's not what you say now, it's what you say next."

The priest put a hand on Weston's shoulder, and Weston knew it was both for reassurance and to mask a frailty, because he needed to lean in for a bit of support as they neared the end of the block. Weston read the signal but said nothing, and turned back toward the house.

"You know, with your understanding of languages and theology, you could consider other careers," Father O'Halloran said in seriousness. "You could be a linguist, or do diplomatic work, or teach."

"Do you question my devotion and my calling?" Weston asked, his tone far more determined on this subject than any other.

"I do not, my son," O'Halloran told him. "I see the love for God in you, and a faith stronger than any I have known. There is no doubt in you about the divine, and that is the single greatest hurdle for any man of the cloth. It is a hurdle that many never clear in a lifetime."

"I have a doubter's proof," Weston said softly, and O'Halloran smiled.

"I believe you must," the priest replied. "But you will continue to be questioned. You are very young. The Church will try to put the brakes on your path to the priesthood and delay your ordination. It is unusual to accept a man to orders before he is thirty, for good reason. The Church gives men an out, a way to escape to secular life, to lovers, to families, time to change their minds about what they will leave forever behind them. This life is not for everyone. Most importantly, the Church should never be used as a place to hide from the world; that motivation is common, and it is the worst of all possible reasons to seek the collar."

Weston thought about this, and paused. He understood, and O'Halloran could not, that there was nowhere for him to hide from what he was. He gently took the old man's arm, saying, "C'mon, Father, let's get home so you can relax."

O'Halloran leaned against Weston gratefully, thinking, not for the first time, that the young man was truly the angel his appearance suggested him to be.

15

WESTON LOOKED DOUBTFULLY OUT THE windshield at the long low cinderblock buildings after he had removed the key from the ignition. He sat still, closed his eyes, and listened to the sounds coming from the shadows beyond the open garage bay doors. They were interesting. A pneumatic wrench squealed in crescendo and abruptly stopped, a battery tender hummed in another location, and his sharp hearing caught the solenoid click of a dead starter ahead of a frustrated epithet.

And running through it all, the music, the voices, rapid-fire Spanish, giving the place life and personality. He thought he recognized a few of the words that the fishermen who worked with Grandpa had taught him, and the demons inside moved and pulled with curiosity at some of the more vulgar ones. They understood it, and it was from them that he gained the gift of understanding many tongues. He could inexplicably speak languages he did not know well, or understand what was said to him, and he knew this to be a part of his diabolical legacy.

When he knew it was of no use to delay any longer, and not wanting to disappoint Father O'Halloran or his friend, he opened the driver's door and swung his legs to the ground, pausing a moment before standing up. He was unused to the outrageous adolescent growth that had recently made him even more freakishly tall, not wanting to stand out in any way. And he hadn't gained any weight since his mother had died, which prompted his schoolmates to call him *Ichabod Crane*, and worse.

He was grateful that Ms. Margaret had taken such a protective interest in him, ensuring that his pants were taken out as he grew, giving the world one less item of ridicule. His appearance was contrary to his usual desire to disappear, even though the good priest did his best to reassure Weston that his height and everything else about him was a part of God's plan.

He made his way to the front door of the shop and pulled it open, painfully aware that all those who were waiting for their repairs had nothing else to do but stare. There was no one sitting behind the desk, which presented him with another problem. But a kind patron, an older gentleman, tilted his head toward the open door into the shop and nodded.

Weston poked his head through and sighed. There were at least five different men working busily, and it would be awkward to interrupt, as if it wasn't awkward already. So he stood still just inside the garage, knowing that his presence could not go unnoticed for long.

As usual, he was right. His unsubtle height and other incongruities were not missed, and soon he was approached by a gentleman of indeterminate age, with copper skin, a young, smiling face, and black hair that was peppered with silver. He was wiping his hands on a rag.

He stopped a few feet away to look Weston over. He took in the sturdy blue jeans, broadcloth shirt, and spectacles. The big feet and broad shoulders that the boy hadn't yet grown into, but would make for an impressive man. The long wavy hair that was a decade or more out of fashion, the incredible height, the angel's face.

"You must be Weston," the man said kindly; if any of what he saw bothered him, it would be impossible to discover it. "I am Erasmo Jimenez. I take it you are the one who keeps Father O'Halloran's transmission from giving up between his visits here." His accent was strong, but Weston found it lovely.

Weston nodded shyly, acknowledging his identity and his avocation. It seemed to bother Erasmo not at all that he didn't speak.

"You like transmissions? I've got a tough one. It's old, and wants to give up on me," Erasmo laughed. "C'mon, you can help me with it. It will probably give up all of its secrets to you."

Erasmo showed him the car, and left him to tinker away on his own, so Weston assumed that this vehicle had been left behind. It was unlikely that his new boss would put him to work on something while the owner waited on it.

Surprisingly, the profanities and the rattle and hum of the machinery in the shop interfered with the distraction of his demons, as these things attracted their attention from him. He could focus even more at solving the problem, and in half an hour, he'd decided that someone had grossly abused the clutch and been overly rough with the gearstick.

The car was old, with the antiquated configuration that put reverse forward, opposite the lowest gear. He checked the gearbox and found that the dog clutch arms were loose, and this made them respond poorly or incompletely to the shifter, so he adjusted them and cleaned the interface gaps. Then he tightened the connections between the clutch mechanism and the pressure plate to reset the tension needed by the hydraulics to allow the car to respond when a driver depressed the pedal.

When Erasmo returned to check on him, two hours and fifteen minutes had elapsed, and he was just finishing closure of the gearbox mechanism.

Weston gestured to the engine, mimicking turning the key, and said, "Try now."

Erasmo's eyes got big, but he nodded. "OK, kid."

Weston flushed, waiting for some exclamation of disbelief, but Erasmo had taken him at his word. He was unused to the most basic of respects. The man slid behind the wheel, still looking surprised, watching Weston through the windshield, and started the car. The death rattle from the gearbox was gone, and the stick wasn't jumping.

Erasmo smiled and waved at Weston to join him in the passenger seat. He reversed down the ramp and pulled out of the bay, then drove the car first around the cinderblock structure, and then around the block.

He laughed delightedly when they were halfway around the block and pumped his fist. "*Ese*, you fixed her! You did it, *Loco!*"

When he didn't return to the garage, instead turning the opposite direction on the main road, Weston was confused, but said nothing. Erasmo must have noticed that he was nervous, because he glanced over and said, "You must be hungry. It's lunchtime. My wife always cooks for me, and it's the least I can do. The house is crazy, though, forgive me."

Weston nodded politely, not sure how to feel. He looked down at his filthy hands, grimed with engine oil, and felt awkward.

They drove on in silence for ten minutes, finally pulling up to a tan brick house with a front yard that sloped down to the sidewalk, in a nice neighborhood. A chain link fence enclosed the back yard, where two enormous dogs chased one another. The dogs came to the fence and barked at Erasmo and Weston as they got out of the car.

"Don't worry about them, they make a lot of noise and aren't good for much else. Well, maybe sleeping and eating. They might lick you to death, so don't let them get you on the ground," Erasmo said, and laughed. He led Weston through a side door off the driveway, which put them in the garage, where there were three cars in various states of disrepair.

"You can see that this is my overflow. All the drivers in this house have to park on the street. Luckily, my wife tolerates me," Erasmo told Weston, and Weston was glad he didn't have to say much. He could tell that Erasmo loved his family.

They entered the house into a laundry room, and Erasmo called through to the kitchen. "Adrianna, *estamos aquí!*"

Almost immediately, a dark petite woman even smaller than Erasmo appeared in the doorway.

"Hello, Weston, I hope you like Mexican food. I am glad you could come," she said, smiling as she looked up at him. "Erasmo, he's so beautiful!" She exclaimed, and Weston blushed again, hyperaware of his filthy hands. He curled them tightly against his shirt. He was surprised to be called beautiful.

"You can wash your hands here," Adrianna said kindly, indicating her laundry tub. "Don't be shy, we are used to dirty hands in this house. Erasmo will show you what soaps to use to remove the grease, and he can teach you when to use gloves so that you don't get permanent staining."

While he and Erasmo cleaned their hands, there was a commotion in the hallway. Suddenly, three giggling teenage girls appeared, putting their heads round the doorway to peek at him.

"Oh no, no, no, no, no," Erasmo scolded them. "None of your nonsense, *m'ijas!* Wash your hands and make sure you help *su Mamá.* Let Weston be."

"*Papá,*" frowned the youngest with a pout, but the three of them disappeared again, muttering something that sounded to Weston like *bonito,* which made him blush even harder.

"Don't worry," Erasmo told him, handing him a soft towel to dry his hands. "Like the dogs, they make a lot of noise, but they are harmless. I won't leave you alone with them." He laughed again at the relief he saw in Weston's eyes. "Let's go get something to eat."

16

THE FOOD WAS DELICIOUS, AND there was so much of it. Weston sat down to a plate loaded with black beans, rice, tamales, and eggs. There were two kinds of salsa, and a stack of warm tortillas. Erasmo poured tamarind soda for all the kids, including Weston. Adrianna brought coffee for her husband, and when everyone was seated, they prayed.

It was an alien experience for Weston, sitting in that warm kitchen at that crowded table, elbow to elbow with strangers, but strangely feeling as though he belonged there. For a moment he just sat and enjoyed it, realizing that this was God's kindness and charity at work. There was love and laughter here, too, swirling around him. Everyone talked and laughed together, and it was so different from what he was used to.

He had only been shown kindness by a few people in his life, often in cases where there was some expected duty involved. His mother had loved him desperately, but he felt she had always been afraid for and of him. Father O'Halloran and Ms. Margaret had taken him in, but he didn't fully understand their motives, thought it was more compulsory than voluntary, despite their abundant demonstrations of quiet affection for him. He knew his time with them was transitory, a stop along his journey, not yet realizing that it was the closest approximation he would get to having a home after losing his mother.

He was unused to acceptance and fellowship for their own sake, recalling the sterile, hostile meals he had endured when he was still boarding at school. The isolation and cruelty of those days before his mother had died, before Father O'Halloran had rescued him from that existence.

And no one asked him to talk, or even seemed to expect him to. It was possible to fit in here and at the same time be forgotten. But not entirely. Whenever he glanced up from his food, it seemed a different dark-eyed Jimenez child, usually one of the older girls, was looking at him with curiosity and interest.

Finally, Erasmo spoke, his voice cutting right through the din of his children's chatter. "Marta, Weston fixed your transmission today. We bought the car used; I just haven't had time to get a look at what was wrong with it," he added, for Weston's benefit.

The oldest girl's eyes widened in delight as she looked at Weston with something new in her eyes. Thankfulness. *"Muchas gracias,* Weston," she smiled gratefully, but couldn't resist the little test.

"English, please," scolded Adrianna.

"De nada," Weston answered, just as Adrianna was giving this instruction.

All eyes at the table looked at him with astonishment and respect.

"You're just full of surprises, *m'ijo,"* Erasmo laughed and put a warm hand on Weston's shoulder.

"Thank you for lunch, *Señora,"* Weston said shyly to Adriana.

"Anytime, Weston. I am happy to feed you up," she smiled at him warmly.

Without being asked, Weston stood up and began clearing his plate. He carried the empty plates of a few of the smaller children as well, and took them to the sink. "Can I help clean up?"

"That's very kind, but we'll take care of it," Adrianna said, getting up to give him a hug. "You are a sweet young man."

"It's time for us to get back," Erasmo said, patting his full belly and stretching. He kissed his wife on the cheek and looked at Marta. "Well? We need a ride."

She smiled delightedly and jumped up. Turning to her mother, she said, "Leave those dishes, *Mamá*, I will take care of them when I get back." She kissed her mother, who smiled in happy surprise, and waved her on.

Erasmo seated himself in the front passenger seat, and Marta frowned slightly in disappointment. She brightened when Weston opened the driver's door for her, though.

He climbed into the backseat behind her, and they pulled out of the driveway and headed back toward town.

"It really is fixed! Thank you, Weston! Now I can take the *niños* to school, and I can get a job, right, *Papá?*

"Concentrate on your driving," said Erasmo in mock seriousness. "We shall discuss it."

She delivered them back to the shop, safe and sound. As they were getting out of the car, she asked, "Can I help with anything at the shop later today?"

Erasmo smiled at her while he was shaking his head. "I wonder why the sudden enthusiasm to help."

"Daddy, you know I don't mind helping you," Marta protested.

"*Claro*, but you also don't volunteer," he laughed, putting a hand on her cheek. "*Besos, m'ija.* I will see you at home later. Drive safely, and straight back to the house. Your *Mamá* will be expecting you."

"Yes, *Papá*," she said softly. Then, to Weston, she promised, "See you soon." And with a wave and a secret smile, she was gone.

17

"DON'T JUST PUSH THAT FOOD around on the plate, young man," Ms. Margaret's gentle scolding brought Weston out of his reverie. He was tired from a long day of work at the shop and not enough sleep in the days before. He'd wanted to go straight to his room and sleep when he got home, but didn't want Ms. Margaret to think he didn't appreciate all that she did to care for him. So he had gone through the motions of setting the table and pretending to be company for her. "If you lose another pound this summer, Father O'Halloran will think I starved you!"

At this he smiled, and it reminded him of something he had always wanted to ask her. "Why do you call him Father O'Halloran if he is your brother?"

"I suppose it is out of respect," she told him, smiling to herself.

"Because he is the oldest?" Weston pressed for a better explanation.

"Not really," she replied, gesturing at his full plate. So he took a bite of food to oblige her and she was encouraged to say more. "Although he was mostly grown by the time I came along. I call him that because it is what he wants to be called, child."

"Ms. Margaret," he began shyly, "Do you know why some priests use their last name, and others use their first name after 'Father?'"

"It's a good question," she paused to consider it. "I never thought about it before."

"I mean, isn't it confusing in your family? There are nine Father O'Hallorans out there in the world." He punctuated his question by pointing his fork toward the window.

"Use that fork for what it was meant," she reminded him gently, and he went back to eating, hoping she would keep talking. He loved to hear her rolling Irish brogue, inherited despite living her entire life outside of Ireland. "Well now, there are only four Father O'Hallorans in our family. We then have a Father Eoin, a Father Ciarán, a Father Ronan, a Father Cillian, and a Father Macgregor."

"Wow. So what happens when you are all together at the same time?" Weston asked.

"As you can imagine, that doesn't happen very often," she said, and she looked genuinely sad, but she chuckled. "But perhaps you'll see it for yourself someday. There's a lot of Father O'Halloran this, and Father O'Halloran that, I suppose."

"So why do you think *our* Father O'Halloran doesn't use his first name?" Weston asked.

"Padraig never liked his first name, as I understand it," she told him. "I think it's a lovely name myself, but the problem is that no one ever called him that. He was always 'Paddy' and he hated it. I think he was relieved to leave it behind. So when I say that I call him what he prefers to be called, I mean to say, I do it out of respect for my brother and his wishes."

"Ms. Margaret?" Weston began, but yawned exaggeratedly.

"Yes, dear?" she inquired, looking at him critically.

"Will you tell me more about your family?"

"If you like," she consented. "But right now you're about thirty seconds ahead of putting your face in those potatoes. Go to bed. I'll clear tonight, and you can help me tomorrow."

As if he needed a reminder of his weariness, he punctuated her statement with yet another yawn, but couldn't resist asking another question. "What shall I call myself when I am a priest?"

"I'm sure you'll make a wise choice when the time comes," she smiled at him indulgently.

"I just think-" he started to say something and decided to stay silent.

"What is it, child?" Ms. Margaret asked, always wanting to encourage him when he felt like talking, which was not often.

"I mean, Father Seraph?" Weston shrugged.

"What is it? Father Angel, essentially," Ms. Margaret tilted her head. She was trying to understand him. "That's not so bad."

"I know. It just sounds kind of…pretentious."

Now she really did laugh, which surprised him. He was often unintentionally funny. But he knew she wasn't laughing at him.

"Well, then. Go to bed, Father *Weston*," she teased, shooing him up the stairs.

18

WESTON WASN'T SURE HOW THE argument started, just that he was suddenly at the center of it. He had been playing a peaceful game of Monopoly with the Jimenez children when Marta and Iliana started arguing.

"He is taking *me* to prom," Marta protested. "You don't need an escort for your birthday, and besides, *Papá* will be with you."

"You had Martín!" Iliana shouted, throwing down her gamepiece in disgust.

"*Sí! Nuestro primo, ¿de veras?*" Marta replied, the argument devolving into Spanish given its ferocity. "*¡No puede ir con un novio!*"

"*¡Weston no es tu novio! Solo es amable,*" Iliana retorted unkindly.

Weston sat quietly, uncomfortable in the midst of the maelstrom, and before long, Adrianna appeared in the doorway with a frown.

"Ladies, please. Why the shouting? You have a guest," she motioned to Weston. "What is going on?!"

"*Es que Marta cree que Weston le pertenece,*" Iliana responded.

"English, please," Erasmo emerged from the next room. "What is this about Weston?" he asked, seeing that Weston wore the expression of a hostage.

"He doesn't belong to me," Marta hissed. *"Mamá*, tell Iliana that Weston cannot take her to her *quinceañera* because he is taking me to prom!"

"I don't see why I cannot do both," Weston said softly, and the entire family turned in surprise. "I am happy to escort Marta to her prom, but I can also attend Iliana's *quinceañera, ¿por qué no?*"

Iliana squealed with delight and jumped up to hug Weston.

"Spoken like a man in fear for his life," Erasmo nodded approvingly, ignoring Marta's attempt to plead her case. He looked critically at both his elder daughters. "Recognize kindness when you see it," he advised them.

"Weston, that *is* very kind," Adrianna gave him a hug of her own, despite knowing it might embarrass him further. She turned a stern gaze on her daughters. "Apologize to him, and to each other. Weston, if I hadn't already told you, we will pay for your tuxedo rentals. Children, wash up, and come help get the table ready for supper."

Weston wondered if he had done something wrong, because suddenly Marta was no longer making eye contact with him, and she looked very angry. He busied himself putting away the Monopoly board and pieces, arranging the money neatly in the compartments and then followed the others into the kitchen.

Abuela Jimenez was in there, and she smiled gaily at Weston as she attended her cooking. He peered over her shoulder at the *posole* she was making, watching her nimble fingers add the hominy and the spices. It smelled wonderful. She was humming along to the radio. He loved being in this warm kitchen that barely held all of them, crammed together in love and the industry of preparing a meal. He washed his hands and joined the preparations, taking the warm tortillas from Adrianna and placing them on the table.

The back door opened, and Eusebio, Erasmo's brother, entered with his wife and children, adding to the confusion. The dogs were jumping at their feet and Adrianna was shooing them out while Eusebio kissed Abuela.

The song on the radio changed, and Eusebio and Erasmo gave a small shout, reaching for their respective wives and beginning an elaborate dance right there in the kitchen. Weston leaned against the counter and watched. Eusebio's wife, Omahyra, was laughing, but he noticed that Adrianna was quietly trying to protest. It was clear she was not as facile with the steps as her sister-in-law, but Weston could see that she and Erasmo were very happy to be dancing together. He saw Marta watching them closely and had an epiphany of his own.

He made a point of sitting next to Marta at dinner, which seemed to please her. Iliana sat with her grandmother and was not remotely affected by the seating choice he had made. He smiled. It was easier for Iliana, always harder for Marta, the eldest child, based on what he had observed among his schoolmates and here, in this house.

After dinner, he helped clear the table, helped Adrianna with the dishes even when she demurred, trying to send him off with the other children. He stayed to dry them with Abuela, and Marta joined them. When they were finished, Marta let herself out through the screen door to the backyard. He followed her, and stood silently next to her on the sidewalk for a few moments before bumping her shoulder lightly and letting himself out through the back gate.

She followed, and they went down the alley in silence. He turned left when they reached the street, intending to take the long way around the block with her. It was a fine evening, and although the days were getting a bit shorter, twilight was still a long way off.

They continued for a time without speaking, the soft rhythm of their sneakers on the pavement accompanied by the sounds of the neighborhood kids playing a game of pickup baseball in the corner lot. Some of the younger Jimenez children had joined them, and they paused to watch for a few moments. Marta waved to her younger brothers and sisters.

"I am sorry about earlier," Marta said softly. "She just makes me so crazy sometimes. You are lucky to be an only child."

"Am I?" he replied thoughtfully. "It can be lonely."

"She tries to do everything that I do," Marta sounded annoyed, and he knew she hadn't even heard him, she was so caught up in her altercation with her sister.

"She wants to be like you. She admires you," Weston told her, surprised that this was not obvious to her. "She may even be a bit jealous."

He did not look down at her, but sensed she was looking at him. "Do you think so?"

"It's obvious," he nodded.

She smiled. "I didn't know."

"She really wants your approval, that's all," he told her. "Perhaps she is a bit overbearing but maybe she thinks it is the only way to get your attention."

"Wow. I never thought about it." Marta considered this. "I *could* be nicer to her."

"You are already a great sister," Weston reassured her. "I just wanted to tell you what I thought."

"Thank you, Weston," Marta briefly grasped his hand, and, surprised, he squeezed hers, but let go.

"I should tell you," Marta began, and he could hear the amusement in her voice, "Iliana's dress is peach colored."

"And?"

"And the escort has to wear the matching color," she told him, unable to suppress a giggle.

"Why in the world didn't you stop me?" Weston laughed too.

"I don't know," Marta said. "I was a little mad, and I guess I thought it served you right. And even if I wasn't mad, I can't wait to see you dressed up *como un durazno gigante*."

"Should I be afraid to ask you what color you will wear to prom?" he asked.

"That is a surprise," she told him, shaking her head. "But I will let *Papá* know what I want you to wear."

"Now I am terrified," he told her.

"As you should be," she teased, and Weston could tell that everything was right again, so he turned back toward her house.

19

WESTON'S FINAL YEAR OF HIGH school drew quickly to a close, and as graduation approached he was busier than ever.

Physically, he had gained weight and muscle, both from the exertions of his after-school job, but also because the crew at the shop spent time after hours trying to outdo one another with free weights. Erasmo kept an old weight bench in the corner of the shop, and it was there to provide an outlet for the frustrations of the work, but it had become a rite of passage for any who came through the place.

"C'mon, Clark Kent," the men would call to Weston, impressed with his not insignificant displays of strength.

"*Ay, Loco,* he really *is* Superman," they would jostle each other, adding more weight, and after a year of this, he was truly transformed. He enjoyed these sessions, and realized a secondary benefit. He could wrestle control of himself more easily when the demons tried to push him around.

The sleek young man in the unfortunate peach tuxedo was so fit and poised at the *quinceañera* that the insults of Iliana's brothers and their friends died on their lips, and none dared do what they had planned, which was to ask Weston whether his suit was pink. And females of every age envied Iliana her choice of escort.

Similarly, he was gracious and chivalrous with Marta at her prom, understanding that his presence was providing her with some special teenage status he did not understand, since she had brought a date from another school. No one could tell that he was two years her junior, and since he was able to honestly say that he was also graduating from high school that spring, it made no difference. She was lovely and happy, and he was attentive to her, which he could see pleased her.

But after the dance he resisted her efforts to get him to attend any parties, insisting that he had made her father a promise, and taking her directly home. Even though Erasmo and Adrianna looked surprised at their early return, they consented to allow Marta to take her car back out to join her friends. Weston declined, not wanting the complication of sending her any mixed messages, and slightly afraid of Erasmo, he used that as his excuse to bow out.

Thus Marta's disappointment was blunted because logically she understood that a young man who worked with her father might actually be in peril if he were to cross the line with her. She pouted briefly, but he walked with her out to the car.

"You're leaving after graduation, aren't you?" she asked him sadly.

"I am," he nodded.

"Are you worried about *Papá*?" she asked earnestly. "I would never tell him anything about us."

"It isn't that," he shook his head, and then laughed. "Well, some of it is that. I think you should think about what *you* really need."

She leaned into him, looking up into his face, searching for something, and shook her head.

"What?" Marta's voice betrayed her frustration. "Someone who will stay? I don't care that you are leaving. I mean, I do, but I want you to see me. I want you to touch me."

"I think you'd regret it someday," he shook his head. "Perhaps sooner than you think."

"Is there something wrong with me?" She threw up her hands in frustration. "Or maybe with *you*?! Are you gay or something?"

"There isn't anything wrong with you," he told her, addressing the true concern. "You're amazing. Smart, beautiful, fun. I just don't have the right thing to offer you. I don't have what you deserve."

"Which is what?" she asked, her anger departing because he did nothing to inflame it.

"A future. The kind of love you should demand of anyone who wants to be with you," he explained.

"It's true, then. I didn't believe *Papá* when he told me you were going to become a priest, but you are really going to go through with it," she said softly.

"It's what I want," Weston explained.

"More than me?"

"Think about how you feel right now," he told her. "It feels right to you; it makes sense. But don't you want the object of your affection to feel the same way about you? I care for you, Marta. I cannot be the one for you. And nothing about my decision takes anything away from you. Nothing at all. I know you are my friend. I need your understanding about this most of all."

"I thought I could change your mind," she admitted sadly and began to cry. He pulled her close and held onto her, her tears soaking through his shirt, cold by the time they reached his skin, and with difficulty he ignored the taunts of his resident familiars, who asked him in the most vulgar ways imaginable what difference it would make if he took what she offered him.

20

WESTON FINISHED CLEANING UP AFTER Mass, glancing out the open doors to the lovely afternoon sunlight beyond. He loved empty churches, the way the light filtered through windows of varying size and color, the cool pillars, the stone floors echoing beneath his feet. The smell of incense that was unchanged and, he thought, welcoming, waiting for him in every Catholic church he'd ever been in.

He stepped out to the vestibule, absently touching a searing drop of holy water to his forehead, genuflecting, and crossing himself. The air was still, but the demons were restless, whispering to him from the shadows at the top of the façade that faced the street. The sun was starting its descent to the west, but still unbearably hot on the sidewalks.

Notre Dame Seminary was a haven for him where it may have been a hurdle for others. He was by a decade the youngest man admitted to his accelerated program, which put him on track to earn his Master of Divinity in ten semesters in lieu of sixteen. It was a prestigious track, one usually reserved for older students who had come to the cloth in the latter part of their third decade, after earning degrees in secular disciplines and finding they could not deny their desire to seek religious occupation.

He was grateful for his seminary studies, the exhausting routine, the endless scholarly and liturgical examinations. Grateful even for the disapproval of many of his instructors, understanding their prejudices about his extreme youth; he welcomed their inquiries about his personal fitness, feeling some satisfaction that most of them behaved differently once they had spoken with him about his faith.

He was relieved to find that Father O'Halloran's kind reassurance about the spoken word was true. Weston was infinitely more confident in his control over what he said, understanding that his fear might let the demons take their reign. The priests who had taught him in parochial school had recognized his intellect, but they would not have recognized the erudite, well-spoken young man who contributed eloquently to discussions and composed prayers that evinced a maturity that was not possessed by many of his peers. Indeed, the silent, withdrawn young man who had been brought to Terrebonne Parish was gone. In his place was a mature, forward-facing seminarian who, while not necessarily ambitious, was anxious to acquire the learning and training he needed to assume the collar.

And the demons were quieter than they had ever been. The sanctity of the sacraments was a torture to them, and though Weston's flesh was also affected, burned or blistered by the divine, these hurts were momentary, and he welcomed them as his burden to carry.

21

WESTON FINISHED HIS MASTER OF Divinity in eight semesters, largely because he decided to forego semester breaks and vacations to continue his studies and pursue his scholarly writing.
He would take the bus to Terrebonne for brief periods at named holidays, usually traveling on Christmas Day as he had been a participant priest at the Nativity Mass at midnight on Christmas Eve, an assignment more senior priests and his fellow students avoided if they possibly could.

Similarly, he did not leave during Spring Recess, as it was called at NDS (Weston assumed the secular term 'Spring Break' was associated with so much sinful behavior that the Catholics had to disassociate themselves from it). This was typically taken in the final Holy Week leading up to Easter, and he enjoyed most of all the expressions of faith related to Christ's Passion and Resurrection. The relative periods of immense traffic for Mass, the observance of the Stations of the Cross, Maundy Thursday, Good Friday, and Easter itself alternated with significant time for quiet reflection while preparing the empty church for the onslaught of the faithful. He could not bring himself to trade the routine, the ritual, the beauty of these celebrations for his own selfish need for rest.

Father O'Halloran and Ms. Margaret had, in the latter years, come to spend the Holy Week in New Orleans, so as not to create any conflict for Weston. This brought him more pleasure than he had thought it would, and it was nice to retire from all the busy preparations of Easter to a quiet dinner with them.

They would return to Terrebonne Easter night, wisely watching Weston try to avoid falling asleep as supper neared its end, knowing he would rise before the dawn to prepare for Easter Monday. His tireless love for his chosen vocation gave them a great deal of pride, and not a little relief that he had found his place in the world. Father O'Halloran suspected that this zeal was to keep Weston from dwelling on the hurts he had suffered in his short life, and had no perspective on the real reason for the young man's drive. He knew that Weston's faith and piety were real, inspiring even to himself, and he was unsurprised that Church leadership was beginning to take notice of him.

In the first semester of his final year at seminary, he was assigned to an advisor for his practicum and thesis. As his focus was on demonology and the Global Church, he was channeled to another prodigy, a priest from South America who had risen quickly through the Church's ranks, and was said to have been nominated to the bishopric, which would make him one of the youngest to wear the red sash should he be appointed.

Father Kedron was on special assignment from the Vatican, and Weston had ignored the whispers that the reason he had come was to evaluate and groom the young prodigy at NDS. Father Kedron had accepted many prior assignments to teach at the seminary, and he was a refugee from his home country of Venezuela. He too, was a linguaphile who spoke three languages fluently, and had scholarly understanding of Latin and Greek.

Weston's first meeting with him was inauspicious, a harbinger of things to come. He was summoned to the Archdiocese in early fall for an initial discussion of his thesis, and was presented to a fit man of not quite forty years with piercing dark grey eyes, relatively fair for his provenance, and a trim and fit figure. His advisor seemed a bit too pleased with Weston's appearance, and Weston's familiars seemed to respond to the man in a very uncomfortable way.

Weston supposed his reservations to be the work of being in the presence of a priest who had true political ambitions, as he could ascertain no piety, but he promised to be charitable and give the relationship a chance. He discovered that his first impressions were not wrong.

Father Kedron was non-plussed upon learning that Weston's command of Latin, Greek, and Aramaic were better than his own, surprised that someone only nineteen years of age could also read and write those tongues as well as speak them. Weston presented him with a completed thesis, asking honestly for his opinion, wanting a dialogue about scholarly edits as he was contemplating his doctoral thesis in Moral Theology and had been accepted to the Catholic University of America for a two-semester residence to complete his Doctor of Sacred Theology the following year.

Weston's earnest innocence amused Kedron, but the older priest was cautious in his own way. The youngster had indeed garnered the attention of the Vatican, and as much as Kedron's petty and jealous heart wanted to make Weston suffer, to teach him his own brand of humility, his love of advancement won out. He knew that if he were to take the young priest as a protégé, his name would forever be connected to the meteoric rise of this gifted student. And he also had to admit that Weston's face and form were pleasing to him, and these were currencies Kedron well knew how to exploit. Perhaps the young man was a candidate for his own secret sect, the *Dei Gloria*.

For now, he would have to control himself, thinking he could manipulate Weston and feed his own appetites. He made every accommodation for the young priest, approving his thesis and promising to present him to Rome the following summer.

W

I expect too much of others. Father O'Halloran always said so. But not as though it was a bad thing necessarily. Perhaps more a weakness, or the wish of one hopelessly naïve to the realities of this world. I assume people are inherently good, or at least better than I.

While I have no comment on my own goodness, inherent or not, as I am not fit to judge, I find in times of despair that there seems to be a race to the bottom. A contest to somehow prove one's own worth greater than another's, costing dearly in lost love for humanity.

I am surprised by vanity and pride where I find it in my fellow priests. And in Church leadership. Perhaps it is true that power is absolute in its ability to corrupt. Their reasons for taking orders seem lost to time, whatever ideals they brought to seminary, if indeed they did so, abandoned for the climb to power. They hunger for advancements and singularity that I do not seek.

Yet even such thoughts as these cast me in a sinful light, as I am pronouncing judgement too often. I do try to love them, and I pray for all of them. I do not understand them, despite my desperate attempts at the exercise.

The contempt the Morningstar wishes me to have for humanity has found home in their hearts and minds. It is a contempt I do not harbor, for I see so many with so little, and it costs me nothing to give what charity and love I possess.

I am attached now to the Dominican order, and these brothers are the vainest creatures yet; seeming to be most concerned with the cut of their tailored cassocks and their slim skirts. I yearn for the quiet servitude of the Jesuits, but it is not to be. Kedron wants a trophy, and I gather that I am his steppingstone to greater things, as I have attracted the notice of Rome.

22

ORDINATION WAS BITTERSWEET   Weston underwent
blessings in conclave, and then took vows publicly during the
Graduation Mass.

Father O'Halloran came, and of course Ms. Margaret, who cried,
as she had for the ordination of each of her brothers. To Weston's
great pleasure, Erasmo Jimenez came with his family, and
surprisingly, most of the staff from the automotive shop came along
to extend their congratulations and share their pride in his
accomplishments.

It was a celebrated honor, to be sure. Yet Weston knew it meant
he was now on a journey that would take him away from everything
he had known before. It was both a beginning and an end. The
sacred Alpha and Omega.

He was now Father Weston Seraph, OP, M.Div., made official
by those few words at the center of his diploma. At twenty, he had
prevailed in his petitions to be allowed to assume the collar; just a
semester earlier, they had reassured him that awarding him the
Master of Divinity was assured, although his fitness for the cloth was
still being debated rigorously among seminary leadership, who had
requested advisement from the Archdiocese. Weston knew that the
endorsement of the Dominican Order had helped improve his
supplication, and knew that Kedron had campaigned on his behalf

with ranking Vatican contacts to secure the permissions needed to ensure his promotion.

It was a question of canon law, which required one to attain the age of twenty-five before becoming a candidate for the priesthood. Given the educational requirements, and the emphasis on the knowledge of at least one ancient language, most scholars, no matter how precocious, could not finish the minimum requirements at that age even if they started out of high school. But the Church will bend the rules, even break them, when there is a clear benefit to do so.

Although the Archbishop had been firmly against it, counseling that a man must reach a certain maturity prior to contemplating such a grave responsibility as the vows entailed, Weston knew his professors and the seminary Chancellor had argued on his behalf, not wanting his scholarship to be lost to secular academia.

Kedron's argument had been the most eloquent of all, delivered in that lilting accent, suggesting that the Church could ill afford to turn away any who sought priesthood and showed fitness for the work. But in Weston's case, he had argued, you have a man whose love for God, for the Church, shines from him like a beacon. He has mastered the old languages and throws the energies of his youth toward the causes of charity and evangelism in a troubled society, Kedron told them. He reported that Weston's career would have the longevity to do real good in the world, and exhorted them not to be led by prejudice of any kind, which should have no place in their hearts and minds. He finished by reminding them that Weston had lost his own family and found a new one in the Church, asking them to consider their responsibilities to the young applicant as Brothers in Christ, asking them to recall their own ordinations, asking them to lead Weston as all new priests were led and mentored in their ministry.

Beautiful as it was, Weston knew it to be self-serving. Without his ordination, Kedron had no excuse to keep him close, and less reason to present him to Rome in the coming year. Weston would go on to his doctorate, and Kedron would be recalled after his sabbatical, leaving Weston under the mentorship of another.

It was not yet known to Weston that his ordination had been secured more personally, by the highest office in the Church.

23

WESTON TRADED ASPIRANT'S ROBES FOR the tailored cassock of the Dominicans, but he kept the Converse trainers that Ms. Margaret had purchased for him. He disdained the pearl rosary given him by the Order, giving it instead to Marta, knowing she would love it, and kept his beloved wooden rosary with him when he went to Rome.

He owned nothing of personal value to discharge prior to taking on his duties, and his last errand was to the eye doctor to ensure that his prescription would serve him. Most of his personal effects were forwarded to the priest's dormitory at Catholic University, where he would begin his one-year residence in the fall.

His official work for the summer was as a scholarly cleric in Kedron's retinue, which essentially translated to something between a valet and a manservant. It was the Catholic version of a personal assistant, and Weston was surprised to find that he was not alone. It appeared that because Kedron was likely to ascend as bishop in the near future, a number of young priests in Rome were positioning themselves to curry his favor.

Weston was considered the least of these. Not just because of his extreme youth, but also because, he learned, one can come from a family of Catholic priests, similar to the O'Hallorans, and these legacy priests came often from wealthy families whose money contributed to the Church's banks and whose political influence afforded the

Church another kind of capital. His provenance was hardly distinguished, and there was a kind of snobbish disdain for Americans that subtly pervaded Vatican culture. It was so like his experience at parochial school that he should not have been surprised.

Weston simply wanted to immerse himself in his duties and disappear, as he felt it was the best possible balance for a priest to humbly do good works without expecting any recognition. But his status as the youngest modern priest in the church made him a curiosity, and he was invited to meet with many cardinals and prelates who wanted to examine him. Kedron, of course, invited himself along to all of these events, but Weston was grateful to have someone who was willing to teach him the protocols, even if the reasons were not remotely altruistic.

Some of them wanted to test him. He'd been given an assignment by Father Kedron to review the Church archives on the Inquisitors' diaries. Not a pleasant task, to be certain, as it required him to bear witness to a number of atrocities the Church had endorsed in the name of eradicating evil from the world.

In many cases, Weston observed, they had probably introduced it. The Morningstar's hand was present in these pages, and he waded through volume after volume, his exhausted mind transitioning from Latin, to Spanish, to Portuguese, with Italian and French occasionally.

What he found was driven by superstition and prejudice, but in some of the accounts he recognized something he valued for his own scholarship. The presence and proof of a not insignificant number of what he believed to be true demonic possessions. Hidden among the cases which could be ascribed to mental illness, and those driven by misogyny, religious discrimination, and racial profiling, were events that spoke to him. First-person accounts of diabolical acts that were perpetrated with random abandon and violence, or stigmata of possession that he recognized from his own experiences, things that could not be explained away by a modern rational mindset.

In an effort to understand better the similarities between these selected incidents, and selfishly wanting to comprehend such events in the context of his personal affliction, he began to catalogue them in a notebook that he kept on his person to augment this scholarship. In one of the Vatican libraries, working alone late at night, a kindly cleric came to stand at his elbow and inquire about what he was reading.

"This is the work of the *Dei Gloria*," the man recognized it immediately, and if he was curious about Weston himself, it was not obvious as it had been with so many others.

"I am Weston," he introduced himself, and the man nodded gently, as though this was known to him.

"You are *Father* Weston, and I am Father Nicolò," the elderly man told him, but his tone held no hint of rebuke, only a reminder. Weston marveled at the formality and hierarchies that were observed without fail in this unusual and fascinating place. "I am an archivist and librarian here. I notice you coming late at night, and you read, and you read. Do you never sleep?" His English was broken and heavily accented, as if he had to painstakingly pick every word, so Weston surprised him by answering in Italian.

"I sleep poorly, Father, which is perhaps God's blessing, as He has given me much to do," he replied.

"You are too young to be so afflicted," Father Nicolò said. "Insomnia is usually the province of the old." He quietly perused the tomes that Weston was examining, and then motioned for Weston to follow him.

"If it is demons that interest you, you must have access to other collections," he protested, taking out his keys and leading Weston through the stacks.

"I was not given permission to-" Weston protested, understanding that the Church's secrets were legendary, and She kept them under the watchful eyes of Vatican leadership. He did not want to cross a boundary, wanted to be obedient to Kedron's directives.

"*I* am the gatekeeper here," the old priest reassured him kindly. "So few of us really seek knowledge here, where it is overshadowed by the quest for power. So few of us can truly discern what is important."

He unlocked one of the gates, and admitted them to a narrow aisle which contained many volumes of varying age and size. He narrowed his eyes and sneezed soundly, twice, excusing himself. "This dust will do me in someday, but it is not such a bad way to go, is it?"

Weston smiled and remained quiet. He understood the great privilege he was afforded in this. Father Nicolò searched briefly and then spread his arms to indicate the section that should interest Weston. "Here, my son. Here you will find more evidence of your quarry. These are some of the diaries of our most prolific exorcists, both within and without the *Gloria* sect. Work on these and then we will decide what you should see next," he nodded, as if pleased with this decision.

Weston must have looked as lost as he felt. There were hundreds of books here. A lifetime of research.

"Let the Lord guide you. *Ce n'est pas la mer á boire.* It is not as if you must drink the sea tonight, my son," Father Nicolò chuckled. "You can give the clerk my name and you will be admitted to this collection at any time," he said kindly, and leaving Weston with such assurances of his wisdom and his assistance, he departed.

By the time Weston returned to his study table, his personal notebook, containing months of research, had disappeared.

24

ONE HOT SUNDAY IN JULY, Weston received a note following Mass from one of the other clerics, instructing him to meet Father Kedron. The address on the note was outside Vatican City, but one of the gate stewards informed him that the *direccione* was within walking distance, and gave him rudimentary directions. These were improved upon by a local flower vendor, and Weston was surprised to discover that his destination was a very grand hotel.

He recognized some of his contemporaries taking up station in the lobby, one of whom came over to escort him in the lift. They rode to a high floor, walking down the long hallway to a guestroom halfway down the corridor. As they approached the door, it opened abruptly, and a young woman emerged. She was lovely in a very simple way, but something was wrong. When she saw the two priests she turned dark frightened eyes on them briefly, and flinched away, hurrying back toward the elevators on unsteady legs. Weston's own familiars were piqued by her presence, and he felt the pull of their interest about what was inside the room.

His escort evinced no visible emotion, leading Weston inside. It was actually a fairly lavish suite, and they were admitted to a stylish entryway with a small corridor leading to a seating area. There was another room opposite, likely a bedroom, and it was from here that Kedron emerged, half-dressed, the top half of his cassock unbuttoned and hanging, the shirt and sleeves dangling from his waist, his torso and chest bare.

He was slightly breathless, but smiled brightly at Weston in greeting. "Hello, my friend, thank you for meeting me here."

Kedron moved past them without any obvious concern about the state of his clothing and led them into the living rooms on the other side of the suite, taking a deep draught from the remains of a glass of wine on the countertop in the kitchenette. Weston was suddenly certain that Kedron had not attended Mass that morning, and further, that the man wanted him to know it, wanted Weston to see him in this setting, had meant for him to see the woman leaving.

He opened the freezer and cracked the ice tray, shaking cubes into a kitchen towel which he applied to his left hand. Weston could now see that the knuckles were bruised and swollen, and he was angry, although he swallowed any sign of it. His demons were stimulated by this display, the blunted sexuality, the violence that had recently occurred at the hands of this priest.

It was another kind of test. Was Weston loyal to this brotherhood that he had been invited to join, that was a requirement, really, for his training and deployment as an exorcist? But he knew that Kedron believed him a prude, not understanding that Weston was mature enough to acknowledge his own desires without the exercise of them.

"How are your studies going?" Kedron inquired, and for not the first time, Weston saw something dark and all too familiar in those eyes. "Ready for your S-T-D?" he asked suggestively, and the other priest chuckled.

"Very well, thank you," Weston answered politely, wanting to frustrate their mockery. It was a veiled reference to his plan to attain his Doctorate in Sacred Theology, which carried the unfortunate acronym STD, for its Latin name, *Sacrae Theologiae Doctor*. "I look forward to returning to formal education."

"I'm sure you do," Kedron observed mockingly, and accepting a towel from the other priest, he dried his torso before putting his arms into the sleeves of his clerical robe and carefully fastening the buttons.

He replaced the icepack on his hand and winced briefly before facing Weston with a look of utter curiosity.

"You've been summoned to Castel Gandolfo," Kedron remarked wonderingly. The third of their number now stared at Weston with an incredulous expression and a new respect.

"Close your mouth, Alejandro," Kedron said, and his tone betrayed what he'd been trying to hide. He was furious.

Weston said nothing, letting his sincere expression of shock convey his feelings. Castel Gandolfo was the Pope's summer vacation home.

"You know nothing of this?" Kedron asked him.

"No, Father," Weston told him.

"Alejandro, leave us," Kedron demanded, and the other priest departed readily, hesitating only to afford Weston a second meaningful glance.

When the sound of the outer door closing reached their ears, Kedron remarked petulantly, more to himself than to Weston, "*I've never been invited to the private residence.*"

Weston kept his peace, correctly recognizing the volatility of the situation.

25

THE DRIVE OUT TO THE hills of Alban took nearly an hour with traffic, but Weston didn't mind, as he took in the beauty of the landscape. Father Kedron sat silently beside him in the back of the Audi that was driven by another one of his clerics, quietly seething.

At the residence, they were shown into a formal receiving room on the top floor. French doors opened to the patio beyond, and after a short wait, the Pope attended them. Weston followed Kedron's lead, kneeling quietly and waiting to be acknowledged.

Kedron was greeted warmly, and he spoke to the Pontiff for a few moments in German, probably assuming that Weston did not know the language, but the Pope's eyes betrayed a suspicion that they were understood. It was small talk, nothing of importance, simply a ploy to make Weston understand that Kedron was known to this man.

"Father Kedron, I thank you for all your faithful service." Here the Pope held out his ring once more, and Kedron, obviously confused and visibly wounded, recognized the dismissal. He knelt dutifully and kissed the ring before departing the salon with one of the Papal secretaries, who closed the doors behind them, not before giving Weston a look of utter hostility.

The Pope turned to Weston with a smile of genuine warmth and said, "Please be at peace, my son." He indicated the open doors, inviting Weston to join him on the patio outside, and they sat together in the late afternoon sunshine.

One of the Papal assistants returned, handing His Holiness a small package and pouring wine from a carafe chilling on the table nearby.

They sat quietly in silence for a time before the Pope asked, "Are you enjoying Rome?"

"Summer is lovely here," Weston replied.

"I agree. Though it is a bit hot for me." The Pope looked out at the sky.

"What does Your Eminence do on vacation?" Weston asked, his natural curiosity getting the better of him. Internally, he scolded himself for asking such a question. *You get a private audience with the Pope and that's your question?* He felt like an idiot.

The Pope chuckled, and seemed enchanted to be asked. "*Bundesliga* keeps me entertained. Although it's probably terrible for my blood pressure. You like soccer?"

Weston shrugged. "I'm a Saints fan," he replied.

"Ah. American football. Did you play?" It was a common assumption due to Weston's size.

Weston shook his head. "I'm not very gifted at team sports."

"But you *are* an athlete." The Pope indicated his physique.

"Solitary pursuits, Father," Weston explained. "I lift weights. I run occasionally."

"Physical strength contributes to spiritual health," the Pope nodded. "I am glad you have an outlet."

The Pontiff reached for the package that his assistant had delivered and passed it silently to Weston. It was the notebook that had disappeared from the Vatican library.

"You'll forgive me for the intrusion on your work," the Pope explained. "I read your thesis, and it was the reason I told them you had earned the right to the collar. But I felt that I could take a better measure of you from your private writings."

Weston was both confused and surprised by these words.

"Oh, I know you would have gladly given it over had I asked for it directly," the Pope waved gently at it. "But then others would have known I had made a Papal request."

"My earthly possessions belong to the Church," Weston responded respectfully.

"Indeed. But you travel more lightly than any priest I've ever known," the Pope remarked. "It would be wrong of me to keep your notes. You are quite a discerning scholar. I don't think the Vatican library has had a more faithful or diligent patronage in a century or two, at least. Are you certain in your desire to leave us to further your education? You can do this work without the additional learning."

"I want my work to have the utmost credibility, in a currency that the Church recognizes," Weston replied.

"I understand this," came the easy answer, and Weston observed that the Pope appeared sincere. Weston knew he was also a politician, but had others to do any dirty work or deal in unpleasantness.

"Exorcism," the Pope began, pausing to carefully consider the word. "Publicly, the Church has abandoned the practice. It cannot now be undertaken, even contemplated, without involving an Archbishop of this Church. And permission to perform the ritual is almost never granted. That's the public relations speech, which I expect you to know and to understand."

"Privately, you shall have more work than ever. I have asked Kedron to train you as one of the *Dei Gloria*. This education and training can be concurrent to your formal university studies."

"You shall be tested as you have never been tested before, my son. And you understand the cost. Be respectful of your betters, as I know you will, but you answer to this office and myself alone."

26

PAIN AND HARDSHIP MARKED WESTON'S path to induction as one of the *Dei Gloria*, and he suspected that much of his suffering was a private lesson from Kedron.

But what another human could subject him to was nothing compared to what his own demons had already done. Coupled with the creative cruelty of the other boys at parochial school, he was mentally and physically prepared to deflect bullying in all its forms, understanding that the ones he faced now were performing a rite of passage.

The sect was the arm of the Church tasked with maintaining order and righteousness, which unfortunately meant that such priests were always at the heart of the unpleasantness involved in eradicating evil from the world at large.

Exorcists came from their ranks, and the descendants of the Inquisitors as well, so the sect attracted those pragmatic enough to function as spiritual enforcers of the faith. Although there were canon laws protecting human rights, the ultimate justification for intervening in a number of political arenas was found in the Scriptures.

The Church still quietly sanctioned its own brand of espionage and subterfuge, and involved itself in a great many private political endeavors. Its bottomless coffers had allowed it to rewrite and maintain its own history, but in the modern world these medieval practices had persisted despite public outcry. The Church had allowed that the Inquisition was a terrible spot on its history, and publicly denied any such coercive practices in eradicating sin in the present day, but the work had simply taken on a new face. Publicly, protective outreach. Privately, the priests of *Dei Gloria* remained a paramilitary arm of the Church, one with the expected enforcers and spies.

Weston knew that his work, while less appealing to most, was the more righteous of the justifications, and given his own history, he performed these tasks with the reverence and faith they required. It was what he had wanted, and he knew Kedron would have kept him away from the other side of it, where dark operatives were recruited from the laity, and priests lived more like secular men. Kedron himself behaved like the underlord of a criminal network, perhaps getting too close to what he was purporting to eradicate.

Ultimately Weston finished his studies and his tests of faith, and was sent to oversee a dying parish in New Orleans, cover for the assignments that brought him back and forth to Rome and sent him out to hunt demons.

And when Kedron was installed as Bishop, Weston heard even less of his doings, but this was a relief, as he believed he was never meant to involve himself in such shadowy dealings as some of his *Dei Gloria* contemporaries. He still had to answer directly to the Pope.

27

JUST AS SUDDENLY AS IT began, it was once again in flux, as only three years after that fateful summer in Rome, there was a new Pope.

Weston performed as he always had, uncertain how he would now receive his orders, and heard very little for many months. He expected he would see Rome again soon, and sure enough, the following summer, he was summoned by the Vatican.

He was welcomed to the visiting priest's quarters but received no further instruction regarding his duties, so he assisted with the many Mass preparations, explored the city outside the Vatican's walls, and spent many pleasurable evenings continuing his scholarship in the Library, renewing his friendship with Father Nicolò.

He was now able to compare his own experience with the data he gathered from the writings of others. His interests were no longer theoretical, they were practical.

"Promise me you shall donate your diaries when your career ends," Father Nicolò teased. "You have the loveliest handwriting I have seen in five hundred years of journaling."

"I would not have guessed you were a day over three hundred," Weston shot back. "And your eyesight at such an advanced age is to be questioned."

Out of a politeness he did not really feel he inquired about Father Kedron, but was told the man was abroad on Vatican business. To Weston's great relief he was not expected to return during the remainder of the year.

It was three weeks before he received a Papal summons, and he worried about his parishioners back home in New Orleans. He didn't like neglecting them for politics. It didn't seem fair to him. He was grateful for the kindness of his brother priests who covered for him during these absences, but theirs was a kindness coerced by what the Archbishop deemed dutiful, less than out of any sense of friendship or charity. Furthermore, his vocation proscribed him from returning these favors in kind. He could not lift any liturgical burdens from them as he was required to respond when his skills were needed elsewhere.

He was invited again to the Castel in Alban, unaware of what he should expect in the new leader of the faith. What he found, he felt when reflecting upon it later, was no less than a miracle.

The new pope awaited him in the courtyard with one nervous cardinal attending him. Seeing that pristine robe made Weston's errant thoughts run to such incongruities as when he had last had a haircut. He couldn't remember. But Father O'Halloran's words came to him unbidden, *a priest is just a man*.

It was as if the Holy Father was impatient to meet him, and Weston climbed out of the car and found himself face to face with the Pope. It was immediately a very different experience than he'd had before in this place with this man's predecessor.

There were no layers of bureaucracy separating them, no doors, no levels, no formality, no cadre of staffers. Weston knelt immediately and took the man's hand, kissing the ring. But where many of these observances were perfunctory, and one had the suspicion that the recipient of the obeisance wanted only to reclaim his hand as quickly as possible, this time, the Pope held his hand warmly, even using it to restore Weston to his feet.

"Father Weston, I am told you use your first name?" the Pope inquired, but smiled, perhaps realizing that it sounded rehearsed.

"May the love of God be with you always." The man blessed Weston, making the sign of the cross.

"And also with you, Your Eminence," Weston replied.

"Cardinal Mazuri and I were just discussing your doctoral thesis," the Pope told Weston.

"I'm flattered," Weston said, adding, "I'm surprised to find you both still awake."

The Pope laughed, and Cardinal Mazuri was thus encouraged to politely laugh as well, though it was clear he found nothing funny. Weston was acutely aware that he probably should have kept his comment to himself.

But the Pope surprised him. "You're quite popular with the Vatican librarians," he imparted. "Father Nicolò says you are something of an inadvertent comedian."

The Pope put his arm through Weston's, leaning a little, and it reminded him of his adolescent walks with Father O'Halloran. There was a familiar comfort to it. Cardinal Mazuri's expression was one of censure, but he turned to open the wide doors of the palazzo and entered the Great Hall ahead of them.

"You are hungry? I hope you will take lunch with me," the Pope said, and turned to Cardinal Mazuri, saying, "Manolo, would you address that issue we discussed this morning? God be with you."

"But, Your Eminence," the cardinal stammered, and Weston thought he understood the consternation. But the Pope merely made the sign of the cross in his direction and led Weston onward to the stairs.

When they reached the second-floor landing, Weston asked softly, "Are you *supposed* to be alone with me?"

"Of course I am not," the Pope replied. "My son, I am not supposed to be alone with anyone. Or ever. My secretaries would follow me to the bathroom if I let them. And I suspect some Popes have." He chuckled. "But they will forgive this old Jesuit if he does not take to all this frippery with ease. I am a humble priest. I cannot recall which of the Popes was asked if he would enjoy sleeping in a Pope's bed, and do you know what he said?"

"'Not really, as I suspect I shall also die in it?'" Weston asked, not sure if such had been the response. It would have been his answer.

"You understand!" The Pope gently pinched Weston on the forearm in congratulations. "I think that our blessed mortality is God's not so subtle way of letting us know that we are all equal in the end. When I face my Maker, I will have no secretaries to speak for me then, will I?"

Weston could hear that he believed what he said. The Jesuits were famously opposed to positions of advancement and power. Among them they represented the smallest number of bishops, archbishops, and cardinals within the Church hierarchy. It was rumored that after the conclave of cardinals had chosen this man as Pope, he had sought permission from his brotherhood to accept the promotion. For all that he might disclaim it, this man had to be influential indeed to have risen through the ranks of the Church. Perhaps kindness and humility had won the day. For once.

28

LUNCH WAS A PLEASANT AFFAIR during which neither of them discussed the Church. The Pope wanted to know about Weston's life before he became a priest, what books he read, and his favorite music. His Eminence admitted he had never heard of Fall Out Boy, which was not a surprise, but made Weston promise to play their music for him sometime, which was.

They spoke of Weston's mother, and the sadness of losing a parent at a young age. The Pope gushed about his love for San Lorenzo football, meaning soccer to Weston, but agreed that if one were to pick a team to support, the Saints were a good choice. Weston laughed, telling His Holiness that his preference was an accident of the geography of his birth.

Two hours slipped by, and when Weston realized it, he was concerned. "I am sorry, Father. I have been inconsiderate, I am sure you have much to do."

"Don't concern yourself, my son," the Pope replied. "This is my *vacation* house. I can at least pretend I am on vacation. But I do have one more question. Your passion for this unusual work is unparalleled. Where does this devotion spring from, I wonder?"

Weston started to answer, but paused. He closed his eyes, and said a small prayer. "Because while many of us must operate on faith alone, I have a personal knowledge of the darkness that lives among us."

The Pope was silent, waiting for him to say more, listening with his whole being. And it was this attentiveness, this sincere desire to know more, that Weston responded to. "Holy Father, I must unburden myself to you. There is something I want to show you, something to reveal."

"I will bear witness to whatever you wish to share," His Holiness responded with enthusiasm and curiosity.

"Uncomfortably, and perhaps strangely referring to our earlier conversation, I need you to accompany me into the bathroom," Weston told him, and was grateful when the Pope laughed.

He followed Weston readily, saying, "You have a mark, or a stigma to show me?"

"Something like that," Weston replied, "but I am not going to disrobe; we need the mirror."

When he had positioned them shoulder to shoulder before the glass, he raised his eyes and peered into it, and was gratified to see the Monster looking out, its reflection there for the Pontiff to witness. And it spoke, on seeing whom Weston had brought there, saying in its unintelligible language, *"You dare!"* before retreating once more.

The Pope grasped Weston's arm and gasped in alarm. Weston turned to leave the room, returning with the older man to their seats on the veranda.

"*¡Dios mío!*" the Pope exclaimed, reverting to his native tongue and crossing himself. "And it spoke to us!"

"It was angry that I revealed it," Weston admitted.

"I understood it, although the language is unfamiliar," the Pope said, surprising Weston.

"You understood?" Weston was astonished.

"It said, 'you dare,' correct?" the Pope inquired. "The language is similar to something, but this is not one of my strengths, so I am not sure why I know this!"

"As far as I can tell, it most closely approximates Aramaic," Weston replied calmly.

The Pope nodded slowly, and surprised Weston by reaching for his hand and holding it with a tenderness that the younger priest did not expect.

"I assume that you have shared this with my predecessor," the Pope stated this confidently, so he was surprised by the answer.

"Forgive me, but I have never revealed this to another," Weston replied. "I hope you can understand my reasons. The last Pope removed me from the hierarchy of reporting, making himself specifically available to me, but still I did not tell. I waited."

"For what?"

"For you, Your Holiness. I knew God would tell me when the time was right." Weston was afraid, but relieved in a way that even he had not anticipated when the burden of the secret was lifted. *The truth only hurts once,* he remembered.

"Tell me everything," the Pope whispered, not letting go of Weston's hand, leaning in to hear.

So Weston confessed it all, the strange connection to the Morningstar, what he remembered about growing up, the demons that attended him, his attempts to first vanquish and then understand them, his path to a vocation that would use the knowledge and faith he had gained to help others.

Hours passed, and at several points, the Pope needed to send away those who came to remind him of other meetings and other responsibilities, but he refused them all, remaining with Weston. He never once interrupted, nor did he relinquish Weston's hand.

When it was over, and Weston felt as though his every word were spent, he received absolution and Holy Blessings. He was given penance and accepted it with humility. His voice was raw and hoarse. He knew that none of this really made him clean, but he did feel better for the unburdening.

"I see that the Lord is at work within you, my son. It is a terrible battle you undertake for our Church. But the greater battle is for your own soul."

Weston nodded quietly.

"Through your brotherhood, the *Dei Gloria*, the Church monitors the supernatural," the Pope observed wisely. "And through my offices are the *Dei Gloria* monitored."

"Meaning I am to be monitored," Weston responded quietly.

"Yes, but no more than we all are. You will continue your work. You will continue your strange and necessary arrangement with your Pope. You will answer to me alone, following your unique path, responding to the needs of the faithful."

"And if at some point I am corrupted? I need to know that any untoward eventuality can be contained," Weston said.

"I will give the order myself," the Pope promised sadly. "Yet I know that what we ask of you will likely claim so much of you that there will be nothing left to erase."

"Even without it," Weston said, "I know what my faith requires of me, Your Eminence, and I make my sacrifices willingly."

"For that, my son, you have my gratefulness and my admiration." The Pope's tone held both abject love and profound grief.

29

WAITING FOR WESTON WHEN HE reached the residence late that evening was a tooled wooden box, placed without ceremony atop the monastic bed in his room. Inside it, nestled on the purple velvet of the Papal Office, were two identical silver crosses, ornate, embossed with symbols of the Church, of careful and loving workmanship.

They were heavy, longer and wider than Weston's hand, the links of their chains robust. They were also beautiful, polished to a gloss that reflected the lamplight from their cradle within the folds of cloth that held them, and indeed, seemed to trap that light within.

There was no note, but Weston recognized these holy symbols for what they were, and he knew from whence they came. The Redeemer Crosses, the only two ever made. Legend was correct, he quickly discovered, they contained hidden blades. But that was not what made them special.

For they were cast from the silver coins that Judas had tried to return following his betrayal of Christ.

carter

30

WESTON JOGGED OVER THE GRASSY curb, hopping down when he reached the concrete, then dashed across the driveway in front of the main hospital doors, his robes swirling, ignoring the stares of the few curious onlookers who were surprised to see a priest moving so athletically, or perhaps one so young.

He weaved his way around wheelchairs and gurneys and found the elevators, pausing to peruse the directory, finding the floor he wanted. He rode up to the ICU, unsure whether he would even be admitted. His instructions had been cryptic at best, but he was here to investigate the injuries of one suspected victim of the possessed. He'd been told it was a critical case; if the victim died, they might not learn enough of those responsible to act.

He shouldn't have worried, the Church had far-reaching influence, and endless resources.

The nurses' desk was a busy control center, encountered immediately upon exiting the elevators, and where he had expected a somber, quiet place, he was met by the cacophony of beeping monitors, hushed voices, and ringing phones. The staff moved in their own preoccupied but coordinated dance, and the place was walled with windows, which admitted sunshine to battle the constancy of despair along with breathtaking fifth floor views of the surrounding valley.

The nurse facing the bank of elevators was obviously stationed there for control of visitor traffic; her dour face brightened slightly when she saw him. As he approached, she said, "You must be Father Weston, we were told to expect you."

He nodded in confirmation, and her face became serious once more. "Would you clip this to your clothing?" she asked, handing him a laminated blue visitor badge. He attached it between the buttons of his cassock and followed her around the curve of the unit's broad hallway. The nurses' station was the center of a hub, the rooms surrounding it, such that no patient was far from view or help.

When they entered the room he thought she had made a mistake, because the bed at first appeared empty. But just as quickly he saw that the mistake had been his, because the patient was so small her form had been obscured by the nurse's silhouette.

He was left alone with his shock, because the strident beeping of an alarm elsewhere prompted his escort to give a hasty apology and depart to assist with that emergent event. Weston barely noticed.

In the bed, on the snowy sheets, nearly disappearing she was so small and pale, lay the ruins of a child. His information must have been incorrect. He'd been told she was seventeen, and he'd expected an adult, or at least a facsimile of one.

She barely took up any space, certainly she did not fill the bed either side to side or lengthwise. Her long chestnut hair was pulled up away from her face, under bandages that appeared to hold something in place against her skull. Her cheeks were covered with tape that held tubes and wires in place. At a glance, he would have guessed her age at ten, or perhaps twelve. As he got closer to the bed, he could confirm that she was older, her bone structure evolving from adolescence to womanhood, her proportions womanly, but miniaturized.

She had a pixie-ish beauty despite the swelling and bruising of her face, long dark lashes rested against smooth skin. She had a cast on one arm, and her exposed skin was as pale as the sheets upon which she lay. Despite all the evidence of terrible trauma, he could see that she was exquisite.

Her monitors beeped out a rapid tone, her heartrate, racing along at the staccato speed of a rock drummer, her heart dealing with the many insults done her body. He suspected it was the red number on the screen; the others were green. She appeared deeply asleep, and the machines breathed for her, a rhythmic hiss and hum. Bottles and bags hung from poles on both sides of the bed, flowing into her arms, flowing away into lines that ran beneath the voluminous gown she rested under.

He was witnessing the evidence of extreme physical trauma, a horrible beating, perhaps worse. It seemed not an inch of her had been spared. There was evidence on her arms alone that she had been cut, burned with cigarettes or cigars, and marked with some other sharp object.

Weston did not realize he was involuntarily shaking his head.

"Devastating, isn't it, Father?" A male voice spoke out from the doorway, and Weston turned to see a young doctor in blue scrubs and a white lab coat. His credentials said *Dr. R. Weitzman, Emergency Staff Physician.* He had a kind, bearded face, and a cheerful demeanor, but his eyes were sad, and tired.

"I'm Raphael Weitzman," the doctor explained, reaching for Weston's hand, and smiling at Weston's surprise.

"An angel's name," Weston observed.

"Yes, I think my mother wanted me to be a rabbi," Dr. Weitzman shared.

"Well, my mother probably thought I'd be a doctor," Weston told him, making a joke. It felt necessary under such serious circumstances. It sealed their understanding.

"I try to visit every day," Dr. Weitzman said, indicating the girl on the bed. "I was the one – I took care of her in the emergency room," he explained.

"I was sent by the Church, and I am afraid I have very little information," Weston admitted. "I don't know her name, and I'm not sure what you can tell me, if anything, about her history."

"It's okay. Clergy are usually considered family, and Father Paul said something about your arrival. In this case, she needs as many people praying for her as possible," Dr. Weitzman said, waving away Weston's concerns. He tapped on a computer monitor next to the bed, and said, "Carter Thomas, seventeen years old. Local resident, a student at the Catholic high school here, supposed to graduate this spring. Lived with her father, who died suddenly three weeks ago. She was brought to the Emergency Department four nights ago, after someone witnessed a moving car dump her body on the county road just outside of town. A local deliveryman called for an ambulance and they brought her here. I was just finishing my shift, but I couldn't leave her; I stayed until nearly dinnertime the next day."

"She was thrown from a moving car?!" Weston couldn't mask his concern.

"Yes, as if that's not bad enough, but those are the least of her injuries, unfortunately," Weitzman told him. He inclined his head to invite Weston to step out into the hallway.

Once they were outside the room, Weitzman pulled the slider and said in a soft voice, "I ascribe to the belief that she can hear us, in spite of all that is going on, and I don't like to discuss unpleasantness in front of a comatose patient."

Weston nodded, liking this man more with each moment that passed.

"She was tortured, for some time, apparently, as the surgeons tell me that her injuries are of various ages. She was raped, sodomized, the works, by more than one piece of shit," Weitzman said bitterly, not bothering to apologize for the profanity, assuming the priest would understand. This one did. "But the fall from the car gave her a pretty serious head injury; she has some significant brain swelling, so perhaps, God willing, she won't remember what happened to her."

"That would be a blessing," Weston concurred.

"She has to live first," Weitzman said angrily, and his tone prompted Weston to place a reassuring hand on the man's arm. Weitzman looked surprised, and then grateful. He continued. "I have young kids, Father, and I have to tell you, if she was my daughter, I would have walked out of here and committed murders."

"Understandable," Weston commiserated, sensing that Weitzman needed to talk about this, and realizing that he probably had no outlet for all the suffering he had to witness and absorb.

"She's in a medically-induced coma," Weitzman explained, opening the door once more and reentering the room. "But there's a fighter living in that tiny body. And I want to show you the other thing. It was done right before they dumped her."

He led Weston to the bedside and gently lifted the sheet and carefully moved Carter's left arm. He lifted enough of the gown away from her side to expose her left flank from her hip to her ribcage. She was heartbreakingly thin, those tiny ribs in stark relief beneath her skin. And on the expanse of flesh there, beneath a snowy gauze covering, Weitzman showed him what else had been done.

The black wings branded onto her skin were instantly recognizable to Weston, and when he saw them, he understood personally the heat of his own homicidal rage. It was a message for him, a message that the Church had already received. The demons he had learned to control were closer to the surface than ever, delighting in this development, encouraging this response.

31

WESTON LEFT THE HOSPITAL IN the ensuing days only to drop in at the visiting priest's quarters to shower, or stop by the church to attend Mass. He took his few meals in solitude, late at night, in the church cafeteria, or after hours, at a twenty-four-hour truckstop out by the Interstate.

There were few changes in his charge, and they came slowly. The bruises began to fade, and her heartrate slowed, but still she did not awaken. The neurosurgeons remained guarded in their assessment of her potential for recovery.

For his part, he prayed, sometimes alone, often accompanied by Raphael Weitzman, which he suspected the staff found strange, but neither man cared. Weitzman often found Weston all by himself, at odd hours, in the church's nondenominational chapel, during breaks in the chaos of the emergency room.

One afternoon, Weston was surprised by the appearance of a teenage girl who came to the doorway of Carter's hospital room. She looked a bit afraid and overwhelmed to be there, so he stood up and walked over to her.

"Hello," she said shyly, looking up at him. "I – I'm Hayley. Carter's friend? We got permission to visit her, but I was afraid. Father Paul at St. Gregory's told me you'd be here so I wouldn't be alone."

"That's very nice, Hayley. She needs her friends more than ever," Weston told her reassuringly. "I will be happy to stay while you visit. I'm Father Weston."

"I know," she smiled, and blushed as well. "I have seen you outside the church school with Father Paul."

Weston returned her smile. His exposure to teenage girls had been limited given his own parochial schooling, but they all seemed to smell like bubble gum and flower perfume, and this one was no different. She was understandably nervous, but that was to be expected. He was thankful that most of Carter's injuries were covered by the sheet today, and her face was less swollen than it had been. Still, he imagined it was upsetting for Hayley to be here at all, much less see one of her contemporaries lying injured in the hospital.

She stopped short of the bed. Weston stood beside her. "You can talk to her if you want to, she can probably hear you. Also," he gently steered the young woman closer to the bedside, and freeing Carter's hand from the sheet, he laid it against the coverlet, saying, "You can touch her if you like. It won't hurt her. It's another way to let her know you are here."

He turned to grab the chair he'd been keeping vigil in, placing it so Hayley could sit next to her friend. She sat down reluctantly, but took Carter's hand. Then she smiled, relieved. "She's warm!"

"Of course," he told her. He could see that she was overcoming her initial uncertainty, so he said, "I'm going to get a Coke. Would you like one?"

Hayley nodded absently, her concerns about being left alone there were departing. Brave soul. He stepped out, pulling the door partly closed behind him to give the girls some privacy.

When he returned, he paused outside the door when he heard Hayley's voice. She seemed to be telling Carter about all the recent events she was missing at school. Something about prom, and perhaps graduation. He just stood in the hallway, out of sight, thanking God for Hayley, and for friendship. He hoped it would have the power to heal.

While he was standing there, Raphael Weitzman came up beside him, giving him a quizzical look. He was curious about Weston's posture by the door, and the two cans of soda in his hands.

"Her friend is here," Weston whispered a short explanation. "I wanted to let them alone."

Weitzman put a friendly hand on his shoulder and nodded, peeking in through the window. "It's nice she has at least one visitor who knew her before all this."

They stood in companionable silence for a short time before Weitzman said, "Well, I will come by later. I start my shift in half an hour, and I should go wade into the fray."

"See you, man," Weston said in farewell, and shortly after Weitzman disappeared down the stairwell, Hayley emerged from the room.

"I will come back," she said breathlessly, peering at her phone. "My mom's waiting for me downstairs. I have to go."

"I'm glad you came," Weston told her, handing over the soda he'd brought her. "Is it okay if I walk you downstairs?"

"Sure," Hayley agreed, giving a nervous giggle. He found it endearing.

"Can you tell me a bit about her?" Weston asked, as they waited for the elevator.

"She's my best friend," Hayley said, with a small sigh that sounded tearful. She swallowed some of her soda, and seemed to regain some poise. "A sweet girl, really. Very Catholic, you know?"

Weston nodded, but wasn't sure he understood what that meant to Hayley.

"She is smart. Good in school. She lived with her daddy after her mother died a few years ago. Her mother had cancer," Hayley whispered the last statement, and Weston thought she wasn't aware she had done so. "We have been friends since kindergarten."

"When was the last time you saw her?" Weston asked, still unsure about the timeline of events around Carter's attack.

"She was at our house after her daddy's funeral for a few hours," Hayley told him. "I asked her to stay with us – my mom said it was okay – but she had decided she was going home. She was old enough to live on her own, and we are close to graduation. I thought it was kinda cool. Scary too, I guess. Anyway, she went home that day, and I haven't seen her since. She missed some school, but we all thought maybe she was taking a break, or that she was with her uncles. I guess I should have gone over to visit her," she said softly, tearful again.

"This isn't your fault, Hayley," Weston told her, thinking it was good she hadn't, as she might have become a victim as well. "I will see you next time?" he asked, when they reached the front doors of the hospital lobby. He leaned out and waved to the woman in the car at the curb, who he assumed was Hayley's mother, and Hayley nodded and went out to the car.

She reached for the door handle and stopped. She turned back, and jogged back to him at the door. "I almost forgot, Father." She dug in her bag and pulled out an early generation iPod with headphones. "She left this at my house. It was her mother's. She took it everywhere. It only has one song on it – weird, right? – but I wanted to give it back to her."

Weston accepted it, looking down at the tiny box with the jumble of wires and earbuds that fit in the palm of his hand. He was about to thank Hayley, but when he looked up again, she was already at the car. He watched her get in, watched the car drive away.

It was time for him to start investigating, but he was finding it difficult to bring himself to leave Carter when she was yet so vulnerable.

32

WESTON SPREAD THE HASTILY JOTTED directions on his knee and reviewed Weitzman's instructions about how to reach Carter's address. He shook his head. His own handwriting had deteriorated since his ordination, perhaps because he wrote even more, but probably because he was usually in a hurry, and legibility was becoming less and less a priority considering his other burdens, but the physician's tangled scribbles were almost as confounding as hieroglyphics.

He only made one wrong turn, easily corrected, and soon he was on the county road west of town. It was a warm spring day, quiet, much too early for the sounds of the summer bugs, but the trees were beginning to bloom. He rolled the windows down and set his collar on the passenger seat, leaving the top of the cassock unbuttoned, enjoying the breeze coming through the windows.

He slowed after about five minutes, needing to concentrate, since Weitzman's directions only got him to the general area. He started looking for numbers on the dilapidated mailboxes that lined the road and made his way toward the one he wanted.

He found it among a cluster of others situated next to a dirt access road. There was a shabby sign that said *Bloomfield Park*, which appeared to be the vastly optimistic name of a run-down trailer park. Weston shivered, thinking of his own childhood, identifying even more with the unfortunate child lying in that bed back at the hospital.

He turned in, listening to the familiar crunch of the gravel, watching the dust stir up in his rearview mirror as he made his way down the bumpy lane to the cluster of homes set back a short distance from the road. There were a few scrubby trees here and there, and the place at one time may have been a handsome settlement, but it had fallen into disrepair. Some of the mobile units were so dilapidated that one might assume they were abandoned, but he knew better. It was more likely than not that someone lived in them.

He parked in a central location, replaced his collar carefully, and climbed out. Some of the plots were marked, and some were not, but he soon worked out the numbering sequence and was able to locate Carter's home. It had been well-maintained; it was an old unit, with the aluminum-tin sheet construction of forty years earlier, white with a blue stripe. Its foundation was plumb, and there was raked gravel in lieu of a yard. The carport was freestanding, but had recently been painted and was in good repair.

Weston stood for a few moments, listening carefully. The front door was severely dented but sealed with crime scene tape. There was a phone number listed on the seal; it was probably the contact for the detective leading the investigation. Weston whispered it to himself a few times and committed it to memory. Then he trudged around to the back.

Cinderblock steps had been fashioned as an egress from a back door. There was some spotty crabgrass that made up a tiny yard. An ancient oak and some cottonwoods lined the boundary at the bottom of the yard, beyond was a recently tilled but fallow field stretching to the horizon. He approached the back door, but it was similarly sealed. It was then that he noticed the smell.

It was subtle, came to him on the breeze and then was carried as quickly away. He hadn't noticed it in the front. It was the smell of rot, but not dead leaf litter, an animal. The smell of a decaying rodent, but this was too forward, it had to be something bigger.

He backed away from the trailer, and the scent faded. He took another step, and one more, and was about to abandon his concerns, when his eye caught on something incongruous. There was something under the trailer, in the open crawl space behind the cinderblocks. It was bright white, too white to have been there very long.

Weston knelt down next to the cinderblocks to confirm what he was seeing. It was a body, seemingly in peaceful repose, a bearded man, not too old, not too young, lying on his side, stiffly straight, facing outward. The white was his funeral suit, shirt, vest, tie, pants, and shoes. There was no jacket. His eyes were closed, and other than the fact that he was dead, there were no signs of violence.

Weston leaned forward to confirm that this was the source of the stench. It was, but it was too subtle for the body to have been there very long. He sighed. He knew the Morningstar's handiwork; had been the recipient of so many such messages. He climbed slowly to his feet and brushed dead leaves and dust from the skirt of his cassock. He caught movement from the corner of his eye, and turned to look. Sitting on the steps, watching him carefully, was a large blackbird.

He reached out to it, and it puffed up its feathers, squawked, and took off so abruptly that it left behind a feather. Large and black, it fluttered and flipped on the breeze before coming to rest near Weston's foot. He turned to follow its progress, but it had disappeared.

When he returned to the car, and glanced in through the open window, there were more black feathers scattered across the seat, these too large to have come from a bird. He blinked in disbelief, and shook his head, closing his eyes and putting a hand on the warm metal of the car door to support himself. His own demons were singing to him, and he fought desperately to shut them out without success.

When he opened his eyes again, the feathers were gone. He shook his head, and sighed, accepting that he would be living with his torment for whatever duration this time, and turned to the trailer next door. Weston's knock on the door brought an irritated inhabitant, whose angry words cooled when she saw the priest on her step before begrudgingly agreeing to assist him in calling the authorities.

The patrolman who responded took only twenty minutes to arrive, and when he saw the priest sitting on the back steps, talking to himself, he just shook his head. He was young, and assumed the man was praying, which he felt was appropriate for this horrible case that somehow, even now, was not getting any easier.

33

WESTON RETURNED TO THE HOSPITAL after giving his statement to the patrol officer, who assured him that he would be in touch before hurrying to call for backup and an ambulance. He was afraid, Weston could see it, in the way that people are when something is both unexplainable and thoroughly disturbing. This certainly qualified.

There was no change in Carter's condition. He read to her for a while, and then remembered the iPod. He retrieved it from the pocket of his cassock and pulled his chair close to her bed. He fiddled with it for a moment, found the tiny power switch and moved it to green, then gently placed one of the earphones in her ear, fumbling a bit. He put the other in his own ear and pressed the disc on the front to start the music.

The song started, and he followed the lyrics easily, thinking it was an inspirational tune, but he realized halfway through that someone was making some kind of promise, and it was a love song of sorts. Hayley was correct, there was just that one song, set to repeat over and over. It must have been very meaningful to her, or perhaps to her mother. The message seemed to be that one person would be there for the other and love them, and protect them. Perhaps a ballad from a mother to her daughter?

The song made him sad, and then slightly uncomfortable, as if he were intruding on something private, so he removed his earpiece and put it on the coverlet, leaving it to play just for her. Shortly after, the nurses came in and shooed him out so that they could attend to her wounds, and bathe her.

He wandered back down to the chapel, and grateful that the voices of his familiars had quieted once more, kneeled to make his own prayers. When he finally came out of the reverie of his wandering thoughts, he realized he wasn't alone. In his peripheral vision, he could see someone sitting across the aisle from him. It was too early for Weitzman, so he crossed himself and turned to the other visitor, assuming it was a patient's family member looking for his blessing, seeking solace in the familiar symbol of a holy man.

"Hello, Father," the woman said, directing a shrewd gaze at him. "The nurses upstairs suggested I look for you here." She handed him a card, and said, "I'm Lieutenant Green. I'm the lead detective on Ms. Thomas' case."

Weston accepted the card as she showed him her badge, and thought it interesting that she hadn't used Carter's first name. He sensed anger and frustration from the policewoman, and he suspected that this was her way to keep an emotional distance. The situation was not easy for anyone to stomach.

"Can I buy you a cup of coffee, Lieutenant?" Weston offered, to break the tension.

"I was about to ask you the same thing," she said, and he could see that she was relieved somehow.

"Dutch treat, then," he said, and laughed at his own joke. He was bright enough to recognize that he made stupid jokes when he was nervous. To his great relief, she laughed, too, understanding the irony of a priest on a date. Besides, both knew that the hospital cafeteria here did not bother to charge clergy for coffee, and he suspected that cops got their coffee *gratis* as well.

It was slow in the cafeteria, as it was between the lunch rush and dinner, so they took their coffee over by the windows that looked out onto a central green space. They were far enough from the other scattered patrons for privacy.

"I'd like to thank you for calling in the incident at the trailer," Green began, taking a sip of her coffee and watching him closely as she did so. "But I also have to ask you what you were doing there."

"Ah," Weston nodded. "The Church sent me to investigate, because Father Paul of the local diocese notified Church authorities."

"I see. And what prompted him to do so, I wonder?" Green still didn't see the connection, but she suspected she knew everything else, how long he'd been in town, what he'd been doing, and where he'd been seen.

"The mark. The brand on her skin," Weston replied.

"The black wings? Are what? Some Satanist cult?" she asked.

"Something like that," Weston replied, thinking carefully how he wanted to proceed.

"Father, that's not an answer," she rightfully protested. "What is the nature of the Church's involvement here? Is the unsub one of yours?"

"The unsub?" Weston asked, honestly not understanding her lingo.

"The unknown subject, the perpetrator, or perpetrators. Is this the work of a priest? I have to tell you, if the Church has sent you to protect someone, our prosecutors don't take kindly to that kind of interference in this county."

"Protect? If this was a priest, I would bring him to you myself," Weston said, and his tone betrayed his offense and his honest distaste for whoever had done such a thing. "The Church involves itself for any suspicion of demonic acts." He said it directly, expecting to be taken seriously.

"Do you expect me to-" Green began, but then stopped, and sat back in her chair, studying him carefully. "You're serious." She was quiet, waiting for him to say more, but when he didn't, she sighed.

After an uncomfortable silence, where both refused to break eye contact, she finally spoke. "I would be grateful to hear whatever you have to say, Father. Goodness knows, I don't seem to be making much progress with this. And your discovery today just adds to the dilemma. Demons? I wish it were that easy. At this point it's the only thing that makes any sense."

"It's okay," Weston reassured her. "I am used to disbelief. Anyway, demonic influence is only proven by exclusion of all other causes. I, like you, remain skeptical until I get more answers. Quite often there is another, more orthodox cause for the unexplainable."

"So you're what?" Green asked. "A church detective?"

"Only incidentally," Weston replied. "I am an exorcist."

"Is – the girl?" Green's eyes wandered upward, as if she could see Carter through the floors above.

"No. No. But possibly those who attacked her were," Weston explained his suspicion. "I went out to her home to get a feel for the place. I was hardly expecting to discover a body."

Green was watching him very carefully now, and he had the feeling she was assessing him from moment to moment, from statement to statement, like a human lie detector. Which, of course, she was, professionally speaking.

"I believe you," she said. "It didn't make the department very happy either. But it helped us close the loop on another open case."

Weston didn't follow, and he could see that Green didn't care. She was weighing something else, deciding, resolving an internal struggle of her own.

"The staff tell me that you have barely left the hospital to attend your own needs. You have stayed here with her for days. Raphael Weitzman sings your praises, and he is a skeptic of the first order. Not to mention your conflicting philosophies," Green said, probably referring to their differing faiths. "He said he *prayed* with you, for Christ's sake. Sorry." She said the last as an afterthought, more because she did not want to offend than for what was said.

"I have an assignment," Weston said simply. "But my first concern is for the victim's spiritual integrity."

"Meaning that she is still vulnerable to attack by these..."

"Possibly. I hope to be led to the answers to these and many other questions," Weston told her.

"Where do you propose to begin? Divine intervention?" Green asked, and for the first time she sounded bitter and tired.

"The Lord works in mysterious ways, Lieutenant. I suspect you are here for a reason," Weston replied gently. "I think we can help each other, but I think you are deciding whether you can trust me. It is understandable."

"I do want to trust you," Green said. "I'm just not sure I can get past this other thing."

"It is unnecessary for you to believe what I believe," Weston assured her. "Differences in perspective can be advantageous if they can overcome bias."

"I feel like I am losing my mind," Green confided, probably not meaning to.

"Let me make it easier for you," Weston said. "I'll start the sharing, and we can see where the conversation leads. The man I found was her father, right? White suit, calm repose. He was removed from his coffin recently, and his embalmers did a good job, because he is only just beginning to rot. Someone put him there on purpose, probably for me to find."

"But how-?" Green asked, astonished.

"Lieutenant, I am a priest. That alone would give me more experience with the dead than the average person," he reminded her. "But I am also a member of a very special order, and I have seen the fantastic and the profane ways in which humans can hurt one another. We probably have more in common than you realize."

34

"FAIR ENOUGH," GREEN CAPITULATED. "There was a disturbance at the local cemetery yesterday. We usually ascribe such mischief to the youth, but this was not the handiwork of a bunch of bored kids.

"The coffin was dug up, the seal was stripped, and after taking the body, they closed everything up, and put the dirt back into the hole. Awfully disciplined, I'd say. Most graverobbers have a fetish; they know if they get caught, they will be arrested. They don't hang around for cleanup after they have what they want. And they don't just give the body back, or leave it for someone else to find."

"Ignoring the details for a moment," Weston said, taking a sip of his coffee, "Is there any scenario in which you would say that this is *not* connected to what happened to Carter?"

"That's just it," Green said. "I can't believe the two events aren't related."

"So why the father? Why now?" Weston asked, but answered his own question so that Green could see it through his lens. "Whoever was involved likely had a relationship with the two of them, and possibly perceived him as an impediment to getting what they wanted from his daughter. This desecration was purposeful."

"I think you missed your calling, Father," Green told him, and he could see she was beginning to relax a bit more. "From all we have learned, he was a good dad. Very protective of his daughter. But he did have some unsavory friends. And a criminal record."

"I see." Weston stretched his arms upward and then pulled them across his chest one by one. He needed a workout; he was getting stiff. Running his hands through his hair absentmindedly, he asked, "Can you tell me what you know about her mother?"

Green raised an eyebrow, unsure why he was changing the subject so abruptly, but she humored him. "Tragic, really. She had some sort of weird lung cancer. She was only 32. The girl was 12. Divorced from the father, but they had a lot of contact. She made sure he didn't drink himself to death, and had regular visits with their child.

"After she died, the courts tried to step in, and suggest placement for the girl, but she argued strenuously on her own behalf. She wanted to go and live with her father, and apparently she convinced the *guardian ad litem* to advocate for that as well. A remarkable little girl. I think she fought for it more than he did.

"To his credit, he got clean and sober fast. Went to counseling, enrolled in a trade course and became a master machinist. Worked at the local plant. Her teachers report that he was appropriately engaged with them, the girl was at school every day, clean and well fed. They suspect that most of that was her doing; she had to grow up fast when the mother died. Sounds like she picked up where her mother left off, in terms of keeping him on his feet. Perhaps even did a better job of it."

"Children can have a profound effect on their parents," Weston observed.

"I wouldn't know," Green said, her mouth twisting bitterly. Weston suspected she didn't even realize she was doing it. There was something here that touched a nerve with her, something that kept her aloof, kept her from using Carter's name, something she identified with and didn't necessarily want to process.

"And his history? If you can share it," Weston asked, wanting to distract her from whatever was causing this distress.

"An old drug conviction. He wasn't the prime target at the time, according to the prosecutor. But he refused to roll over on the bigger fish, which in hindsight was probably smart. He did a short turn up at Fort Madison, got quite a bit of time shaved off for good behavior, and stayed out of trouble since. On paper, anyway.

"But he kept those friends he had, and I can't say they followed his good example. Most of the core group belong to a motorcycle club with St. Louis roots. If anything, their behavior deteriorated. But he kept ties with them. Chiefly because of childhood friendships, we believe, and one of their trustees is a first cousin on his mother's side."

"Unfortunate," Weston nodded, because the story was neither surprising nor unusual. Changes in lifestyle for criminals without change in associations were largely unsuccessful.

"So you suspect these men of the crime?" Weston asked.

"Yes and no. They have a strange code. They have little qualms about mistreating their women, but they usually shy away from hurting kids, generally because it raises the risk profile without the reward. And so many women gravitate to them anyway, because they trade their bodies for drugs," Green explained. "And even though some of these groups have gotten involved in sexual slavery, this kid would be a poor target. Too many people to ask questions about her disappearance."

"But no one did." Weston remembered Hayley's words, about the assumptions everyone had made about Carter's prolonged absence. He made a mental note to ask Father Paul if she had been missed at Mass. "And the lack of concern from her attackers about her disappearance might be an effect of demonic influence. It tends to create chaos and disorganization, lack of forethought about consequences. What about alibis for the group you're describing?"

Green shook her head and smiled, looking out at the people moving about beyond the windows. "I might have to tell our Captain that he needs to be recruiting from the Church in the future.

Funny thing, that.   All persons of interest seem to have utterly disappeared."

Weston nodded.   "I suspect when they are found, *if* they are found, they will already be dead."

Green's gaze snapped back to his face.   She seemed to be processing this statement, then said, in a tone that belied the feelings he was sensing from her, "Another intuition, Father?"

"No.   Demons covet flesh, but tend to destroy it when they get it," he told her.   "This time I am speaking from experience."

35

BUT IT FELT AS IF this time he was wrong. He wasn't sure how he knew, but they were still out there, and this was a development he dreaded. It meant more destruction. His heightened senses were alert to the possibility that he would hear more about these demons before it was over, and it frustrated him that he would likely be unable to prevent further harm.

It did confirm the need to protect the girl, though. He said none of this to Green; it was important to him to be careful and purposeful with her. He would need to inquire whether she would permit him to see the inside of the trailer. He felt broaching the subject now would be a step too far, so he deferred his request.

"Thank you for the coffee, Father," she said ironically, and perhaps a bit warmly. He could see a spark of mischief in her eyes, and she shook his hand. "We'll be in touch."

"Thank you, Lieutenant." He stood and watched her walk away, waiting until she was out of sight before taking their empty cups to dispose of them. Then he had a second thought, and kept his, carrying it to the elevator.

Instead of going to the fifth floor, he pushed the button for the lobby, and as he'd suspected, he found Green standing near the elevator bank. She looked sheepish.

"I thought I would save you the effort of having to retrieve this from the trash," Weston told her as he stepped out of the elevator. "I'd be happy to provide a formal specimen. I understand your desire to clear me as a suspect." He handed her the cup.

"I'm sure you have an alibi," she said, abandoning her chagrin. She was too pragmatic to be truly embarrassed.

"Probably," he smiled down at her. "But she was in that trailer for a long time. And suspects sometimes return to the victim out of a narcissistic belief that they cannot be discovered. When you have your answer, will you consider letting me look inside the trailer?"

"Since you're cooperating with my agenda, I'll take you there myself," she promised.

"Until then," he said, turning back toward the elevator and joining another family that was riding upward. She watched him until the doors closed with an unreadable expression on her face, then turned toward the exit and other concerns that lay beyond it.

36

ONE OF THE YOUNG NIGHT nurses, Jordan, caught him as he came off the elevator. He handed Weston the iPod with a careful smile.

"I didn't know if you had the charger for it," he said. "I noticed it wasn't playing and plugged it into one of the ones we had at the desk. If you give it to any one of us when you leave, we can make sure it stays charged."

"That's very kind," Weston nodded. "God be with you."

"And with you, Father," Jordan said. "I'm glad you're here. We all are."

"Thank you," Weston told him, putting a gentle hand on the man's shoulder before turning toward Carter's room.

He was happy to see that Hayley had returned and was sitting beside the bed reading. He passed her the iPod and she nodded her understanding, putting the earphones in place for Carter and starting the music. He decided to leave the two of them alone, so he backtracked to the elevators and returned to the ground floor.

The late afternoon sunshine was rapidly fading into early evening, and he decided to walk the handful of blocks to the church.

He found Father Paul in the sacristy, preparing for evening Mass, so he assisted with the setup, retrieving white gowns for both of them and locating a green stole, helping the other priest arrange it over his clothing.

"Will you stay?" Paul asked him, earnestly wanting his assistance, and Weston thought, his company.

"Of course," Weston answered, wanting to attend the Mass, so he was surprised when he felt the other priest place a green stole over the white lace of his own surplice. Paul's hands gently smoothed it in place and rested against Weston's chest for a moment longer than necessary.

Weston was used to such treatment, and understood it; humans need physical closeness, and priests were deprived of it. Most of such expressions signaled loneliness, rather than attraction, although he was aware that his physical form was coveted by some of them.

As soon as Weston glanced out into the sanctuary, he saw what Paul had anticipated. It was a large gathering, and it would help to have a second priest for administering the sacraments and perhaps with any confession scheduled as well.

"There was a Lieutenant Green here asking about you," the other priest told him.

"I know, Paul," Weston said carefully. "She is the detective working on the case. We had coffee together at the hospital this afternoon."

"Suspicious," Paul replied. "Intense."

"Occupational hazard," Weston replied, smiling. "I told her why I was here, so perhaps I made it worse."

"Great. Now she thinks we're both crazy," Paul told him, shaking his head.

"Maybe not. But I think she is starting to feel crazy herself," Weston told him. "None of this makes sense. Someone robbed the father's grave and dumped the body at the house."

Paul's eyes rolled heavenward as he crossed himself. "I knew there had been a vandal at the cemetery, but I had no idea."

"I'm surprised they haven't called you yet," Weston said sadly. "We'll have to reinter him with the usual blessings. We should consider the Roman rituals this time; I can help you. I'd like the man to have some lasting peace."

"I appreciate that," Paul said. "Thanks, man."

Both men turned toward the murmuring coming from the church, realizing that they were running behind. Weston glanced at the clock and noticed that the minute hand had slipped past the hour. The altar boy was looking nervous waiting there on his own.

"Are they getting restless?" Paul smiled, looking beatific and boyish.

"Nice to know I'm not the only one who fails to start on time," Weston replied in reassurance, and followed him out to give the benediction.

W

My eyes open onto an unfamiliar darkness. Too many days in strange places attending to evil things. All while battling my own.

They cannot overpower me anymore; it is an exercise they seem to have abandoned for now, although strong emotions wake them. Physically, as I have trained my body to be strong, they cannot challenge me. They go for me when I am most vulnerable to their influence, while I sleep they contaminate my dreams. I suspect they think that such deprivations of rest will wear me down, but I will continue to fight against the kind of dominations they succeeded at when I was a child. It is a hard-fought control, nothing so complete that it could be called independence.

The Holy Father granted my request for a car; I think the experimentation I began at Jimenez's shop can be perfected in a larger engine. The Charger is theoretically ideal, but actually retiring them to captivity? Perhaps not a respite for my own familiars, but for the pseudologues, the minions that it plagues me with, perhaps for them.

My prayers enrage them. They punish my flesh still whenever I touch the sacred, but where there should be roadmaps of scars I have none, because whatever profanity holds me rejuvenates. Nothing I learn about the behavior of other demons applies to the legion within me; the Monster found a way to bend the rules to its own satisfaction. I should thank it.

Eventually, I promise myself, that flaw will be the answer to my salvation, though I give my earthly form to see it to its end.

37

CARTER DECIDED TO TAKE A drastic step toward her own recovery about three days later, when she pushed out her ventilator tube with her tongue.

Weston arrived that morning amid the kerfuffle that it caused, since her timing had been the worst possible. She had done it during shift change, the alarm on her respirator going crazy, bringing everyone on the run.

He hovered in the hallway outside the room and watched the skirmish, every caregiving role duplicated at that time of day. But after a few tense moments everyone seemed to relax. He watched as their movements slowed, and they smiled at each other in relief, watched her surgeon giving instructions to the nurse.

Weitzman showed up, too, wanting to check in on her after he'd finished the night shift.

"What's going on?" he asked, when he saw Weston in the hallway, looking concerned.

"Not sure," Weston murmured. "I just got here, too."

Weitzman, unlike the priest, was in his domain, so he walked into the room to investigate. Weston saw him speaking with the surgeon.

Moments later, another physician came on the run, smiling a quiet hello to Weston before entering the fray. He slowed considerably when he saw that the mood in the room was apparently not what he'd expected. An emergency page to respond, but the patient was stable on arrival.

Weston watched all of it through the window, admittedly fascinated by all these coordinated processes, but honestly just wanting to catch a glimpse of his young charge. Finally, it appeared the group could disperse, and eighty percent of the people in the room made their way back out of it, on toward home or the resumption of their duties.

Weitzman and the two other physicians wandered out near the end of the group, and drifted together toward Weston.

Raphael very considerately introduced him to the other two physicians, and the surgeon explained that though he was only caring for her burn and some of her other skin wounds, he'd been rounding when the crisis started. "All's well," he said, before ducking his head and hurrying off.

The second physician, the one who had come on the run, was the attending doctor on the case. He was the intensivist, responsible for the ICU care and the ventilator. He shook Weston's hand and smiled. "Yusef Adebonojo. Very good to know you, Father. My friend Raphael has told me very much about you."

Weston nodded, but his eyes must have given away his concern.

"She is all right, Allah be praised," Adebonojo said, his eyes crinkling as he smiled. "She scared us all this morning, got our hearts started, but she is perfectly fine."

Weston still didn't understand what had happened, so Weitzman said, "She pushed her breathing tube out – with her tongue." He laughed.

"You have seen she has so many tubes and wires, and these are important for the care of the critical patient," Adebonojo told Weston. "This is why you may have noticed we keep the soft restraints on her arms, they are there to keep her from inadvertently removing any of the monitoring equipment, especially from pulling the breathing tube. But some patients confound us, and get the tube out with their tongue!"

"So of course, this is an emergency, because we don't know if they are ready to breathe on their own," he continued. "So the alarms go off, and everyone gets to work, and it looks very scary. I am grateful that Dr. LaSalle was rounding, since I hadn't quite made it in when I got the call. She is fine, doing great without the tube."

"She's alright, then?" Weston asked, just to confirm.

"She's great," Adebonojo repeated and nodded, putting a reassuring hand on the priest's forearm. "I have a personal theory, completely anecdotal, that when a patient is either strong enough to pull out their tube, or in this case, wiggle it out with their tongue, that they have probably earned the right to a trial without it. She is young and was very healthy before this incident. So we will watch her closely and see how the day goes."

"If she gets worse, they will put the tube back in, but it looks like she knew what she was doing," Weitzman laughed. "She's breathing fine. She will still be out of it while some of her sedation wears off, but her vital signs look just fine."

Weston realized that the two men were both relieved and pleased by this development. He sensed this, and it made him feel better. He realized that he was still recovering from his own adrenaline burst from witnessing the urgency of the event.

"You can come in and see for yourself. C'mon," Adebonojo beckoned warmly.

Weitzman begged off. Patting Weston on the shoulder, he took his leave to get some rest.

Weston followed Adebonojo to the bedside. He sat down in his usual chair, grateful to be off his feet, wanting to slow down physically and mentally.

Carter's face was even more exposed without the tube and all the tape, and seeing her mouth was affecting him. It made her seem even more vulnerable, lying there with the open mask around her neck. And it completed the lovely symmetry of her face, now much less swollen, the bruises faded away, revealing only the appeal. He felt the first stirrings of an attraction to her that he did not want to have, and he lied to himself throughout those early days that this was brought on and could be explained away by protective concerns. His own demons were piqued by this, which made it worse. He did not want to be an additional threat to her well-being, neither did he want to have to listen to their internal dialogue about his thoughts.

Adebonojo went about his business, checking on those things he needed to know, and before long, he gave his farewell and departed to see other patients.

Weston found that being alone there with her was suddenly unbearable, and went to seek solace in the chapel.

38

THAT EVENING, WESTON OPENED HIS eyes and found Carter awake, looking directly at him with a curious and amused expression. He hadn't realized how exhausted he was, hadn't remembered falling asleep there in the chair, didn't even know what had awoken him.

He sat up slowly and looked around. The lights in the ICU were dimmed, and it was dark outside the large windows. Visiting hours were surely over.

"You're not Father Paul," she said, in a slightly groggy voice.

He adjusted his spectacles and said, "No. I'm Father Weston. Father Paul was here earlier."

"I had such a bad dream." Her brow wrinkled as if she were struggling to remember it but didn't really want to. "Do you have some water?" she asked suddenly.

"No, I – let me get the nurse for you," Weston offered, starting to get up.

But her expression stopped him. "Father, please stay. I don't want to be alone."

It was a plea for a small mercy, made in a small voice that did something to him. It occurred to him that fear should never be the province of someone so young. It was accompanied by a searching expression in her large lovely eyes, and he noticed that one was green and the other brown, which took nothing away from her beauty, indeed made her even more striking.

So he leaned forward and stretched out to press the call button where it was secured to her blankets to summon the nurse. Carter surprised him by capturing his hand in one of her own, holding it tightly, curling her slim fingers into his palm.

He gently switched hands, so that he could maintain contact less awkwardly, and moved the chair closer to her bed. It was the first time in his life that he was so aware of the touch of another. He had comforted many parishioners, and objectively he understood his role in this was the same, but his feelings betrayed something that felt nothing like the purely pastoral concern he'd had for them. This felt personal, and oddly intimate, and entirely foreign.

The nurse on duty was Jordan, the young man who had been kind enough to help ensure that the music player was charged, and he was surprised and pleased to find Carter awake.

"Well. Good evening, young lady," he smiled kindly as he looked her over. He nodded at Weston and raised his eyebrows to communicate that everyone's shared optimism about the girl could be celebrated with this sign of recovery.

Weston, for his part, watched Carter carefully. She seemed cautiously polite with Jordan, and was still confused about why she was in the hospital. She looked from the nurse to the priest and seemed to be carefully scrutinizing their faces and movements.

Yet there was no recoiling from either of them, both of them clearly male, and the purported source of her injury was kidnapping and sexual trauma, which was suspect given the demonic aspects of the case. Irrespective of what she did or did not recall, he felt that she would be, subconsciously at least, very uncomfortable with the two of them, no matter the associated benign roles of their vocations.

She *was* afraid, he could tell, in the way that one becomes in an unfamiliar situation, and it was evident that she remembered very little of what had occurred in the time before she was injured. But she appeared to ascertain that she was in a protected place, and he watched her trying to sort out how it had happened.

"Why am I in the hospital?" she asked, directing her question at Jordan, who was moving about, checking on her vitals and looking her over.

"You were brought by ambulance. You were unconscious," Jordan told her, neutrally. "Give me a moment here, sweetheart, and then we can talk." He placed a hand on her forearm and stroked it gently, before getting out his stethoscope and listening to her heart and lungs. He listened over her belly and put a hand against it, pressing lightly here and there.

"Any pain anywhere?"

She shook her head, still watching him closely.

"Can I change your bandage?" Jordan asked her, but it wasn't really a question. "If you roll up on your side, toward Father, I can take care of it."

She frowned, but allowed him to turn her gently toward Weston. She was far too weak to help or resist, he realized, understanding how frightening that must be.

"Father, can you just put your arm around her shoulder, there?" Jordan asked. "If that makes you uncomfortable, I can grab one of the other nurses."

But Weston shook his head silently, and pulled her toward his side of the bed in what should have been a very awkward half-embrace. But she turned those enormous eyes to him, and he looked down at her with a gentle smile, trying to reassure her, hoping that whatever the nurse was about to do would not be painful.

She just looked up at him, unblinking, trusting, even though he was a stranger. And it was both torment and blessing, to be this close to her. He found he wanted her trust, wanted to earn it, even though he understood the danger of it.

And he was thankful to Jordan, who skillfully rearranged her gown and the bedsheets so that she was never exposed to either of them, beyond what was required for her care. He tried desperately to remain unaware of the graceful curve at the side of her breast above the area that had to be bandaged. Such were the new impossibilities of his existence as he knew it. He was awake to the world in a different way, only because she was now in it.

Once Carter was settled among the pillows again, Jordan turned away and took a seat in front of the computer monitor and typed rapidly for a few minutes, clicking boxes and scrolling on the screen. He then turned back to his patient with a smile, and rolled his stool over by the bedside.

"Now, then. What would you like to talk about?"

"Water," she replied in a hoarse voice, and something about her expression was wise. She was confused, but trying to be funny at the same time. Or perhaps it was completely inadvertent. The overall effect was charming.

Jordan laughed. "It's always water. I have to ask your doctor if it's okay, but I think we can make it happen. Do you mind starting with a bit of ice, and we will go from there. Let me just make a phone call. Anything else?"

"Are you going to tell me what happened to me?"

"I would be delighted," Jordan told her. "But I don't know all of it. While I make my call, can you think about what you remember?"

She nodded slowly at him. Weston liked the nurse's response immensely. While there was probably certain training involved, he felt that most of it was Jordan's understanding and care. He was balancing the understandable need to protect Carter in this fragile state with her absolute right to have answers and gain what comfort she could from knowing the truth.

39

SHE LISTENED CALMLY AS JORDAN told her how long she had been in the hospital, listened to him explain that she had suffered a brain injury as a result of falling from a moving car. Carter heard about the surgeries to clean her wounds, the placement of a monitor in her skull (here Jordan warned her that a patch of her hair had been shaved away, but reassured her that she would be able to hide it), the need for the breathing tube.

He asked her carefully what she remembered, but she shook her head, looking bewildered and overwhelmed, and she murmured only that she had bad dreams but could not recall details.

Over her head, Jordan gave Weston a significant look, and neither of them was sure whether to be relieved or not.

"Your dreams might be your memories," he told her. "But sometimes, the pain and sedation medications can cause nightmares, and even hallucinations." When he said this last, something in her eyes changed, as if she was grasping at something important, but Weston saw her mentally push it away, not ready to think about whatever the statement triggered.

She said nothing more, and Jordan tucked her in, leaving behind the ice chips he had promised, and assuring her that he would be back to check on her. Weston knew visiting hours were long over, and asked Jordan if he would get in trouble if Weston stayed on the ward.

"Oh, honey, I'm already in trouble," Jordan said with a smile. "They can say whatever they want to me about rules. I only have one: Patient care over hot air. She needs you here." With that, he disappeared into the hallway.

Weston smiled. He liked it when people felt comfortable enough to be less formal around him, and he realized it was a first. He had never before been called '*honey*.' Jordan's heart was absolutely in the right place.

"I don't understand," Carter waited until the nurse was gone to turn her attention to Weston. "I was in a car accident?"

"You don't remember it?" Weston asked, wanting her to find it for herself. "What do you remember, what's the last thing you can recall?"

"My daddy," she whispered finally. Her head dropped forward, and the veil of her dark hair obscured her face. Her hands, palms up on the coverlet, opened and closed slowly. Weston heard, rather than saw, that first tear drop onto the blanket. "Oh, Daddy..."

Her tiny shoulders shook with grief as she pulled that memory back. "He really is dead?"

"Yes," Weston told her. "You went to his funeral," he told her, as much to inform as to prompt her recall.

She nodded sadly. "I know I did. I drove myself, even though everyone said I shouldn't. But I needed to do it. I remember sitting in the car afterward, afraid I wouldn't be able to leave him there. I didn't want him to be alone."

"I used to worry about that, leaving him alone. He got sad sometimes. I knew he was sad that I was going to go away to college, but he always told me not to worry. He used to say, 'Listen, gal, you was gonna grow up sometime. You have to go away, and God will take care of me, just like you say.'"

"I always made him pray, told him that God was looking after us. Mom, too," Carter said, and she must have assumed Weston knew the history, because she didn't explain herself.

"I was sitting in the car, and the rain was coming down, drumming hard on the roof. Suddenly, it stopped, and the sun peeked out – you know, when the rays streak down through the clouds, they call it something…"

"God's Glory," Weston said, and she nodded again.

"Yes! And that's when I knew it would be okay to leave. I knew God was there. I felt it so strongly. I knew he wasn't going to be alone. But I don't know where I went after that."

He watched her consider this for a few moments and then she shrugged, pushing her tears away with the back of her hand. He reached for the box of tissues and offered them to her.

"Thank you, Father Weston, you're so kind," she said, and hearing her say his name was nearly an undoing. She blew her nose loudly, and started crying again, completely silently, which fascinated him.

"I don't think I went home right away," she said. He could see that she was exhausted, and he wasn't surprised. Whether or not she remembered all that had occurred, waking from what she had experienced over the last several days had to be confusing and frightening. The work of trying to make sense of it alone would be wearying. Weston saw her give up on her attempts to recall anything more. She leaned back against her pillows and gave him that searching gaze once more.

"Will you stay with me?" she whispered, tears still flowing from her eyes. "I think I can brave the bad dreams if you are here."

He nodded solemnly, not trusting his words. He fished in his pocket and discovered his rosary and one other item. The music player. He held it up.

"Your friend Hayley brought this in. You left it at her house," he explained, and she brightened a little. He reached forward with the earbuds. "May I?" Weston gently placed them into her ears. "Perhaps this will help you relax."

He took another tissue from the box and dried her tears. Then he started the song, and by the time he had pulled the blankets up over her arms, she had fallen into an exhausted sleep. He gently wrapped his rosary around her hand before taking up his vigil in the chair beside the bed.

40

WESTON AND THE STAFF WATCHED Carter's body recover, which was no surprise. She was young, she was healthy, and she was determined. It was her mind that remained a concern.

Her bad dreams persisted despite successful weaning from sedatives and pain medication, and Weston suspected that her dreams were her remembering. She refused to look at the brand on her side, and he felt this was some additional subconscious way she protected herself from the worst of it. He suspected that she recalled more of it than she let on, but he refused to push the issue.

One afternoon, while she was at physical therapy, he went to the chapel to say his prayers. He hadn't been there more than fifteen minutes when Lieutenant Green found him. She sat respectfully at the back, but was obviously anxious to speak with him, so he curtailed his rosary and joined her.

"You still want to see the trailer?" she asked, her manner slightly more relaxed with him than before.

Weston nodded. He picked up the house phone and asked the hospital operator to connect him to the diocese. He had done this so often that the operators all recognized his voice. He asked for Father Paul and was transferred.

"Paul, Lieutenant Green and I are going out to the house. Would you be willing to come sit with Carter after her treatment so that she doesn't have to be alone?"

Paul agreed readily, and Weston followed Green to her car.

"Father, you are going to restore my faith in humanity," she remarked ironically, although he detected no insincerity in her tone. If anything, she sounded surprised. "Just climb in the front, there."

"Thank goodness. If you'd put me in the backseat, I would have worried," Weston said, surprised when she gave a short laugh. "I guess this means I am no longer a suspect."

"If you ever really were." Green sighed, climbing in and turning the key. "Turns out, you were easy to eliminate. You're a secretor."

"I'm a what-now?" Weston smiled at her cop lingo.

"It means that you secrete your blood type in your saliva. Some of the population can leak red blood cells and other proteins in bodily fluids. Fascinating, certainly, but it helps in criminal investigations," she explained.

"You got that from my coffee cup?" he asked incredulously.

"Father, you'd be surprised what we can learn from those things. Your fingerprints were on it as well."

Weston laughed. He liked Green. She was thorough, and her personality was like the shield she wore clipped to her jacket. She hid behind it and hoped it would keep the world at arm's length.

"Are you from here?" he asked her, wondering what she would say.

"Technically, yes," she admitted, moving her arm in a sweeping motion at the vista outside the windshield. "I grew up in the next county. It's pretty much like this one. My daddy was the sheriff, which probably doesn't surprise you. I became a cop despite that," she told him. Then, giving him a sidelong glance, she added, "He was a religious man."

Weston felt this was mostly for his benefit, to explain away anything in her manner that had been skeptical of his occupation, so he asked, "And you?"

"Oh, we were Catholic. Went to Mass every Sunday, confirmation, First Communion, the works. But it never felt like the answer to any of my questions," she said. "It felt like I was never going to belong. When I got older, I realized that following the tenets of a belief that was born in the Bronze Age didn't make any sense to me. I couldn't reconcile the fairytale, couldn't understand why people swallowed such outrageous fables."

"Of course they are fables," Weston agreed with her, and he could register her surprise from the corner of his eye. "But all religions have them. I think it is because stories resonate better with human beings. It is easier to believe in a beautiful mythology. After all, that's what faith is – knowing that the stories are the work of other persons, but believing anyway that there *is* a higher power, a greater reason for our creation. And I think that the fables differ because one size does not fit all when it comes to the serious business of contemplating one's existence."

"You are really good at this," Green said, and quickly added, "I understand your love for it. I didn't mean-"

"You have not offended me," Weston told her. "You have your own religion, you just don't call it that. We are not so different, you and I. Both seeking the truth, working against injustices."

"I'm failing miserably, then," Green said bitterly, and again he heard and felt her fear.

"We all do. I cannot eradicate the world's evil in a lifetime. I need help. We need one another. We would do well to embrace the differences and find common ground. Isn't that the Golden Rule? There are human laws, human truths that are universal. You are upholding them by enforcing the law and bringing those who break those laws to justice. I uphold them by providing an example of faith, a path to that same justice. We are certainly more alike than not. I meant it when I told you that I don't need you to believe what I believe."

"I thank you for that, Father," she said. "I am unused to being given the benefit of the doubt."

"Which is why it is so difficult for you to afford it to others. It is a luxury that you think you do not have. You must first have empathy for your own condition before you can extend it to another," he told her.

"But what if the world questions me at every turn?" she asked suddenly, and it was as if something inside her had broken free. "What if my church tells me I cannot love who I want to love, what if society constantly questions my fitness for my work?"

"God made you as you are. God doesn't care about the what, God cares about the *who*," Weston said. "And the only thing that should matter to you is what you think about your fitness for the work. Are you fit for it?"

"I'm damn good at my job," Green told him, and he could hear both pride and confidence in her voice.

"I noticed," he said calmly. "There you have it."

She stopped talking, and he knew she needed to distance herself from him again, rein in the emotions that she probably hadn't wanted him to see. He understood it; she couldn't unlearn this self-protection any more than he could jettison his own demons. But he knew she saw him differently than she had before, and her renewed respect was enough.

41

THE TRAILER WAS IN SHAMBLES. It was clear that Green could make no sense of it, but Weston certainly could. Chaos was the very province of demons. They had little regard for human order; certainly a hallmark of the possessed was a loss of organization or care for possessions or person. Destruction of objects and property were common, and the afflicted person often exhibited deterioration in hygiene and self-care.

The denting that Weston had noted on the outside of the trailer doors on his first visit were minor findings compared to what had gone on inside. The interior paneling had been stripped in places, and there were holes in the cabinetry. Broken fixtures had left crystalline glass fragments on the carpeting. Food was rotting in the refrigerator, and on the countertops. Furniture was pushed out of place and overturned.

There was stagnant standing water in the bathtub, and the toilet looked like it had been repeatedly used without being emptied. The flies had come and since died, but the maggots still lived on the filth in which they had been laid.

The stench alone would have been unbearable, but there was the scent of something darker inside, something he recognized from the serpent and its familiars, the scent of decay and death.

And there were no animals. The broken screens and perforated siding should have allowed small rodents and perhaps birds, snakes, and raccoons to follow, but nothing lived here other than carrion worms. The scent of decay should have attracted rather than repelled curious hungry creatures looking for easy shelter, but there was no evidence of such activity. Their instincts had warned them off.

Green stood to one side, watching Weston and saying nothing at all. She appeared curious about his reaction, but if he had a particular opinion about it all, she couldn't discern it.

He picked his way through the detritus and went down the short hallway past the bathroom and into the bedroom at the very end of the trailer. Here he found something that surprised him. It was obviously Carter's room; it had frilly white curtains with pink polka-dots and a matching bedspread. They appeared to be homemade items. The throw pillows were fuzzy and sparkly, and there was a stuffed ballerina doll that had her name embroidered on its chest. It looked like a well-loved childhood treasure.

None of that was surprising; it was by all accounts the bedroom he would expect a teenaged girl to occupy. What was odd was the order there. Nothing was out of place. The fabrics were not torn, her many collected treasures were lined up neatly, and her closet was organized.

The bed was made, but he had a curious thought, and glanced at Green who had followed him as far as the doorway. He looked a question to her, and she shrugged, so he tugged down the coverlet and the top sheet.

The sheets were marked with spots of old blood, and he recalled what Weitzman had said about her many superficial wounds of various ages. The spots were random, scattered on the underside of the top sheet and the exposed mattress sheet. Weston pushed his spectacles more firmly onto his face and considered this. She had been tucked into this bed every night, of that he was certain. No matter what she had suffered at the hands of her captors, she had slept, or at least been kept, in this bed with the covers up around her.

It made no sense. None at all. While he puzzled over it, he pulled the sheets and the blanket back into place and arranged the pillows as they had been before, putting the ballerina gently in her place of pride at the center. It was a crime scene. Green nodded at him, thankful he was restoring it. Although for what? The crime lab had come and gone, and he doubted that Carter would ever want to come back here.

"Seen enough?" she asked with a shiver, although the day was warm. The place was beyond creepy.

"More than enough," he answered, and they retreated to the front door and out. Green restored the tape seal at the doors after checking that they were secure front and back.

"She said she had a car," Weston asked. "Where is it?"

"No idea," Green replied. "We have an all-points bulletin out for it; I suspect we will find it was the vehicle that she was tossed out of."

Weston nodded, that had been his assumption. He followed Green back to the car and mirrored her movements, climbing back into the front seat. They sat quietly, both of them staring through the windshield at the trailer in front of them.

"I'd love to hear your theories," Green invited, and she sounded like she really wanted to know what he thought.

"It's a mess," Weston said, somewhat noncommittally.

"Yep. And no criminal mastermind would do such a thing," Green said. "We have tons of evidence. They left all kinds of tells behind. Drugs, do you think?"

"Possibly. I have problems with the sustainability over that amount of time," he told her. "The chaos lends itself to supporting my theory. But in cases of possession, the afflicted are stationary. They don't get into cars and have the capacity to drive away."

"Exactly my thought," she laughed and shook her head. "If I had known *what* to think. I wonder if in the end all the hair and fiber we found will even close this thing."

"Better to have it and not need it," he told her.

She started the engine and then turned toward him, as if she wanted to say something. But she didn't, so he stayed quiet as well.

At the end of the dirt lane, she turned back on the access road to town, and it wasn't until they slowed to a stop at the junction with the county road that she decided to tell him what she'd been holding back.

"You were right about something else," she said, and he could tell it bothered her.

"What's that?" he asked, already knowing what she was about to say.

"My three suspects, the ones we talked about up at the hospital, the ones I told you were probably good for this? We found them. All three murdered, in geographically different places, on the same day, at about the same time."

42

INSTEAD OF PULLING UP TO the drop-off, Green parked in an empty slot outside of the ambulance bay by the Emergency Department that was marked *Law Enforcement*, and followed Weston up to the ICU. She had put off getting a statement from Carter, for which Weston was grateful, since he knew it had the potential to be very traumatic.

Green had wanted the girl to have a chance to absorb all that had happened, and she had hoped that time would assist with her ability to discuss the events from the lost three weeks. She was also sensitive to the fact that what Weston, Father Paul, and the physician staff had shared with her suggested that what Carter did or did not recall was not likely to be of any great evidentiary value, but did have the conceivable risk of causing a setback in her recovery.

Green introduced herself, and Weston was thankful that she asked Carter if they could talk. Carter consented, and Green asked how she was feeling, and remarked that she had heard that Carter would be allowed to graduate on time. They talked about various local happenings, and the lieutenant got some family history, asking about surviving relatives and the like.

Her focused questioning, when it began, didn't get very far, because Carter still denied knowing much detail. Carter admitted that she was having dreams, but was never sure how faithful they were to what had actually occurred over the three weeks she had been missing.

Finally, she started to discuss Carter's social life, whether she were a typical teenager, a bit about her friends. Finally, she asked if Carter had a boyfriend, and Weston saw something in Carter's eyes that looked defensive.

"I'm a *virgin*," she said firmly, not answering the question she had been asked. Both Green and Weston noticed it. After a few moments, she said, more calmly, "No boyfriend. I never had one."

The tension in the room was palpable, and Weston could see Green deciding to wrap it up, when Carter spoke again.

"I know what you think," she said, her eyes traveling from Green to Weston and back again. "I have been reading my chart. No one asked me if it was true, and it isn't. I am still a virgin. I would know if I wasn't, right?"

She was angry, and this made Green nervous. Weston could see it, she was balancing the need for information on one hand and the desire to avoid interfering with whatever protective mechanisms were at play in Carter's understandable denial, if that was what was happening, on the other.

Weston said nothing, but was pleased at Carter's strong assertion, because it fit with what he already knew about demonic possession and diabolical control.

"I simply need to rule out-"

"Whether I was having rough sex with my boyfriend before I went missing?" Carter's eyes blazed.

"If there is anything you don't want to talk about, it is okay," Green tried to reassure her. "You don't have to answer any questions about the men who kept you in the trailer, or any other questions, for that matter. I don't want to upset you. You did nothing wrong."

"I am a virgin," Carter said it again, and although her voice remained firm, a silent tear slipped from her left eye and rolled down her cheek. It seemed it was important to her to be believed on this point. She reached out and gripped Weston's hand tightly.

Green tried again. "So those men never tried to-"

"What *men*?" Carter looked truly bewildered at this. "I never said they were men."

"Okay, Carter." Green sighed, and Weston could tell she no longer wanted to ask questions, because she assumed this was part of an elaborate denial. "Let's just take a break. If you want to talk to me in the future, I can come back."

She smiled and handed Carter her card. Weston excused himself a moment to walk with her out to the hallway.

"I'm sorry, she's not ready. That went badly," Green shook her head.

"Don't beat yourself up. Nothing about this is going to be easy. She's a tough one," Weston ran his hands through his hair and sighed. "I had no idea that Jordan let her read her records, but you have to admit, it's fair. She has the right."

Green nodded and her shoulders slumped. He could see that the case was defeating her. He wanted to do something for her, but didn't want to be presumptuous.

"Lieutenant, would it be okay if I pray for you?" he asked.

He was rewarded with a wan smile. "I would really like that, Father."

And before he could finish sketching a blessing in her direction, she was gone.

43

TECHNICALLY, CARTER WAS WELL ENOUGH to leave the ICU. Practically, no one on the care team felt it was prudent to move her. The psychologists worried about the step-down unit making her feel less secure, the surgeons wanted to ensure that she was still getting proper burn care, and it was evident that the ICU staff were protective of her. Hospital administration, despite a low patient census, were putting pressure on everyone to free up the bed.

Ultimately, it was Green that came through, without even being asked. She spoke to the medical director in her official capacity, ensuring that it was understood that since one or more of the perpetrators could still be at large, Carter remained in protective custody because she had nowhere safe to go. In lieu of stressing local taxpayer resources and assigning a patrolman to hospital duty, she suggested that the ICU was a saner alternative due to the twenty-four-hour staffing and its status as a closed ward.

She promised to assist the social workers in finding a community alternative, either with a foster family or a safehouse as soon as she possibly could.

But the social workers were stymied because the patient told them she was an adult who could still live on her own. While that was subjectively true, from a legal standpoint Iowa didn't recognize her as such because she was not yet eighteen.

Weston was in limbo. He read the local papers every day, and quartered the county in his car when he could be away from the hospital, looking for something, anything, that would provide a clue about his missing demons. Occasionally, if there was no longer a suitable host, they departed, and he wondered about the dead bikers.

Rome was reporting nothing of an abnormal spiritual nature from that area, and he knew that perhaps they had all been thwarted. The Monster in the mirror had little to say, although it knew much, and Weston was working hard on his anger, which seemed to seep into his daily life. He knew it was sleep deprivation and frustration, and this couldn't be sustained for long.

On his way back to the hospital one afternoon, he detoured to the local Dairy Queen. It always amazed him that in the most remote rural places in America, where there were barely any services to speak of, there seemed to be a Dairy Queen at every exit.

This community was no different, and the restaurant was located just off the highway, near the truckstop. It was somewhat inconvenient to the hospital, but Weston was confident that with his driving, he could get the ice cream back to Carter before it melted.

He chose his favorite, an Oreo Blizzard, and after a moment's consideration, got one for her as well.

She had just finished another round of physical therapy when he arrived, and her eyes lit with pleasure and delight when she saw him. It made his heart hurt a bit to have that expression directed at him, and he schooled his demeanor accordingly. She was seeing a priest, nothing more, even if he could no longer see her as one of the faithful. He saw only the young woman before him.

"I wasn't sure what you would like," he explained apologetically as he passed her the ice cream. "I hope it's okay."

"It's my favorite," she replied happily, accepting the spoon and digging in.

They ate together in silence for a while, and then he set his ice cream aside. He watched her eat, finding it made him happy to see her finish it off. It made him happy to see her do anything, and that deeply concerned him.

"Have you given any more thought to what your plans are after you leave the hospital?" he asked, and this elicited a frown from his charge.

"I want to be free to decide for myself," she said, her brow furrowing. "They act like I am not a grownup."

"They want to protect you, and they have to follow legal guidelines. I do understand your frustration." He thought about the irony of his own adolescence. He had been in seminary at her age.

"They are talking about assigning a *guardian ad litem*, suggesting that my trauma might cause me to make unsafe choices," she said bitterly, setting her cup aside. "I know about those, I went through that when…" She fell silent, and he could see she was thinking about something she did not want to discuss.

"I asked Father Paul to look into helping me become an emancipated minor, so that I can make my own decisions. After all, I have been taking care of things at home for a long time, and I don't need guardians looking over me, strangers trying to control my next move."

She was so well versed in these maneuverings from her parent's divorce, her mother's death. And she didn't seem concerned about the future, which he found very interesting.

"Would you want to be able to go home?" he asked, anticipating her answer.

She shook her head and closed her eyes. Without opening them, she said, "No. I don't need to go back there."

"Is there anything I could bring you from there?" he asked, wanting to do what he could. "Clothes? Any personal items?" He thought of the stuffed ballerina, but again she demurred.

"I just…I can't." She spoke with a finality that made him think of something else.

"Carter, I think you remember more than you have let on," he told her, trying to temper his directness with gentleness. "I would like you to tell me what you remember."

She smiled, but her eyes were scared. "So the ice cream was a bribe, Father?"

"If it was, you've already eaten it, and I didn't get any information, so I'm a terrible interrogator." Weston returned the smile, and added, "I came to investigate what happened, because Father Paul asked for my help. The Church sent me. As much as I would like to stay on indefinitely, I am assigned elsewhere, and I have to return to my own parish very soon."

It was the truth, the Vatican had signaled that there were other tasks that required his attention, and he knew he had neglected St. Constantine for far too long. But his heart was now here, with her. He understood that it was safer for both of them if he left.

She nodded, and swallowed hard, and he could see she was fighting off tears.

"I'm selfish about you," she admitted. "I didn't want to believe that you would go, but I knew someday you would have to. I feel loved by you. I feel safe with you."

Her word choice was interesting, but he reminded himself that she saw him through one lens only. He was a symbol of a Church that brought her comfort.

"I would stay if I had the power to do so," he admitted, knowing it wasn't an empty promise. "But my life is not my own, and I must go where the Church sends me."

Again she nodded, and said, "I will tell you what I remember. But only you."

She asked him to close the door, and he went to it, pulling it closed along its track. The glass of the cubicles was a blessing, because there could be no suspicion of impropriety. They were essentially in the equivalent of a large fishbowl next to the nurse's station, and all that happened could be seen but not heard.

"I went to see a friend, after — after the funeral," she began, and he knew she picked that as a starting place because it was benign, and safe, and straightforward. Not the sadness of the funeral nor the fright of what came next.

"Hayley, right?" Weston asked, to encourage her.

"Yes, that's right." She smiled a little. "She asked me if I wanted to stay with them. It was really nice. She is very sweet, and her parents have always been kind to me."

Weston stayed silent, waiting for her to continue at her own pace.

"I guess in hindsight I should have stayed there," she wrinkled her nose in regret. "But I just wanted to go *home*, you know? Sleep in my own bed, look at old pictures, get back to picking up without him. I didn't want to put it off, knowing I would have to face it sooner or later."

"Could you tell me about your parents?" he asked, wanting to give her something safe to lead with. "I have the general information about them, but I would love to hear the story from you. I really would like to know more about your life."

"Okay." She seemed relieved to be given another benign topic to discuss, and she considered it for a few moments, probably wondering where to begin.

"It was always me and my mom when I was little," she began. "She loved my dad, but he went to jail before I was born, and they got divorced at some point. She was honest with me about what happened to him, and she visited him in prison, but I didn't meet him until he got out. I think I was three or four years old."

"Mom took care of him. She would take me to see him regularly. She wanted me to know him, and I think she thought it was important that he was in my life. He was a very kind man. He had a drinking problem, and maybe some drugs, I don't know. I kinda think he gave up the drugs after he went to prison. I remember sometimes he was a bit off, he talked funny and walked funny, but to me, it was normal. I know now how sad that sounds."

"It makes sense," Weston said. "That was your reality. Children are blind to everything but the essentials. Value judgements must be learned."

"Yeah. He was just my dad," Carter agreed. "But Mom never once said anything bad about him. If he was sloppy, or mean, she would leave me in the car. I could read the signals when I got older. She tried to make sure he ate and took care of himself. I remember once she had to help him in the shower, and I offered to help, but she refused. She didn't want to expose me to certain things. We celebrated his birthday, and he never missed one of mine, even if she had to go out there and clean him up and drive him into town."

"I was in the sixth grade when she got sick, in the seventh grade when she died. They wanted to put me in the system, and it was so much like it is now, with everyone talking over my head and across me and not asking me what I wanted. Well, I refused to be quiet in court, and I wouldn't let anyone speak for me. The judge listened. I told them that my daddy could take care of me. Daddy cried in the courtroom, because he was scared to be held accountable for my well-being. But I was responsible for both of us. He was also heartbroken, because Mom was the love of his life, and he knew she had never given up on him."

"The social workers were ordered to visit the trailer, and see if I was okay. They were court-ordered welfare checks. I could see they wanted him to fail. It was all so hateful and prejudiced. So I made it hard for them. I would lock them out, or just make sure we were gone when they arrived."

"They finally gave up. The place was clean, I was doing well in school, and Daddy gave up his drinking for good. He got training through the local community center, and got a great job. He was my best friend," Carter said, with a little sob.

"I guess all those years of not taking care of himself caught up to him. He was still so young. He was only forty-two when he died. It was a heart attack."

Weston nodded. "Very sad."

"His friends came to his funeral. All those bikers. I realized how much of an influence he had, a life I never knew about."

"You didn't know his friends very well?" Weston asked, hoping this wasn't getting too close to dangerous territory.

"Not really. He kept me away from them," she explained. "Or perhaps he kept them away from me. Occasionally we would get a visitor out home, but I trusted my instincts. Most of them were harmless. And the others, I just paid attention and kept my distance."

If any of what she was saying had any deeper effect on her, he couldn't find evidence of it. She betrayed only a tiny shiver, but he suspected it was because they had arrived at a place in the narrative which was disturbing.

Weston stood up to retrieve a blanket from a shelf. Turning it into a makeshift shawl, he draped it over her shoulders and resumed his seat. She smiled at him gratefully and reached for his hand. He took hers in both of his and turned his whole body toward her, showing her he was there to listen.

"I knew when I got home that something was wrong, but I ignored the feeling I was getting, thinking it was just because I was returning to a place that he was never coming back to. I sat in my car a long time, letting it get dark outside, wishing I had left a light on."

"I remember climbing the step and thinking about going back to Hayley's. I was really creeped out by this sense I had of being watched. But the lady next door is pretty nosy, so I must have thought it was her. Somehow it was just off."

"I don't remember how I got inside…there's something there, like maybe the door opened for me, or I found it unlocked, which was odd. I never forgot things like that."

"There were three people in the trailer, I think women, but something was so inhuman about them, something off." She paused, and took a shuddering breath.

"Can you remember what it was?" Weston prompted her gently.

"Yes, because it is somehow the worst thing about all of it," she told him. "They smelled awful, like I imagine dead people would smell, but they were alive. They were like zombies. They all moved at the same time, but it was their eyes…their eyes…"

She stopped, and he could see that this was difficult. He considered asking if she wanted to stop, but she tugged on the blanket with her free hand and went on.

"Their eyes would move *after* their bodies moved. And they would all track me, their eyes moved together, following me. When I slept, if I slept, one of them was lying on the bed next to me, on the coverlet, just staring at me with those dead doll's eyes, whenever I woke up. It was terrifying."

"They kept chanting some poem, I could never really catch all the words, because they mumbled it. There were a few words that rhymed, something about a *beast, beast, beast* and they said that over and over, like it was what animated them."

"Sometimes they took turns with me, like they were watching over me. And sometimes they were all touching me at once. They would put me in the bathtub and all three of them were trying to wash me, but they were so rough, and they were touching me… down there-" Her voice dropped to a whisper, and her cheeks turned pink, but she kept going.

"They told me they were getting me ready. For the Prince." When Weston heard this, he flinched, but if Carter noticed, she did not indicate it. The demons, and the serpent-man had always referred to him in this way. "He was coming, and they were preparing the Bride. I was the Bride, apparently. But it was like they didn't know they were hurting me. They just said I had to be *clean.*"

"They never fed me. I think I had some old Cheerios in a sandwich bag in my backpack, and I ate a few here and there. I had secreted a pack of gummy bears in my room, and I had those. I drank water from the sink."

"I tried to talk to them, tried to ask questions, but they didn't answer – I don't think they could. They were sitting around in clothing that they had soiled. One of them didn't have her shoes, and that was really disturbing. It was like they had forgotten who they were."

"None of it made any sense. They were cleaning me up, but they would burn me with their cigarettes, or find a freckle on my arm and pick at it until it bled, telling me that this would make me more acceptable to this Prince. And they treated my room like a shrine. They didn't let me get dressed, so I would be naked and bleeding, but every night, the three of them would walk me down the hall and put me in bed. They would tuck me in, pull up the covers and everything."

"Two of them would stand in the corners of the room, just staring. The other would lie down beside me and stare at me, unmoving, presumably until they felt it was time to get me up."

"One of them would even sing parts of 'Someday my prince will come,' from Snow White, you know?"

"I'm not sure what was happening to me, I wasn't able to fight them. They seemed so strong, much stronger than they should have been. The only time they tried to actively hurt me was if I tried to leave the trailer. They would tackle me, punch me, and throw me against the wall. There were three of them, and I am not very big."

"I don't know how long it went on, but I felt myself slipping, losing time, waking and not knowing what they had done to me. I was sure I was going to starve to death. They were keeping me for the Prince, and they seemed to despair that he would come, but they persisted in their argument that I had to stay."

"One morning, I was really scared. I felt like I couldn't go on. The sun had not come up, but I climbed out of bed on my own, and fought to get a nightgown on. I told them, 'I am the Bride, and I will take you to the Prince.' I thought if I fed into their delusion, I might have a chance to escape. So instead of fighting, I played along."

"I talked them into getting into the car with me," Carter said, and her wonderment at this was evident. Weston was impressed. It was a gamble she had taken, but a very smart one. She hadn't lost her spirit, she had taken control of a very uncertain destiny, knowing that the price she might pay was with her soul.

"I remember driving out to the county road with them chanting that awful verse, and I was trying to decide where I should go, and then – well, then it all gets confused. I can't remember much after that, but there was something, something-"

Weston watched her face moving, her eyes focused on an indeterminate point in space, as she reached for it, concentrating on the memory.

"I feel like at some point there was someone else in the car, but that seems impossible. I just get the sense that there was someone else, but that's all I can say. After that, it's just nothing. Nothing in my dreams, nothing until I woke up here. I guess that's when they tossed me out."

She sat back against the pillows with a sigh of relief, as if glad to have unloaded the burden of the nightmare, grateful she could stop talking. She gripped his hands tightly, as she had throughout, but she hadn't cried. Weston was concerned about the latter, but proud of her. He was horrified by the implications. It was nothing like any demonic possession he had ever encountered or read about. He was certain that during his time reviewing exorcist's diaries in the Vatican library he had read of no accounts of shared possession.

He also noticed that she mentioned nothing about being branded, being burned.

"I'm sorry. You said they moved together. Can you describe it to me again?" He was apologizing for going back to it, but he needed to hear it in her words one more time.

"Yes. In synchrony, which is a terrible word for it. Think of synchronized swimming; it is beautiful, but there is something forced about it. This was – it was scarier than any horror movie. They moved *together*. It was so unnatural, and I never got used to it. It is the thing that dominates my nightmares." She looked at him expectantly, as if she needed confirmation that she'd told him enough.

"Thank you, Carter," Weston was sincere. "It helps me to understand." There was still so much of it that he did not comprehend, and he suspected he might never get any satisfying answers. And parts of it bothered him, as though she were remembering what the demons wanted her to remember, and that was worst of all.

44

WESTON KNEW THERE WERE STRIKING discrepancies in male and female possessions. Perhaps due to differences in social and psychological factors that he did not pretend to understand.

Males tended to go on violent rampages and then commit suicide in an equally violent manner. Females tended to waste away with occasional enraged outbursts. Their deaths were usually ultimately due to starvation or dehydration-related heart failures.

But although sexual shaming and hypersexual gesturing were a part of demonic manipulation, actual sexual potency was not. Demons talked a good game, and though the imaginations of religious folk were titillated by the idea of a sexualized demon, there was no basis for it in reported histories.

Their aim, if they even had one, was to destroy. Anything remotely creative was abandoned, including procreative function. Pain, degradation, sexual self-mutilation, all of these were common. But he had never heard of any connection between penetrative sexual violence and occupation by evil spirits.

Carter's story didn't fit her injuries, but he knew she was telling him the truth of what she had experienced, as she remembered it. She believed her history of those strange events.

So he sought Weitzman's opinion. It was a delicate subject, and he debated whether he should even broach it. He waited until the next time they were alone in the chapel.

Weitzman was surprised to see him. "I thought you were leaving us," he said, settling on the bench next to Weston.

"Eventually I must. Probably not for another few days," Weston told him, and they sat together in silence for a time.

"Raphael, I need your help," Weston said, deciding that he would appeal to the scientist and the father who wore the white coat.

"If I can, I will," Weitzman replied, looking concerned.

"It isn't me, I'm fine," Weston reassured him. "It's just, I need you to help me understand the clinical side of this. Carter is convinced she wasn't violated, and if it's a defense or a denial, I can't see it. Can you tell me about what was found physically when she came in?"

"I did her examination myself, with the social worker and a nurse, because we had to document it and the specimen collection for the rape kit. It's not an exact science, but there are patterns of bruising that are indicative of forced intercourse or sodomy, bruising and tearing, and she had both of those. Pretty severe, suggesting multiple attacks."

Weston thought about what Carter had said about the bathtub ritual she had been subjected to. "I don't question your expertise, but did the kit show anything? Any bodily fluids?"

"Hmmm. As a matter of fact, no semen was found." Raphael paused to consider it.

"But that doesn't rule out the possibility," Weston prompted.

"Not really. But it is strange. If nothing is found there is generally evidence that someone tried to cover it up by using soap, or vinegar. I don't recall either of those findings," Weitzman admitted. "What are you thinking, Father?"

"I'm thinking that none of this makes any sense," Weston admitted. "I understand her inability to remember the most traumatic parts of it, and the value of denial, but is it possible that she remembers it correctly?"

"It is possible," Weitzman said gently, but what he didn't say spoke volumes. Finally, he opted for the direct approach. "There are many ways to hurt someone. The instrument might not be a body part." He sighed. "My mother would be upset with me for having such a conversation with a holy man, but right now we are just two people discussing something we care about. Human beings are far too creative when it comes to hurting one another. We both understand that too well."

W

I know now what Father O'Halloran meant about understanding the man in the priest.

I thought I knew what I was giving up, knew what I was denying myself, but I was wrong. Overconfident in my ability to overcome temptation, because I thought I had always done so, thought I had been fighting it and them all my life.

It's different if the object of your desire is something you want. For the first time, I have found something I want. Something I cannot have, at least not in the way the weakest parts of me want to have it. I have learned at this late day what appetite truly is, what longing truly feels like.

She reduces me past all of the layers, demonspawn, priest, man, until I am only Weston.

I could regret my vows, but I do not. Had I known her before them, it might have given me pause. Were I not this priest, I would never have come to know her.

The Monster in the mirror tells me she is mine, that whatever I want is mine. Take her, the Morningstar urges, reflecting my naked torso with luxuriant enormous black wings covered in iridescent black feathers. They are beautiful, but it does this to mock me, to remind me that now she is marked. Marked for me. She suffered for me.

It won't be easy to deny it, deny the demons, and most of all deny myself. But I will. If she is for me, then that really means she is for we. Never.

They shall never have her. That knowledge is weighted with an inherent and important truth, one that I accept.

Neither shall I.

45

WESTON RETURNED TO NEW ORLEANS with a heavy heart. He had relinquished Carter's spiritual care to Father Paul, whose presence he was grateful for, but he couldn't believe that she would be safe. It was vanity to think he could protect her better, and he recognized this sin as he always did in himself, because it was the one he abhorred most.

She did not attend her graduation ceremony, perhaps correctly recognizing that her presence there would be a distraction, both to others and to herself. She did not want to be an object of pity or part of any spectacle.

She had parted from him reluctantly, nearly back to normal, a teenager in blue jeans and tennis shoes standing in the sunshine on the sidewalk in front of the rectory. She had embraced him, wrapping her arms around his waist, and burying her face in the front of his cassock, inhaling his clean, familiar scent. He had relished her touch, but he let go before she did. Indeed, for a moment it seemed she was unable to release her physical hold on him.

He knew that even though he could drive away from her, he would never be free of her. He hoped that the same was not true for her, that time would find a happy place for her, a soft landing, a quiet life of love and laughter. As much as it hurt him, these wishes were sincere.

46

THE SUN WAS SHINING THROUGH the stained-glass windows of the cathedral at Notre Dame seminary on a temperate Sunday in late September. Weston had volunteered to give the Homecoming Mass, and one of the senior parish priests caught up with him in the sacristy afterwards.

"The Archdiocese called down. Someone from the Bishop's office wants to give confession. They asked for you. Some VIP, probably. They are waiting for you in the confessional."

Weston nodded, finishing his few remaining chores. He decided it would be alright to remove his surplice, as he had to hustle across campus for the Archbishop's lunch once he was finished.

He climbed into the confessional and settled onto his seat. He pulled the screen cover and said, "God be with you, my child."

"And also with you, Father," an all too familiar voice answered with a touch of happy mischief. His heart was lifted immediately when he recognized it as Carter's. VIP, indeed. "It has been sixteen weeks since my last confession, because I was unable to find anyone who would tell me how to get to St. Constantine."

Weston smiled, and gave her a gentle reminder that she was there to unburden herself of her sins. He shook his head in amusement. She sounded healthy and in good spirits.

He tried to hear every word of her confession and managed to assign an appropriate penance and blessing, but being so near her again was the ultimate distraction.

"Please come out," he heard her plea once she had exited the confessional, because she knew it was customary for him to wait, and maintain her privacy should she want it. "I cannot come in, and I would dearly love to hug you."

He laughed, obliging her, and had barely pulled aside the velvet curtain when she threw herself at him. It felt like home must feel, like love, and this one time he didn't bother to arm himself against this casual affection.

"I don't understand," he admitted, holding her at arm's length. She was altogether too pretty in her navy dress with the round white collar, prim and sophisticated, her shining hair pulled away from her fairytale face in a casual knot. She would have benefitted from high heels, being so petite, but she wore simple modest black ballerina flats. Her legs were tanned but bare.

The child he had first seen in the hospital bed was gone, replaced by a young woman with poise and grace. She smiled at his consternation. "I have been here since July. Father Paul found a clerk's assignment for me with Bishop d'Anjou, at his office here in the Archdiocese. I told him I wanted to surprise you, but I don't have a car or a cellphone, and I have been waiting on the kindness of others to bring me to St. Constantine."

"Ah." He nodded. No wonder the older priest had thought her a VIP. She was employed by the Church offices. "I am so delighted to see you," he told her. "Unfortunately, I am running off to the Archbishop's lunch. Can I meet up with you afterward?"

"Of course," Carter laughed. "But only if you will let me walk with you now. I am expected there as well."

So they hurried through the sunshine to their engagement, and though he was surprised to be seated at the Bishop's table next to her, he probably should not have been. She was a very capable and smart young lady, and she had the advantage of knowing he was invited. She'd probably made the seating chart.

Afterward, he asked, "Can I escort you home? Where are you staying?"

"In the nun's dormitory on campus, actually, until I can find a suitable place of my own. They were kind enough to take me, and I have everything I need. I am within walking distance of work, it's a safe neighborhood, there are plenty of churches… but it is too far from St. Constantine."

"I've always thought that was the worst thing about it," he agreed, teasing her.

"So you went to school here?" she asked, as though she already knew the answer. "Everyone seems to know who you are. I don't think the nuns approve of me seeking your company."

"I did my undergraduate work and my master's thesis here. It's a small place, very insular. I think most of the graduates are like family," he told her, wondering about but not commenting upon the last part of her statement.

"The Bishop seems suspicious of you as well," she observed, and he wondered at her keenness in picking up on the politics of the matter.

"The Church is one big hierarchy," Weston explained. "Theoretically, he is my superior, but the Vatican has instructed otherwise. I get my instructions directly from Rome."

"That's a bit of an understatement, isn't it?" Carter replied. "I hear them talking, and they don't hide their feelings. You only answer to the Pope. You never told me this."

"Would it have mattered?" he asked.

"I suppose not, but you are not just an exorcist," she said. "You are some sort of special priest. They resent you."

"What the priests of my sect are asked to do is extreme, very juxtaposed to the most conservative conclaves of the Church," Weston said, wanting his words to sound as forgiving as they could.

"I don't think they resent it so much as they fear it, fear the need for such as I."

They walked quietly along the campus sidewalks toward her dormitory. Finally, he said, "What about you? Why here?"

"I don't know," she admitted. "I had my diploma, and I actually had a scholarship to go to St. Kate's, but in the end, I couldn't see myself there. Everything about my life and who I thought I was had changed, if not actually, then existentially."

"I needed to be away from there, and in my most honest moments, I realized that I needed you," she admitted in a small voice. "I missed you, and knowing that I could see you or talk to you anytime I wanted to seemed to give me something to look forward to. Thank God for Father Paul. He understood. He called in some favors to get me here, I think."

"Undoubtedly," Weston agreed.

"And once I was here, even though I couldn't quite figure out how to get to you, I knew it was the right thing. I felt safe. I sleep better at night knowing that you are in the same town."

"Yes, but you have been here for months!" he protested. "You could have called me."

"I know." Carter stopped walking and turned those enormous eyes his way. "But I didn't want all that space between us the first time we spoke. I just had faith that it would happen as it should. Also, the time alone, trying it out on my own, has been good for me. I have tested out my independence, and I am doing okay. I hope that makes sense."

"It does," Weston reassured her, wanting her to know he wasn't upset. He was pleased that she was finding herself. It didn't hurt that she was doing it here, although he knew it complicated his life. He knew he wouldn't be able to stay away, and he wanted to maintain some semblance of professional distance, for both their sakes.

47

WESTON MANAGED TO RESURRECT THE old Buick that he had inherited from Father O'Halloran. When the Church had approved his request for a more powerful vehicle, he had pledged to donate it, but no one from Catholic Ministries had ever shown up to claim it. A bit of rudimentary maintenance on his part got it road safe once again, and he gave it to Carter to use.

She was as delighted with the ugly thing as he had once been, and it made him happy to do something for her.

A secondary benefit was realized almost immediately, because she began driving across town every Sunday to attend mid-morning mass at St. Constantine. Then she would hang around and help with the cleanup while he wound up his chores, waiting to take him to brunch.

They would walk together to the diner a few blocks away, and she always insisted on buying breakfast.

"I am gainfully employed," she boasted, snatching the check off the table that first time. She pretended to study it carefully before remarking, "Besides, you are a cheap date."

Afterward, they would return to the church together, but he would never invite her inside. In its emptiness, its only use was as his residence, and such was not proper, even though the two of them observed the utmost decorum.

So she would dawdle there on the sidewalk, near the car, and they would talk, sometimes for an hour or more before he finally sent her off.

One Sunday, he asked her, "How's the apartment search coming?"

She had talked about starting to look for a more permanent place to stay, but months had passed without her remarking on it again. He wondered if she were reluctant to be truly alone, living by herself.

She smiled a secret smile. "I found a place, but it is only a couple blocks away from where I am now."

"Terrific," he said. "Will you need help moving? I can think of a volunteer."

"It's kind, but I won't need very much," she shook her head, and started to laugh. "I am becoming a novice, taking the path to the convent. I have declared myself to the Mother Superior at Our Lady. The Carmelites make the most sense, and I have always admired their charitable works."

"Is this what you want?" he asked her gently, recalling what Father O'Halloran had said to him about using the Church as a place to hide. If he were truly honest with himself, he was saddened. If she were cloistered, he would have little opportunity to see her.

"It's what I have wanted for a very long time," she nodded. "It was why I picked St. Catherine. The nuns there are the Sisters of St. Joseph of Carondelet, renowned as teachers. That appealed to me very much, and I was to take my education and orders there. But I think charity suits me better now."

"You are young for the cloister," he remarked, surprised by what she was telling him. But he recalled Hayley telling him that her friend was 'very Catholic,' and he wondered if her knowledge that Carter wanted to be a nun had been the reason for that observation.

"Are you being a hypocrite?" she asked, teasing. "The famous Father Weston, youngest priest in the free world?"

"Big word," he said, smiling. "What does it mean, again?"

Carter pretended to ignore him. "The Bishop recommended me. I think Sister Mary Matthew would like to say no, but I don't think she dares. She doesn't love the idea. She wants me to go to college."

"That is smart of her," Weston said, having to defend the soundness of the argument.

"I have enough of an education from my life," Carter said with conviction. "And you should know about it, because I have another request."

"Oh? You are doing just fine making decisions for yourself, you don't need my approval," he told her, wanting her to know he was proud of her, even if a bit worried about the decision she was making.

"I know that. But what I do want is to assist you. I have raised special circumstances in my request for orders. Since I seem to attract demons, I think I could apply my charity to those who are similarly afflicted. Accompanying you when you perform exorcisms would make an excellent use of my personal experiences with the profane."

"I cannot see the Mother Superior agreeing to that," Weston shook his head and adjusted his spectacles, his calm voice belying the storm that raged in his blood. She wanted to do this work, and with him. He wanted to lock her in a safe place where she could never be hurt again. "Or the Church, for that matter. Have you discussed it with the Bishop?"

"Not hardly," she said, rolling her eyes. "But I don't need to. I have a friend who knows the Pope."

W

In the end, I was alone in protesting the idea.

His Holiness already knew her story.

He is a firm believer in self-determination and free will. He questioned me simply about whether she was fit emotionally. And I gave him the only answer I had. I simply do not know, that is the truth of it. Then he asked me if I thought any human being fit emotionally to battle the Devil. Checkmate.

I'm not sure I am prepared to expose her to the evils that I combat on these assignments, the exorcisms that can take days or weeks, the demoralization of demons. More importantly, I am not sure what I am exposing her to in myself. If I accept her help, haven't I furthered the cause of whatever diabolic power wanted us together in the first place?

The Morningstar delights in my suffering. It mocks me from the mirror and tells me that I am much more interesting now than I have ever been. I can see it believes that my resolve shall weaken, and her presence will hasten my use as its instrument.

The Church sanctions anything that furthers its aims. The eradication of evil will always be a greater justification than any other. Greater than the Pope, or the institution.

Greater than this lowly priest plagued by the very pestilence I am asked to dispatch.

The most selfish parts of me rejoice that she will remain close to me, but they are the parts I can never trust.

48

"WHAT DO YOU THINK?" CARTER asked, showing Weston the haircut that Sister Mary Matthew had administered. It was brutally short and uneven, purposefully so, Weston suspected.

He found her even more devastatingly beautiful, and though it gave her a haunting vulnerability, he knew better than to underestimate her. She was strong in a very particular way, something he guessed she had inherited from her mother.

"No matter how awful, no one will see it," she concluded. "I am going to wear my mother's wedding ring as my bride's ring. That way I can have her with me always."

"I like that idea," Weston told her. "I have something for you to look at after your declaration Mass. I will see you tomorrow afternoon, following the ceremony."

And he witnessed her take up the coif with the other novices, and come into the Church he loved.

She was surprised when she saw the white minivan with the cross at the front, but seemed a bit disappointed.

"What's wrong?" Weston asked. "It matches your clothes."

She was used to him making nervous jokes, so she shook her head. "I like the old car, because it used to be yours."

"Well, this one was the Pope's," he told her, rewarded when she laughed aloud and looked skeptical. "Okay, so he rode in it once.

The Church bought it just for that. He won't be back for it, or if he comes back, they will probably buy him another one. I suggested I could use it. I think he agreed, but not for me. For you."

"That's insane," Carter protested, but Weston shook his head.

"His Eminence knows about what happened to you, and he celebrates the sacrifice you are making in dedicating your life to this cause. He takes such things very seriously, he respects them."

"What is he like?" Carter asked suddenly, and he was relieved because there would be no more argument over the car. He had already delivered the old Buick to Catholic Ministries, and this time, they had taken it.

"He is a very good man with a very difficult job," Weston said honestly. "I think he is perfectly suited to it."

"That's comforting to hear," she smiled at the fond tone he betrayed when speaking of the Pope. "You love him."

"I do," Weston admitted easily. "He is easy to love, and that is important. It makes my work less burdensome. I hope you will get to meet him someday."

He spent the better part of the afternoon explaining to her what the car could do. When she understood that it wasn't just a car, she seemed to accept the gift more fully.

"One more thing," he told her, holding out an old wooden box. "I believe in destiny, because it is another type of faith. It means that I accept that God has a plan for me, and there are far better persons than I who recognize the truth in that. His Eminence gave this to me; it is the second of a pair, and I didn't understand until you declared your vocation that it belongs to you."

She looked at him questioningly, and opened the box. He watched her admire the elegant item nestled in the velvet within.

"It's just like yours," she whispered, running a finger lovingly over its surface. Enormous eyes looked up at him. "But I can't possibly-"

"You can, and you must," he told her. "This is the Cross of the Redeemer. From them both come our greatest charity, the blessing of redemption, the gift of Christ Himself."

Carter allowed him to lift the chain over her head and settle it around her neck. She arranged it against her snowy garments, curling her fingers more tightly around it as Weston told her its secrets.

And so they began the work of facing down the damned.

Together.

49

THE HIGHWAY CURLED THROUGH GENTLY rolling hills, over bridges that spanned the interstate and under train trestles carrying freight between Texas and Chicago. It continued as a four-lane, persisting wide and smooth even as they traveled farther and farther from the Interstate.

Carter saw fallow fields that had probably held corn and soybeans, scattered cows and the rare sheep. Three skinny horses grazed behind a rusted shed.

They passed an evangelical church with a lettered marquee that read, *Give Satan an Inch and He'll Be the Ruler.* She glanced at Weston, and his eyes told her that he'd seen it, too. He smiled a little. The Bible Belt. Carter didn't smile.

She thought it a kind of grim reminder of what they were about to face. This one was going to be bad; they all were, but already the landscape, the church, the barren fields were too much for her. It was too close to what she had known, before.

Weston reached out, taking a hand off the steering wheel, sensing her distress. She clasped it gratefully. It was warm and strong, a reminder that she could use him to anchor her in place, hoping that wouldn't be needed, hoping that she could master this fear to help him once more.

"Are we meeting the doctor beforehand?" she asked, hoping that there was to be some rational discussion about the case, in relative peace and quiet.

"She's at the house," he told her. "I can drop you off at the church and meet her alone. I would understand if-"

"No." Carter spoke with a flat finality. "I want to help."

When he didn't respond, she said, in a softer tone, "I need to help. I'm praying for strength." Weston gave her hand a squeeze.

The grey light of late afternoon accompanied them the rest of the journey. They turned down a dirt track between mailboxes stacked five to a side, but the driveway ended near a smart ranch house surrounded by scattered old oaks and maples. The winter grass was dun-colored and listless, and the property was bounded by empty fields. A pole barn was set back from the house on a separate track, next to a light post. An electrical line ran from the barn to the corner overhang of the roof.

There was an ancient tire swing hanging from the largest tree in the front yard, pushed idly by the breeze. It should have recalled happier things, but the quiet sadness of the place made it more ominous somehow, like a gallows.

They stepped from the warmth of the car into the biting air, their feet crunching on the grass. Weston led the way onto the porch, and Carter glanced around, noticing the dead poinsettia that had been forgotten there. She remembered the file saying that the trouble had started during the Christmas holidays past, and apparently no one had bothered to remove it. She supposed the family had more important concerns.

Weston knocked on the door, and it was opened shortly by a middle-aged Hispanic woman who nodded somberly and let them in. As soon as the door opened, Carter knew. She felt it. Something here was wrong, very wrong. It was a feeling that countless girls had experienced before they disappeared or died. A feeling that comes on just before getting into a stranger's car. A feeling too many of them ignored. As Carter herself once had.

The woman introduced herself as the family's physician. She gave her name as Emilia Esparza, and led them through a short entry hall into the front parlor. Carter could see the tire swing through the window, and she shivered. Several more somber faces. Parents, worn down, despairing, exhausted. Siblings, afraid, traumatized. The psychiatrist, the local priest. Mistrusting expressions mixed with vague hope and not enough relief that they had finally come.

The house was cold, the old steam radiators fighting to keep it habitable. There were homey crocheted afghans on the backs of the furniture, the nimble work of a great grandmother that was likely long dead. Rows of photos on a mantelpiece still wearing a plastic holly wreath. The empty stocking pegs like a handful of crooked metal teeth. The sadness was palpable.

Carter heard Weston murmuring something to someone, but she had moved away, past the family to the barren, empty fireplace. Searching through the photos to find what she wanted.

Eventually, someone, usually the mother, would offer to show them a picture of the afflicted. Wanting them to see the person that had been, before they met the horror that existed now. Carter always had to look, to remind herself why it was so important that they had come, that no matter how terrible, there was a person in need of their help, that perhaps she and Weston were the last hope for redemption.

Seeing the faces helped her fight. She didn't really see *these* faces, they were all heartbreaking, young, wholesome, smiling. The pride of their families, their parishes, the bright hopes of their volleyball teams, church choirs, small town dreams. Instead, she saw the same face in these picture frames, rendered repeatedly. Only one. Her own.

50

WESTON WAS PRAYING WITH THE family when she came out of her reverie. She touched the smiling face in the photo once more, as if to reassure this person from the past that she understood, before joining the group once more. More than one curious set of eyes traveled over her, and she was self-conscious in her pristine habit, feeling like an impostor, wondering if she could do what was expected of her.

When the prayer concluded, a gentleman nearing middle age separated from the group, and he, like the doctor, were obviously not members of this average midwestern rural family. His face betrayed what appeared to be an Asian origin, and he introduced himself as Jean-Marc Wong. Carter found it interesting that he had a French first name ahead of his Chinese surname, surely unusual anywhere, not to mention in landlocked flyover country. This was the psychiatrist. He had a casual confident manner that made her nervous, as she had always wondered if psychiatrists were able to resist analyzing whomever they encountered.

He handed Weston his card, and said, "Perhaps we could meet in my office for a more comprehensive discussion." His expression was meaningful; it was clear that he desired their conversation to occur away from the family, perhaps even away from this setting. "But I wanted to be here when you met Rachel, to take you in so that the family wouldn't have to. Would you like to meet her now?"

"Of course," Weston nodded somberly. "I'd like to see her."

"It isn't very pleasant in there," Dr. Wong warned them, looking at Carter in her snowy robes.

She made no reply, just waited expectantly to be shown the way, marshaling her nerve for what she knew was to come.

They went down a short hallway off the living room, and Carter's skin began to crawl. Gooseflesh rose on her arms, and she doubted it was due to inadequate heating. Outside the last door on the left, Dr. Wong paused, and she could hear whispered words from inside the room.

Then he opened the door for them, and Weston and Carter went through. Wong closed the door behind the three of them. The room was cold, the window to the back yard open, blowing the filmy pink curtains back and forth. The stench was nearly unbearable, it was obvious that the girl was living in her own filth, that she had soiled herself, and it was unlikely that anyone had the energy to keep up with the cleanup this required. Still, the linens on her bed looked reasonably fresh, but Rachel herself did not. There was nothing left of the fresh-faced girl in her school picture. This wraith was a wasted wreck, a grimace of distaste marked her expression, and her eyes were fever-bright points of light.

She wore only a Taylor Swift tank top that was much too large for her, although Carter suspected it might have fit her once, with nothing beneath it. This left nothing to the imagination, her ribcage and hipbones standing out in stark relief against pale skin marked with many injuries, most likely self-inflicted.

Her head swiveled to look at them, and she focused on Weston first, her frown deepening as she continued to whisper the same repetitive phrase over and over again. The names of the apostles, *Andrew, John, Philip, Bartholomew, James Alpheus, James Zebedee, Thaddaeus, Thomas, Simon the Zealot, Simon Peter, Matthew, Judas Iscariot*...and so on. Interestingly, the demons under Weston's skin did not respond to Rachel as he had expected.

She did not pause or comment on their presence, but something odd happened when she reached the name Thomas. It caused a sort of break in the rhythm of her speech, as though she were choking on it whenever she reached it. And her attention had definitely shifted to Carter as she did so. She moved off the bed, slowly approaching the nun with an intense gaze, and when she reached the name Thomas again, she said, "Thomas, Thomas, Thomas, Thomas the Doubter, Thomas the Unbeliever, Thomas, Thomas, Thomas."

Finally, her voice rising to an unbearable volume, she leaned in and put her arms around Carter, moving her face against the snowy bib of her gown, finally shouting as she writhed and jerked, that skeletal form pressed against Carter, "Thomas the SLUT, the SLUT, the SLUT...aren't you, Carter?"

Dr. Wong looked horrified and reflexively he reached for Rachel, intending to pull her away, wanting to contain her outburst, but Weston gently shook his head, and made eye contact with Carter, not understanding but seeing hers, and the distress in her eyes. But she, too, shook her head, and instead of pushing the young woman away, she embraced her, taking that battered form into her arms, unmindful of the ordure that was soiling her clothing, ignoring the physical insults that were visited upon her.

Even in her emaciated state, Rachel was larger than the diminutive Carter, and eventually her spasms carried them both to the floor, and still Carter waved the men away, as the girl's mantra continued, only now she whispered just one word under her breath, saying, "*Slut, slut, slut, slut, slut, slut, slut, slut...*"

Carter held on tight, enduring the blows, enduring the sexually suggestive movement, and she closed her eyes and began to sing, stroking the dirty hair gently, ignoring the worst, and Rachel's sobs came finally, in a ragged alien croak. And Weston knew he loved Carter more than he could bear, and the demons inside of him rose up in response to her, as they had not for this lonely unfortunate they had come to save.

51

WHEN RACHEL FINALLY CALMED, CARTER nodded at Weston, who gently lifted the girl in his arms and sent Dr. Wong to fetch the family doctor. Carter climbed gingerly to her feet, knowing that she would have some bruises to show for the ordeal. She straightened her clothing as best she could, and turned to see Dr. Esparza in the doorway.

Carter noticed something she hadn't when they were first introduced. The doctor looked tired and somewhat despairing. Carter reached out and touched her arm, not wanting to overstep any boundaries, but the woman seemed to appreciate this.

Dr. Esparza smiled at Weston, seeing how tenderly he held the girl. "Perhaps this would be a good time to bathe her, while she is calm," she observed, and she took Rachel from Weston as one would take a baby from the arms of another.

"Would you like some help?" Carter asked, knowing it would be needed and wanting to spare Rachel's mother from the task.

"That's very kind, yes, I would," Dr. Esparza replied.

After the bath, once Rachel had been dried and dressed, Weston came in to carry her back to her room. Carter was surprised and touched to see that he had changed the linens on her bed. Mercifully, Rachel slept. Carter sat close by the bed, and she could hear voices from the living room down the hall, and the front door opened and closed at least twice before Weston reappeared in the doorway.

His raised eyebrows seemed to ask if he should come in, and she nodded, cautioning him with a finger to keep quiet.

"I sent the doctors home," he whispered in her ear, and she shivered inadvertently at this forced intimacy.

She nodded, and got up from her seat, indicating he should sit down. He did so, and she went into the adjacent bathroom briefly to get a drink of water. When she returned, she wandered about the room, looking at Rachel's posters, her stuffed animals, at the clothes in her open closet.

Carter sat down at the girl's small vanity table, and examined the many photographs that Rachel had secured in the frame of the mirror in happier times. Many smiling young faces, often the same handful of girls, and as she'd wondered, one particular boy. The vanity top was otherwise neat and organized, which she found interesting as well.

Calling on her own very recent experiences as a teenage girl, Carter sat and thought for a moment. The vanity had a small drawer. It was not locked, and inside it Carter found pens in a rainbow assortment of colors, several stickers, a green paperclip, and the odd mismatched earring. She felt the underside of the drawer, but it was smooth.

Getting to her feet, she studied the room once more. She crossed over to the side of the bed opposite Weston and knelt on the carpet, then put her head almost to the floor to look underneath the bed to see if anything was trapped there in the frame. She knew that there was likely nothing placed between the mattress and box spring, because it could be easily discovered by Rachel's mother, and would have been found by Weston or the many others who had been changing the bedsheets recently.

She stood up again and turned in a full circle. She caught Weston's eye and smiled, wondering what he thought of her snooping. He looked amused and not entirely clear about what she was doing, but that didn't surprise her. Boys didn't have the same kinds of intrigues that girls did.

There was a hanging jewelry organizer at one end of the closet, and another closet organizer with multiple cubby holes into which Rachel had placed socks, belts, and scarves at the other end. The lower left cubby was obscured by the edge of the accordion door, and there were multiple winter hats stuffed into it. Carter gently pulled them out one by one, and saw that the bottom surface of the recess looked bulky. When she removed the fabric covered insert, she discovered a small journal covered in fluffy pink fur, with an attached pen in the shape of a unicorn that was attached to the binding with a Velcro loop.

She retreated to the stool by the vanity table and opened the book. It was a diary of sorts, filled with painstaking loopy cursive writing. Every *i* was dotted with a heart. She flipped backward to just before the Christmas holidays, and then back to before Thanksgiving and began to read.

Weston watched Carter's expressions change with the words that were written on the page, at times dreamy and faraway, at times she smiled, but as she advanced through the recent record of Rachel's life, she looked sad. When she reached the last written page, she frowned. The date was just before New Year's Eve of the prior year.

Carter spent some time flipping to random pages here and there, probably to learn as much as she could of Rachel's thoughts and her normal state of mind before the trouble started. Finally, she closed the book with a sigh, stroking the fur cover absently.

She carefully returned it to the place where Rachel had secreted it so skillfully, replacing the insert over it, and stuffing the winter hats back into place in the haphazard way they had been stored, keeping this stolen confidence.

And just in time, because as she settled herself again on the stool, she had no sooner come to rest when a timid head peered in from the hallway. Rachel's mother, looking very nervous, her hands fluttering near her abdomen, where she clutched the outer apron from Carter's habit, which she had been kind enough to launder. Her eyes went from one to the other, beseeching. Her exhaustion was evident in the slope of her shoulders, the hollows under her eyes.

"Oh, she really is sleeping," she exclaimed softly, stepping into the room. She looked upon her daughter with a mixture of fear and pity, and avoided coming nearer the bed. "Do you think you can help her?" she asked doubtfully.

"Let's have faith that God can heal her," Weston whispered in response.

The woman nodded violently, and closed her eyes tightly, trying not to cry. She sniffed loudly, and said, "I was just about to make some tea. Would you like some?" But this was too much for her fragile state, and she began to sob.

"Come," Carter urged, going to her and pulling her away from the bed. "I will help you with the tea, and then perhaps we can sit down with Father and talk." She led her from the room, not wanting the commotion to awaken Rachel, and Weston kept his vigil until Carter returned to tell him the tea was ready.

52

"WHERE IS THIS HOST HOUSE?" Carter asked, as they turned out of the driveway in the dark. Rachel had allowed her mother to give her medication before they had left, and they had promised to return the following morning.

"Not far," Weston assured her, and she was surprised when he turned back down into town rather than head back to the four-lane.

He pulled up to a handsome restored Victorian that was two blocks behind the town square. The porch light shone out on the fallow lawn, the glow not quite reaching the driveway or the street, but it was warm and inviting.

There was a wraparound porch with rocking chairs set out front behind the railing, and Carter heard the barking of a what sounded like a small, very determined dog. Weston led the way up the walk and rang the bell, which sent the dog into a veritable frenzy.

Carter was even more surprised when Emilia Esparza answered the door, accompanied by a Parson Jack Russell Terrier that was jumping as high as her waist as he scolded her for letting them in.

Much to the dog's surprise, Weston caught him at the peak of his jump, snatching him up midair, and he stopped barking.

"Oh, I am glad you like dogs," Dr. Esparza laughed. "That's Jack. I know, not very original, but it suits him."

"He was about to give himself a stroke," Weston murmured, holding the dog against the sweater he wore over his cassock, and stroking Jack's ears. For his part, the dog looked half indignant at being interrupted in his duty, but was well on his way to granting forgiveness for the insult given Weston's close attentions.

"Some guard dog you are," Dr. Esparza said, tapping Jack gently on the nose. "Please, come in."

"I didn't realize you were our hostess," Carter said, following the doctor into the house. "Thank you for your hospitality, Doctor."

"Oh please, call me Emilia," she begged. Glancing at Weston, she said to Carter, "Your Mother Superior already phoned to check on you."

"Oh, dear," Carter lamented, looking out the windows on the darkness outside.

"I told her you were bathing," Emilia said, a mischievous gleam in her eye. Looking at Weston, she added, "I didn't tell her that you were also staying here, Father."

"Thank you very much," Weston responded, but continued, "I know that was what we originally arranged, but I think I will stay at the priest's residence over at St. Luke's." He didn't want any possibility for mischief to arise in anyone's imagination; more practically, he did not want to be sleeping one room away from Carter. It was doubtful he would get a moment's rest with such a torment.

At that moment, the telephone began ringing again, the metallic dinging of a landline located somewhere at the back of the house. "That'll be her again," Emilia said, excusing herself, and Carter looked hopelessly over her shoulder at Weston as she followed, not wanting the Mother Superior to have any *other* excuse to castigate her.

When the two women returned, Weston was still standing in the hallway, cradling the dog, who appeared to have made himself at home.

"Oh, Father, you can put him down," Emilia said, embarrassed. "I should have taken him from you. He's absolutely rotten already."

"It's perfectly okay," Weston said, smiling down at Jack with genuine good humor. "I know it's late, but do you have time to talk with us tonight about Rachel? It would be wonderful to learn more about her. I will completely understand if you would rather wait until tomorrow."

"Not at all," Emilia told them. "I sleep very little these days anyway. Oh dear, I nearly forgot – you haven't eaten! I made chili and cornbread, I hope that will serve. I wasn't sure what you'd like."

"It sounds perfect," said Carter, unable to betray her delight at the prospect of a meal, pulling and lifting impatiently at her head covering to take her wimple off, and running her hands through her short hair. Emilia returned to the kitchen to prepare for dinner, leaving them alone in the front hall. Jack, perhaps understanding that food was the subject of their conversation, squirmed out of Weston's arms, leaping to the floor and following his owner.

Carter busied herself picking dog hairs from the front of Weston's sweater, wanting an excuse to stay close to him for a few moments more, disappointed that he wouldn't be staying in the house with them. He held still and quiet, and she could feel the warmth of his breath on the top of her head. After a brief interval, the loud ticking of the grandfather clock nearby brought her back to her senses, and she stepped away.

"Do you think – would you have time to hear my confession before dinner?" she asked shyly.

"That depends on how terrible you've been recently." He smiled and punctuated this cheeky remark with a glance at his watch.

"Well, part one, then," Carter replied smartly.

"We should have time for part one, surely," he nodded, gesturing toward a small study through one of the doors off the hallway. He followed her inside, and slid the pocket door behind them, careful to leave it gapped open several inches to preserve propriety. "How would you prefer we do this?" he asked, seating himself in an old-fashioned armchair.

"Traditional, can you turn away?" she asked him, retrieving a cushion from the small couch near the wall and placing it on the parquet before kneeling carefully facing the wall.

"Bless me, Father, for I have sinned," she began. "It has been six days since my last confession."

Weston remained silent, waiting for her to say more, but she was quiet, perhaps marshaling her courage or trying to remember what she wanted to tell him. He found her adherence to this exercise was frequently more thorough and thoughtful than his own.

"I have sinned against another. I intruded on Rachel's privacy, and I did not have permission to examine her things, and I came between her and her parents, from whom I should have sought approval to know more. I have been unchaste, and disobedient, because I do not always wear my veil and coif as I should when in company. I have been uncharitable in my thoughts about Sister Mary Matthew, who is only trying to teach me by her excellent example how I must approach my vocation," she told him.

He waited, because she seemed to be finished speaking, but she continued into the silence. "I have had unclean thoughts about my confessor, and I have been inappropriately intimate with myself."

Weston shook his head at her way of admitting to masturbation, but had to acknowledge that it was a very ladylike way to put it. He spoke briefly of clinging to God's example in living day to day life, in rejoicing in chastity for the sake of the privilege of being the Christ-bride, then gave her penance and blessed her as she mirrored the sign of the cross over her own breast.

Then he got to his feet and helped her to stand, ducking down to retrieve and replace the cushion she had used. As he led the way out of the room, he adjusted his spectacles and said, "Let's help set the table. Part two tomorrow, then?"

She resisted the urge to give him a little push, as if they were schoolchildren, and watched his broad back moving along ahead of her as they made their way down the hallway toward the kitchen.

53

EMILIA'S CHILI DID NOT DISAPPOINT, although Weston thought he could have eaten cardboard, it had been so long since his last meal. She also served excellent wine, which was a good sign; she was an understanding Catholic. Most priests love their wine but other than during Mass they don't often get it. It is considered an indulgence for one who has taken a vow of poverty. Sympathetic parishioners feed their priests often and well, and keep the wine flowing.

Carter glanced at him shyly when she accepted her wine, because he knew that technically she was not old enough for it, but he nodded gently. Emilia did not seem concerned about it. After half a glass the young nun was flushed and smiling, and she was prudent enough to stop there.

They helped Emilia clear, and talked companionably in the kitchen while everyone pitched in to put away leftovers. Weston loaded the dishwasher, and then Emilia poured out more wine, and they sat at the kitchen island together. It was more informal, and Weston suspected it might be an easier place for her to have a difficult discussion.

"I was the physician on call when Rachel was born," she smiled, remembering happier times. "I was new in town, it was my first year in practice, and I hit it off with the family right away. The entire family have since become my patients."

"She has always been a typical kid. She had a normal childhood, seemed genuinely happy and well-adjusted – all her siblings do, too – and never really got into trouble. The family is very involved with the church, she sang in the choir, and participated in the local youth group."

"She was baptized and confirmed. All was well."

"Rachel started having trouble last fall, just after the Thanksgiving holiday. She seemed anxious, and withdrawn. She was rude to her grandmother. Her mother spoke to me about an intestinal illness just after the holiday, and Rachel was uninterested in family trips to go Christmas shopping. She was sleeping a lot, and crying a lot, so her parents brought her to see me."

"She denied any problems, but she was defensive and angry, which was very unlike her. There were altercations with her siblings, and she scratched her sister's face. She was still going to school, and the week before it let out for the holiday break there was a decline in her attention to her hygiene. She stopped showering altogether, and her math teacher reported she hadn't performed well on one of her exams."

"The family then noticed that she started talking to herself in her room, but they were disturbed by the changes in her voice, and the shocking things that came out of her mouth. Profanity, shouting, and intrusive repetition, to the point where no one in the family had any peace."

"At that time, her mother insists that there were still glimpses of the old Rachel. For example, she refused to go to Christmas Mass, claiming she was unclean, and it was around that time she stopped going to the church altogether. Father Lucas initially tried to visit the home and see Rachel, but she was violent with him, and told him to keep away from her. She said some pretty ugly things, considering. Father Lucas is beloved in this community, and he does a lot of good."

"He initiated the inquiry about the exorcism," Weston told her.

"I assumed so," Emilia replied, and then paused as if trying to remember where she had left off. "After Christmas, I got Jean-Marc involved. We are lucky to have him, too. He is a general psychiatrist, but he also makes prison visits, and he completed a pediatric psychiatry fellowship. He is wonderful with the most difficult kids, you know?"

"Anyway, he evaluated her but couldn't really pin down a diagnosis. He explained to me that some of the psychotic disorders are challenging to diagnose in adolescence, and the picture never really fit. He couldn't get much from Rachel at that point to give him any clue as to whether there had been a psychological trigger, and she deteriorated so quickly after that it was harder and harder to be around her, much less try to counsel her or gain further insight about her psychopathy."

"She stopped eating, stopped bathing, and became more and more removed from the world around her. She would refuse to speak, only grunting or chanting, often profane and very personal in her attacks. She refused to use the toilet, soiling herself and sitting in it, refusing to allow anyone to clean her up. We have to do it forcibly now, involving her parents, which is heartbreaking for them. She was exhibiting hypersexual behavior, which was so unlike her that we all became very concerned. After New Year, she started to self-harm, and Jean-Marc and I tried to coordinate a hospitalization to begin antipsychotics and hydrate her. Tube feeds were considered."

"She destroyed her hospital room and attacked one of her nurses in a very calculated manner. Horrifying. The administration approached Jean-Marc and I to suggest she would be better served elsewhere."

"Her family would not think of institutionalizing her, so we have been coordinating her care for the past several months at home. Sometimes we can get her medications right, and she is quiet long enough to drop a nasal tube and get some nutrition into her, but then she shifts again, and pulls all the tubes. Her strength when she rages is impressive, and we have had to restrain her at times. Even when she won't let us get near her, she doesn't leave her room."

"Jean-Marc has increased her antipsychotics to levels that are unheard of for a young woman, with mixed efficacy. He wondered if she was hebephrenic given her repetitiveness, but discarded the diagnosis of schizophrenia for now. He initiated further discussions with Father Lucas and myself because he was at the end of his rope. He's a Buddhist, but he felt there seemed to be such a religious bent to some of her chanting, that he wondered if there were other avenues to explore, knowing that the family has a very strong Catholic tradition."

"He is a thoughtful man," Weston told her. "Demonic possession is only confirmed when all other causes of affliction are ruled out, particularly psychiatric causes. It is dangerous to leave certain metabolic and psychologic disorders untreated while pursuing exorcism. Historically, the majority of exorcisms were probably performed on the mentally ill. The church takes a very conservative approach to exorcism now, considering it an exercise of last resort. I cannot perform one without permission from the Church. Yet in some cases, it is effective on the mentally unstable for the very reason that it works on a diabolical actor."

"I don't understand, Father," Emilia said, looking concerned. "I know the Church had to grant Father Lucas permission to ask the diocese to look into the case. I assumed since you were here, we would finally have help."

"I will do my best," Weston said. "Sometimes the rite of exorcism is a panacea to a suggestible mind that *thinks* it is possessed, especially when a person, like Rachel, has been so faithful to the Catholic church. In these cases, exorcism may be effective."

"Like a placebo?" Emilia asked.

"Just like that, especially for one who has spent a lifetime in devout observance of the faith, one for whom the Church has been an integral part of their life," Weston replied.

"We all have our own personal demons, if you will," Carter added. "It does not have to be a demon with a capital *D*. In Rachel's case, I suspect it started with guilt over sinful behavior coupled with a more personal shaming from someone very important to her."

Emilia looked from one to the other of them, amazed. "How did you come to such a conclusion? You just met her."

"I need more information, to be sure. I promise I will explain it all when we have everyone together. I'd like Dr. Wong, Father Lucas, and the family to hear what I have to say," Carter said softly.

Emilia Esparza looked shell-shocked. "I feel so terrible that we may have missed something so fundamental," she lamented.

"Sometimes a set of fresh eyes can see it," Weston said. "Don't be too hard on yourself. You were focusing on what you knew, all the evidence you already had. Preconceived ideas are the most difficult to overcome, and what Carter is going to tell you was only incidentally a medical problem. Also, she has a unique experience with demonic possession, so she was looking at the problem from that angle first and foremost, and she found something else."

54

THE NEXT MORNING DAWNED SUNNY and cold, and Emilia and Carter shared a quick breakfast of cold cereal and juice while they waited for Weston to return from the rectory. When they heard the Charger coming up the street, they went to the front door to get their coats. Emilia crated an acrimonious Jack, and pulled her keys off a hook by the door.

Carter was surprised to see that Weston had a passenger, but she should have anticipated that he would want to include Father Lucas in their discussion. Sunlight made the day seem more hopeful, if not warmer, and even the old farmhouse looked less desperate and sad in a new light.

Dr. Wong had already arrived, helping Rachel's mother administer morning medications before the others got there. Rachel's father was already gone, as were the other children, and Carter realized it must be a school day. They crowded around the kitchen table and Rachel's mother, Elise, served coffee and tea.

"Owen took the boys to school," Elise told them. "He'll be back soon."

"Good," Father Lucas nodded. "He should hear what Father Weston has to say."

"How is she today?" Carter asked. "Is she awake?"

"She seems more herself this morning," Elise nodded sadly. "It comes and goes."

"May I see her?"

"Of course," Elise gestured toward the hallway but did not get up, probably not ready to face the possibility that there could have been a change in her daughter since last she'd been in. Weston and Father Lucas stood to accompany her, but Carter shook her head.

She took the long walk down the hallway to the bedroom and knocked. She opened the door and let herself in. It was quiet; Rachel seemed to be resting. She was wearing a clean cotton nightgown that made her look younger than her seventeen years. Carter realized with a start that had she lived in this town, she and Rachel would have attended the same schools together, that they were not so very different at all in age and background.

Carter sat down in the chair next to the bed and began to pray for Rachel. She prayed softly, but aloud, because she always felt that there was magic and healing in a prayer.

"Heavenly Father, please help Rachel to see that there is always and ever room for her in Your grace. Help her understand that forgiveness was Your first and best lesson, and that she must also forgive herself before she may be well again-" Carter jumped and stopped praying when she felt a strong hand clamp down on her wrist. She looked into the sad and desperate eyes that watched her from the bed.

Rachel was shaking her head slowly, tears flowing from her eyes as she whispered, "Unclean. I am unclean."

"You are beloved of God," Carter told her gently. "You are beloved of your family and your friends. You must allow them to help you. You must ask them for help. They love you, but they do not know what you know. Show them how to help you; they want nothing more than your safety and your happiness once more."

But Rachel merely turned her head away, toward the wall, and said no more. So Carter finished her prayers, feeling that hand tighten on her wrist as she outlined for God what she thought had happened, knowing that Rachel was following every word.

When she was finished, she blessed Rachel, and made the sign of the cross over her, and whispered, "Only you can decide when to stop carrying this burden. Even Jesus needed the Cyrene to help Him with the Cross. You do not have to do this alone. I, like St. Simon, will help you."

Then she left Rachel alone with her thoughts, and returned to the kitchen.

Rachel's father still had not returned, so Carter said, wanting to introduce the subject gently, "Does Rachel have a friend named Penny?"

"Penny Wilson?" Father Lucas asked.

"His name is Rutherford," Elise explained, "But he has been called Penny for as long as I can recall. I don't remember why."

"He's named for Rutherford B. Hayes, the former President," Emilia said. "When he was little he told his teacher that Rutherford B. Hayes was the president on the penny, because he got mixed up. He's been Penny ever since."

"Do you know him?" Carter asked, reasonably sure of the answer.

"Well, not really. He goes to school with Rachel," Elise replied, glancing up as the back door opened and Owen stepped in, accompanied by a gust of cold wind that was unsuccessful in penetrating the warm kitchen. He looked relieved to see all of them, and worried.

"Who's that?" Owen asked, wanting to clarify the last thing his wife had said.

"Penny Wilson, dear. The Sister wanted to know if we knew him," Elise said.

"Just Carter," Carter corrected her gently. "I am just a novice. I have not completed my vows yet."

"Well, what about him?" Owen asked in a demanding tone, when a furtive movement near the hallway captured everyone's attention. Rachel stood there, eyes reddened from crying, hair wild, her nightgown hanging from her wasted body. She carried something almost shyly, hidden against the folds of her pajamas.

Elise stood up slowly. "Darling, what is it? Are we making too much noise?"

Rachel shook her head, one quick shake that rearranged her matted hair before she looked at Carter. She raised her arm out straight, and Carter could see that she held her diary in her hand. She took one step forward, and looking worriedly at all the important adults in her life sitting there together, pressed the book into Carter's hands and then backed away, sobbing in grief when she encountered the far wall, as if she wanted to disappear through it.

Owen looked on helplessly, but went to her, saying, "Rachel, let's get you back to bed."

He led her firmly away, and she turned desperate eyes on Carter, as if beseeching her to help. Carter nodded and smiled at her, putting the diary on her lap and folding her hands over it securely.

When Owen returned, he turned angry eyes on Carter. "What is that?"

Carter understood the anger; they had been living this nightmare for months, and their daughter had responded to a stranger.

"It's her diary," Carter said.

"Do you know what's in there?" Elise asked, suspiciously. "Is this why you asked about Penny? Fathers, what is going on?" She looked to Weston, and secondarily, to Father Lucas, wanting answers.

"I think you should hear what Carter has to say," Weston said softly, with such quiet authority that it surprised her.

"What's in her diary is her voice, her words, her life," Carter said. "It is a life that she was too afraid and too ashamed to share. "But I think that by entrusting it to someone else, she is hoping for help."

"I would do anything to help her," Owen said, still angry, and Carter began to suspect that he knew something he wasn't ready to say. "But I thought you were here for that. She has a demon."

"What if I told you that an exorcism isn't the right solution for this particular...demon?" Weston asked, and now he was sure who had pressed Father Lucas into action.

"I know she's possessed," Owen insisted, getting very red in the face.

"Owen," Elise protested softly, putting a hand on his forearm, urging him to sit down. He finally did.

"Demonic possession is very rare," Weston observed. "But it has been long believed that a demon will change someone's behavior for the worse. Please hear what Carter has to say. She has a special kind of expertise in this area."

"Demons are chaotic, and destructive. Both internally and externally. While I was struck at the severity of Rachel's appearance and behavior, I noticed that all hallmarks of change were isolated to her person. Her walls, furniture, window, and door have not been moved or damaged in the least. Because Rachel, the person, respects these things as items that you, her parents, worked hard to obtain for her.

"Her desk and vanity were orderly and neat, her closet undisturbed. Everything that shows signs of decay are directly related to her person, and according to Dr. Esparza, that is an extreme departure from her usual state of being. She has abandoned hygiene, decorum, and self-care."

"But she knew your *name* the first time she encountered you," Jean-Marc protested.

"Not such a feat of impossibility as you might think," Carter said, turning to him. "Can everyone in this room attest that they have refrained from discussion or mention of Father Weston and myself in reference to this visit? Within this house, were our names *never* spoken aloud prior to our arrival? And when we came, we were introduced. It is possible that she heard it before. It is an unusual name for a woman, never mind a nun's novice."

Father Lucas and Emilia were nodding. "It is possible," the priest agreed.

"Even probable."

"But the religious chanting, the changes in her voice and her appearance?" Dr. Wong was showing the same signs of distress as Emilia had the night before, not wanting to think he had missed something fundamental and endangered his patient.

"She has been raised in a strict Catholic household," Weston pointed out. "Our faith can be a source of strength, but it can also provide the roots of our shame, can it not?"

"True," Father Lucas supported this.

"But Carter has another attribute that gives her an advantage," Emilia spoke this time, something dawning in her eyes.

"Which is what? She's a stranger! What advantage?" Owen demanded, not letting go of his ire.

"I was most recently a teenage girl," Carter said simply.

"I'm sorry, I don't follow," Jean-Marc looked confused.

"Probably best that you don't," Emilia said with a trace of humor, urging Carter to continue.

"It is a singular state of being, often a difficult one. The landscape is marked with peril, from mean girls, boys, and societal expectations," Carter explained. She could see that Elise was beginning to understand, and she knew that Emilia could follow, having once been teenage girls themselves. "Not to mention the pressures of being a 'good girl,' which is even more complicated by religious standards."

"Imagine you have committed a sin, perhaps the biggest one of all for a young Catholic girl trying to hold up under enormous pressure. And imagine that while you know it is wrong, you are conflicted by what you feel inside. And you think you have made the decision for the right reasons, because you have been led to believe that you are loved, you are special, you are the only one," Carter said.

"Then imagine that into this conflict comes a complication of even more enormous proportions. You tell yourself that it will be fine, because you still believe in the fairy tale. Until everything you thought was true is not. Until someone you thought was in love with you pushes you away, and ridicules you, and suddenly your sin is enormous, and you are alone. Worst of all, you are personally shamed for your mistake. Not once, but twice." Carter looked at Owen.

"So this boy, this Penny, they were lovers?" Elise asked, starting to understand but not wanting to believe it.

"And she thought it was okay, because she thought he loved her, and wanted to marry her," Emilia continued, filling in the details. "And she got pregnant."

"That may be what was wrong with her at Thanksgiving," Elise wondered aloud.

"And then you called me because she was so sick in December," Emilia said. "But she really deteriorated at Christmas time. So something happened. She must have lost the baby. But she also must have told Penny. And he must have shunned her. Shamed her."

Elise put her head down and quietly sobbed. Her tears dripped onto her lap.

"I know it was a demon," Owen said quietly, and when the others looked at him, he was crying, too, from eyes red and raw with suffering. "My Rachel is not a slut! It has to be a demon, and I told her so!"

Elise sucked in a ragged breath, and her head jerked around to look at her husband. "You *knew*! And that's all you said to her! That's all you did for her!" She was nearly shouting, and Father Lucas stood up, looking helpless. "You left her *alone* with all of this!" She screamed out her frustration and stood up so abruptly that she knocked over her chair.

Weston and Father Lucas corralled her, and Father Lucas took her in his arms. Like Weston, he was relatively young, but he took the situation in hand. "Elise, let's get your coat. Let's get some air."

It was quiet for a time, the silence punctuated by Owen's sobs. Weston picked up Elise's overturned chair and sat down next to him. "God will forgive her, Owen. God will forgive you," he said, taking

Owen's hand in both of his. "But she cannot get well, cannot accept God's Grace, without knowing she can forgive herself, which she will not do without *your* forgiveness, your acceptance, and your understanding."

"My little girl is ruined," Owen mumbled, but he did not pull away.

"Must she be lost forever for you to see it?" Weston asked. "She is showing you that she will sacrifice her life to pay for her sin, and she is determined to follow through. Are you prepared to lose your daughter because you have set yourself in judgement over her? In Matthew, Jesus tells us, *'Judge not, that you be not judged. With the judgement you pronounce you shall be judged, and the measure you give will be the measure you get.'* Good God, man, will you pay for your pride with her blood?"

"She will recover from Penny's abandonment, but she cannot survive yours," Emilia told him. "And she has heard you proclaim her wrong, but you have not shown any wrath toward the boy. His sin is just as great, and yet, he too deserves forgiveness. They are children still. She needs your love, Owen."

"Father Lucas and I will hear her confession, if she will give it," Weston told him. "But you must go to her. You must ask her if she is ready for forgiveness, and you must be her strong loving father here on earth, an example of the Father in Heaven, whom you have told her, all her life, loves her always, no matter what. Without this, no medication, no exorcism, no friend can cure her. Dr. Esparza and Dr. Wong cannot restore her. Only your love can save her now."

55

JEAN-MARC, FATHER LUCAS, AND EMILIA followed them out to the car when it was time to leave.

"I thank you, Brother, for coming," Father Lucas embraced Weston warmly and turned to Carter. "Thank *you* for seeing the heart of the truth."

"No wonder Rachel had no true psychiatric diagnosis," Jean-Marc said, still looking a bit shell-shocked, but smiling.

"I'm surprised 'teenage-girl syndrome' never made the DSM," Emilia remarked, still trying to make him feel better. "But I missed it, too."

Emilia hugged Carter tightly, holding on to her for a long time. "You are a very special person. The Church is lucky you have chosen to bless them with your talents."

Then they stood around awkwardly, in the way caused by goodbyes that are complicated, five strangers who would never forget each other, yet were unlikely to ever meet again.

"Do you think they'll be okay?" Carter asked, still wanting a happy ending for Rachel. They all did.

Father Lucas sighed, and put a hand on Jean-Marc's shoulder. "I hope so. I'm thinking of asking Dr. Wong to share some of his Buddhist wisdom with Owen."

"We'll do everything we can to get them across the finish line," Emilia said, waving Rachel's diary at Carter. "And when the time is right, I will return this to her and assure her that no one else has seen it. Well, almost no one." She gave Carter a wink, and turned back toward the house, not looking back. Jean-Marc followed.

"God be with you," Weston told Father Lucas.

"And also with you," he replied, smiling hopefully.

When they were getting back onto the Interstate, Carter asked, "Do you think they will be able to forgive each other? Owen and Rachel? Elise and Owen?"

"A very wise person once told me that forgiveness is not a line you cross, it is a road you take," Weston told her, and she could see that he was optimistic about the possibility of a happy outcome. "Now, let's rename a few state lines."

now

56

WESTON ALWAYS KNEW WHEN CARTER arrived for her confession. She preferred to wait in the queue at Constantine's with the other parishioners, and take her turn behind the screen. Somehow he always got a sense of her, like a tiny whirlwind, her feelings jumping around nervously, guilt, embarrassment, excitement, even.

But he concentrated on everyone, needing that person to feel, and to know, in whatever ways he could convey it, that they were the focus of his attention for as long as they needed it. He was patient, and courteous, hearing each of them out in entirety, unmindful that he would be here long past the end of posted hours. In the early days he had worried that this would upset them, as he was keeping those who waited beyond their expected time, but perhaps not surprisingly, this was a welcome development.

He stayed until he was done. And the other priests, as they had in other places he had been assigned, ridiculed him. Their arguments selfish, they thought the faithful might start expecting it of all of them, but they were wily enough to couch them behind other concerns. Such as the worry that keeping the church open after dark in that neighborhood might invite criminals.

"Did Christ turn away such?" Weston had asked calmly, adjusting his spectacles nervously to hide his displeasure. "I am a servant of my parishioners, not a shopkeeper."

He heard the nervous laments of a grandmother about whether celebrating *Día de los Muertos* was a sin. He reminded her that when one engages in prayer, works of mercy, and penance for the departed, these actions are in keeping with the faith.

"But Ermelinda, remember not to be gluttonous with the tequila, and you should be fine," he told her, making sure she could hear the teasing in his voice, before sending her off with blessings.

He heard the third confession of a young man who had committed a drug crime and remained in hiding. Weston had been surprised that he had unburdened himself so openly, and even more surprised when he had returned twice more. He was truly repentant, and seemed lost. Once again, Weston counseled him to consider turning himself in. They talked a bit more, and the young man admitted he was afraid of going to prison. He was afraid of being alone, without his friends.

"Are they truly your friends?" Weston asked, both he and the boy knew he did not expect an answer. "You are never alone. You have God. Your mother will always love you, no matter what. Love is found in forgiveness for those who ask for it. God will give it. Your mother will give it."

"What about the State of Louisiana?" The young man grumbled softly. "I'm sorry, Father."

"I understand." Weston remained silent for a time, giving the young man the opportunity to say more if he would. After a minute or two, Weston heard his quiet breathing turn into soft sobs of grief, and still he sat, saying nothing, waiting.

"I should go, you are very busy," his penitent sniffed sharply on the other side of the screen.

"I am here for you right now. Only you," Weston reminded him kindly, and was surprised when the young man asked, "Can I see your face, Father?"

Weston slid the screen away immediately, and the young man seemed relieved. "Father, can I ask you a favor?"

"Anything I may do for you, I will try to do," Weston told him.

"Would you go with me when I turn myself in? If – I meant." He amended himself, betraying only the uncertainty of it, but he was considering it, and it seemed to relieve him of some of the weight of the burden he was carrying.

"I am honored to be asked. Of course, if that is your wish, I will do so," Weston assured him. "Do you have your phone with you? I would like to give you the number for the rectory. I am the only priest living here presently, so you may call it and reach me at any time."

These, and many more, before *she* was sitting next to him in the small space beyond the screen.

"Bless me, Father, for my sins," she asked softly, then remembering herself, "It has been sixteen days since my last confession."

But when the time came for her to speak, he heard only a heavy sigh.

"What is it, my child? Carter?" The quality of her silence had changed, and he knew she was crying. He marveled at her ability to do it so quietly, but he felt her despair, and felt ill-equipped to help her. He chided himself for being prideful, if there was help to be had it would come from divine faith. But Weston, the man, dearly wished he had an answer for whatever this was.

After several minutes, he heard her moving, then a sharp sniffle, as if signaling the end of something, and the rustling of her habit as she wiped away her tears. "I-I am sorry. I have wasted your time. I must go and start the meeting now."

"Carter, will you be alright?" he asked, the only question he had at that moment.

"Yes. Thank you." He thought he could hear a small smile in her voice. "It always helps me to help another."

"Alright," he said, releasing her with a blessing, frowning at the swiftness of her departure, almost like the flight of a frightened bird.

Soon he was distracted by other woes, and other stories, doing his best for each one who had waited so long for whatever small comfort he could provide, sadly unable to derive any for himself.

57

WHEN THE MEETING FINISHED, CARTER found Weston in the rectory office, reading poetry. His hair was more unruly than usual, and she knew he was nervous or worried. He would repeatedly push his hands through his hair, making it stick up in odd directions. He was entirely unaware that he did it. She always wanted to reach out and smooth down these cowlicks, and this private admission made her bashful. She suspected that what she felt came from the sense of safety she achieved fully only when with him.

But lately she was restless, and that was disrupting the easiness between them. She was afraid she dared not speak of what was consuming her every thought when she was with him, but knew her thoughts were sinful and needed to be confessed. She had considered approaching another priest about becoming her confessor, but she knew the gossip about Weston, and didn't want to contribute to any suspicion about his fitness as a clergyman.

Their arrangement was so unusual, and coupled with his independence and the fact that he did not answer to the Bishop or Archbishop simply fueled the pettiness and snide comments that she felt others wanted her to hear. She hoped he was unaware of the talk, in her strange way she wanted to protect him from ugliness. For all that she was so young, she felt that she had a worldliness that he always seemed to lack. He always seemed a bit naïve, even awkward at times.

Neither did she want to discuss her sins with anyone else. She had never gotten used to this kind of intimacy in her life, and it felt comforting to unpack her innermost flaws with someone that she knew had a healthy respect for her. She'd had Father Paul for confirmation and her teenage years, and now Weston. Like the Magdalene, she knew she was judged by her church superiors, and they were suspicious about her pursuit of her vows, suspicious about her relationship with this priest.

"How was the meeting?" he asked kindly, and she knew that his concern was for her. He was asking about the meeting rather than asking what he really wanted to ask, how she was doing.

"It was moving this week, very emotional," she observed. "I'm sorry about earlier."

"You know that we can always do confession face-to-face," he told her. "A lot of priests do it that way. A bit less formal, more like a conversation with a friend." But seeing her expression, her skepticism at this last, he added, "Or a sympathetic stranger."

"More likely a jealous one," she observed, crossing herself and apologizing.

"You think the other priests are jealous? Of me?" he gave her a quizzical look, which confirmed her earlier thoughts about how obtuse he could be about the way he was perceived. Or perhaps he was above caring about it. He was that rare person who was neither petty nor a fool.

Rather than answer him, she said, "The Mother Superior gives her confession to the Bishop. She suggested I should do so as well, but fell short of ordering me to do it her way. I guess I can ignore it for now. I wish I could be less disobedient."

"Yes, I have been meaning to talk to you about your radical defiant nature," he murmured, aware that she still hadn't stated a preference regarding her confession, so he offered the alternative again. "I can open up the sanctuary again. Or you can wait for another time."

They both glanced out the window. It would be dark soon, and it was agreed that when not on assignment she was to return to the convent and be cloistered within before dark.

She sighed. "No, let's just try it informally."

"I was about to make tea. Would that make it seem less threatening?" he asked, and was surprised when she laughed, and pleased.

"I don't think of it as threatening, per se," she told him. "I would like tea, yes."

He felt he should have given her an opportunity to refuse to enter the dwelling, but merely led the way up the stairs, knowing that it would be cold and impersonal to share tea with her in the church cafeteria, if more proper. She followed without comment; given what they had been through together, there was no bright line that separated them anymore. At any rate, they had upheld the odd honor system under which they were dually bound with admirable dedication.

He liked having her with him in the kitchen, and he recognized his error in this.

"Do we have to repeat all the usual phrases?" she asked earnestly, accepting the tea with a grateful comment.

"Not necessarily," he told her, taking a seat across the table from her and offering sugar and honey. "I have some milk, if you'd like it."

She shook her head and sipped her tea with a faraway look, then jumped right in. "Don't you want me?" she inquired, knowing just how wrong it was, but unsure what name to give this sin, it was so enormous.

His shoulders slumped, as if he physically bore the weight of what he had to say.

"Carter, a priest is not a stone, not an oak tree, not the Church," he told her. "A priest is a man. I am a man, with all the attendant weaknesses of any other man.

"This closeness to you – I am in near-constant agony of the sin of lust," he admitted. "But I need not act. To do so would be to ruin the trust I have fought to gain over a fleeting gratification. It is not a competition of bad impulses, our human condition. I think it important to keep the promises that I have made, to you, to the Church, and chiefly, to myself."

"And of course I have these feelings for you. But I must be a better example. I am the shepherd who must care for the lambs."

"Shepherds protect lambs so they can use their wool and *eat* them," she grumbled, waving the air. "I know, I know, it is a metaphor for protection, the lamp at the golden door...I *do* feel safe with you."

He smiled, not bothering to correct her. He wasn't the Statue of Liberty, but perhaps in her frustration she was being ironic. He chose his next words carefully. "After what you have experienced, that is incredible. Safety and trust. I won't demean them by taking a carnal advantage."

"What if I wanted you to?" she asked. Her directness was almost painful, pointed like a blade. Yet she was not taking the role of a temptress, she was not attempting to seduce, simply stating a position.

"Ah. I cannot. I took my vows with open heart, open eyes, open mind, knowing what I put aside to do so." He hoped she could not detect the lie there, that the decision would have been impossible had he known her prior to making it. "You can still relinquish your intended vocation and refuse orders, live another life, have a husband, a family."

"As could you."

"No. My vows are the only things restraining the demons."

"Will you send me away?"

"I probably should. Can you continue the work we have started? I will not hold you to it, if you'd rather be elsewhere," Weston told her.

"You are the only one who will ever love me like this – as I am – so I will stay and help you."

"Do you think I am weak? That perhaps I am only hiding from the life I could have?" he asked her, realizing that the question subverted their roles.

"I only know you to be incredibly strong. And I thank you for your honesty," she told him. "In my deepest heart, I knew the answer before I asked the question. But it had to be spoken aloud."

"Were I another man, any other man…" He started, but his voice trailed off, as there was no point in continuing.

"Were you another man," she began, reaching out to touch his face, "This conversation would be unnecessary."

58

"YOU'RE A PESTILENCE," TATSUO TOMO spat in his rage. Seeing that the Collector still survived, he made a suggestion. "Just die."

The Collector, inscrutable, simply smiled. It took overwhelming effort, but he was pleased that he achieved it amid this suffering. He had once thought his time in the bamboo forest the worst imaginable; perhaps he had forgotten the reality of that time, but the immediacy of his current situation made this a living hell.

Unable to die, unfortunately an unintended consequence of the Blood Gift, likewise was he unable to feed in this dark place. He barely had the strength to hold his head up, but he dug deep when it was time for defiance. Tatsuo Tomo's dark magic bound him here, impaled upon his own sword.

Time had a surreal quality. It passed, but one could not discern whether hours or decades had gone. He had a real time of panic, alone, listening to the echoes of his own screams through these black catacombs where he could smell the souls of many deaths. The stench was thick in the air, a miasma of untrammeled evil.

To pass the time, he murmured passages he had memorized long down the centuries in his father's library. Words from a book that was worse than banned at that time and in that place, was forbidden, was a death sentence to any who dared keep a copy should such an offense be discovered. Latin, or Spanish, the words were, he could not remember. Or perhaps Portuguese, which he surmised had been his father's original provenance.

The words infuriated Tatsuo Tomo, so the Collector persisted, stretching the limits of his memory for new and different verses. And those minor beings who persisted in petty torments of his flesh were rendered powerless to approach, impotent in their assaults.

In his weakest moments, if recall failed him, he turned to his Shinto and Buddhist prayers, and as he had suspected they would, these served just as effectively to frustrate their tortures.

And out of the darkness and the quiet of the refuge he created with these verbal talismans came another, Father of Deceit, Akenomyosei, ready to manipulate.

"You cannot know *all* of the words, because some of them were simply left out." It adopted a conspiratorial tone. "My story, because it was deemed inauthentic, its author discredited, or improperly credited, however the Creator wanted it to be believed. Those chapters were never canonized, never made the final edit, if you will. A Divine work of propaganda. The origin of such an exercise was not taught to the pureflesh by me, rather by God."

"But I can teach those lost words to you," it whispered, its voices everywhere, and nowhere.

The Collector refused to acknowledge any of it, and his pain crescendoed as his torments worsened. He did notice that he was unable to become inured to it; as his tolerance for pain understandably increased, his ability to experience it was manipulated in novel ways to ensure that his agonies were ceaseless.

And when, after hours, days, or centuries, he still lived, Tatsuo Tomo came to finish him, believing that the power of *Hōfuku* had frustrated his purpose. Certainly, the samurai sword carried the power of the souls it had dispatched, a magic of its own making, and the Death-Bringer determined to take it away.

Yet when this adversary tried to pull it from the Collector's body, extract it from the stone wall of the catacomb, it was unable to move it at all. With the rage and terrible power of a *djinn* Tatsuo Tomo stormed about, seething, unable to hide his frustration and irritation at this unexpected development.

The Collector patiently endured these furies, as they were repeated over time, he began to make of the entire proceeding a mockery. He marshalled his strengths in the interim, wanting only enough power to laugh at the demon's failures. And having done so a hundred times, and a hundred more, he made a curious offering, appealing to what he had guessed of Tatsuo Tomo's intentions.

"You want my sword? Then, by all means, just ask me for it," the Collector asked, finally, but received no answer on that day, or for many days after. He knew that this exercise of will was helping him find a renewed purpose, a new determination to survive at all costs. But Tatsuo Tomo merely continued his tantrums, too proud to answer the inquiry of a human.

And then *she* came, in the same guise in which she had ensnared him, but he knew her now, had catalogued her betrayal, had learned of the weakness in himself that had responded to her, and her tricks were now known to him. But she had been sent to save face, to respond to the question asked on behalf of the puppet master, Tatsuo Tomo.

She answered his question in the affirmative, admitting that the sword was indeed an item they desired to have. And because, as he correctly surmised, they did not believe that one such as he might read their intention, and could not know that he had guessed their real motivation to possess the weapon, he acquiesced.

He himself pulled the sword from the stone, from his flesh, having understood almost from the first that only he had such an ability. He relinquished it readily, as more of his lifeforce poured out of him, and as he was no longer supported by the inherent strength of the steel, he collapsed, and they were arrogant in their assuredness that his demise was certain.

So rigid in their assumptions were they that they never questioned his submission. But the Collector knew that Tatsuo Tomo would deliver the sword to Azuma, thinking it a painful mockery, not realizing it to be a strategic mistake.

For whatever interference this place created between them, the Blood Tie persisted as long as they both lived and breathed. A personal token, the magic of *Hōfuku* would strengthen the bond, allowing Azuma to find it, and know his distress.

The Dragon would return it personally to his hands, and together they would unleash their own brand of retribution upon their enemies.

59

WESTON CURSED AND THREW THE wrench, then cursed again when he realized it was the one he needed. He knew the beast was nearby, outside, somewhere in the neighborhood – his familiars had been chanting that childish refrain all afternoon. His patience was further taxed by the Death-Bringer's minor demons, who seemed to have taken an interest in his activities and who appeared out of nowhere whenever the beast was about. They slid over his skin like an ill wind, ruffling his hair and adding to his existing petty torments.

He slid out from under the car to retrieve the tool; for good measure he cranked the volume on the speakers, blasting Fall Out Boy. He drummed an angry riff on his thighs and screamed along with the song before sliding back under the Charger.

After another twenty minutes he had still failed at identifying the issue. He climbed out and leaned over the top of the engine, removing a housing cover next to the twin cooling fans he had installed. He frowned down at the connections as he wiped his hands absentmindedly on a cloth.

The relay loop was set up properly, and the circuit was too new for a faulty wire. He drummed his fingers on the skin of the fore panel and flexed his tired shoulders while he considered his next move.

"C'mon, idiot," he said aloud, ashamed at his loss of control. Too much frustration, not enough sleep, too many *G.D.* demons. He could barely think.

The loud music was helping, and he thumped along with it and tapped on his chest before having an epiphany. Painstakingly, he went over all of his connection points, hearing Erasmo in his ear. "If it isn't obvious, *m'ijo*, don't forget the small details."

That did the trick, and he found the broken connector clip.

"Too easy, *too easy*, you're off your game," he whispered to himself as he removed the faulty part.

He dug through odds and ends on his workbench, finding what he needed. He took the replacement clip back and opened the circuit. He reached to turn the last wire into place and felt rather than heard a strange rushing sensation and he jumped clear of the metal, wanting to avoid a shock.

Then the strangest thing occurred. Every hair on his body stood on end, and he could feel the charge jump from the contact to close the circuit, but Forcas' annoying little familiars followed, sliding off his skin and into the loop, just as if they had been sucked down a drain.

He realized what had happened and didn't hesitate, slamming the clip in place with a click, and it was done. The screams were those of a furious horde, but somehow they were trapped, within the car, within the electrical circuit, which was now closed. They couldn't escape. And because the flow of electrons was circular and contributed to a relay that was used when the engine was running, there was no egress for that energy. They howled with rage.

Suddenly, having his own demons under his skin seemed peaceful after the physical barrage of the afternoon, and he smiled. The only disappointment was that his own familiars hadn't gone the way of the pseudologues, but he'd effected another victory against the darkness. He'd been trying out a variant of such a maneuver since he was an adolescent. It was the reason he'd wanted the car. He never expected he'd find the answer accidentally.

He didn't know if he could do it again, but he recognized that wins like that were few and far between. He wondered what Forcas would do about it, but didn't dwell on it. He would chew that food when he had to.

60

WHEN HE SAW THE BEAST crossing the road, whatever he was, Weston knew that all his planning for a confrontation hadn't meant he could control the timing. It was happening now, and Weston didn't hesitate. He crossed back toward the front of the car, taking the most direct approach.

Not slowing, he released the cross from the Charger's front grille and held it out in front of him. The creature seemed amused. *Not for long*, Weston thought grimly, tired of the impasse.

"I told you-" it said, its accent indeterminate.

"Not Catholic, right?" Weston smiled. "It doesn't matter to the cross," he added, surprised at how reassuring his tone sounded.

As soon as the points hit their target and delivered the charge, the beast dropped like a stone, felled like a tree falling in a forest, and Weston knew he'd made some sort of terrible miscalculation. The flesh did not render. This was no demon.

He reached the man, kneeling down beside him, his hand feeling flesh that was warm as his own, humanoid. Too quiet. He put his ear to the chest and gasped. No heartbeat.

"Lord, forgive me my vanity and my transgressions," Weston whispered, and raised both fists above his head, bringing them down on the man's chest with all of his considerable strength. He did so realizing that the Taser had done what it could to any human victim; it had initiated some sort of cardiac arrest.

That done, he listened again, and miraculously, the thumping beat of an angry heart resumed. He put his hand against the chest and tried to get something, anything, through the maelstrom of babbles coming from the car. When he isolated it, he nearly pulled away. A bestial rage like nothing he'd yet experienced, animal, primitive, and ancient. And the smell of male musk as the form began to change, the muscles rippling, hair scurrying along the skin, enveloping the man within the beast.

The thing was not fully conscious, the thought pattern jumbled and confused. And these emotions were buried deep, the being not yet capable of awakening. Weston knew his time was limited. He'd been ready, but expecting this confrontation to culminate at Constantine's.

He prayed for strength, and he needed it. He managed to get the man across the rear seat of the car by dragging him in by the shoulders. He was not as large as Weston but again as tall, and truly it was like moving a dead weight. Weston was thankful this had happened one of the rare times he was not wearing his cassock, imagining it would be an added burden to this problem.

He probably broke land speed records getting across town, wondering how he would handle dealing with what he felt was the inevitable traffic stop. He'd have to decide in the moment what to do; he knew the car was in the condition he'd prepped it for and could easily outrun almost any other street-legal vehicle. Even the supercharged 350 small block V8 police interceptors would be no match for the Charger.

Conversely, he had no idea when his captive would awaken. And how was he to explain his now very hirsute friend to the authorities? He couldn't very well claim he was rescuing a drunk acquaintance. The murderous thoughts that were already breaking through from the backseat didn't bode well for a healthy outcome for himself or any involved peace officer.

Not bothering to put the car into the garage, he slid to a stop by the alley door at the back of St. Constantine and wrestled with the padlock for several agonizing seconds before he managed to get the door open.

The back-passenger door had aligned to the opening closely enough for Weston to heave the body through the doorway. It was now completely transformed, the coat of the wolf surprisingly soft against Weston's arms, but unwieldy.

He dragged it as gently as he could a few feet farther on the linoleum, and took the time to lock the door to the alleyway behind them. He kneeled next to the beast, placing his arms underneath its limp form and staggering to his feet. It was beginning to twitch, and he could hear its rhythmic breathing catch and continue. He hoped they would make it to the cage, but could only hope. Time was not on his side.

Weston ran for the stairs, and just as he was about to take the first step down into the familiar darkness, he felt it. Death. Homicidal rage. The beast the demons had sung to him about all his life had awakened, and he was not ready. But it did not move, not knowing that he could feel its calculations.

And when it reared up in his arms with tooth and claw, he held on and took a literal leap of faith. Man carried beast off the landing, and they rolled together in a struggle for life and death down the stairs, coming to rest at the bottom, Weston refusing to give up his hold though he was savagely bitten and clawed.

He ducked his head away from the snapping jaws, adjusting his purchase on the wolf's torso and squeezing unmercifully, until this effort was rewarded with a yelp of pain. He held on, not allowing the animal to fill its lungs, compressing it as he dead-lifted the snarling creature and pushed through the doors to the basement gymnasium, praying he could keep his feet.

He was tiring, and he knew that if the wolf got him on the ground again, he would pay with his life. At the door of the cage he found the last bit of forward momentum he had, and all but threw the wolf inside and reversed direction immediately, pulling the door closed, hearing the satisfying click as the mechanism closed and pushing off with his legs to clear himself from the reach of the bars. Scrambling backward, he sacrificed balance for safety, coming to rest several feet away as the wolf slammed against the metal. Praying the tongue would hold, Weston lay on his back, panting, unable to catch his breath, bleeding from a number of bites and fierce gouges.

He crawled several feet away, retrieving the key from its hook on the wall and pulling himself up to sit against it, appreciating the coolness of the painted concrete against his back. He stood on shaky legs, trying to master his fear as he approached the cage once more.

Icy blue eyes watched with intelligence and murderous intent, so he feinted right before jumping back to the left to put the key into the lock, turning it as quickly as he could, managing to secure the bolt but unable to escape another vicious swipe that cost him flesh and blood from the back of his left forearm. He screamed in pain, the depth of this insult worse than the others and not numbed by the adrenaline of his former desperation.

The wolf raged and snarled, pacing and battering the bars of the cage, his muzzle dripping saliva and blood as his jaws snapped at the air. His growls were like words, and Weston left him behind, the beast threatening a bloody revenge, and found the strength to crawl to the top of the stairs, where he collapsed in exhaustion, unable to find sleep but unable to move.

W

I want to keep Carter out of this, now that it has begun. I just don't know how. I have known all my life that once the beast arrived, it would set in motion the events I cannot avoid, the herald of the end times. My call to the battle, my time to die.

I hide the wounds made by the beast, and carry on with the evaluation of the newest files that the Vatican provided during my most recent visit. But Carter is wise, and she knows something is bothering me. I defer her questions, promising to explain everything in time.

I don't tell her about Iowa, wondering whether it would be wise to take her back there. It is the one loop I have yet to close, the one bit of unfinished business I must see to before I can leave this place. I have to know she will be safe. I have to know that the ones who have tasted her flesh won't track her down to finish what they started. They cannot elude me forever, and I devise a plan to deal with them without her assistance.

I have evidence that they have returned to that place, and it is likely that they seek to finish what they started.

Perhaps another priest would be willing to help me, but I am loath to expose anyone unwittingly on such a dangerous errand.

61

AMAOKE FOUND WESTON AT THE back of the sanctuary at Our Lady, saying his rosary. He sat politely at the other end of the pew, putting the kneeler on his side up with the tip of his boot because he felt it would be rude to put his boots on it.

The priest glanced over at him, and nodded, but did not curtail his prayers, for which Amaoke was glad. He felt guilty for interrupting anything he recognized as sacred. He sat, listening to the rustling whispers of the ritual, yet unable even with his augmented hearing to pick up exactly what was said, so practiced, quiet, and formulaic it was.

Sometime later Weston pushed himself up on the bench, and lifted his own kneeler upright using a hand still encircled by the tiny wooden beads. He kissed the wooden cross in his palm, and made the entire talisman disappear into the pocket of his cassock.

He stepped out into the aisle, genuflected, crossed himself, and finally turned his full attention on Amaoke.

"You look good, my friend," he remarked, giving Amaoke the once-over.

"As compared to what?" Amaoke growled back, half in jest and half because he hated to contemplate weaknesses, especially those he had left behind.

"I'm just sizing you up," Weston replied. "I invited you to dinner, but I really need to go for a run. You can wait for me in the cottage or come along if you want."

"I could use a run," Amaoke readily agreed. "You going like that?"

"You think I should?" Weston, joking, pulled on the front of his cassock.

"I don't know," Amaoke said. "It's New Orleans. Probably not much of a stretch of the imagination to see a man running in a dress. Won't be the first time. I'd be happy to chase you."

Weston laughed, coming near and grasping his hand, pulling Amaoke in for a man-hug. "I've missed you. I'm glad you're recovered."

"And I should thank you for covering for me at work," Amaoke said sincerely, and then could not resist adding, "Especially after I nearly ate you alive."

"The least I could do after tasing you and putting you in a cage," Weston said. "So we're even."

"Cool."

They walked out to the cottage and Amaoke waited for Weston to change. He took the warmups the priest offered him and shed his work boots for his own Converse.

"You're not running barefoot?" Weston teased.

"*Fun-ny.*" Amaoke gave him a look, and said, "When I do that I am usually naked, too."

Weston put up his hands in surrender and they went out together into a cool dusk perfect for a run. And run they did.

The priest was fit, but better suited for anaerobic endeavors, and Weston was unsurprised that he could not match Amaoke's cardiovascular fitness, especially for running. It was a natural talent of the Wolf. Luckily, Amaoke was happier to have a companion, as wolves are naturally pack oriented, than he was to exploit an inherent competition between friends. Weston was grateful when it was over, but had to admit it was the best workout he'd had in a long time.

They showered at the rectory, taking advantage of its multiple bathrooms, and went down a few blocks past the Archdiocese to Fontainebleau for pizza.

The local place was crowded with college kids, but they managed to secure a high-backed booth, probably, Amaoke surmised, due to the magic that Weston's good looks and priestly collar worked on the pretty hostess.

She brought beer for Weston and Amaoke, saying, "It's on the house."

Amaoke pushed his across next to Weston's, and the priest did the same with his water glass, like a trade that was deemed acceptable by both parties.

"Sorry we couldn't do this sooner," Amaoke said, while they waited for their food.

"No worries, man," Weston told him. "I'm just glad you're okay."

"Nothing like a gentle reminder of my place by the Morningstar," Amaoke remarked with a touch of bitterness. "I was concerned about you as well; I left you alone with Forcas."

"As predicted he was disinclined to accept my invitation into the house of God," Weston smiled. "Although I imagine there will still be a reckoning for interfering with his minions."

Amaoke raised his eyebrows, waiting for Weston to say more, but he didn't. Their pizza came and they ate in silence. Amaoke wondered if the latter subject of their conversation had killed it entirely. They paid their bill and walked out; as soon as they hit the sidewalk, Weston started talking again.

"I knew you were coming into my life; it was foretold," he told Amaoke. "I just didn't know when, or what it would mean."

"Poor bastard," Amaoke said, happy that he could see Weston was smiling next to him.

"I didn't know what your presence meant for me," Amaoke finally admitted. "I just knew that I had to understand who you were. It was like something I expected to happen in my life had finally been set in motion."

"Exactly," Weston agreed. "Wherever I am headed, you're headed there, too."

"Strange. And you seem like such a nice guy," Amaoke said, laughing a little.

"You lost me, Brother," Weston admitted.

"The problem is obvious, I should think," Amaoke said. "Don't you think we feel this way because this is what the Morningstar wants?"

"Possibly. But when have you ever embraced his plans?" Weston said.

"Almost never," Amaoke said softly, thinking of the Berserker in the snowy woods of his past.

"Well, I for one am glad we found each other," Weston said. "Now I don't have to feel so alone planning the ultimate defiance."

"Do you believe that's possible?" Amaoke detected the hope in the priest's voice and stopped walking, turning toward him.

"Possibilities keep me from losing my mind," Weston told him. He put his arm through Amaoke's both to encourage this new closeness and to get him walking again. "And I find nothing in you that seeks the Monster's approval or even suggests that you have stopped looking for a way out of becoming a means to its end. In that effort we are united, I think. Tell me if I am wrong."

"No." Amaoke was incredulous. This was a conversation he had waited a millennium to have.

"So let's help each other through it. We are on this road together and of a similar mindset," Weston said reasonably. "My entire career has been dedicated to trying to thwart it when I can. And Carter has been of great help to me, although my reasons for keeping her close have been more selfish than utilitarian."

Amaoke stayed away from that subject. He felt it was not his place to make any comment about another man's woman. He felt this way even though he was ignoring the fundamental terms of their relative vocations, because he knew his instincts were not wrong.

"And yet," Weston said, "I have a favor to ask of you, because for this errand, I want to leave Carter out of it."

Amaoke looked around. They had arrived back at the groundsman's cottage at Our Lady.

"If it involves interfering with the Morningstar's evil, count me in. Being around you has made me realize that I have been too passive in my resistance. What have you got in mind?"

"Can we go over the details sometime soon?" Weston asked. He wasn't ready to relinquish the pleasantness of their evening discussing the particulars of hunting demons.

"Do you mind if I ask Aleta to join us? I value her opinion," Amaoke asked him. "She is open-minded and has a keen intellect about difficult problems."

"I would welcome that, if she is willing," Weston consented, though he felt sure that Aleta wanted no part of his company.

"Let me discuss it with her, then," Amaoke followed Weston into the house and retrieved his messenger bag. He turned to the door and nodded to Weston in farewell. "This was good, man."

"Absolutely," Weston bumped his fist against Amaoke's, and watched him walk back out to the street, wondering if such an alliance had been the Monster's intention all along. Hoping against hope that what he'd told Amaoke about denying a predetermined fate wasn't wrong.

62

"I'M IN JAPAN," AZUMA SPOKE into the phone, her frustration so pervasive that she was unaware that she was clenching her jaw.

"*Aijin*, my apologies," *Ni* replied. "Can you repeat that? I don't think I heard you properly."

"I am in Japan," Azuma repeated. "And don't say it. I know I was just there with you and it is impossible, but let's just say I ran into...an obstacle. I'm at the house in the mountains."

"But-?" *Ni* heard all that was said and curtailed her question, understanding that certain magics should not be questioned. And by the sound of her mistress' voice, this was not her own doing. It didn't help that *Ni* was still groggy from the dual insults of jet lag and the unfortunate circumstance of travel that meant she was Azuma's safest food source. She badly needed her own blood meal.

Rather than ask another fruitless question, she asked the most practical one. "Are you safe?"

"I am, thank you." Azuma sounded angrier than a wet cat, and *Ni* knew better than to press any further. It was extraordinarily rare for the Dragon Goddess to betray any strong emotion, so when she did, it was best to proceed cautiously. She was still fragile from the loss of the Collector – they all were. She was gratified that Azuma's ire was not directed at her.

"Shall I take up any errands for you while I am still here?" *Ni* offered, doubting that Azuma's reply would be in the affirmative.

"No. Be ready to return on short notice. I will instruct Konoye to bring the jet home in the morning. For now, go back to sleep."

"With respect, *Aijin*, you should let me arrange some security," *Ni* offered. "I'm sure *Hachi-*"

"Konoye will call you with departure details." Azuma rung off, and it took *Ni* less time to surrender to sleep than she might have expected.

The afternoon sunshine blasted the peak with unseasonal heat, but Azuma was too distracted to enjoy the mild air. She looked for a time over the void, finally shivering despite the warming breeze, reminded of her nakedness, though she was not really sensitive to the cold.

She wandered inside, weary to her bones, having made too many time zone changes in the past two weeks without proper recovery, and then, for the Sorceress to send her home so unceremoniously. . .

It was infuriating for many reasons. Not the least of which was the sheer display of power, a power perhaps more dangerous than any Azuma had ever encountered, and she wasn't too proud to admit she was afraid of the woman. She had simply *disappeared* three people with a word.

And apparently, in Azuma's heart of hearts, she considered this a home. How else had this become the destination of that tersely given order? It made her miss the Collector even more. If indeed this was her home, he had made it so. And she sorely needed his counsel. She wondered what he would make of the events of the last several weeks.

She snagged a kimono from her dressing room and pulled it on, briefly wondered why the sash was missing, but not in a mood to remedy it, she did not bother searching for it in the adjacent sleeping quarters. She took the back hallway, unaware that in her concentration, indeed her consternation, she was chewing on her lower lip. So savage was this distracted assault that she drew blood, and stopped short on the stairs, remembering something.

The man with the silver cross. A priest, perhaps. The Wolf had called him *brother.* And he, too, had appeared out of nowhere. More of the Sorceress' handiwork? Something else? It was a priest who had set the recent disaster with Iara in motion. Was there a connection? She promised herself she would revisit the files that *Ni* and the Collector had compiled.

For a moment it so frustrated her that she wished for Akenomyosei. It would have something to say about the encounter, and even in its misdirection there would be a kernel of truth, perhaps something she could build upon to get answers.

She looked around as if waking from a dream, realizing she had no idea what she should do next, or why she had come down the stairs. She needed sleep, that was the most responsible course, and if *he* were here, she would be forced to comply. No matter, there were several arrangements to be made before she could take her rest.

She was forced to use the secured landline to make calls, since her cellphone was still at the hotel in New Orleans. Her first call was to RSI, where she discovered that *Ichi* was expecting to hear from her. Azuma smiled. *Ni* had alerted her.

Azuma gave hurried instructions, *Hachi* was to be dispatched with her vehicle immediately, to make the trip up the mountain. There were other less pressing items to attend to, and her final call was to Konoye Ko, her pilot, to provide instructions regarding the return of the jet and her staff to Japan.

Very little time had passed, but the afternoon light was just beginning to fade a bit, the first warning of night to come. There was nothing further she could accomplish, so she took a brief dip in the koi pool, refreshed by the crisp cold of the water, before climbing the stairs to her rooms.

She removed her kimono and toweled her hair thoroughly, walking through to the bedroom with grateful thoughts of much-needed sleep. But such a respite was destroyed by what she saw, like a ceremonial offering lying crosswise on her bed, Akiko, dead and staring, the missing sash still wrapped around her neck. And placed carefully in her left hand, a lacquered sheath with the thousand painted butterflies that Azuma recognized instantly. The sword *Hōfuku*, the Collector's lost weapon.

All criminal handiwork carries the signature of the individual. Creativity and suffering together were the province of her Collector, but this was too petty for him. Azuma recognized the message and through her rage she did not realize that she was smiling. Tatsuo Tomo, in his desire to punish her, had given her a gift. She would not refuse to use the mistake to make the Death-Bringer pay.

The moment she touched the sword she received the second provident blessing, for *Hōfuku* carried another message, opening the Blood Tie which had been strangely silent, but no longer. Her Collector was *alive*.

W

I know it really happened. I could have believed it a dream, except that I fell asleep at Our Lady and when I awoke I found myself at St. Constantine.

And I felt the others, felt Amaoke's distress and real fear for my safety. The anger and frustration of the adversary, the righteousness and perhaps even amusement of the spear-bearer. She seemed drawn to the Wolf.

And my own demons, with their inability to react in time, their relative silence in that place and since, has meaning beyond what I can fathom in these early moments. When she sent us all away from there, I think her magic pushed them out. Perhaps they are trying to reorient themselves and locate me since the displacement. I do not doubt their eventual return, but I revel in the first true silence, the first true isolation of self in my life.

I smile because her power, while unexpected, was like a familiar friend to me. It was not as fundamental as a filament nor as utilitarian as an outlet, but it was, somehow, electrical. She has harnessed something inherent while I have only created rudimentary conduits. I am in awe.

I sense no reason I should not return to check on my friend, but I have no car and it is the middle of the night. I have no means to travel and I am in my long underwear. I decide on a telephone call; I appreciate the irony that landlines are now the province of priests and doctors.

If it rings on that end I cannot know, because the line is answered supernaturally promptly.

"I'm fine," Amaoke reassures me, and I can tell he is still trying to keep Aleta from waking. "But I bet that hair of yours is a mess."

He hangs up in the middle of my laughter.

63

AMAOKE HEARD AND FELT THE rumbling vibrations of the Charger when it first turned down the block, the engine noise bouncing off the brick of the venerable old neighborhood houses. It shattered the quiet of the tree-lined street for several seconds until Weston shut it down.

Amaoke put his feet down and rocked himself to a standing position in one practiced move; the dogs were apparently too comfortable to be disturbed, and they snored away in the warm afternoon sunshine.

He walked to the garden gate in time to see Weston step off the sidewalk onto the path that led between the yards. He gave a short wave as he came bounding up.

"Hey, man," he said, with good cheer, as he grasped Amaoke's hand and pulled him in for a hug. "Good to see you."

He wore jeans and a black pullover sweater over his shirt and collar, and had on his faded grey Converse sneakers.

Amaoke smiled. "I've been meaning to ask you – do you wear those under your robe? In church?"

"Always," Weston nodded. "It's my small rebellion, but I do have a practical reason for doing so. These shoes are thick soled, and the rubber prevents transmission of electrical current. Obviously, these aren't the shoes the Church provides for me, but thankfully, an old friend gets them for me for Christmas every other year."

"In the same color?" Amaoke asked, not sure why anyone would choose it.

"I think it is her private joke. She is the sister of an old mentor of mine. The only girl in an old Bostonian Irish Catholic family of ten. All nine of her brothers took vows. She is the self-proclaimed black sheep of the family; she refused the convent *and* refused to marry," Weston told him. "I think she believes that every priest needs to own something that isn't black. I think it might also be a reminder that life does not exist in black and white, there are always shades of grey."

"They make them in a bunch of colors these days," Amaoke observed, grinning wickedly. "What happens if she sends you a yellow pair?"

"Hopefully you'll take in a roommate after I've been defrocked," Weston laughed.

"Not a chance," Amaoke said without hesitation. "And you're late. I'm starving."

They had reached the door of the carriage house and Amaoke frowned at the cat, who had taken up station in the chair he'd abandoned. It gave him a challenging look and then yawned, stretching its legs dismissively before putting its head back down.

"You're lucky I'm done sitting," Amaoke murmured, amused.

"Are you talking to the cat?" Weston laughed, his quizzical expression showing that he didn't understand the exchange.

"Him? A rhetorical exercise," Amaoke replied, reaching inside to grab his jacket. Shrugging it on, he gave the cat one last glance. "Just two old nemeses, sizing each other up for battle."

Weston saw Amaoke's expression and tried not to laugh. Entirely unsuccessfully.

"If you knew him, you'd understand," Amaoke said, leading the way out the back gate. This time they followed the path to the alley. "Do you mind walking?"

"Not at all. Eventually, I will get you into that car," Weston assured him confidently.

"If I need a ride, I will call Carter. She seems to take safety seriously," Amaoke replied, marveling at how easily they fell back into this relaxed banter with each other. It was nice to have a friend now and then within a long lonely life.

They walked over to *Joey K's* on Magazine Street, and ordered enormous cheeseburgers with fries. Then Weston ordered something called brownie pie, trying unsuccessfully to feed some of it to Amaoke.

"You don't know what you're missing," Weston told him, apparently perfectly content to finish the whole thing off by himself.

"I trust my nose," Amaoke tapped it gently. "I don't smell anything in there I recognize. Is it food?"

"Chocolate is a *food group*, dude. You haven't lived."

"If that's living, I'm not sure I want to," Amaoke told him.

"So how is Dr. Madison?" Weston asked, and Amaoke knew that the change in the direction of the conversation meant that it was time to be serious.

"Not sure. Not entirely happy with me," Amaoke said, wanting to avoid discussing what Aleta had said to him a few nights before about Weston's motivations.

"Or me? For putting you in the path of danger?" Weston's astuteness was uncanny, and Amaoke wondered about it. Sometimes he came dangerously close to mind-reading.

"She doesn't want to take part in any of our discussions about the near future," Amaoke told him, putting it as kindly as he could.

"Does that bother you?"

"Sure. She has a terrific mind. I'm sure her perspective would be helpful," Amaoke said, knowing he wasn't sure about that. He suspected that her fear for his well-being might interfere in an entirely objective application of her intellect to the problem at hand. "Besides, I was put on this path, whatever it is, before I was born. When I have tried to veer from it, I have been reminded that I cannot escape it. Not that I want to, except to have some control over avoiding further destruction caused by my...*condition*." He smiled, aware that the word had been overused and set up as a euphemism for what he really was, almost a code-word for werewolf at this point.

"I believe you can help me. I want to better understand your life, and your faith. I have done some reading, but cannot absorb a worldview from a book," Weston told him, setting aside his empty plate.

Amaoke sighed. He signaled for the check and paid it, ignoring Weston's protests. He knew that the priest was poor, and he had more than he could spend if he tried. It wasn't until they stepped back out into the sunshine that he decided to share something.

"When you and I had our encounter," he began, not able to come up with a better word for it, "I had a vision, a dream if you like. I met someone very important to our faith, and it was almost like meeting God."

"Raven?" Weston asked, and Amaoke nodded, surprised.

"Such a beautiful being. Seemed so above humanity. At first, I couldn't tell whether it was a male or a female, which makes sense, but the signature energy for me was male," Amaoke said. "It reminded me, in a more positive way, of the Morningstar."

"How do you mean?" Weston asked, and he was walking so close to Amaoke that their upper arms touched every few steps.

"Well, when the Monster comes to me, it also presents as a sexless being, and it is disturbing," Amaoke attempted to explain. "Dehumanizing. Which is perhaps why my mind wants to assign a gender to a god. And then you look so much like the Morningstar, it makes me wonder why. You seem so human."

"So you wanna see my junk?!" Weston laughed.

"I think just knowing that you *have* junk is reassurance enough," Amaoke said, pleased to be understood, despite the awkwardness of the exchange. "Because *it* doesn't."

"I understand. It doesn't have a belly button, either," Weston added, and it seemed a non-sequitur at first. Seeing that Amaoke didn't follow, he asked, "You know why we have them, right?"

"In theory," Amaoke said. "But your point?"

"The Morningstar has no hallmarks of humanity. It is a created being, not a natural one," Weston said. "And think about why humans need such things as belly buttons and junk, and you uncover an essential truth, one that it doesn't want us to consider. It lacks the power of creation, something that all pureflesh have, in theory, as you say. Or at least the potential for it. In that way we are all more godlike than the Morningstar."

"Not all of us," Amaoke shook his head, looking around, surprised that they had reached the carriage house once more.

The cat had not moved, but the dogs had gone back into the house in the time that had passed during their absence. Weston picked the animal up gently, settling in the chair with it on his lap, and Amaoke sat down next to him.

Glancing over at the purring cat on the priest's lap, he shook his head and said, "It figures."

Weston smiled down at the cat briefly before revisiting their conversation. "What do you mean, *not all of us?*"

"Whatever it did when it interfered with my birth, or perhaps even unrelated to its interference, I cannot procreate. Not that I am saying we qualify as pureflesh in any way."

"How do you know?" Weston wondered aloud, and Amaoke gave him a look.

"Well, when a male meets a female…" Amaoke began in a mock-serious voice, and then paused for effect. Weston threw back his head and laughed delightedly.

"They did teach us the birds-bees thing in Catholic school," he said to Amaoke when he was able to control his mirth. "I guess I meant that I am surprised that you would know that."

"Because you suggest that no female would ever get close enough to me? That hurts me, Brother."

"Not that," Weston said, smiling a little to indicate he heard Amaoke's teasing tone. "But you know what you are, and still you took that chance?"

"Not really," Amaoke said. "Not in the way you think. I lived for a very long time as a wolf. I discovered it then. But later in my life, I married. Once." He looked out across the slanting sunshine on the yard, and stopped talking, surprised that he did not want to revisit that source of Nanatha's pain. "It never happened for us, and I am fairly sure that the fault lay with me."

"But what if it had worked? Even as a wolf? And you'd borne some hybrid human-beast like yourself?" Weston wondered aloud, and managed to keep any judging tone out of his voice.

Amaoke had never thought of that, and it wounded him deeply, because the priest was right. He'd been irresponsible. "As if I needed another reason for self-loathing."

"I apologize. That was shitty of me. It would be wrong to judge you – not that I want to, God knows," Weston said softly. "Listen, man, I wish I could confirm or deny, but I can't, obviously," Weston told him, reaching out a hand and touching Amaoke's shoulder. "But in a perverse way, it makes sense. Because the Morningstar cannot create-"

"-nothing it tries to create can either," Amaoke finished the thought. "But I agree that if such a thing had been its aim, I would have served its nefarious purposes." He shivered despite the mildness of the day.

They were quiet for a time before Weston spoke again. "I did find it interesting that you said that Raven seemed sexless as well. That follows. But you also said he had male energy. Can you tell me why?"

"Not sure. You have a theory?"

"I have several, but first I want to share something with you that I've never told anyone," Weston said. "For reasons you'll understand I have kept this to myself. But I get what you said about Raven. It's just, when I think of God, I have always thought of that divine power as female. In the Church, we encourage the faithful to pray to whatever version of the Trinity is meaningful to them, as the Godhead is all of them. You'd be surprised how many of them are most comforted by the infant Jesus.

"Think about it, a baby is far less threatening than an adult. Babies are not considered judgmental beings, they need from us only the basic things we can all provide. Some think the Holy Spirit is the best choice. Many more draw comfort from the idea of an omniscient father figure. I think it is the same thing we have been discussing. Humans need to *humanize* their god – or gods – singular or plural. I think the patriarchy of the past several millennia have driven this in organized religion.

"But society is changing. Some Lutherans are now praying to Father/Mother God. And there are many so-called pagan religions – I know, pagan only because they are other than Judeo-Christian-Islamic – which had female gods, often in the image of a mother. And Jews have always been matrilineal, acknowledging that the family line followed from the mother.

"So you are saying that you think it has something to do with our influences?" Amaoke asked. "What energy we assign to god? That to you the divine is female?"

"Ok, yes. But perhaps it is driven by my love for my own mother. And the mother part is important. Stay with me. It is no difficult task to trace your ancestors through your mother because there is a fair bit of certainty who she is. But who do we count on to tell us who our father is?" Weston asked. "How do you know who *your* father is, for example?"

"My mother told me about him," Amaoke replied, not yet following where this was going.

"Exactly. Our mothers tell us, this is the guy," Weston punctuated the statement by stabbing the air with his finger, and the cat opened one eye to warn him that he needed to hold still. "That's powerful, but they have a great reason to do so. What if they know that the guy that provides protection – and I mean from way back, when we sat around fires – can't do it, but will blame her for the failure? She can fix it handily, and who's the wiser? Our mothers are the only ones who ever know the truth, really."

"I never pegged you for a cynic," Amaoke interjected.

"Oh, I'm not impugning the virtue of our mothers. That's not it. But it serves the Morningstar to draw power from them, draw attention away. Is it because of this ability to create? Which I argue is the very reason it hates humanity so bitterly. But I digress. What if it has done so on such a grand scale to hide the fact that the Creator is also devoid of gender, wanting us to anthropomorphize such a being and diminish Its significance? Worse yet, give humans another avenue for division – if having a *male* god forwards the cause of patriarchy generally and perpetuates the undercurrent of misogyny in such a society?"

Amaoke considered this for a time. "In my culture, despite there being strict gender-defined roles, it is universally agreed that everyone is needed to satisfy the natural order. And in my mother's language, and some other Inuit languages, there aren't any gender specific pronouns. No he, she, him, her, or his. Just they, them, that person."

"Non-binary address? Fascinating," Weston mused. Seeing Amaoke's confused expression, he added. "I think it's brilliant, but I don't want to wander too far out in the weeds."

"You lost me," Amaoke admitted with a laugh. It was clear that Weston was warming up to something, and when he got excited, it was both contagious and at the same time, almost manic.

"I'm saying that if we can work out the understanding of *why* the Morningstar did what it did to create us, maybe we get to the *how* of its destruction," Weston said. "I know it envies us our flesh, our procreative function, and our status in the eyes of the Creator."

64

"CARTER WAS ATTACKED BY DEMONS nearly three years ago," Weston finally said, changing the subject. Something about his tone made Amaoke notice that the temperature had dropped as the late afternoon became evening. He hadn't noticed how much time had passed as they sat on the patio talking.

"That's how I met her," he explained. "I was assigned to the case when the local parish priest requested help from his Archdiocese. I was called for an exorcism that never took place."

Amaoke listened carefully, and he heard something in Weston's tone that told him something was off. Very off. Weston was afraid. He sat through a silence that started to get uncomfortable, but he rode it out. He simply had no response to make.

Finally, he reached out to touch Weston on the elbow, which prompted the priest to start talking again, but disturbed the cat enough that he dashed off into the darkness of the trees.

"I never located a trace of the demons responsible, and local law enforcement ran into a dead end when all persons of interest conveniently disappeared, and then were found murdered," Weston explained. "It is the only errand I have undertaken for the Church where there was no ultimate closure."

"Difficult for Carter, I imagine," Amaoke said softly, thinking of Aleta.

"I suppose so," Weston allowed, but didn't have to say more.

"She doesn't know?" Amaoke asked.

"She doesn't remember," Weston said, and betrayed his frustration by running his hands through his hair, making it stick up and out in interesting patterns. "She had some early recollections about what happened to her, but they never aligned with what was suspected about the attack. That wasn't so surprising, actually. When the possessed were finished with her, they pushed her out of a moving vehicle, and she suffered a head injury."

"Perhaps not so terrible to lose those kinds of recollections," Amaoke allowed, waiting to hear more.

"I have no issue with the loss of memory," Weston agreed, but something was bothering him. Soon enough, he got to it. "I fear that one of these days she will wake up and remember the details. She remembers being afraid, remembers many of the oddities, but has no full recall of the worst. Even less appealing is the idea that these demons are still about in the world, searching for her, frustrated in their failure to use her up for their own ends. It was clear that they held her, had a plan for her, and then tried to destroy her."

"I convinced my superiors that she needed ongoing protection, but with no demons to send along, I had to return to my other duties. Her local priest worked hard on her behalf, which resulted in finding her placement in the office of the Archdiocese here. A regular entry job, clerical. But she told the Bishop that she had been called to orders, that she wanted to be cloistered with the Carmelites and take up the coif – become a nun," he added, by way of explaining the term to Amaoke.

"It was a blessing and a curse, her desire to obtain religious vocation. Because she is some sort of diviner, she senses the supernatural, attracts it even. She is irresistible to the possessed, and the demons are drawn to her. The Church has exploited this, rightly thinking that she makes the perfect assistant for an exorcist. It meant we were assigned to work together, which is good on the one hand because I don't have to leave her behind when I am on assignment," Weston told him.

"But a problem because you are repeatedly exposing her to the very trauma she suffered, knowing she could recall the worst of it at some inopportune moment," Amaoke concluded without needing Weston to explain.

Weston nodded, and was silent once more.

"And because you love her." Amaoke leaned back in his chair and put his feet up, staring out into the yard. He had been avoiding the subject, but now that his own life was taking this path, he wanted to acknowledge truth and allow himself to know Weston, and let himself be known in return. The Morningstar had wanted to keep them apart, perhaps wanted them in competition, each man weakening the other, and he doubted it would understand an alliance outside of its own plans; something based on understanding rather than necessity. It didn't escape him that their relationship may have been playing into the Monster's hands.

The priest's silence confirmed it, but Amaoke needed no affirmation. It explained many things, and complicated many others.

"Recently, there have been some unexplainable events that are likely related to these same diabolical actors," Weston said. "I cannot bring her along, and yet, to go alone seems imprudent, knowing what was done. It was at least three afflicted during the original attack, and the behavior described was unlike anything written in our Church archives regarding demonology."

"And Carter remembered nothing helpful at the time?" Amaoke asked.

"What she remembered was suspect from the beginning because it did not align with what was known. Although I do believe that she is telling the truth of it as best she can. I suspect she was duped, for a very specific reason. But I am operating with caution regarding the memories she does have. At the least, returning to that place with me would imperil her beyond just her flesh. I say that because I think it is what the demons want me to do, bring her along for the confrontation. I refuse to expose her soul again."

"Say no more. I am happy to volunteer," Amaoke said, unsurprised that his feelings fully aligned with the strength of his statement. His instincts were leading him somewhere, so he added, "You'll have to teach me what you need me to know."

"It's fairly simple," Weston told him. "I may still have a chance to recover the afflicted souls. It will require performing the ritual and trying to avoid being attacked myself. It is important to preserve the life of the one in the demon's possession if at all possible. No matter how ugly, no matter how frightening, the pureflesh should be spared if possible. Essentially, I need you to watch my back."

65

AMAOKE FROWNED AT HIS CLOSET. He hated packing generally; this endeavor was even more difficult. He had no idea what he might need, or whether he would have to do laundry. He should have asked more questions.

Weston had been vague on the details, telling Amaoke about what the local priest had reported to the Church, which was somewhat more than what he had reported to the local authorities, out of necessity.

The priest had seemed most excited when he caught sight of Amaoke's old timber axe just inside the patio door. He'd lifted it gingerly from its place, looking at it with curiosity and an expression that Amaoke had learned to worry about. Unhealthy interest was just that...unhealthy.

"Dude, is this your weapon?" he asked.

"I'm slightly concerned that you think of it first as a weapon," Amaoke replied. "It's a logging tool."

"Yep, sure, that's why you keep it here, by the door. For logging," Weston nodded sarcastically and sighed happily, hefting it and spanning the handle with his arms. "It just doesn't look like any other axe I've ever seen. It's mean-looking, like once, I saw a fire axe. It was brutal."

"It's old. These were also custom made to fit a logger's stance and height," Amaoke explained, taking it gently from the priest's hands. Weston had looked as if he were about to swing the thing, right there inside the dwelling.

"It's beautiful. But you don't generally carry any weapons," Weston observed, and Amaoke gave him a look. Weston returned it with one of his own. He was serious.

"And other people generally do?" Amaoke asked. Finally, to yank Weston's chain, he said, "I can swing an axe."

"But as a wolf? How does it work? Like the movies, where you can use your arms and take up a weapon?"

Amaoke chuckled at Weston's overly anxious tone. But then he paused. The Wolf, no. But if the Beast were to take up a weapon? Would it be possible? The Beast was more like a man, both more facile and terrible.

But then he shook his head. "As a wolf I don't need a weapon. I *am* a weapon."

Weston considered this carefully, and Amaoke could almost watch the progression of his internal dialogue.

"Yeah. But bring the axe," he recommended in all seriousness, reaching out to run an admiring hand along the handle once more. Amaoke had no intention of doing so, knowing that they needed fewer liabilities, not more.

66

AMAOKE AGREED TO TRAVEL by private car but only on the condition that they take a vehicle other than the Charger. Weston looked wounded, but had agreed. After all, he *had* assaulted Amaoke with it.

The morning of their departure, Weston was surprised by a knock on his door before the sun was up. He went to answer, thinking it one of the priests from the rectory next door. But instead, he discovered Amaoke on the stoop, wearing a dark watchcap over twin braids that reached nearly to his waist, his messenger bag slung over one shoulder.

"Didn't trust me not to show up at your place in the Charger?" Weston asked, surprised that it was cold enough for his breath to fog in the air.

"I know you are a man of faith," Amaoke observed quietly, smiling gently at Weston's teasing tone. "In my tradition, when we go out on an important errand, we leave together, from the same place, at the same time. The men gather at the *qasgiq*, or the central dwelling in the village, to burn wild herbs, bathe in smoke, and pray for success."

"Thank you for reminding me to be reverent," Weston was sincere, and thought once again that enlisting Amaoke felt right to him in more ways than just his extranormal skill. Weston had correctly assessed him as a spiritual man, and his wisdom would be welcome.

"I don't question that," Amaoke said honestly, and added, "Besides, I needed to involve myself directly in the choice of vehicle."

Weston laughed aloud and grasped Amaoke's hand in greeting, pulling him inside with the handshake. "I'll be ready in a few minutes. We'll take the minivan, even though it isn't as cool."

Cool or not, Amaoke was disturbed to discover that the larger, ostensibly safer vehicle did not engender any restraint in Weston's driving style. It was little consolation for Amaoke to realize that after his recent mishaps a wreck was unlikely to kill him, because the attendant suffering would be significant.

"I could teach you to drive," Weston said, when they had reached the highway, amused at the look of horror on Amaoke's face. But then he saw him consider the offer, if only briefly.

"I never learned," Amaoke said, shaking his head. "For reasons you can probably guess. Also, the old Yup'Ik in me believes it is unwise to move at a speed you don't generate yourself. I am sorry that I will be unable to share the burden of driving. Carter is better help for you there."

"In theory," Weston said. "She *can* drive. I just love doing it so much that I rarely let her. I don't mind the road time; it relaxes me."

"Control freak," Amaoke murmured, just loud enough for Weston to catch it, and turned his face to the window.

"Can't hide it, huh?" Weston laughed and reached to turn on the music. It seemed nearly every song was too loud and angry for Amaoke's taste, but he understood that this was the priest's version of a battle ritual, and he respected the need for it.

67

THEY REACHED THE SLEEPING TOWN after fifteen hours on the road. Amaoke suspected it would have been longer had Weston not been the driver, but he had avoided any law enforcement snares despite setting the cruise control at ninety, or even higher.

They had followed I-55 going north, crossing the Missouri river at dusk and continuing up US-61 to Iowa City before veering west toward Des Moines, although they followed I-80 for only a short stretch before turning off on county roads that led them into the broad emptiness that existed in-between.

It was after midnight. Once they got past the arc sodium lights on their tall poles that blazed above the truckstop just off the highway exit, it got very dark, very fast.

There were long stretches of farmland before they reached the town itself, just a moderate collection of older buildings that fronted the main street, typical Midwestern Americana. There were at least four churches by Amaoke's count.

Neighborhoods were set back off of the central part of the town, with avenues set on an ordered grid. Other than a fairly large modern high school that was next to the road at the edge of town, the schools were away from the busiest traffic.

A bluff on the southeastern side of town was lit by a long building a handful of stories high, obviously a hospital.

Weston slowed for none of it, although he did observe the posted speed limit through town. He increased his speed once they passed the high school, and after several minutes slowed again to make another turn down one of the county roads. The blacktop here was pitted and scarred, and there were dormant fields on either side of the road punctuated by an occasional farmhouse and barn, at this hour only shadows of variable size and shape.

The minivan slowed to a crawl when they neared their destination, and Weston stopped entirely on the crown of the road, the hum of the windows descending sounded loud in the country silence of late winter. There were stacked mailboxes on Amaoke's right and Weston looked like he was trying to see something through the open passenger window.

"I'm pretty sure this is it," he said, and Amaoke thought that this forgotten spot on the planet was the perfect place for nefarious events to happen. Weston started to roll up the windows, and Amaoke could understand why; they turned down a lane between trees and heavy undergrowth and deadfall that seemed to reach for the car. But Amaoke stopped him, making a silent sign to leave his own window open, trying to ignore the creepiness of the dark wall of vegetation only a few feet away.

Because he smelled something, dark and familiar, not just the dry rot of the leaves, or the small ground animals in their burrows, but a signature not unlike the scent of the Ungalek, or Forcas, or whatever he was calling himself these days. It was a carrion stench, putrefaction, faint but not far off. And he heard something that didn't make sense. Footfalls in the field beyond, stealthily creeping, then a pause, as if their progress was being tracked.

"No time like the present, I guess." Amaoke reached across the console to touch Weston on the arm. He held up a hand for the priest, signaling that he should stop the car. He popped open his door, thankful that Weston had disarmed the dome light and alarms that heralded the act.

"What's going on?" Weston asked *sotto voce*.

"I'm getting out here," Amaoke told him. "Keep going."

"You don't know where the trailer is," Weston protested.

"But I can find *you* at any time," Amaoke replied, tapping the side of his nose, and then he was gone.

He backtracked down the lane several yards and shook his head. He guessed he should be grateful that it was so deserted. He took a deep breath, realizing that he was no longer used to the cold after so many winters in the South, and reluctantly started to undress. It was rare that he planned a change, so he reckoned it would be wasteful to ruin his clothes if he knew in advance.

He piled the discarded garments and his shoes in the dry culvert among the weeds and stepped into the trees a man, emerging from the deadfall on the other side of the divide as a wolf.

He slunk silently along the fringes of the vegetation on the field side until he came level with the place where he had asked Weston to stop. The scent of death was stronger here, but he could no longer hear any movement. There wasn't much to see, as there was no moon, although his eyesight would serve well enough in the dark.

He sniffed the air and headed off in the direction parallel to the lane, following the natural boundary across the field. There was a marshy brook at the corner near the fence, and he trudged through the water to hide his own scent out of habit. He slid beneath the fence and stepped out of the trees into a rudimentary yard behind a trailer when he heard the furtive noise once again, so he sprinted across the space and ducked under the trailer skirt where he could hunker down and peer out. This gave the field mice the shock of a lifetime, and they scurried for cover.

His precaution was rewarded almost immediately. A woman stepped out of the trees, in nearly the same place he had emerged moments before. It was her scent he had been tracking, but there was something very wrong with her. She smelled dead, but she was not dead. It was sickness, to be sure, but still altogether human.

Her movements were beyond strange, jerky and disjointed somehow, but also rhythmic. There seemed to be an unusual timing to her gestures. She turned to her face side to side as if looking for something, but not as a normal person would do so; this had an odd precision, like an automaton, and it was one of the most frightening things he had ever witnessed. Probably because there was nothing natural about it.

As if compelled, she made her way toward his hiding place, but he noticed that there was some looseness about her walk, as though her joints couldn't keep her aligned with her trajectory. Like a drunken robot. It would have been comical were it not so terrifying.

She painstakingly knelt at the gap in the trailer skirt, posed as one would a baby doll on hands and knees, and her head turned slowly in the same way, swiveling up and around as if moved by an invisible force, and his earlier observation persisted, it *was* the way a little girl would turn a doll's head, looking beneath, searching. The movement of the eyes lagged behind the movement of the head, but fixed upon Amaoke where he was hidden in the dry leaves.

In an eerie voice hoarse with misuse and neglect, she said, "The Prince has come." Then she got up and disappeared, moving away through the dark yard.

Amaoke slipped through the gap and followed her, at a cautious remove, but it did not matter, she paid him no further attention. She was moving as if impelled toward something.

The putrid scent was increasing, and now Amaoke could make out two other figures, standing near a carport built next to the trailer on the end of the row. They stood out in dark relief against its light-colored paint. Weston's scent was stronger here as well, but he could not see the priest.

He paused at the corner of the adjacent trailer to watch. There were three women, all enveloped in the stench of their own death, but he could hear them breathing, could hear their hearts racing away in their chests. One of them had a staccato rhythm that was not regular.

They were emaciated, and their clothing was tattered. One of them had no shoes. There were other scents that clung to them, and if he concentrated he could separate out the smell of dead leaves, blood and old violence, and an odd perfume, concentrated, like attar of roses.

They stood still, together, but only for a moment, as if awaiting something. Then, as one, they turned, in synchrony, toward the back door of the trailer, moving toward it. When they reached the steps, they lined up, side by side, and three faces turned upward, their eyes lagging but finally focusing on the door.

As if at their silent request, it opened, Father Weston's cassock skirts swirling at the threshold, and the white surplice he wore seemed to glow against his dark clothing and the shadowy interior of the trailer.

"The Prince is here," the three women spoke the words in unison when they saw him.

In response, he stepped down onto the cinderblocks at his feet, and he seemed to be floating, his robes rippling and his hair moving in the breeze.

He clutched his silver cross in one hand, and a small book in the other. It was not a bible, but he read from it in Latin, in a clear voice that seemed to carry further than its volume might allow.

Each word seemed to fall onto the women like a burning ember, and they flinched away and writhed in synchrony, turning toward the field and their escape.

But the Wolf had come around behind them, and now crouched between them and freedom. Amaoke bared his teeth and snarled a warning.

"The beast, the beast, the beast," they intoned, and advanced on him, reaching for him, but their movements were weak and slow, and he easily evaded their grasp.

Yet they couldn't seem to resist Weston, turning this way and that, wanting to keep him in sight, as if his figure compelled them to look, even as they were repelled by the sacred words he spoke. Amaoke could see that Weston was struggling with the efforts of his prayers, focusing on the women, and he did not notice the movement behind him just inside the trailer's back door.

But Amaoke saw the glint of the eyes, the curve of a lovely pale cheek, and smelled the feathers on her cape, the brimstone signature of her provenance. He knew her from the gathering of demons on All Hallow's.

He dug his claws into the soil for purchase and dived around the women on the lawn, feinting left to avoid colliding with Weston, and leapt through the doorway, landing on her, trying to find purchase with his teeth in her neck.

She was strong, and they rolled together through the open front door, opposite the one he had hurtled through. He yelped when his ribs slammed into the railing next to the stairs, and landed on the ground.

The woman hissed at him, almost laughing, but those eyes were angry, and she advanced on him with a smile he didn't much trust and liked even less. He rolled his head on his shoulders and got unsteadily to his feet, and then saw the minivan, like a beacon, to his left.

She grabbed him roughly by the ruff of his neck and started to twist, but he had other plans. She was expecting to control the wolf, but Amaoke called the Beast, lunging toward the vehicle as he did so.

He used this off-balance momentum to bump the Dodge cross at the front, praying he was right, and it lit up with that ethereal blue glow and clicked outward. He concentrated with all his might, effecting a reversal of the transformation on his left hand, feeling the hairs receding as he rediscovered the fingers he desperately needed to pull the crosspiece out of the grille.

He allowed her to roll on top of him; if his shifting form surprised her she didn't betray any alarm. Indeed, she straddled him with a look of triumph, ready to hook her claws into his face, as the Beast receded to allow the man to return.

Amaoke didn't hesitate to deploy the Taser, hoping that he had it aimed properly, and as she leaned slightly upward to get purchase, both points found their homes in her form. Her wail of pain and frustration was otherworldly, and she seemed to implode with a pop that affected the pressure in his ears, and dispersed like smoke. Motes of dark matter and plum-colored feathers rained down on Amaoke, and overall he found it very satisfying. He was also thankful in that fleeting moment that the Taser had not had the same effect on him when Weston had deployed it.

He lay there in the gravel for a moment, having a harder time than usual catching his breath. He was fully human, and his ribs were broken. Again.

68

SHIFTING BACK WAS A NECESSITY, but it was agonizing with cracked ribs. He slunk slowly back around behind the trailer, using the carport as a shortcut, and found the priest standing over the near lifeless forms of the three women.

They were like fallen marionettes, as if their strings had been cut, and Amaoke was sure that this had occurred the moment he had dispatched the demon.

Weston knelt next to them, looking distressed, and Amaoke realized it was because they were all still alive, but not in very good condition.

He reached out to Amaoke, and turned dark sympathetic eyes on his friend. He touched the Wolf gently on the nose, and Amaoke gave a whine.

"I'm sorry, Brother," Weston said, seeing that Amaoke was somewhat listless and obviously in pain.

Amaoke licked his hand and turned away, trotting down through the yards to retrieve his clothing. By the time he returned, carrying the bundle in his teeth, Weston had roused the woman in the trailer next door.

When he came out, he found Amaoke leaning against the minivan, his clothing and the spent Taser at his feet.

"Smart, very smart, my friend," Weston said. He slid open the bay door on the car, and reaching behind the second row of seats, he folded down the third row, then made a soft bed out of his winter coat.

"Can you get up there?" he asked, and before Amaoke could move, Weston decided for him, lifting the wolf with ease and surprising gentleness into the back. "Rest. I think it's wisest you stay like this for a while. You'll understand why when it's all said and done."

He packed Amaoke's clothing into the messenger bag, and recovered the Taser, locking the wolf into the minivan. Amaoke didn't bother to pay attention to what Weston did after that, just curled up on his good side and tried to sleep.

Weston wondered what the woman thought of the priest who had now disturbed her twice to call the police about the empty trailer next door, not knowing that she had called them herself about the noises she sometimes heard from it. But he didn't dwell on it, because he wanted to get back into the trailer before the authorities arrived. He retrieved a small flashlight from the glovebox and climbed the steps.

Inside, the damage and defacement of three years prior was unchanged. He wandered the length of the living space, and then angled his shoulders to take the short hallway past the bathroom into the bedroom.

Carter's decorating was still in place, her things untouched, with one glaring exception. Sitting on her bed, posed next to the plush ballerina pillow he'd noticed before, was a tiny, ratty, soiled Choo-Choo Charlie. He recognized it immediately, though he hadn't seen it in over twenty-five years. It had been a gift from his Grandpa, a weathered occupant from his own crib. He shivered, realizing that he had probably averted some disaster by not bringing Carter back to this place, although what it meant he still could not decipher.

And on the mirror, written in fresh plum-colored lipstick, were the words

sOMEDAY mY pRINCE wILL cOME

He placed his doll in the pocket of his cassock, but left the message for Lieutenant Green to find. He switched off the flashlight and went back out into the yard when he heard the first sounds of the sirens.

69

THE FIRST OFFICER ON THE scene was the same patrolman who had responded to Weston's call three years earlier. He was still young, but understandably more experienced, and this time he rolled his eyes when he saw the priest, and let out a heavy sigh, probably understanding that it was going to be another long night.

The ambulance had been first to arrive, followed by the fire department, and their efforts had been to stabilize and transport the three women behind the trailer, all of whom were in serious need of medical attention. The medical trucks were just leaving as the patrol car arrived.

The officer made the mistake of leaning against the back of the minivan, which brought Amaoke to his feet with a snarl. The cop nearly jumped out of his skin.

"Jesus, your dog is impressive! What is he, some kind of Malamute?" If he thought it strange that a priest had a dog, it wasn't mentioned.

"Something like that," Weston replied, moving several feet away to encourage the policeman to follow. "I think he's not very happy being cooped up after the long drive."

"Lieutenant Green is coming out. She asked me to hold on getting your statement until she arrives," the officer told him.

"I understand. I'd like to go down to the hospital, if I could. I'm worried about these women. Could you ask the Lieutenant if she'd meet me there?" Weston asked, shrugging out of his surplice and folding it carefully. "I really should feed the *dog* and walk him before I get tied up with all of this."

"You'll be there waiting?" the patrolman, whose name was Petersen, asked, looking skeptical.

"Of course," Weston promised. "I'm headed back to town anyway. Tell her I'm getting the coffee warm. She'll get the message."

"I hope you're right," Petersen said, still looking doubtful. "Just don't make her have to look for you or it'll be my neck."

"Yes, officer. I won't," Weston promised, and climbed into the car before Petersen could change his mind.

He headed back into town, pulling off the road on the near side of the turn for the county road, opening the back hatch to let Amaoke out for a few minutes. Once he got the wolf settled again, he turned back toward town and pulled in at the IGA, which was open 24 hours.

Weston ran in and picked up stew meat and bottled water. He opened the meat and set it down in back near Amaoke before resuming the short drive up to the hospital. He parked in a far corner of the lot and backed into the space away from the lights. He cracked the windows and said, "Don't kill anyone, okay?" before locking up and jogging toward the Emergency Department entrance.

He found Weitzman on duty, and other than raise his brows in Weston's direction, the physician was too busy to talk. Weston went downstairs to the cafeteria and ordered two cups of coffee and sat at the windows to wait for Green.

About ninety minutes passed, and no sign of Green, but then Weitzman showed up, looking careworn and exhausted.

"Hey, man," he greeted Weston as though he still saw him every day, and three-plus years hadn't passed. Weston passed him a cup of coffee.

"It might be cold," he apologized, but Weitzman waved this away.

"It's got caffeine, that's all that matters at this point," he said. "I hear you're involved in this mess upstairs."

Weston nodded and said nothing, hoping Weitzman would share whatever news he could.

"Minus the signs of frank assault, this is too much like before, but these three aren't going to survive the night," he said. "The marks on their skin, the dehydration, malnutrition. But this stuff seems longstanding, a chronic process. They've suffered some sort of neurotrauma and seem to be in shock from starvation and neglect."

"All three have doll's eyes and didn't respond to cold calorics, and one of them is in frank heart failure from atrial fibrillation." He saw Weston's confusion and said, "Essentially they are all brain dead, their bodies just haven't succumbed yet. None of them is over forty, and I suspect them to be younger, although it is difficult to tell because they have been so poorly used. Is it some sort of cult?"

"Of sorts," Weston allowed, not wanting to lie to his friend, but unsure what to say. "I'm so sorry."

"Me, too. It gives me the creeps," Weitzman admitted. "Other than that, I have missed you."

"Same. But you'll be happy to hear that your original patient is thriving," Weston thought to give the man some good news.

"That *is* good news, thanks. I needed to hear something positive," Weitzman smiled for the first time. "I thought this shit was over. I was ready for it to be safe and boring around here again."

Weston realized Weitzman didn't have the whole picture. He'd assumed that Green had given him more of the details of the investigation years ago.

"You really don't know?" Weston looked at his friend and shook his head. "This is the end of it. It was these three that were holding her before. The danger dies with them."

"What about the other stuff?" Weitzman asked, talking about the perceived physical assault on Carter. Weston was sad he couldn't expound on the theories he'd compiled about that, but he didn't want to contribute to Raphael's bad dreams. "I know there's at least one more."

Weston said nothing, knowing that it was more than one, but not an individual that could be named or captured.

"C'mon, I want to show you something," the doctor said, and Weston, resigned, got up to follow, already suspecting he knew what Weitzman was about to reveal.

They visited all three women in the ICU, and one by one Weitzman showed Weston the identical marks on the emaciated torsos. Instead of wings, each had a single black feather tattooed over her ribs.

"It's not a brand, but you tell me that's not the same thing," he protested, searching Weston's face for answers.

"It isn't, my friend," Weston told him. "These women were marked because they failed. They lost the prize, and Carter lived. This was punishment, a living hell that lasted three years."

Weitzman was surprised at the profound sadness in the priest's tone, and he waited quietly while Weston administered the last rites lovingly to each of them.

70

WHEN THEY RETURNED TO THE Emergency Department, Green had arrived. She looked up from where she was standing at the central desk and approached them. She nodded at Weitzman briefly as he went back to work, and turned to Weston.

"I gave your coffee away," he told her, by way of greeting.

"Not the worst news I've received tonight, Father, but it's close, it's close," she smiled wanly, and he could see how tired she was. "How are you?"

"Not sure yet," he answered honestly.

She sighed. "Am I going to find evidence that these three were involved in that cluster we worked on three years ago?"

Weston didn't answer.

"Never mind. I don't really want to know right now," she said tiredly. "You'll stick around a day or two?"

"Of course. I'll be at the Holiday Inn Express by the highway," he said, resisting saying more, but she knew him too well.

"Getting smarter?" She touched him on the arm with an expression of wry amusement. She looked at her watch and groaned. "Coffee at your place at ten a.m.?"

It was code to meet back there in the hospital cafeteria later that morning. His place of 'residence' from three years ago. Versus her place, which was the conference room on the third floor of the precinct, down the hall from her office. He suspected it was infinitely more private here in the hospital, and they'd be avoiding the peak mealtime rush.

"See you then," he promised, not telling her to get some sleep, since he knew she wouldn't.

He retreated to the car and drove back out to the highway and checked into a motor inn with rooms that could be accessed from the parking lot. His appearance didn't seem to faze the man at the desk, who Weston assumed had seen it all. This priest and a werewolf would fit in with the type of clientele he served, Weston thought to himself.

He parked up outside the door of the room and let Amaoke out, leading him inside and helping him get settled on one of the beds.

"You'll be more comfortable up here with those ribs," he remarked, but got only a doleful look from the Wolf. Weston was happy to see that he'd eaten the stew meat, and he gave him some water from one of the bottles he'd purchased.

He went back out to the van and closed it up, finding the doll in his pocket and examining it briefly before tucking it away in his bag. He still wasn't sure what it meant, but he had an idea. More importantly, it made him feel a pang of loneliness. He missed Momma and his Grandpa, even now.

He returned to the room and stretched out on the other bed, grateful to see that Amaoke was resting peacefully. He switched out the lamp and the locomotor rumble of the wolf's breathing soon lulled him to sleep.

71

"YOU'LL RECALL THAT OUR ORIGINAL persons of interest were found murdered at about the same time," Green reminded him when they sat down with their coffee the next morning. "We lost all three women during the night, which makes your prediction somewhat prophetic, if that isn't too redundant." She twisted up her mouth as she finished her statement.

"Initial ID on the three from last night is based on fingerprints taken at postmortems this morning. It tells us that they are, in no particular order, a known girlfriend, common-law wife, and live-in to our three dead bikers," she said. "Evidence collected from the murder scenes three years ago suggest they are good for the killings of their men. Carter's missing vehicle was found abandoned on the county lane that runs parallel to the drive into the trailer park, about half a mile away. Smells like something died in there, and the one woman's missing shoes were in the trunk. The lab says there are stains on the backseat consistent with Carter's original injuries, so it would appear they pushed her out of her own car, and have been using it ever since. They must have kept it garaged somewhere, because the BOLO on that plate has been active three years running. So I've got, what, some sort of cult ritual here? Slow starvation and self-harm leading to this conflict with you last night?"

"Which brings me right to it – the Church got reports that strange things were happening here?" She looked at him with that probing expression that always made him feel as if she knew answers he wasn't about to give her.

"Something like that," he responded with as much innocence as he could, but she didn't buy it.

"Because there *have* been odd things occurring here lately," Green said. "A number of calls, complaints, really, from your girlfriend in the next trailer there. Disturbances next door, but when we respond all is quiet. She does have a history of drinking and meth use, so it is difficult to sort out what's what. But we've had some pets mutilated in the area, and whoever it was graduated to livestock, killing some horses. Parts were missing."

"Father Paul also reported some minor desecrations at the Catholic school as well. He said he hadn't seen you, which I think feels like the truth, but I didn't think he was all that surprised to hear you were back in town. I remind you that it would be a bad idea to withhold information or lie to me."

"We're clear as ever on that point," Weston replied, intending to say as little as possible.

"And now I have a woman's shoe, size 7, purple. A Louboutin, which I doubt belongs to anyone in that trailer park. Just the one. And some feathers, also purple, recovered from the gravel out front. The lipstick on the mirror was new, and it was, oh wait, it's actually plum," Green said, consulting her notebook. "Pantone color 19-3220 TCX, according to my criminologist. It's important, I guess, because the shoe, the feathers, and the lipstick are all exactly the same shade of...plum, did I say? Which seems impossible to be coincidental. Classy stuff, I'm told. And those three on the slab don't fit that profile. So it seems I have a loose end of sorts."

Weston ignored this, and refused to take the bait. "Perhaps with all the activity out there...?"

"It could be that the place has attracted some nuts secondary to the notoriety," Green allowed. "There are some cuckoos that might get a charge out of having a tryst at a crime scene." She shook her head. "I hate this case. So if we think this was a cult set-up, then

Carter was being prepared as some sort of bride for this 'prince?' Who was he? Some visiting VIP? One of the ranking biker leadership?"

"And they have been coming back around – for what? Waiting for the prince? And why? Their bride got away," Green pointed out, and then got a look on her face that Weston couldn't read.

"She *is* safe, right?" Here Green looked at him carefully. "If I were to ask NOLA PD to do a welfare check, they'll confirm her safety?"

"Sure," Weston nodded, fairly certain that she had already set that process in motion. She was nothing if not thorough. "She's in residence at the Carmelite cloister at Our Lady of the Blessed Sacrament."

"Well, I'm glad there was ultimately a rational explanation for all of this," she said, with a biting irony in her tone that he felt was for his benefit. She also scribbled down the information he'd given her about Carter's whereabouts in her notebook before leaning back and looking him over carefully.

They sipped their coffee companionably for a few minutes, and then she stood up to leave. He stood up as well.

"I like you, Father Weston," she began, pulling on her jacket. "But no more coincidences, okay? If you feel the need to pay our little hamlet another visit, you call me first, or we're going to have a misunderstanding."

He could tell from her tone that she was scared; she knew it wasn't the whole story and her expression said that this time she didn't want to know.

Weston took the hint and was driving east out of town thirty minutes later with a bearded Amaoke in the passenger seat beside him. When they took the onramp onto the highway, Amaoke pulled his cap down low over his eyes and reclined his seatback to nap.

"You owe me a pack of razors," he said grumpily, and Weston smiled, knowing they were alright.

72

RETURNING TO NEW ORLEANS, AMAOKE discovered an old army knapsack in the bottom of the coat closet by the patio door. He'd forgotten about it; he'd come to refer to it as his 'drifter's pack.'

He'd picked it up somewhere on the West Coast, up Portland-way, in a surplus store. It had weathered well, literally, surviving his periods of homelessness over the last thirty-five years. For the same reason, he didn't carry it every day. It was a reminder of lean times, and its appearance betrayed something about him that he didn't like to admit was a part of his truth.

But it was unfussy, sturdy, and could hold enough for him to carry his life around on his back. Because this homecoming was not really to stay. It was a stopping point on the way to the rest of it. First to follow Weston to the heart of his Church, and then on to Africa to find a woman who probably didn't want to be found.

The pack sat open on the bed, the top like a yawning dark mouth, and it saddened him. This place felt like home, and something in him knew that when he left this time, he wouldn't be coming back. It was so final. And bothered him more than he had expected.

He realized with even greater clarity why Aleta was such a threat to the Morningstar. She gave him a reason to abandon the madness of the future for a present peace, no matter how curtailed. And he was still wrestling with what he was going to tell her.

When she'd declined his invitation to hear all that Weston had to say about what they were facing, he had respected her decision, but it felt isolative. He had to process and plan without the benefit of her wisdom and certainly without her company.

She had retreated to the solace of her sister after the Dragon's visit. He could not decide whether he was an idiot to have avoided telling her the events of that night, because he did not like to keep anything from her. He owed her the honesty of what he knew. She didn't want to be spared. But he sensed she might be avoiding a goodbye, and he could understand her need to move past whatever distress and lack of control he had brought into her life.

It was the last part that stung; he assumed she was strong enough to move on; he knew he never would.

So preoccupied with these concerns was he that he did not at first notice his unwelcome guest. Too late he recognized the insidiousness of that scent, death, char, the mineral signatures of sulfur and ozone.

"Are these as comfortable as advertised?" the Morningstar could drive one crazy with the inanities of its approach. It held one of his Converse sneakers in those spade-claw hands.

"Try them, take them, I don't care," Amaoke replied, some part of him was finished with being reactive to its intrusions; he had learned that such was probably what it wanted. It always found a way to put him off his guard anyway. And the fact that it wore Weston's face was both more and less disturbing, because he recognized that his relationship with the priest had probably blunted his response to seeing it. It was an odd emotional exercise; for centuries he had despised it, but now it was the face of a friend. He suspected that it was just such a conundrum that the Morningstar intended to generate. He wondered if it was going to comment on their recent road trip.

"I can see you're going to be no fun at all," it shook that floating mass of hair. "Aren't you even the slightest bit curious about what will happen to her once you leave?"

"Whatever it is, I don't have to worry. You talk so much about it that I begin to suspect that whatever plan you had for her has failed. If you could have gotten to her, it would be done by now," Amaoke observed astutely but perhaps not at all wisely. "But something about her has frustrated all your efforts."

"To the contrary, my beloved wolf-child, my intent has been all along to strip away her defenses," it replied.

"She might have found her footing following your performance of proof during your initial visit. Perhaps she would have similarly recovered following *my* visit." Here, the Morningstar frowned darkly, probably recalling Weston's interference. "But now she has learned that my demons reach for her, and most importantly, she got to witness firsthand how much damage I can do to you, with nothing more than a speeding car. I argued with Forcas that you wouldn't be so easily baited, but your responses to your ladies is boringly predictable.

"It introduces doubt that you will always be around to protect her. Even if you planned to be, which you don't. Now, she faces every day with the possibility of your mortality, and coupled with her love for you, that has driven her to distraction.

"When you leave, she will have no contact with you, only the company of her mind, imagining, as such a fine mind must, all the innumerable possibilities of your fate. Add to that the burden of knowing that the supernatural world is not an abstract place created by the mind, but a real part of the world she now looks upon with fresh eyes.

"At any given moment, that world can reach into her world, and there is no way that she can control the ordered life she has built for herself with that kind of variable. So you see, my dear beast, she will slowly descend into a madness of her own creation.

"That type of distractibility can cause someone to lose critical focus and run through the wrong intersection, or misjudge the homicidal tendency of a patient. Accidents happen, but they are rarely *accidental.*"

Amaoke listened to this with mounting horror. The Monster continued, delivering further blows.

"What started out as an independent, self-assured woman slowly transforms. She had control, strength, she was certain of herself and trusted her decisions. And she wasn't arrogant. The arrogant are my favorite; they engineer their own downfalls. It's so delicious really, like watching a train wreck."

"So your brilliant idea to *prove* your story was the first brick to be removed from the foundation. Introduce doubt, and one loses the security of the mental stronghold. Everything becomes shaky, doubt leads to fear, and on to despair. Loss of faith, loss of belief, loss of hope. Utter destruction. Cannot sleep, cannot concentrate."

"Because you lack imagination, certain things like possibility, and resilience, and enduring hope are foreign ideas to you," Amaoke replied quietly, reasserting his refusal to accept the worst, because he had learned that it served nothing of value to do so. "You don't have an answer for those qualities, and cannot fathom them, much to your displeasure. I think Dr. Madison has all the tools she needs to triumph over whatever darkness you have introduced into her world, and I am confident she will."

"Including finding another man to share her bed," it responded dryly, recognizing that its initial approach was failing to find its mark.

But old wolves are old wolves because they have learned self-discipline, and Amaoke masked the anger and jealousy that hearing such a bald truth cost him. He thought his mother would be proud of this self-actualization, never mind that it was such a late development. The best response to some assaults is no response.

Then, because he had no further patience to listen, he turned his back to begin picking out the things he wanted to take with him, not wanting to encourage further discourse. By the time he had found what he was looking for, he was alone once again, with only the emptiness of the space, and his lonely mind. It saddened him to know that the Morningstar was vindicated by his leaving, and that it had left him alone because it knew he was following the course it had set for him.

73

AMBAKISYE GRADUALLY BECAME AWARE OF the hum of the locusts descending upon the grasses beyond the road. The sunlight had not pierced the clouds that hung low over the eastern horizon, but a lightening of the sky heralded another day.

He remained still, not wanting to disturb his wife, and when the inertia slipped from him enough that he was ready to stir, he turned toward her, but she was gone. He stretched out his hand to her side of the mattress, but the sheets were cool. He frowned, wondering where she had gone, because he could not hear her moving about in the hut, and she had been late to come to bed. Or had he simply dreamt that she had, in that strange stillness that he could achieve in lieu of sleep?

He rolled back, using the momentum to slide his feet to the floor and sit up. He rested there at the edge of the bed, shaking off a feeling of unease. He shivered involuntarily, then stood up and stretched slowly before sliding his feet into sandals and wandering outside.

The heat was already stifling, sun or no, but nothing stirred. He thought to call for Yabluu, but something stayed his voice, as if it would be wrong to disturb the silence. Not even the goats stirred, which was strange, as their near constant protests for food were the singular feature of their wakeful state. Yet the shed was dark and quiet.

He glanced toward the water reservoirs; both were full, confirming her return, as her first task of a morning was to gather water. But there was no other sign of her.

He walked up to the road, the cacophony of the insect horde increasing in his ears. He was mesmerized by the beauty of their pink gossamer wings made even more fanciful by the rosiness of the sunlight that had finally managed to break through the distant storm clouds. It made him yearn to bring his paints out and capture it; but he couldn't shake the feeling of disquiet enough to make such a wish tenable.

He turned in a full circle, scanning the entire horizon. To the north and west, in the far distance, were more locust clouds, or perhaps a dust storm just starting to develop. The haze was substantial, but still far out over the plains, and wouldn't make it to the clearing any time before nightfall, if ever, unless the wind changed drastically.

The remnant of his left arm throbbed strangely, and he wondered if the storm was affecting him; it was unusual for him to be aware of it for any reason anymore. He massaged the truncated muscles absently, and turned back toward the hut.

On his way back across the yard, the chickens were finally out scavenging, the boldest of them scolding him as though he were tardy with their feed. He almost laughed at them; he understood well why some men referred to their wives as hens – and thanked *Enkai* for blessing him with a wife who was more like a cool breeze running through his life. At her worst he wouldn't have equated her with these pecking, fussing creatures.

Their commotion had awakened the goats, and he turned them out in the yard, scattering food for the hens behind them. He turned back to the shed and mixed the grain mash for the goats, then returned to the kitchen and chopped sour apples to augment it.

These chores done, and still no sign of Kusini. Yabluu turned up when he was butchering a blooded grebe, chattering away at him about some grievance and eyeing the discarded bits at the periphery of his butcher block. He waved her in, teasing. "Bloody cannibal. Where's your lady gone?"

He ate at the window, looking out on the morning, distracted. It was too hot to burn brush, so he puttered around in his makeshift studio, making do with the natural light, too restless to create, organizing brushes and paints and pieces of wood that Kusini always complained could be kept elsewhere, which was probably her euphemism for discarded. He knew he was being irrational, that sometimes when he did something she thought he might never do, something he procrastinated over but never changed, she would show up just to give him that look she had, of pleased surprise and amusement. She was a magical being, on occasion his own magical thinking had attracted her attention, and he was superstitious, wanting to wish her back on this strange day.

But the shadows shortened and lengthened, and still she didn't return. At dusk, at a crossroads, he decided against shattering the peace with the roar of the generator and the blaze of light it could provide, instead ushering the goats into their pens and securing the roost.

In the hut, he burned candles and fed the beast that lived in his skin without tasting the food. He tried to read but couldn't concentrate. Alone in the dark he felt the strange disreality of their shared life, and finally shook his head. It was possible he had forgotten something she had told him about an errand. Or she could have slipped out shortly after she'd returned, sensing the distress of others. It had happened many times over the past two hundred years, yet he couldn't shake his sense of foreboding.

He rattled about without accomplishing much, before giving up and giving in to his ennui. He left the candles burning, like a beacon he knew was unnecessary, and stretched out on the bed, seeking rest.

It felt like only seconds later when his eyes opened to an unnamed dread. Full dark had come down, and the hours had advanced. The earth was moving, in a way he'd not felt before, and the sound was like a thousand thunderous crashes, a wave of rushing air ahead of something gargantuan. He could hear small clay sculptures diving from their niches, down and down to their deaths on the mosaic of stones in the floor.

He rushed to the door, pulled inexorably to investigate, finally connecting what he heard and felt to experience. Recalling that Kusini had stood with him, near the western edge of the Gorge, looking out on the expanse that spread out ahead of them, sky above, river below, the Mbulumbulu obscured by the thundering herds of the stampeding wildebeest, blundering blindly onward under a migratory imperative.

He could make no sense of it at all; such behavior had never driven the beasts themselves this far east, this far off the life-giving river. But it was the only frame of reference he had, and he knew with an awful clarity that whatever needed to be done to avert disaster was impossible. It was too late. The herd was nearly upon them, and would tear through the clearing with destructive finality, heeding the safety of none of the existing lives, not those of their kindred livestock, not his own, and the homestead would be razed to the ground.

The air was thick with dust, and it was only when he felt that first trickle of blood from his nose, and a force that drove him to the ground, that he realized a terrible magic was at work. Having no experience of this side of her power, he could not know that his wife was the progenitor.

The pressure wave was unrelenting, and the forces were unbearable, the winds rising around the hut, making the dust cloud even more impenetrable, and he was blinded utterly. The wind carried to him something that sounded like her distress, like a scream, like his own name, but before he could be sure, it was snatched from his ears into the vacuum of the void. Eerily, he heard no lowing of the wildebeest or any other animal, and he struggled against the forces that pushed and pulled him, finding his feet, steadying himself against the hut's outer wall.

He pushed off, into the maelstrom, certain he could wander far out on the plain or encounter mortal danger without warning in such an assault, when he caught sight of a bright flowing form in the dark, coalescing like light in the darkness. It was a small glimpse that came and went, and he moved toward it, continually feeling dragged away, dragged under, by the wind that wanted to carry him away. The dust and sand particles stung his skin, alighting like wasps, and this added insult, despite his great strength, made him despair. He was losing the battle, the pressure so great that he felt like a man drowning, starved for breath, sobbing with effort, realizing that the bright flamelike dance at the center of his vision was created by the flowing folds of his wife's abaya as it whipped and floated about her.

He moved forward, wanting only to reach this beacon, coming infinitesimally closer over epochal periods, until he could see her own distress, and the strength she expended to control the chaos that surrounded them. Her arms outstretched to the sky, every inch of her skin abraded and bleeding, the strain of her posture to hold the atmospheric blast, and her eyes, turning to him, golden and aggrieved, mouthing something that was carried from her lips and thrown to the heavens without the sound touching him.

And when he made it to her, reaching out for her, she collapsed against him, unable to hold on, and he closed his eyes, knowing that without her strength they would both succumb, but he didn't care, they were together, and it was more than he could have hoped for in an ending. To lose everything but have no worry that either of them was left not knowing what would become of the other.

But as she sheltered under his remaining arm, the storm subsided, as though she were at the eye, its innermost calm. He sat and held her, watching as she lost her battle with an exhaustion he could not fathom, as her eyes drifted closed and then fought anew to remain open. She was gasping with an unknowable exertion, and trying to talk, but he shook his head, letting her know she didn't need to explain.

And when her eyes closed again, unable to maintain her grip on her consciousness, every mote of dust, every speck of sand fell directly to the earth anew, as if her power had been the only thing keeping them aloft. Ambakisye's first unlabored breath was an audible gasp.

Under the starry dome of the heavens was an impossible sight. The innumerable dead, the martyred, the maimed, the tortured, had climbed atop the earth to walk again. Their eyes – oh, the eyes were aware with an awful intelligence, red, glittering, with the hunger of the centuries. And they had come to a stop as one, gazing at him momentarily as he held his wife's listless form, before falling to their knees, wave upon wave of them, a prostration of thousands, as they murmured to him in one voice.

"Msifune Mfalme, Msifune Mfalme..." hailing him as their king.

And he looked down at his beloved Kusini, who inhaled sharply and gulped in air, suddenly jerking upright in his lap, and her eyes, when they opened, were the color of fresh blood...

Then mercifully, from another place, she was saying his name, more and more urgently, and he surfaced from this vision, relinquishing a bad dream to return to a world of reason, afraid to tell her that he feared he had seen the future.

74

CARTER SURPRISED HIM THAT MORNING, Flying across the church campus in her usual state of disarray, as soon as she entered the cottage she pulled off her veil and wimple with more impatience than Weston had seen from her before.

When she bent at the waist and began pulling off her robes, he turned away and even took a few steps into the kitchen, unsure what he would do if he had to see her undressed. He called upon as much fortitude as he could muster, hoping it would be enough, hoping he could refuse any direct offering.

But what she'd done was strangely more difficult for him to deal with than her nudity. Under those white skirts was the simplest smocked sundress, with a sunflower pattern that was completely disarming in its ordinariness. It was overwhelming to him, even more intimate to see her in this secular attire, after becoming accustomed to all the yards of material that separated them, not only a physical barrier but also a philosophical one.

Her shoulders, arms, and legs were bare, her skin glowing with youth, her face flushed, expectant, asking silently for his approval. He was quite certain she could read it on his face.

"Now you," she demanded, frowning pointedly at his cassock skirts. She stepped closer and reached for the buttons, but then he did recreate a physical distance, feeling as though balance and gravity had suddenly been robbed of him. He stepped away and held up a restraining finger, at once sorry when he saw her hurt expression, so he used it to tap her playfully on the nose.

Her shorn hair was particularly uneven, its lack of artfulness purposeful, the Mother Superior wanting to strip her of all vanity, but it gave her an appeal that was unmatched by any other woman he had known. But he had no time to be distracted by her charms, as he realized her impatience with his inertia when she crossed her arms.

"If you start tapping your foot, I will wear this cassock all day," he warned her in a teasing tone, watching her crumple up her discarded clothing and stuff it into her bag. Smart. She knew to leave no evidence of a disrobed nun for the cleaning lady, who was clearly on a mission to catch the two of them *en flagrante delicto*.

He withdrew into the bedroom and was relieved to find an old pair of Levi's and a clean grey t-shirt that Ms. Margaret had purchased for him. He'd last worn it to change the oil in the Charger, but it was currently clean. He dressed with economy and transferred all of his pocket junk, putting his cross around his neck and dropping it inside his shirt. Finally he replaced his spectacles and returned to the front of the cottage.

"Probably should exit through the garage, eh?" he nodded toward that door and opened it for her, dashing across the dark space to open the street doors before getting the passenger door for her. He took her bag and put it into the trunk before climbing behind the wheel.

After a brief pause to resecure the garage doors, they were on their way. Pretending. Just for a day, as she had requested. A normal day, the boy, the girl, some sunshine, a fast car, and a place to go, but no particular hurry.

Muse and Fall Out Boy provided the soundtrack; Weston's favorites, but Carter did not mind, understanding why he liked these songs perhaps better than he did.

He made her laugh by singing along with 21 Pilots, doing a clever word swap, "All my friends are *demons* take it slow...wait for them to ask you who you know...please don't make any sudden moves...you don't know the half of the abuse..."

She knew well enough that his sense of humor could be awkward, at times morbid, especially when he was nervous or particularly stressed. Weston, for his part, was recalling that ironically the song was from the soundtrack for *Suicide Squad,* and although he had never seen and likely would never see the movie, he thought it a strange and tragically appropriate association. Carter had once seen it, and she found it coincident to too much of what was happening to discuss the details with him; the pretext was an apocalyptic battle pitting a group of meta-humans and supervillains against one another. There *was* a sorceress, and a beast (although reptilian rather than lupine), and a half-demon who sacrifices himself for his friends and for the greater good. She refused to think on it further, and she was absolutely against bringing up the parallels.

Not while she could pretend that it was someone else's reality, someone else's life, even for just this one day.

She placed her hand over his on the gearshift, and he surprised her by picking it up and bringing the back of it to his lips. His eyes never left the road, and she assumed it was involuntary, something he did without giving it a thought, and she wondered if she was bringing him down somehow, stripping away something righteous, something that he might need to preserve to prevail.

So she didn't say a word or register her amazement, simply felt that place burn where his mouth had touched her skin, giving her goosebumps despite the warmth of the air that drifted across her bare shoulders through the open windows.

75

AS WESTON HAD EXPECTED, MS. Margaret was delighted with Carter. If she disapproved of their abandonment of the adornments of their respective vocations, she gave no indication of it. She displayed her usual warmth, welcoming Weston like a long-lost son, which still surprised him as much as it always had. Carter's happiness was measured by the wattage of her smile, and he could see how much she was enchanted by their visit.

They enjoyed lunch on the back porch, drinking lemonade while Carter pestered Ms. Margaret for details about Weston's adolescence, having difficulty believing that he had been so serious and so quiet. Not that Ms. Margaret needed much encouragement, and some of what she shared helped him realize that he had underestimated the depth of her feelings for him.

"I had to take out his pants every other week one year," Ms. Margaret shared, shaking her head and giving a soft chuckle. "But he'd had it hard enough, and I wasn't going to give anyone any reason to laugh at him." Her expression was unreadable, and she was no longer looking at Carter, she was looking at him. She sat for a moment and then got up quickly, as though she had just remembered something. She tucked a stray curl of his hair behind his ear, and said, "I also made sure he got regular haircuts, when I could catch him. I'll go get the cake."

"You didn't tell me this was your home," Carter observed, giving him a look that he could decipher no better than his old caretaker's.

"I think when I was here, I was unequipped to recognize it," he admitted, feeling guilty that he didn't get to visit more often. He knew that Ms. Margaret was probably lonely now that Father O'Halloran had passed away.

She came back with the cake, but also had an old photo album tucked expertly under one arm. This she passed directly to Carter, ignoring Weston's expression of mock horror with an innocent smile, before putting her efforts toward serving cake. She did so knowing that no one would take umbrage with a sweet old lady passing out dessert.

After they were full, and the sugar coma was coming on, Carter suddenly noticed the garden swing, and she jumped up like a little girl, asking, "May I use it?"

"Of course, my dear," Ms. Margaret was happy to indulge, and it was obvious that she enjoyed Carter's enthusiasm.

Weston sat quietly beside his caregiver, and together they watched Carter far off down the garden, exploring the many flowers that Ms. Margaret carefully cultivated now that she had no humans to care for. Finally, Carter climbed onto the swing, closed her eyes, and rocked in the breeze, enjoying the sunshine.

"I'm going away soon," Weston said into the silence, his eyes not leaving Carter.

"Oh? Where?" Ms. Margaret's question had a strange tone, far more curious than her usual brusque, no-nonsense approach. It was this that made him suspect that she thought he was leaving the Church for the captivating companion he'd introduced to her. So he let the silence draw out a moment or two, trying to decide whether she was distressed or pleased or something else entirely.

"Abroad. Back to Rome, and then on to Africa," he told her. "I was hoping-"

"What is it, child?" Ms. Margaret touched him for the second time, gently, on his forearm.

"Do you think that Carter could come back here if she needed to?" he asked quietly, not aware how much grief his tone revealed. "She really has no one else, and she may need…"

"A friend?" Ms. Margaret asked. "She is welcome here anytime. I will make a home for anyone you love."

He sat stiffly, refusing to betray the depth of his emotions, surprised as ever at her keen powers of observation, thankful that she knew him well enough that she did not expect him to talk. Ms. Margaret left him alone with these thoughts, knowing what he didn't tell her. He was putting his affairs in order. She recognized it, God knew she did. He was here to say goodbye, but she also knew she was not going to hear that from him. Not directly, at least. So she stood slowly, stiffly, and he half stood to help her, but she waved him away, using the back of his chair to gain her balance.

Once she had steadied herself, she bent down and kissed the very top of his head, smelling his sun-warmed hair, not wanting him to see that she was about to cry. She picked up the dessert plates and retreated into the shadowy coolness of the house, and it was a long time before she was able to return to the porch, and her guests.

76

LATER THAT AFTERNOON, HE TOOK Carter across town, pointing out various points of interest from his life, which essentially consisted of the grocery store, the parochial school, and the church. He drove past the automotive shop, which looked just as it always had, save for a coat of fresh paint.

He turned onto the familiar wooded streets of the Jimenez' subdivision, guessing correctly that the rumble of the Charger off the houses would bring Erasmo to investigate. Any car as purposely loud as Weston's had to be someone he knew. He shut down the engine and looked over at Carter.

"Are you ready for this?" he asked her, smiling. Her expression was questioning. "Brace yourself."

The youngest Jimenez children were now in their early teens, but as Weston suspected they had the same collective personality as always. In only three seconds the car was swamped with a combination of friends and family.

"Weston! Weston!" They raised the usual chorus, jostling him as he stepped out of the car. Guillermo, now fourteen, slid past him to sit behind the wheel, stroking it lovingly with both hands and nodding appreciatively.

Guillermo suddenly glanced over at Carter, who hadn't gotten out of the car yet, and nodded at her too. "Hey." He tried out his adolescent charms on her and Weston gave him a playful shove.

"Out of the car, *Rico Suave*," Weston laughed at Guillermo's boldness.

"*Pensé que eras un sacerdote, hombre,*" Guillermo said. "*¿Puedes presentarme a ella?*" He tipped his head toward Carter and gave her another smile. She blushed.

"Hey man, English," Weston reminded him. "And no. I am still a priest, so what do you think that makes her? She's a nun, dude."

"Ay," Guillermo looked afraid.

"Like the scariest Catholic school teacher you *ever* had, *¿comprendes?*" Weston added, smiling because Ezra, one of Guillermo's friends, was taking the more direct approach and opening the car door to help Carter out. He shook his head. They were shameless, but harmless as well.

Carter took the chaos in stride. She, like Weston, was an only child, but seemed to genuinely enjoy the boisterous, talkative group. Adrianna, Marta, and Iliana ushered her away into the house with knowing looks at him while he popped the hood to show Erasmo the engine. Marta made eye contact with Weston and smiled. He just shook his head, amused.

He was pleasantly reminded that the Jimenez men were demonstrative with physical affection, jostling him, asking questions, patting him on the back, leaning into him. He had missed this kind of male closeness, and he realized that it was one of the reasons he was so comfortable with Amaoke, who was surprisingly receptive to touch. He couldn't know that Amaoke had also been starved of male bonding for much of his own life. In contrast, Weston also appreciated Amaoke's respect for silences, knowing that there would be none of that here.

Finally, Erasmo dragged him away, looking him over and asking him about his work. Weston was amazed as always at Erasmo's resistance to Father Time; other than increasingly silver hair, his face was as youthful as ever.

After Adrianna and Abuela stuffed them to bursting and continued to press food on them, they begged for mercy in order to escape and relax with the family in the living room. Weston helped with the cleanup, and when he was finished, went out to join the rest of the group. Carter and Iliana were engrossed in conversation, so he made the rounds with the other siblings, and after a while Marta was at his elbow.

She had gone on to college, earned an accounting degree, and last he'd heard, was working on her MBA. She handled the accounting for several of the large businesses in town, including her father's, and to her mother's dismay had shown little interest in marrying. She seemed very happy.

"She's lovely, Weston," Marta told him, watching Carter across the room. She was genuine with her praise, but what she left unsaid was unsettling to him. Apparently, he was less subtle than he hoped.

"I recognize the signs," she continued, her attention still on Carter. "Her heart is breaking. You are leaving her, just like you left me once. But this time, the feelings are reciprocated, my dear friend." She stopped to look at him carefully, but he said nothing.

"Oh, Weston," she said, squeezing his forearm affectionately. "I am sad to see you in such distress. Yet I am very glad to see that you are truly loved."

77

IT WAS LATE WHEN THEY headed back to Ms. Margaret's, and Weston knew the older woman was unlikely to be waiting up for them. When they arrived, he shut down the Charger's engine halfway down the block, coasting silently to the curb at the front of the house. The exterior lights were on, but the place was otherwise dark.

He led Carter around to the back, where the lamp over the kitchen sink cast a familiar glow into the backyard, one he recalled from his years as a resident of the home. The night was mild, and it was too early for the dew, so he stretched out on the grass while Carter took up station on the swing.

She was silent for a long time, then came on quiet feet to stretch out beside him, looking up at the stars. Then she sighed, and it was eloquent of so many things that he rolled onto his side, propping his head on his hand to look at her.

"Does Adrianna always try to kill you with food?" she asked, and although she was serious, and he could hear the smile in her tone, he knew it wasn't what she really wanted to talk about.

"Pretty much, yeah," he told her. "It's her way of showing love."

"It's a physical sensation at this point," she said, rubbing her belly. "I feel like a Buddha."

He laughed, then stopped abruptly as she rolled toward him, suddenly they were nearly touching. He ignored the baser attendants of his psyche as they urged him to explore his curiosity about what they might collectively find under that dress. For the first time in his life he was concerned about the state of his breath.

"Thanks for today," she said. "It's been...so lovely. I promise that in the morning I will put my habit back on, and carry on with things."

"Okay," he responded, and realized that he was holding his breath. He had no idea what to say next.

"So what happens now?" she asked quietly.

He sighed. "I don't know. I've fretted over it, fantasized about it...you tell me."

"I'm afraid I am leading you into a sin you don't want to commit," she admitted.

"I did that myself," he reassured her. "I needed no help from you. I was afraid that by agreeing to this...compromise, one day thing, whatever *this* is, I was encouraging you to hope for something I cannot give you."

"I knew that all along," she said. "But I thank you for agreeing to do it."

"I was afraid to say no," he whispered.

"Afraid?!" Carter laughed and pushed at him playfully. "Are you afraid of me?"

"Absolutely," he admitted, and then she was against him, and his arms went around her, feeling that tiny body, nearly weightless in his arms. It would be the work of a moment to pick her up, and he imagined the sweet weight of her, the feel of her bare skin against him, and although the choices he had made burned him, he still knew they were the right ones.

"But I need to leave you as I found you," he told her. "You know my story. It wouldn't be just me and you. It would mean giving you to *them*, and I don't want them to have you. If I could be your man, I wouldn't share you with anyone."

"Even without them, you wouldn't?" her voice was small.

"I *couldn't*. I want you safe, respected, loved. Words are powerful, and to be worthy of you I have to keep my promises. All of them."

She reached out to twist one of his dark curls around her finger. To her great surprise he rested his cheek against her hand and closed his eyes.

"You will always have a place here, you can always come to Ms. Margaret," he told her finally. "She would welcome that."

"I'm not sure Sister Mary Matthew would sign off on that," she said sadly.

"What about Aleta?" he suggested, desperately wanting her to know she didn't have to be alone. What he couldn't understand was that his efforts to provide her with some consolation in his absence were galling, because she was hurting, and she knew that there was no replacement for him in her heart. Her next statement taught him how she felt about this effort, and betrayed the depth of her love.

"Oh, certainly. That should be cheerful," she sneered, the anger in her tone surprising him. "The two lost widows of a useless war."

So he wisely remained silent, and held her there in the grass, until her tears were spent. The stress and exhaustion overwhelmed her, and after a time, he realized she had cried herself to sleep.

In the end, he did have to endure the agony of carrying her, sweet and trusting, to her bed, tucking her gently between the sheets. There he left her, alone, refusing to look back when he reached the door, knowing that if he did he might turn back, and wake her, and damn himself utterly.

W

In the car on the way home, my playlist cycled onward. I had forgotten that I had put her song in there, because it reminds me of her, and I hadn't told her about it, had never played it when she was in the car. I tried to skip past it, but she heard the beginning and stayed my hand, her expression unreadable.

...when the visions around you
Bring tears to your eyes
And all that surrounds you
Are secrets and lies
I'll be your strength
I'll give you hope
Keeping your faith when it's gone
The one you should call
Was standing there all along...

...I've loved you forever
In lifetimes before
And I promise you never
Will you hurt anymore
I give you my word
I give you my heart
This is a battle we've won...

And I will take you in my arms and hold you right where you belong
'til the day my life is through, this I promise you...

I wanted to tell her that I didn't want to compound her pain by forcing her to hear those words, that ballad that had become as much our song as it had ever been anyone else's. Every tear that fell from her eyes burned me like perdition, but she wouldn't let me turn it off.

78

YOU COULD STAY HERE, WITH me," Aleta pleaded. "We could make a life together. You don't have to do this."

"Aleta," he began, not wanting to injure her with too much truth, but knowing it was necessary. "You are afraid. I am as much a cause of that fear and a cause of your peril as the Morningstar."

"You make me less afraid," she protested, unconvincingly.

Amaoke shook his head gently. "You are also afraid of me."

They were both quiet then, an enveloping silence that denied nothing.

"We cannot build on fear," he said kindly.

"I love you," she stated firmly as if daring him to contradict this.

"Yet you remain afraid," he reminded her. "Those are irreconcilable emotions. I cannot bring myself to believe that any relationship built on such shaky ground would be wise. I am certain that you deserve better, much better, than such a relationship as this."

"And it ignores the fact that my life is not my own, can never be my own, until I fulfill or deny my destiny, which I believe led me here, to Weston, to this journey," he told her.

"It led you to me," she pointed out, quietly, and he knew that she was hurt. He also knew she was acknowledging that he was right.

"I do not deny that," he told her, knowing this was the time to tell her the rest. "I was married once." He pretended to ignore her shocked expression as he continued. "There is something about such a relationship that demands the purest honesty, so I will honor you with mine. She was human. You probably think I am about to tell you that I lost her to the Morningstar's evil machinations, but I am not. I married her when she was but a teenager, and I held her in my arms as she died an old woman. The Morningstar threatened her early on, but I have come to realize that it was a message for *me*; it could not fathom such an attachment and assumed our relationship would teach me to avoid such human interactions, that her death would teach me a greater lesson in sorrow and loss."

"But it came for *you* directly, no minions, no harbingers, and it meant to remove you – permanently – from this world and place you out of my reach, out of the reach of all those who love you, all those who benefit from the good you do here. I don't pretend to understand it, but I do know that its response to you is very different. It didn't see my wife as a threat to its greater plans, but you apparently are. It won't leave you alone because you remain a threat, which makes me believe that you will be safest if I leave you. Weston agrees with me," he added unnecessarily.

Aleta disregarded this last, and persisted on her course, using his words now. "You just said your life could not be your own until you fulfill or deny your destiny. What happens if you deny it?" she asked, in a voice that held too much hope.

"I suspect my life would then be forfeit altogether," he replied, not giving himself the escape she offered. "But I also fear that it would change the outcome for several innocents, potentially you, as well. And what kind of man would I be if I selfishly ignored these things, knew that by staying I could have you? For how long? Knowing I had turned away from what was right, knowing that made me the kind of man who didn't deserve to have your love?"

"My mother's people, my people, knew that all things must balance in nature. To turn away from this would be to violate the simplest obligation she taught me to respect. If one knows what is right, what is good, what is necessary, to ignore that course means disaster because it disrupts the sacred balance. This journey is a part of that."

"But what if –" she began again, but he held up a gentle hand to stop her.

"Please don't," he beseeched her. "I cannot tell you what you want to hear right now. If I were simply a man, could I be the man for you? Love you as you truly deserve? I honestly have no answer for that. I am not simply a man, I am something else, someone else. Would that I had some power to change it, I don't know that I could without first knowing the cost."

She seemed utterly lost, for the first time since he had known her, and he didn't want to diminish her spirit, neither here, nor in his memories of her. With a heavy sigh, he told her, "In another life, given any other circumstance, know that I would choose you, I would court you. Is that the answer you seek?"

"It's the answer I need," she replied. "But I want you to love me now, enough to change all of it."

"I will give my life so that you may live. It's the best love I can give you," he told her, gently brushing her cheek.

"Will it come to that?" She reached up toward his face, but he gently pressed her hand back down, and curled his fingers around hers, settling them onto the grip of her crutch. She wanted to be kissed, but their love story was not to end that way, and it was unfair to give her that kind of hope and that kind of pain. So he turned away, not answering the unanswerable, not wanting her to carry any burdens into the future, knowing she would anyway.

79

THE CARRIAGE HOUSE WAS QUIET, and it was obvious that Amaoke was not at home, so Weston decided to take a walk in the neighborhood. It was peaceful and pretty here under the trees, and he could understand Amaoke's sadness in leaving it behind. He suspected his friend was still with Aleta, trying to say goodbye.

When he reached the corner at Washington and Magazine, he saw a familiar figure through the picture windows in the Starbucks on the corner. He thought it no accident; this was the place where he had followed Amaoke on that fall evening of the year before, recalling that it was also where he'd first sensed the Morningstar trying to draw them together.

With a sigh of resignation, he crossed himself before crossing the street and entered the coffee shop. He joined the line, where the Monster was waiting to order, of all incongruous things, and stood aside when it asked the barista for a no-whip peppermint mocha.

"Worried about your waistline?" Weston asked sarcastically. He was in no mood for doing this dance.

The Monster laughed aloud. "I don't think you realize just how amusing you can be. But no. The whipped cream ruins the lovely charred taste of the espresso and dark chocolate," it replied with a facsimile of sincerity.

The barista was still looking at the two of them expectantly. She spoke to the Morningstar. "And what can I get for your brother?"

she asked cheerfully, causing it to bark with mirth at such a suggestion. Weston couldn't escape the irony. Of course, she had to think them an odd pair of identical twins. Him, in his flowing cassock skirts and thick eyeglasses, while the Morningstar was resplendent in midnight blue twill, with a silver shirt, no tie, and a Swiss-dotted pocket square. Not so unusual a sight in New Orleans, with his own alma mater, Notre Dame Seminary, right up the road on the other side of the highway. Lots of people had family members who were clergy, and plenty of them frequented this place, to be sure.

"Nothing for me, thanks," he told her, causing his companion to protest.

"Oh no, dear *brother*, surely you will break bread with me? Perhaps some weak tea, something without a hint of decadence? Day-old bread, perhaps?" It was taunting him now, the reference a reminder of his mother.

"No thanks, just had a bar of soap," Weston replied with a little more heat than he wanted to betray.

"Never mind him, dear," the Monster said to the young woman, who was watching this exchange with feigned politeness. "He's taken a vow of denying himself anything remotely interesting."

With that, they retired to a table by the windows. To Weston's surprise, the staff dispatched someone to bring the Morningstar's coffee. And why not? No one expects the Devil to wait at the bar for his drink.

Weston set his Redeemer Cross on the table with a thump, coiling the chain next to the coffee cup, and the Morningstar drew his hand away slightly with a fussy gesture, and pretended to study the people passing by on the sidewalk outside. It was as good a reminder as he was going to get. As Weston expected, he didn't have to encourage it with small talk. It carried on with what it had to say soon enough.

"Free will was, is, and ever shall be the downfall of humankind. I understand why He did it; they would be boring, insipid creatures without it. Well, even *more* boring and insipid."

"And while it allows them to recognize and exalt their Creator, and return to glorious redemption, it also creates hierarchies, both real and imagined, from which temptation is born. Pureflesh have weaknesses far beyond their physical frailties, and self-determination requires self-realization which can only be carried out in context. That context is comparison with other pureflesh, to the advantage or to the lack, even in similarity difference is easy to find."

"Easier to find than the alternative. And difference creates division. That small grain of sand seems insignificant, but let the wind drive it into the eye and it is virtually a boulder for the suffering it causes."

"Division creates enmity and confusion and blame, which can lead to war, murder, rape, genocide. Pureflesh are easy to convince that a singular cause is just and once believing so can justify that position with religion, or find any other greater-good argument to condone sin on the grandest scales."

"And so I watched, and here and there I suggested, whispered, conspired, and plotted, with no end of pureflesh converts ready, willing, and enthusiastic to the idea of obtaining superiority over their fellows. Which, in and of itself, then can be used to excuse anything."

"I send my own legions in my stead, but I never rest. I have read all your books, your authoritative texts, your manuals of faith. So similar – yet whole peoples have been extinguished over the slightest small variant in interpretation, which has sometimes only been because the intended meaning was lost in translation."

"But all speak of a coming end, when the pureflesh are the prize in a great battle of souls, in preparation for which they must choose a side, redemption versus damnation. After which there will be a reckoning, a tally of the One who will prevail."

"The prize is there for the taking – the Creator will claim Their own. But notice that nowhere is it written that any *must* be saved, so what if all could be damned?"

"Pureflesh need no help getting to sin. Rather, it is those who cling to faith, who exhibit inherent goodness, that interest me."

"God will have an apocalyptic army. I needed generals who could hasten the journey to damnation. Suborning sin as a matter of crafting four immortals of pureflesh contaminated with the debased."

"The first, an incarnate beast to walk among men, magnifying fear. The mother, a pureflesh maiden of superstitious nature, the father's bloody suffering allowing possession and habitation. I have no procreative function, no agency by which to pass my gifts, but by diabolic means I have hijacked the human code. Thus I bring forth my own."

"Next, the luminary, powerful, beautiful. Her father a warrior prince, slayer of men and beasts, her mother the virginal bride who offered a blood sacrifice willingly for the chance to bear his child. She shall inspire awe, and her legacy shall be to frustrate death itself."

"Then, a goddess, rare and exotic, the dragon's blood given, like fire to a corrupt Prometheus, to a samurai who sought power from the dark gods. He abandoned his humanity and fathered by force a child rare and invincible, marrying evil to beauty. My most useful protégé, obedient to her dark nature, understanding its necessity, pragmatic and deadly."

And you, my son, my truest heir, balancing my own traits with those of that sacred offspring, that which has been suspected but never believed, that which I could use to forge a second coming, one of my choosing. You are the best of both of us, that which we could not reconcile is marriageable in you at an atomic level, the profane and the sacred, and your sacrifice will only ensure enduring evil. That you seek martyrdom is of great pleasure to me, a source of fatherly pride, if you will."

When it stopped talking, Weston realized that he had followed most of the diatribe, until the very end. There was a mystery there, a truth, just a granule of it, as usual, wrapped in a riddle. He pondered the words, trying to recall them just as they had been uttered, but it was already escaping him.

The Morningstar pointedly glanced at its wristwatch. "Look at the time! I suspect you have an engagement to attend to. I smell the Beast about, slouching toward Bethlehem, eh?" It smiled at its own cleverness and took a sip of its coffee. "Let's do this more often." Then it flashed its shiny eyes at him and vanished. Its voice echoed back in his brain, the sound of the legions receding, "Give the Jesuit my regards."

80

WESTON TALKED INCESSANTLY DURING THE flight, but Amaoke didn't mind, since it kept him distracted from the fact that he had let his friend talk him into getting onto an airplane. The Wolf did not like breaking its connection with the earth, and in this case, the man that shared its skin didn't disagree. It was the second big breakthrough of the day; earlier he had agreed to ride in the Charger with Weston to the airport.

The Wolf hadn't liked that either, more because that car was the source of some agony that had not been forgotten, slightly less because of the life-threatening way in which Weston drove it.

Something Weston said reminded him of a question he still had, something that had been bothering him since they'd had lunch at *Joey K's*. He'd been distracted by the course of their conversation that day, and all the things that had happened since then made it seem further in the past than it really was.

"The Morningstar said something to me once," he told his friend. "He said that you 'were the most gifted of all of us.' That mean anything to you?"

Weston pushed at his spectacles, a nervous tic he had. Amaoke noticed he did it whenever mention of the Monster was made. He suspected Weston didn't even realize it. He watched the priest consider the question for a few moments before he answered.

"It may just be a vanity," he replied carefully. "But it lies with the truth, so…"

"Just say it." Amaoke didn't think Weston would keep anything from him, but he knew that subconsciously some secrets are harder to shake loose.

"Well, it is so self-absorbed, so fixated on slights to its being. I guess I think of vanity first because it seems preoccupied with appearances. I look like it, so maybe that's it. It also likes to monologue, long rambling flights of fancy."

"It makes speeches to you?" Amaoke leaned forward, finding this interesting.

"It's unavoidable, unfortunately. Every time I look in a mirror, I can see it looking back at me. My reflection is the Morningstar," Weston said, and when Amaoke remained silent in amazement, he continued.

"It speaks to me from the glass. It has plenty to say, not much of it worth hearing."

"How long has this communication been happening?" Amaoke asked, assuming it a recent development.

"Since the first time my mother held me up to a mirror," Weston answered honestly.

"Surely you have no memory of that," Amaoke protested.

"I remember the womb, my friend," Weston said, and nothing in his expression or bearing belied the truth of it. Amaoke was astonished anew; no wonder the man seemed aged beyond his years. "It was with me even then."

"Imagine how frightening, to come to the mirror to wash my face, to brush my teeth, and see those inhuman shiny eyes looking back, out of my own face," Weston told him. "As a kid, I would make my eyes blur on purpose, so I didn't have to see it. Wrecked my near vision. That's why I have to wear *these*." He indicated his thick glasses. "It's impossible to comb my hair, because the curls always appear to be floating around in the glass."

"If I don't stay at the mirror, it continues to talk to me, when I am in the shower, getting dressed, even if I am in an adjacent room. It stirs up the demons inside me, and I have discovered various ways to endure the torture, ways to distract myself, some of them more effective than others."

"Wait, you said demons? Inside you?" Amaoke asked, and the horror of it showed on his face.

"I am essentially attended by a diabolical host, as best I can determine," Weston told him. "I was born with them; I am half-demon, if you like."

"So you are possessed in the same way as those…people I helped you with?"

"Not really. Possession suggests a takeover. My situation is more like a cohabitation, like the worst group of roommates you can imagine. When I was very small, if I didn't do their bidding, they punished me. I always had bruises where they knocked me into walls and tossed me about. When my mom took me to the doctor for regular checkups there was always a social worker that came to 'talk' to me about life at home. She thought I was being abused. I worked hard to keep them from pinning it to my mother and grandfather."

"And now?" Amaoke was very uncomfortable. Weston had just admitted to being host to something essentially evil, something that had a consciousness separate from his own. What he perhaps wasn't admitting to himself was that it was not so very different from his own reality.

"Hey, man, it's cool," Weston reached out to touch Amaoke reassuringly on the shoulder, making Amaoke wonder again how he always seemed to sense what Amaoke was feeling. "I learned how to hurt them, and this physique is less about vanity and more about being strong enough to maintain autonomy over the flesh. My strength has probably saved my life during a couple of really terrible exorcisms, and maybe once or twice in my everyday life."

"You've witnessed some of my other containment strategies, you just don't realize it," Weston told him. "Order and rhythm disrupt them, because they work toward chaos. When it's bad, I pray, but I have learned to add a routine to the prayer to disarm them at their worst."

"Several months ago, when you were spying on me outside the church-" Here, Weston smiled mischievously at Amaoke, but didn't pull any punches with his language. "I was having a particularly rough day. I could sense you were in the alley below, and I had the Morningstar in my ear. I was waiting for a call from Rome, and I couldn't take the voices any longer. I started to pray, and then I started pacing. When it's really bad I add some thumping, and I use the crosspiece in the window because it is a religious symbol, a rudimentary cross, you know? That's what you witnessed."

Amaoke nodded, recalling it well. Having answers to solve the mystery was useful, but he had another epiphany.

"What happens if all that doesn't work?" he asked wisely. A bit too wisely, if Weston wasn't mistaken. He wondered just how much Amaoke had suffered at the Monster's hands.

"Sometimes I lift more weight than I should," Weston admitted. "Once, on the bench, I overdid it, and the bar came down and I couldn't get it back up. Obviously, I don't have a spotter. It was crushing my chest, and I couldn't breathe, but I didn't care. I was relieved. I had found a permanent way to frustrate them, but I should have known better."

"They wouldn't let you die," Amaoke said, speaking from experience.

"Of course not. I passed out, and when I came to, I found the barbell flung across the room. It nearly tore through the sheetrock. Other times, well, sometimes blood and flesh have to be sacrificed." Seeing Amaoke's horrified expression, he hurriedly clarified. "My own, of course. I won't satisfy their true aim, which is to convert me, damning me to their fate."

"You actually have to self-harm?" Amaoke was saddened.

"Sometimes. But I have a few tools that quiet them better than others. There are instruments that survived the Inquisition," Weston said, and his voice was faraway, and he didn't bother to inquire whether what he said made sense to Amaoke. "Can we-can we talk about something else?"

"I think you have more than answered my question, Brother," Amaoke was sorry he'd asked. He wondered what Carter knew. Probably most, but certainly not all of it.

"Have I?" Weston didn't sound convinced. "Me, the most gifted? No. Don't you think it's *her*?" They both knew he was referring to the episode in Aleta's bedroom and the exotic woman with the spear. "She *moved* us. I have never seen anything like it, other than the Morningstar. And that *power*! Whatever it was, it didn't feel evil to me. It felt divine...it felt *godlike*."

81

AMAOKE AND WESTON WAITED IN the luxuriously appointed salon that connected their rooms at the *Domus Sanctae Marthae*, awaiting the escort that would take them for their audience with the Pope.

Their presence in this place had drawn curious glances from the bishops and cardinals that lived and worked there, as well as the visiting dignitaries of the church. It was unusual for a layperson to stay unless he or she were of some diplomatic importance to the Vatican.

Those who passed by in the corridor beyond the doors that opened onto it did their best not to glance inside at the strange man who accompanied Father Weston on this errand. He was obviously not a priest, and they were keen to know more about the reasons for his visit, to have answers about those piercing blue eyes and that endless black hair.

It made Amaoke restless, their fleeting scents of suspicion and fear, and the omnipresent incense that made him sneeze and sneeze.

Weston paced with him, pausing to more closely examine the doors where they folded back against the ornate wallcoverings. "Do you see this?" he asked Amaoke. "The pattern in the door? It is likely to have been done purposefully," he declared, indicating the ways in which the crosspieces of wood formed a series of smaller and larger crosses.

"Sure. The cross is a symbol. But strong faith, strong belief can turn a symbol into a talisman," Amaoke replied.

"Yes. Yes!" Weston was relieved and excited that Amaoke understood what he was driving at. "Talismans have a power that is recognized by dark forces – they respond to them."

"But I couldn't use a cross," Amaoke protested.

"You're probably right – but it isn't because you don't have an inherent goodness. It is because the cross is not a symbol of your faith traditions. And there are even those-" Weston gestured grandly, hurrying into his next statement, "-those who are self-proclaimed Christians, raised in the faith all their lives, some of them amongst the clergy, for whom the cross is not transformed."

"Why not?" Amaoke asked, standing still to try to counterbalance the flurry of Weston's movements, his hair, his arms, his swirling robes.

"Dilution of the religion," the priest replied sadly. "Last year, during the holidays, I saw an ugly Christmas sweater-" Here Weston paused when he saw Amaoke's puzzled expression. "You know about those, right? The red and green sweaters that people wear at Christmas, to be funny?"

"They are ugly. They do it on purpose? I thought it was some compulsory tradition," Amaoke shook his head. "I was feeling sorry for them."

"No, it's - it's a kind of a joke," Weston hurriedly explained, waving that away. "Anyway, this sweater had Jesus on the front. He was wearing a birthday hat with the slogan, *Birthday Boy*. When you see your deity as a pop icon, the symbols lose their gravity."

"But these clergy you describe – surely they don't see Him that way," Amaoke protested.

"No," Weston admitted, "But they no longer truly believe – if they ever really did. You and I, we have borne witness to the fantastic, the unexplainable, the unbelievable. What we have is belief that where there is a Morningstar, there must also be a God…or a Raven. We have the proof that Thomas requested from Christ." He nodded to Amaoke. "Whatever name he carries among that group of faithful."

"Because I do believe that He is One, the same over all humankind. We simply call to him in different ways, by different names. And we take different paths to reach Him."

"Don't let the Catholics hear you say that," said a kind voice in heavily accented English from the doorway. In the heat of their conversation, both Amaoke and Weston had missed the commotion in the hallway that had preceded the arrival of this soft-spoken man.

Weston fell immediately to his knees in genuine respect and love, taking the older man's hand and kissing his ring with devotion. "Holy Father, it is lucky for me that the Jesuits are not Catholic."

Amaoke was surprised and startled when the older priest laughed with abandon and unquestionable mirth. He was also confused, but looking from Weston to the other man he could not discern any answers.

Weston got to his feet and the two priests enjoyed a warm embrace, the elder pulling back after a few moments, holding the younger at arm's length and looking into his eyes with real tenderness.

"Your Holiness, we were awaiting escort to your residence. I hope there was no misunderstanding. We are not late?" Weston asked with concern, and Amaoke knew that this was the person they had come to see. The Pope, the most powerful man in Weston's church.

"Of course not, my son," came the amiable reply, the Pope smiling with mischief. "My secretaries took too long, and it is also quite diverting when I decide to go walking around Vatican City on my own. They all scramble and panic. Ah, how it entertains me, these waves I can cause. Forgive me my vanity."

"There is nothing to forgive, Father," Weston gave his assurances with a bow.

"I was also very curious about your friend. He is the rage of all the gossip since your arrival," the Pope added, with no attempt to hide his amusement at the silliness of such an idea.

At that moment, as if to punctuate what he had just told them, two cardinals burst into the room, red robes flying, eyes and mouths severe, censuring His Holiness silently with their body language, which they dared not do with their words. Trailing behind them was another dark-eyed priest, dressed in robes like those Weston wore, black, but trimmed in the deep red of the bishopric, with a red sash at his waist. He was watchful, and something about his scent was untrustworthy, Amaoke observed.

The more senior of the two cardinals spoke, looking disapprovingly at Weston as he did so. "Your Holiness, Father Kedron was very distressed to find you were not in your apartments when he arrived to escort you to your appointment."

From this statement, Amaoke deduced that Father Kedron was the one with the red sash, probably one of the Pope's secretaries, based on what Weston had already taught him.

"It is deeply perplexing that he required two cardinals to assist him in raising this distress," the Pope replied, not bothering to disguise the irony in his tone.

"Your Eminence," Father Kedron said, directing his gaze at Amaoke, "you are the Father of the Church. We must at all times be allowed to maintain your security."

"God maintains my security," the Pope reminded the three latecomers. "He asks of us that we have faith. How is your faith, good Fathers?" he asked them, looking to each of the men in turn. "It appears I must also be an example of charity," he added, turning to Amaoke. He said, "You are welcome here. Weston has told me a great deal about you."

"Your Holiness, I really must insist," Father Kedron began, but the Pope stopped him with a look.

"I want the three of you to pray. I want you to think on the state of the world, and those things of import that require the power of your faith. I will leave you here, in this private salon, to compose the prayers that bend upon those matters that truly plague the world at large. I will send for you when next you are needed," the Pontiff told them, ignoring their looks of confusion and indignance. He turned, gesturing for Weston and Amaoke to follow him, and pulled the salon doors closed behind them.

Smiling inscrutably, he led them both onward to the gardens. They walked in companionable silence for a time, and Amaoke was lulled by the sunshine and the fresh air, allowing his mind to wander. He had so many questions, but was confident that they would be answered with time. With centuries of life behind him, he had learned a special kind of patience.

"They are angry with you," Weston observed.

"Because when the cardinals convened to choose a new leader, they predicted that one such as I would be more easily controlled," the Pope replied. "They were wrong, so they are angry with themselves. They transfer these frustrations to me."

"They have a point about your safety," Weston argued, wanting to advocate the middle ground.

"If I am unsafe it is from such as those," the Holy Father stopped walking abruptly and laughed. "I am sure Father Kedron hovers over me on many a night, ready to administer a pillow treatment."

Weston looked appalled. He knew Kedron was very dangerous. He had intimate knowledge of just how dangerous.

"My son, do not concern yourself with these matters. He is too afraid to do it himself. He would be the first and only suspect, and he knows this," the old man sighed. "I must admit he is a very useful secretary. He is the best conduit of intelligence from the outside world that we have, although his weakness for the flesh is legendary." He did not miss the distress that remained on Weston's face. "Oh, his partners are all of consenting age. And he is very careful in whom he confides."

Amaoke listened to the balanced tone and decided that this was a very good man to lead such an organization. He seemed to know the personal strengths and weaknesses of his priests and did not presume to judge them.

"But you are not here to speak of Vatican politics," the Pope gestured ahead and began walking again, stopping only when the three of them arrived near a small fountain with a matched set of benches set at angles that advantaged the view of the sunlight on the flowing water. Here he indicated they should rest, and he surprised Amaoke by choosing to sit on the nearer bench with him, rather than the farther, with Weston.

"May I?" he asked, reaching for Amaoke's hand. Weston smiled encouragingly at Amaoke's raised eyebrows.

Amaoke allowed the man to take his hand, surprised at the strength and gentleness of his grip. There was nothing untoward in that touch, it was merely meant to create a point of contact, of connection, a willingness to bridge a physical gap and perhaps a philosophical one.

"I wonder who taught you about faith," he murmured, settling closer. "This must all be quite foreign to you, but you are taking it all in stride. The murmuring, the stares, the suspicion."

"I am used to these prejudices," Amaoke told him, surprising himself with this unexpected admission. "I know myself, after so many long years, I know who I am. It was a hard-won battle, believe me. My mother taught me what is expected and what is forbidden of one such as I; her faith was undeterred by the tests she faced. She sacrificed everything to ensure I understood our beliefs, respected the traditions of our people."

"I come to understand Weston's love for you," he smiled, turning his face up to the sun, clearly enjoying this simple pleasure.

"Why did he suggest that you were not a Catholic?" Amaoke asked, unable to resist getting at least one easy answer before they got to the thornier issues that lay before them.

The Pope laughed again, long and easy, nodding his head. "It is an old Catholic joke about the Jesuits, that we are not *really* Catholic, because we are the unpredictable rebels of the church, often arguing against Rome in her supposed wisdom."

"Weston is very funny, but he is also very observant of formality; I notice that he makes jokes most often when he is nervous, as he is now. I understand this about him. I am sure he was sorry he said it as soon as it escaped his mouth, but he knows my sensibilities run to that sort of rebellious humor."

"He needs this release, and he deserves my indulgence; his work for this Church will ask of him the greatest sacrifice a man may make to God. He has always known it, and I know it as well. That he loves me even though I send him on the most deadly and difficult errands, indeed that I send him to his premature demise is a testament to the fortitude of his faith."

"What he may not know is that he is perhaps more like a Jesuit than I, much like the namesake of our sect. The great martyr, the one who goes ahead to spare others in the name of the greatest good of all." The Pope paused, and shook his head at Weston's demurring. "He lacks the essential vanity that marks his Dominican Order, but I am not sure that they claim him anyway. They would wish that he be required to show much more obedience. I have released him from the traditional hierarchies that exist in our faith, and that also has bred much resentment, even though no other priest would come forward to volunteer to take on his work, his ministry, his place."

The last statement was said with some sadness. "Imagine a parent, and the pain they rightly feel in losing a child. This goes against the natural order, as the parent expects they will never have to face such a loss. Now imagine that same parent, knowing with certainty that they face that grief. I don't know that cowardice is a sin, but to allow another to take a path that you could not yourself take seems to close in on something essentially evil."

"The decision was made before you had to endorse it," Weston said softly. "It is not vanity for me to acknowledge that I was chosen, and what comes is a part of His plan."

"Oh, how I wish that assertion brought me any comfort," the Pope lamented.

82

WESTON WAS PLEASED WHEN FATHER Nicolò appeared in the garden and asked if he could escort Amaoke to lunch.

"We will follow shortly," the Pope nodded his pleasure, although he had likely given instructions regarding the transition. "Amaoke, is it alright if I take a few moments with Weston alone? Father Nicolò will escort you. Perhaps you would be interested in one of the galleries? Lunch is being prepared in the residence. Please get started with something appetizing and we will be there to share the meal."

Weston thought it a perfect segue; he knew Amaoke would enjoy Father Nicolò, and the old priest was practically salivating to meet someone of such an interesting background. Even though the librarian was justifiably curious, he wouldn't necessarily expect Amaoke to make senseless small talk. His heart was happy for both of his friends.

"Thank you, Your Holiness, that was very kind," Weston said.

"I hope Amaoke is comfortable here," the Pope replied, but his tone betrayed his concern about this.

"He has learned to fit in wherever he finds himself," Weston told him.

"Then he has achieved a sort of peace that many never find."

"He is extraordinary, and I am lucky to call him friend," Weston said. "I misjudged him, and I underestimated him, and he has forgiven me. He has treated me with the charity and understanding I have not found in many another."

"He follows the highest law of humanity, the one that supersedes religion, creed, or origin. He gives others the respect he hopes to find," the Pope marveled. "It escapes my imagination that whole societies and too many governments do not recognize the wisdom of the First People."

The Pope stood up slowly, and Weston followed. They walked through the rose gardens, coaxed into blooming year-round by talented gardeners, and Weston thought it appropriate that this month's blooms were a snowy white.

"The Sorceress is in East Africa, and likely lives somewhere near the great mountain Kilimanjaro. Her legacy as a traveling healer and midwife there has been confirmed by many of our missionaries. It is difficult to discern what is real from what is legend, as there are conflicting reports of her advanced age, though she appears but a young woman. It is rumored that one of the coffee plantations in the region has a Doña of nearly one hundred years of age, and it is claimed by many that the Sorceress attended at her birth."

"Are you confident we can find her?" Weston asked. "It sounds like she has a fairly high profile." He had not shared details of the encounter that he and Amaoke had already had with her.

"One might be tempted to assume so," the Pope replied. "But she has an affliction. This condition invites prejudice, at best, and violence, all too frequently, at worst. She has likely learned to hide in plain sight, and if she is as gifted as we assume-"

"She is probably more gifted than we know," Weston declared, but did not explain himself. "Perhaps a priest making inquiries will get a positive response."

"You forget that in Africa, most of the established institutions of the First World, including the Church, have been responsible for some of the most egregious harms. And Christianity has a tenuous hold there, where the people have accepted it, they have merged it with their old religions. You must have a care, my son. You shall have every protection I can extend to you. But Africa is said to be a harsh mother, and her justice does not always look like our justice."

W

In the afternoon, while Amaoke rests, I continue my research.

In the library it is dark and cool, and I realize that this is my true church, where the quiet knowledge of the centuries awaits me. The one place where I have always felt I belonged.

I push through the gate into the archives and lose myself for a time. When I look up, I have a clandestine visitor. He has escaped his entourage once more, and I smile. I imagine he learned to disappear into the busy neighborhoods of his childhood home, and he applies this practical skill these seven decades later to find privacy and much-needed peace.

I respect him more that he communicates his desires directly, without any corrupting intermediaries. I suppose it is necessary as what he asks me for is typically complicated and occasionally has moral implications.

He tells me of Kedron's upcoming journey to South America, and explains that he asks of me one more favor before I embark on my own travels.

The Church must not allow others to act where it carries the responsibility to do so. I understand why I am chosen.

Who understands demons better than I?

83

"*NI*, YOU'VE OUTDONE YOURSELF," AZUMA observed, smiling down at the notes appended to the file she was holding.

Ni remained silent, still thinking about, and discarding, various approaches to their plan. She had done quite a bit of legwork, but the breakthrough had really come from Michael Israel. She told Azuma as much, and then said, "But I think we should keep her out of it."

"I don't disagree," Azuma replied. She picked up her phone and typed out a brief, quick message. Then she took up the file and started reading again. Several minutes later, her outer office door opened when *Jū* let *Hachi* come through.

"*Hachi*, how's your Spanish?" Azuma asked.

"Terrible," *Hachi* dispensed with anything that remotely resembled charm, which startled those who expected such a lovely woman to possess an abundance of it. Secretly, it was Azuma's favorite thing about her.

"Perfect. It will make you more vulnerable," Azuma declared, and seeing *Hachi's* expression, she amended this. "At least in appearance, if not in truth."

"*Aijin*, may I ask what this is about?" *Hachi* could not contain her curiosity, and she knew she could wait centuries for these two to give anything away before they were good and ready.

"I want to use you as bait," Azuma's clarification was anything but. Yet she relented, getting out of her chair and coming around to hand *Hachi* the file. She settled gracefully into the chair next to her, and *Ni* retreated to the windows.

Azuma watched as *Hachi* absorbed the contents of the file, and she knew the exact moment that she reached the narrative about Iara, because she couldn't help but glance in Azuma's direction. *Hachi* took her time, first reading all the original intelligence, then flipping slowly through the photographs, finally concluding her examination with *Ni's* recent discoveries.

"When do we start?" she finally spoke, and there was something dark and hungry in her tone.

"We already have. Michael Israel provided the woman's name, and the itinerary, but I want our involvement to occur in a vacuum. She is still a government official, and I want her to have deniability about all of this," Azuma explained. "This priest," her face twisted up with something that neither *Hachi* nor *Ni* could name. "This man – has a weakness. I think we can exploit it. I also believe that I can get answers about what the Vatican knows. Father Kedron is traveling to Argentina to vet a new female operative. I want to intercept her and send you." Azuma waved away their weak protests and continued.

"Yes, he already knows who she is and what she looks like, so there is no chance to insert you as a decoy. But we can keep her from making their introductory contact, which will rattle him. He will be distracted and hopefully we can use that to draw his attention," Azuma explained. "What I see in that file suggests that he won't be able to resist coming to the aid of such a beautiful and disadvantaged young woman, do either of you disagree?"

Both her priestesses were silent, signaling their understanding and their accord.

"He sent Iara?" *Hachi* finally asked.

"In a manner of speaking," Azuma replied. "Iara was invested in coming to us."

"Is this about her?" *Hachi* rarely showed much that gave away her true feelings, but Azuma heard the jealousy in her tone.

"What shall I say?" Azuma said softly. "I knew what she was from the beginning, and I let her get close because it was the most secure of all the terrible alternatives. That is not to say that I did not sympathize with her plight, and I know you do as well, *Hachi*. If it brings you any comfort, I had the counsel of the Collector from the beginning, and *Ni* shadowed her long before I was involved with her."

Azuma decided that she also needed to address the elephant in the room. "My choosing Iara or Akiko over any other lover does not diminish what I feel for those who are mine, *Hachi*. The choices that any of us make always have the potential to affect others."

"Iara knew full well the choice she was making. But this priest sent her to infiltrate our house. And we must answer that insult. He chose to open a door and walk through it. Now I shall close that door on his head," Azuma promised.

84

WHEN THE TWO MEN RETURNED to their hotel, there was a message waiting for them, a short, cryptic note in an archaic, shaky script. It was apparent that their insistent inquiries had not gone unnoticed. But by whom?

If you want to find the Sorceress, come to Maisha in old town after midnight. I will find you there.

After several days of unfruitful, hot, thankless searching, finally this was something. Amaoke was unable to achieve a sense of relief, however. The whole thing was so irregular that it rang every alarm bell his instincts still carried.

As casually as possible, which ultimately was not very casual at all, he and Weston inquired with the concierge regarding the note. Had the man seen who had left it? Was that person known to him?

To their astonishment, the clerk reported that the note had been left the day before, while they had been traveling up north, sometime after leaving Arusha. He denied having ever seen the messenger before. His greedy eyes conveyed another message, and Weston parted with not some small amount of cash and was rewarded with the further information that the 'staff' had taken the liberty of reporting to the messenger that the American gentlemen had not yet returned from a sojourn in-country. For this outrageous officiousness the clerk had been informed that the message would be the same until Amaoke and Weston presented themselves to the afore-mentioned establishment during its busiest time in the wee hours of the morning.

"What type of place is it? A dive bar, I suspect." Weston directed the question at the clerk, but answered his own question.

The man sniffed as though he, personally, were offended that someone would think such a thing about a local cornerstone, but then he ran a slim-fingered hand fussily over the front of his vest, smoothing out nonexistent wrinkles. He seemed to consider the question, and then spent the better part of thirty seconds scrutinizing the pair of them as they stood across from him at the counter. Weston sighed, reaching into his pocket resignedly, suddenly looking no less menacing than the demons that infested him.

Making the briefest eye contact with the priest, which could not have been pleasant, the man suddenly started stammering, holding up his hands in seeming surrender, "Sir, sir, you misunderstand. It is- it is certainly a busy place where alcohol and perhaps other things are exchanged for money. I was simply considering..." His statement tapered off while he decided whether the two men had taken any offense. "It is just that, well, the two of you..." He cast about unsuccessfully for the words to complete his sentence, and finally settled on looking at the two of them so pointedly that the wolf that lived in Amaoke's skin wondered how much of a head start he might give this little human weasel. His mouth watered, and the clerk sensed the change in the two men, finally managing to squeak, "The two of you, seem, well, *capable.*" He waved over their general forms, and Amaoke and Weston glanced at each other, realizing that they were pretty intimidating as individuals, never mind as a pair.

The Wolf considered. The squeak meant he was more rodent than weasel, probably a rat rather than a mouse, since he had successfully elicited the bribe prior to being spooked. Well, he would earn it, then.

As if instinctually, Weston leaned back against the wall, outwardly relaxing, while Amaoke leaned forward over the small ledge that separated the clerk from his guests. A little good cop, bad cop couldn't hurt. This guy had no idea that it was actually bad cop, worse cop. He asked, as quietly as he could manage, letting the wolf out in his voice, so that only the concierge could hear, "Since you were good enough to tell *him* our plans, perhaps you'd be good enough to tell us how we will recognize him."

The poor little man broke out in a fine sweat, which made Amaoke feel slightly guilty, but only until he realized that in the proper reading of the situation, this man was afraid of the messenger, less than him. He was squirming, not wanting to describe the person who had delivered the note, and who had returned for an update when they hadn't shown up. There was apparently some unpleasantness about the encounter that had been noxious enough to encourage the clerk to avoid interrogation on this point.

"You will," the clerk choked the words out nervously, his eyes wild as they traveled from Amaoke to Weston and back. "Trust me, you will."

With that, short of inflicting bodily harm on the man, there was no further information to be had. Neither of them needed to call undue attention to themselves or their plight; although Father Weston did have official Vatican business in Tanzania, there were some kinds of trouble that the Vatican would turn a blind eye to, and Amaoke shuddered at the idea that they could attract the attention of any police authority.

85

WHEN NEXT THEY LEFT THE hotel, never had emerged a more mismatched pair. Amaoke in chinos and a lightweight Henley, sporting sunglasses that probably disguised his provenance enough that he could pass for one of the young, westernized Arab adolescents who haunted the corner coffeeshops, looking more like catalog models than disaffected petroleum heirs. Weston, showered, bespectacled, and wearing his crisp black uniform with the collar in place, and if that was not bad enough, clutching the chain of his silver cross in one fist.

"You're kidding, right?" Amaoke shook his head. It wasn't that he had ever set foot in a nightclub, but he was pretty sure that they were not going to take to a priest patronizing the place – he guessed it might be bad for business. "You'll never get in."

"Faith, my child." Weston responded, almost keeping a straight face.

They stepped out to the curb, and the doorman signaled for a car, but Weston waved him away. Without turning his head, he said, "We should walk."

Amaoke didn't smell anything irregular, but it was always a possibility that they could be followed, so they set out on foot, walking shoulder to shoulder at Weston's brisk pace for more than five minutes before Amaoke realized that the priest knew where he was going. Weston walked confidently, leaning slightly forward with purposeful, almost religious, zeal.

After a few minutes more, the streets narrowed and got darker, as they left the lights of the central district behind them. Without slowing his pace, Weston shed his eyeglasses and collar, unbuttoned his shirt to what Amaoke would have considered an extreme for someone *not* of the cloth, and shook out that wavy hair before fastening the heavy cross around his neck, letting it fall to the center of a ridiculously muscular upper torso. He looked no different than any other young club denizen in any other city on the planet, and of interest, after rolling up his shirtsleeves just so, he, too, save for that symbol of Christianity, could have passed for one of the ubiquitous young, rich Arab men out with a friend, looking for action.

Amaoke was impressed, and he nodded and smiled a secret smile that he knew Weston could see. Though he did not know him well, he could tell that the man had a worldly savvy that was weighted down by what he had seen and done in his short life. Amaoke suspected that what he already knew about the young priest's life was only the tip of a massive iceberg of tragedy. The fact that he had not descended to madness and despair was impressive. He had learned to appreciate the remarks of the old organist from St. Constantine in a new perspective; from here it was easy to understand Weston's appeal to the faithful. His devotion alone was impressive, and it was not burdened by one iota of falseness. He knew the darkness in a way that many others would never understand, much less believe, and yet his personal faith in the divine was unwavering, even if it had forsaken him in this life.

Weston's relentless pace eventually slowed as he led the way through ever-narrowing byways that were little more than alleyways, into what could only be kindly referred to as a glorified slum. Small, half-dressed children with hungry eyes were still awake, peering out from just inside doorways that opened onto the stone pathways, and Amaoke was reminded of another life, when he had watched the young mothers of migrating Indigenous Arctic peoples herd little ones with eyes and bellies as empty as these. Their mothers were absent, or equally scantily clad, eyeing the two passing men shrewdly, sizing them up as they did every other transaction in this hard life, wondering what two such as Weston and Amaoke were looking for here.

Still, Weston proceeded as though he knew the way. Amaoke realized that while he had slept in the late afternoon, Weston had taken this same route, a trial run ensuring that they would find their way in the darkness, understanding the need for purposeful advance in this nighttime foray, and the potential for violence if they got lost.

Amaoke also realized that Weston's movements had become more complicated, and that they were doubling back and circling the few same blocks, probably to avoid any clandestine pursuit. These maneuvers had started at about the same time that faint sounds of modern music began to reach Amaoke's ears. Weston glanced over at him impatiently and tilted his head slightly, asking a silent question, so Amaoke got out of his own head and put his nose to work, but there was nothing suspicious to be scented. When he was satisfied, he started to notice the thumping bass sounds of the music were crescendoing, and he could hear and smell a crowd of humans nearby. He looked at Weston and shook his head to signal that there were no apparent threats, and the priest abruptly changed direction, heading straight down an alley between two crumbling old stucco structures.

There were no doorways or windows that opened onto the passageway, and as it narrowed and darkened, Amaoke felt the temperature on his arms take a dive, and his night vision was sensitive enough to note that the shadows were gathering and creeping around them – Weston's familiars, curious and unwelcome. As they came to the end of the alley, the space opened into a small square, and they were assaulted with a wall of sound, and colored lights that drew the night crowds like a beacon.

Weston paused a single stride to allow Amaoke to flow past him and lead the way into the establishment. There were two solidly built characters at the door, presumably for security and to collect a cover charge from the scantily dressed youth that crowded the entrance in surprisingly on-trend Westernized clothing. There was much more flesh on display than Amaoke might have expected, but Weston seemed to be unperturbed; rather, if he was, it was not evident in his bearing or his expression.

The menacing fellows considered the two of them for the briefest of moments, before wisely parting to let them through ahead of the queue. They pushed through scattered couples loitering in a short dark hallway that opened out to a surprisingly modern nightclub space.

Strobe lights pulsed in time with the music, greatly annoying to Amaoke, but he soon got used to the assault as he led them some small distance to what he felt was the midpoint of the far wall. It was a good vantage point for watching the ingress and egress of the crowds, and a place where any individual who approached would be obvious, as they would neither be approaching the bar or the bathrooms, and would be slowed by the activity on the dance floor in front of them.

Amaoke positioned himself against the wall, deceptively relaxed, ready at any moment to push off in a hurry if the situation warranted it. The environment was torture for the wolf; too many smells, loud sounds, and noxious lighting were an overload of distractions that he did not want, which he began to suspect was the point of choosing the place. Weston settled next to him, and he seemed to be faring better with the environment. He leaned his head back and half-closed his eyes, either concentrating or praying, Amaoke could not tell which. It turned out to be a useful tactic, since he was attracting the attention of numerous young nubile females, whose approach was only curtailed by the realization that he did not seem interested in his surroundings.

They stood against that wall, the most incongruous of wallflowers, waiting, and watching.

The DJ played a song whose beats were familiar to Amaoke. He realized it was something he had heard spilling out onto Bourbon Street many times some years before. The tune was catchy, and it was still popular with these young people, as the dancefloor crowd began to jump and sway en masse.

One young woman put her head back and gyrated slowly in front of them, obviously dancing just for herself, immersed in a song she loved. A few of the singer's lyrics caught Amaoke's attention. "...gettin' drunk off the thought of you naked..."

His thoughts went immediately to Aleta, and he wondered what she would look like moving to this song. His rush of guilt was profound and immediate, his mind jumping to Nanatha. But he could no more imagine Nanatha in this time and place than he could banish images of Aleta. He wondered just when he had become so complicated, but the anguish was real.

His surprise registered visibly when he felt a strong hand squeeze his forearm in reassurance. The priest was reading and responding to Amaoke's moment of distress—though how he felt it amongst all the distractions Amaoke could not fathom. He glanced over at Weston, but other than re-crossing his arms he remained in his still state of relaxed anticipation.

It was another hour before Amaoke sensed a subtle change in the crowd. The back door was open, providing a much-needed cross current of air, but suddenly there was a minor stir among the clubgoers as the crowd near that door parted to admit a newcomer.

Whether instinctively or otherwise, the group collectively flinched away from the lone figure that made its way toward them.

Although height was a common feature of Tanzanians, this one stood head and shoulders above the frenzied crowd, at least as tall and perhaps taller than Amaoke and Weston. He appeared to glow in the flashes of the strobe lights as he approached, and it wasn't until he had traversed half the depth of the building that Amaoke realized the effect was from the whiteness of his skin.

He wore fashionable baggy denims, and a hoodie unzipped over an open button-down vest. He had sturdy Timberland work boots on his feet that were not unlike Amaoke's own. Amaoke suspected that his had been a fashion choice in comparison to Amaoke's more practical one, given their relative newness.

His exposed torso was like a slab of marble, all wiry muscle and strength, and as he drew ever closer, Amaoke could see both what had frightened the clerk and the reason he had been so sure that they would easily recognize the messenger. It *was* obvious.

The man's handsome face was set in a wide, almost feral, grimace, and his eyes were red as glowing coals. These were not the shiny orbs of the Morningstar, this was something else entirely, and it was effectively disturbing the youngsters in the crowd.

During the final moments of his approach, Amaoke could see cropped blond curls beneath his hood and fine freckles across the bridge of his nose that might have made his visage more childlike were it not otherwise so fierce.

Without breaking stride he walked right up to Weston, and spread a long-fingered white hand across his chest. In an almost intimate gesture, he pressed the heavy cross into Weston's torso and with it created enough pressure to hold the priest against the wall. It was a show of magnificent strength, and from where Amaoke stood, it appeared to cost the newcomer no great effort.

Amaoke could detect no human scent other than the soap that had been used on his clothing, and more subtly, a strangely familiar female scent signature, associated with a hint of cinnamon spice. But no other human scent nor the scent of any other natural creature came to his nose. Just night air and the dust that clung to the man's skin.

Amaoke readily bared his teeth as a warning, and was rewarded with a mocking half grimace from the man that might even have conveyed amusement. There was a flash of strong white teeth between full lips before making a small *tsk* with his tongue against his teeth.

His left arm was concealed by the baggy sleeve of the hoodie, and it did not look quite right. Amaoke decided that perhaps the arm was deformed, but he did not rule out the possibility that the sleeve's irregular appearance was concealing a weapon.

The youth was putting enough pressure on the cross that it was indenting Weston's skin, and Amaoke was concerned that perhaps the priest needed him to intervene. His small wave of dismissal told Amaoke two things. Weston did not feel overly intimidated nor did he need any help.

Amaoke watched as, still smiling directly at him, the other man inclined his head to Weston and said a few words. He waited a moment, and Weston's nod of assent was nearly imperceptible, but the priest made a point of pushing off the wall, successfully reversing the pressure placed upon him. He then made the clearest statement yet, turning and heading for the rear exit without looking back. There was no fear in him. But then, Amaoke thought, a crowd of demon familiars might embolden just about anyone.

The newcomer followed, making his own statement by turning his back on Amaoke, who trailed the procession. It was not lost on him that the club revelers seemed relieved to see the three of them go out into the night.

The stranger took the lead from Weston once they reached the back alley, pushing through the gap beside him. He did not bother to avoid a significant shoulder bump against the priest as he passed.

Weston glanced at Amaoke briefly, and Amaoke thought he might have been amused. He paused long enough to button his shirt over the cross and slide his spectacles on, before turning to follow the messenger.

after

Official record of DNA analysis of metahuman alpha, located on private server at Rising Sun Industries:

Result Completed RESTRICTED
Result Reported   RESTRICTED

Specimen Taken   RESTRICTED
Specimen Received   RESTRICTED
Specimen Identification Number   CLASSIFIED
Specimen COC   CONFIRMED,
                                   Law Enforcement (1)
                                   RSI (2)

Subject Age   RESTRICTED
Subject Gender   Presumptive Male, by history
                   Impossible to determine from available genetic
                   material

DNA Result **presence of uncatalogued species**

Subject Race   INDETERMINATE

Method
Proprietary

RESULT

Determinations

D1. Novel genetic material present; genetic signature reproducible using modified duplication methods given small specimen volume

Conclusions

C1. Uncatalogued species suggests novel humanoid organism, assigned new RSI library identifier, genetic byproduct analysis impossible without further investigation of existing material and direct study of individual

C2. Unidentified genetic material comprises entirety of sample, supernumerary unexplained STR segments present with unidentified chemical bases/unknown chemical bond structure
C3. Lead project science team believes genetic material originated from a single bio-organism (CONFIRMED)
C4. Positive identification of metahuman/humanoid variant; **INDEX DNA EVENT** labeled metahuman alpha (will be added to library catalogue as exemplar for RSI Taskforce MH/UNK progenitor organism; subinvestigation AZ/Defense correlate

** Material characterization project commenced as of report date [classified]

Azuma reread the details of the report on the server anomaly that had cached flagged data instead of queueing it to critical members of RSI leadership. Her IT team had been thorough in their efforts to uncover the cause of the inconsistency and in their analysis of its etiology; assuring her that such a variance would be avoided in the future. They had even outlined the steps they had taken to rehabilitate the faulty coding involved, and that dry indecipherable language comprised the bulk of the communication.

She sent a message to HR approving the overtime hours spent on the project, and authorized a bonus for the entire team. As angry as she had been when she had discovered the hidden data during a correlation search of the database for project AZ, she realized that the nearly three-year delay in evaluating it probably had not greatly affected any scientific outcomes or ongoing investigations other than her own. Her team had delivered, albeit under threat.

It had been a perfect storm, really. The specimen had been forwarded for confirmation of anomalous findings by a criminal laboratory in the United States. RSI had 'friendlies,' these were courtesy agreements to apply their advanced technologies to difficult or unusual cases to support law enforcement or scientific advancement when requested by higher education or industry. It was certainly not a completely altruistic act; in this way, RSI was alerted to any interesting developments or findings in the field of Genetics passively, exploiting the observations of other researchers. This was the first time such a request revealed something unexplainable.

The problem had been her own system, Azuma had to admit. At the time the specimen was received it was simply an alert to unusual findings. It had been taken from a person of interest related to an ongoing investigation, and because that person was not a named suspect, the initial evaluation had been done on a blind requisition. When the materials and paperwork had been received, they had been logged as routine, entering the details and origin.

The main RSI server's operating algorithm had queued the request to the library, because it treated the query as a completed project due to one of the marker fields for 'Results' being filled in rather than null. This had resulted in the data becoming searchable in the file, but inadvertently hid it from further active review by the RSI science team. The agency that had submitted the specimen never sent further inquiry about it, most likely because they were simply forwarding interesting findings, or even more probable, the source of the specimen was ruled out as an ongoing suspect. Because there was no additional communication or subsequent investigation of the file, it was cached with other 'completed' inquiries without ever being seen by fresh eyes.

It was only uncovered when Azuma was attempting to cross-reference the results of the superhuman chimera evaluations, looking for other specimens in the RSI library that showed any unknown chemical bond structures or anomalous genetic material. It was a routine control maneuver, and she hadn't expected a positive finding.

What she found was astonishing, and the fact that it had been hidden by an automated glitch and could have been lost indefinitely infuriated her. Obscure and unhandled was a report of DNA that had been taken from a human (presumptively), but that DNA was not provably human. It did not cross-reference to anything in the RSI library, with the exception of the superhuman chimeras. Yet this specimen was even more exceptional; it lacked the typical CGTA chemical bonds and structures that were partially preserved in herself, the Sorceress, and the Wolf. Its structure was entirely replaced by the unknown chemical bonds found in the chimeras. The investigation into the identity of the source of this fantastic DNA had been frustratingly slow, dead-end really, but Azuma had an educated guess, because there had been four of them in that bedroom in New Orleans.

While her investigation of the bonds and bond structures was ongoing, personally supervised by her AZ team, the correlating details were withheld from her scientists. She had put them to work on the chemical structure but had given none of them any context.

She too was spending time in the lab, working on the bigger picture using her private server and computer resources.

Unfortunately, her urgent trip to Tel Aviv had delayed her review of the full report. The team had briefed her about their initial findings when she was still on the ground at Haneda, before she had even left Japan, but so many additional concerns had inserted themselves in her life that she'd had no time to return to this mystery. She'd instructed the AZ/Defense team to mark the specimen eyes-only, and it had awaited her personal evaluation.

Pleased that there would be no such errors going forward, she glanced back through the fourth of the extranormal files, the one that had been hidden within the system, frowning as she tried to work out a pattern in the sequencing. She looked at the images that had been produced from the other three assays. Before she knew it, *Ni* was at the door.

"*Aijin*, would you like me to bring up the car?"

Azuma glanced out the windows at the darkness beyond. "Yes. Have *Roku* drive so that we can discuss some other business. I will meet you downstairs." She glanced at the clock and stretched. It was after midnight. She was exhausted. She needed to feed. She felt the loss of Akiko acutely, both pragmatically and emotionally. But she reined those emotions in; she had already promised herself that Akiko's death would not go unanswered.

She took her private elevator down to the parking lobby. The hallway was cold, and she shrugged herself down into the warmth of her coat and made the long walk out to the turnabout, where *Ni* was waiting at the door. *Roku* was behind the wheel of the Range Rover, and she anticipated its warmth.

As she approached *Ni*, Azuma slipped off her heels and her escort reached for them silently. Azuma sighed, betraying her weariness. "Thank you, my friend."

But as *Ni* opened first the door to the outside and then reached to let Azuma into the backseat of the SUV, Azuma paused.

Something was there, something she had seen, and suddenly it was bothering her. Her eyes widened and she gasped.

"*Aijin?*" *Ni* was looking at her with concern.

"*Roku*, go on ahead. *Ni*, there's something I need to do. I'd like you to arrange for the helicopter in about ninety minutes. Would you stay behind and ride with me?"

"*Hai, Aijin*," the two responded in unison, but Azuma did not hear. She was already back through the door and running barefoot for the elevator.

Her wandering mind had worked out the pattern in the assays from the new file, and the correlation to the superhuman chimeras. She just needed to see it again for herself and confirm it. The four organisms had a significant percentage of gene similarity, which could only mean one thing. And she understood why she had not seen it before; it was an impossibility. But the science could not lie.

They were siblings.

Acknowledgements

A special shout out to Rob Torgesen at Anderson's Automotive, who walked me (patiently) through the challenges of gas engine transmissions and their electrical mysteries, and was kind enough and imaginative enough to brainstorm the best way to trap demons within them. If the descriptions of car repairs in this story are wrong, those errors are mine alone. Rob takes care of our old cars skillfully and efficiently, and he is one of the hardest-working persons I know.

I am also incredibly grateful to the *real* Father Paul, who suffered through a statistical analysis course with me at St. Thomas. He is either exceptionally diplomatic or his memory is flawless, because he remembered me immediately when I got him on the phone (or perhaps it is because we were the two outcasts in that advanced math class; he the only priest and I, sadly the only woman other than our instructor). He, like me, benefits from the liberal arts education that accompanied his seminary studies, and he is broadly fascinated with many secular subjects and human concerns that fall outside of his vocation. He is unflinchingly honest about the Church, and he has something else in common with our Father Weston – a love of athletic footwear; in Father Paul's case, white Reebok tennis shoes. These were completely unorthodox for a priest during our shared education (not so many years ago, so perhaps they are still), and one of my funniest memories from college is of Father Paul sticking his foot out the rectory window and pulling up the hem of his cassock one day to show me his latest pair, a gift from his older brother. Father Paul was very generous with his time, patient with my questions, and unafraid to admit to the shortcomings of our Church while defending the faith. He was also exceedingly well informed about exorcisms, although said practice has largely been abandoned in the modern era. As with the many others who have assisted in this endeavor, speaking with him made me grateful for the incredible people I have been blessed to know in this life. Ours was certainly a 'situationship' that payed a dividend many years later.

Finally, as I hope many of you have ascertained, **west** is not the end of this literary journey. I realized that to finish the endgame with these characters in four novels according to the original plan, I would have to rob Azuma and Weston of their stories, stories that needed to be told. I hope it isn't too much of an imposition to ask all of you to read one more book, and I thank you again for indulging me.

Timeline

Since the good Father Weston's story takes place in modern society, in the Western culture of the late twentieth and early twenty-first centuries, the prevailing terminology should be familiar.

In lieu of a Glossary of Terms, I decided that what was needed was a timeline. In **north** and **south** there was a natural progression through history. I started taking liberties with time in the latter two novels, much less egregiously in **west** than in **east**, where I shamelessly went back and forth in time (by only weeks or months within a period that spanned less than half a year, but it made things a bit busy).

For those of you that are interested, I include here a timeline that ties together the events of these four novels by the dates of their occurrences. The earliest parts of the timeline include historical happenings to allow perspective about the world in which these events were occurring. The latest parts of the timeline abandoned this practice.

I wanted the reader to have some context about the human history that was occurring concurrent to the highlights of the stories, but near the end of the timeline, what is most important is the shared history of the characters. As for me, putting it together held some surprises. I hope its inclusion contributes favorably to the experience and promotes better understanding of the fairytale.

Morningstar Timeline

c. 1000 – **Amaoke born**, classic Pueblo period of cliff-dwelling Anasazi culture, Leif Eriksson discovers North America, epic ballad *Beowulf* composed

1008 – Murasaki Shikibu finishes *The Tale of Genji*, the world's first novel

c. 1014 – **Noki death, Amaoke first (pubertal) werewolf transformation**

1040 – Macbeth murders Duncan, king of Scotland

1054 – Eastern Orthodox and Western Roman Catholic churches separate

1189 – Richard the Lionheart succeeds Henry II in England

1211 – Genghis Khan invades China

1215 – King John forced to sign *Magna Carta* at Runnemede

c. 1300 – **Morningstar drops Amaoke from the sky**

1312 – Mali Empire reaches its height under King Mansa Musa

1325 – Renaissance begins in Italy, *Noh* drama develops in Japan, Aztecs establish Tenochtitlán, Moorish culture peaks in Spain

c. 1333 – **Kusini born**

1347 – Black death takes at least 25 million people in Europe

c. 1348 – **Kusini tortured by the Ghost and the Darkness**

c. 1350 – **Quuran and Usugan's tribal family settles on the Kuskokwim, the decision to migrate south is made due to cold and famine**

1368 – Ming Dynasty begins in China

1376 – translation of Latin Bible to English

c. 1387 – Chaucer's *Canterbury Tales*

1428 – sixteen-year-old Jean d'Arc leads the French against the English

1438 – Incas rule in Peru

c. 1450 – **The *Ungalek* enters the natural world, captures, and tortures Amaoke**, Florence becomes center of Renaissance art and learning under the Medicis

1503 – Da Vinci's *Mona Lisa* completed

1504 – Michelangelo's *David* completed

1509 – Henry VIII ascends the English throne

1520 – Martin Luther excommunicated by Pope Leo X, Suleiman the Magnificent becomes Sultan of Turkey

1543 – Copernicus theory of earthly orbit around the sun published

1547 – Ivan the Terrible crowned czar of Russia

c. 1550 – **The Morningstar and the Ungalek unleash Amaoke the Berserker**

1564 – William Shakespeare born

1590 – **Kusini descends the mountain, Suhuba dies (unnaturally long-lived due to the aftereffects of Kusini's magic), Bantu massacre on post road following delivery of Mnatoa and Ak'ili's daughter**

1603 – Shogun Ieyasu rules Japan, moves capital to Edo (Tokyo), Shakespeare's Hamlet written

1605 – Cervantes writes *Don Quixote de la Mancha*

1607 – Jamestown, Virginia, established, Pocahontas, daughter of Powhatan, saves John Smith

1643 – Taj Mahal completed

1637 – Shimabara Rebellion, foreigners pushed out of Japan

c. 1650 – **Kusini meets Kenge at Oldupai**

c. 1661 – **The Collector is born**

c. 1666 – **Azuma born**

1667 – Milton's *Paradise Lost* is written
c.1670 – **Megumi born**
c. 1678 – **Azuma sheds the juvenile Dragon and assumes rule as Shogun, Tatsuo Tomo departs natural world**
c. 1684 – **Azuma meets Megumi, defeats Tanagata at Yeso**
c. 1685 – **Azuma transforms the Collector**
c. 1689 – **Azuma's first hermaphroditic shift, death of Megumi**

1704 – Bach's first cantata performed
1732 – Benjamin Franklin begins publishing *Poor Richard's Almanack*
1762 – Mozart tours Europe as six-year-old prodigy
c. 1769 – **Ambakisye born**
1773 – Boston Tea Party
c. 1775 – **Amaoke recovers his humanity and the Berserker is suppressed**
1776 – Declaration of Independence
c. 1779 – **Nanatha born**
1783 – William Blake's first poems published, Beethoven's first published works
c. 1795 – **Amaoke meets Nanatha, Kusini meets Ambakisye**
c.1796 – **Kusini frees Amaoke from the wolf trap, the Beast emerges**
c. 1797 – **Amaoke weds Nanatha, Kusini weds Ambakisye**

c. 1802 – **Ambakisye dies, and is transformed**
1804 – Napoleon proclaims himself Emperor of France, Alexander Hamilton mortally wounded in duel with Aaron Burr, Lewis and Clark begin expedition to Northwest
1836 – Mexican army besieges the Alamo
1845 – Poe publishes *The Raven*
c. 1862 – **Nanatha dies**
1863 – Battle of Gettysburg
1865 – Lewis Carroll releases *Alice's Adventures in Wonderland*
1876 – Sioux kill Custer
1879 – Thomas Edison invents electric light
1886 – Statue of Liberty dedicated
1893 – New Zealand first country in the world to grant women the vote
1903 – Wright brothers fly first airplane
1905 – Einstein's theory of relativity
1909 – Peary reaches the North Pole, the NAACP founded
c. 1910 – *Mjusi* **sells Ambakisye tainted goats**

c. 1982 – **Aleta born**
c. 1990 – **Weston born**; Bithiah and Michael Israel born
c. 1994 – **Michael Ibrahim Israel ben Aharon murdered by the Death-Bringer, Bithiah assumes the name Michael**
c. 1995 – **Iara born**
c. 1997 – **Carter Thomas born**

now (events listed in order of chronology)
- Azuma suppresses Tatsuo Tomo and finishes her final doctorate
- Weston ordained and trained by the Dei Gloria, deployed by Pope, who recognizes his value to Vatican
- Collector harvests Kusini's DNA for project Okori in Africa
- Carter attacked, enters the novitiate with permission of the Archbishop of New Orleans
- Collector harvests Okori project population specimens
- Azuma meets Iara (and Michael Israel) at Prefect's function

- Amaoke meets with Aleta Madison
- Michael Israel jumps off the tower to catch Azuma
- Amaoke meets with the demons at Galatoire's on Hallowe'en
- Iara dies
- Amaoke has DNA test, identifies inhumanity of the Collector
- Milos killed at the place of the fallen
- Collector goes missing
- Weston captures demon familiars of Forcas in Dodge Charger
- Azuma declares Akenomyosei her enemy, gets information about the Collector's disappearance from the courier that implicates Forcas (and Beelzebul)
- Weston and Amaoke have their climactic encounter on the Feast of the Epiphany
- Morningstar visits Aleta
- Amaoke struck by Morningstar's car
- Azuma travels to Israel
- Aleta gets Amaoke's DNA results
- Azuma visits Aleta's home and finds Amaoke waiting
- Kusini discovers biopsies on Ambakisye and others, ultimately her own

About the Author

LJ Farrow's childhood fears were the genesis of these stories. She finds inspiration in the bizarre, the odd, the unexplainable, and the downright scary. A Colorado native, she now lives and writes in rural Indiana. She will always be afraid of the dark.

If you enjoyed **west**, look for **the morningstar**, the final book in the series!

Amaoke, Kusini, Azuma, and Weston must learn to trust one another as they travel to the Place of the Fallen for answers, and they must find common ground upon which to overcome their many differences. Together they devise a plan to derail the evil designs set in motion by the Morningstar.

But the Monster has untold secrets that will challenge what each believes about their origins, and the choices they make could change the course of humanity. Redemption for the pureflesh will demand a sacrifice, and the four of them can only hope that what they have to give will be enough.

Made in the USA
Middletown, DE
27 January 2020